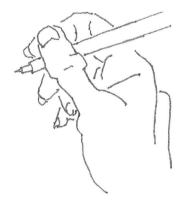

Also, by Kathi Barry Albertini

Stories
45 Seconds – *Open Spaces*
Seeing Red

Poetry
I Remember; I Forget
What Time?

Tribute
Queen of Arts

As Expectations Collide

Fiction

Kathi Barry Albertini

Cover design and photo: Kathi Barry Albertini
Drawings: Kathi Barry Albertini

Shadow Press
27 Chelmsford Rd
Rochester, NY 14618

Printed in the United States of America
10 9 8 7 6 5 4 3 2 1
ISBN: 978-0-9854630-3-8

Dedication

For Clare Marie Matthews – inspiring, adventurous friend who listened to the early versions of this before cancer took her away from us.

And thanks to Bill Biddle, Jim LaVilla-Havelin, Jutta Bauman, John Albertini, Deborah Rothman, Nancy Barry, Rose O'Donnell, Jay Rogers, Christine Zielinski, Susan Domina, Mike Bleeg, and Michael Barry for reading, nudging, and asking.

As Expectations Collide

Fiction

Your Expectations

You try to find
a church community
You look for
a welcoming community
You seek
one that helps the poor
You search for
one where people support each other
You want
your children to know other adults,
who don't look like them,
You hope
your children will develop clear values
You long for
an inviting community that accepts your family
You and your husband have different traditions
You want the community to include traditions from both
You yearn to find a church community that is even more
than you expect.

You read about a church and
hear from friends
You attend a Mass, the church is Catholic
You, a Catholic, see Catholic roots
You also experience warmth, openness, excitement
not common in Catholic churches you have attended.

A woman gives a homily
The priest sits and listens
You sit and listen
Your children remain quiet
She engages them
She engages you
She engages your non-Catholic husband

11

You can see before he speaks,
before the children speak
You have found a community,
a church community
which exceeds your expectations.
You join
You sing
You volunteer.

The community seems eager
to help the poor
to include your family
to invite people of all races, backgrounds, and income
levels
to invent ways to help the poor with food, education, and
clothing
to stretch some Catholic "rules" by including more women.

The woman appears
not only teaching
not only preaching
not ever in the background
but also attracting attention in the broader community
but also speaking nationally in support of Catholic women
but also planning internationally for women's ordination.

You think the Bishop supports
You volunteer more
You think all the parishioners encourage
Your family participates
You think this woman paves a way
You encourage others
You want more women to join the men
You see a new future, for the church, for women
You see your daughter and the woman become friends.

The Bishop removes the woman.

You sing without passion
You volunteer less
You hear dissention
You don't understand
You question
You can't answer your questions
You can't answer others' questions
You can't answer your children's questions.

Naomi

Dear Sam Bonner,

We found a church. And we all love it, Catholic. Yes, I can see the scowl on your face, but read on.

It's called Saint Luke's and we have met so many wonderful people. They, I should say we, have a woman pastoral administrator whose preaching you would enjoy even as you form lots of questions. It works for Zack. I never thought he would agree to attend a Catholic church. But it doesn't seem Catholic, which certainly helps Zack put past criticism aside. Best of all, they run a homeless shelter. They have one part-time staff person, but volunteers do the bulk of the work collecting and sorting food, responding to neighborhood requests for food, and staying overnight with the guests. The volunteers come from all over the city, other churches, college clubs, and former homeless people.

And Vermont? Do you miss the big city? We will probably compete with each other again this winter to gain the "worst weather" title. Watch out, upstate New York will rise to the challenge.

Can't wait to see you and talk!

Hugs,
Naomi

Dear Naomi,

Sorry I haven't answered your many letters. Reading them takes me back to the best parts about divinity school. After a year, you still seem positive and enthusiastic about Saint Luke's. I just wonder. Are you missing anything? What was wrong with divinity school and religion in general still looms large for me even all these years later.

I know we wrote a lot during that time. After leaving divinity school, Buddhist teachings consumed much of my reading time and similarities surprised me. As I wrestled with my love/hate connections to religion, you attended church and put all your energy into singing. You had doubts about the whole Catholic thing. Living away from home gave you some freedom to explore, but you ended up at the local Catholic church. I can almost quote that letter verbatim without looking. "I'm in the choir, pretty far from the silly Catholic dos and don'ts especially about women." Did you say something about spiritual satisfaction? I forget. I suggested books on Buddhism. We argued. We saw parallels, but you went regularly to Saint Still-Accepted-by-the-Vatican. You did question. That questioning seemed healthy.

Do you still question? With Zack being Protestant, your parents very conservatively Catholic and your own doubts, it must have taken a lot of effort to find a place that suited everyone. You haven't mentioned your parents? It doesn't sound like their type of parish. Everything can't be that great, Girl.

Don't get me going. You might pick up a copy of <u>Excellent Catholic Parishes</u> by Paul Wilkes. Yes, I did read it. I'm worried about you and you know I don't worry. Wilkes looks under the hood at those eight parishes. It might give you some things to question about your parish. Call me after you read it.

And, you can probably guess my last bit of advice, on women in the Catholic Church: not happening in our lifetimes, probably not even in the lifetimes of your kids.

You need to come visit. Vermont woods, hiking, farm fresh food...And the foliage, can't beat those trees.

Your,
Sam Bonner

Elizabeth

"No!" Mark doesn't look up. He adds a red block, linking the two blue Lego structures together. He admires the arch and tests to see if his tractor fits.

Clare looks up from her book. "Can't we go tomorrow?" she pleads. "It's so nice by the fire. Please, Mom." She tilts her head and smiles.

Naomi smiles back as she buttons her sweater and adjusts the chain holding a tiny silver cross. She marvels at how Clare's smile touches her even when she knows Clare's intentions. She imagines Zack's smile. She looks away. She glances at Mark moving the tractor slowly through the arch imitating the sound of a laboring motor. Clare can sway her. Mark angers her. What she learned from parenting Clare, helps little in parenting Mark. She applies lipstick without a mirror and tucks her weekly envelope into her purse. "I know, it is nice here." She looks at the glowing logs. "We can build another fire after church. Something to look forward to."

She places Mark's coat in the tractor's path. "Maybe Daddy will be back. Wouldn't he enjoy a fire?" A mention of Zack usually gets Mark's attention. Zack's weekend travel, which he tries hard to avoid, still annoys Naomi. She knows it makes her less patient with Mark. She sighs. She warms to the idea of being together after Mass, though she would prefer being together at Mass. She gathers the papers she needs for her talk with Ben. She smiles.

"We can't leave the house with the fire still burning!" Clare points at the fireplace. She cringes imagining the comforting flames escaping into the room and reads another paragraph allowing her mother to consider, she hopes, the same scary thoughts.

"Your coat, Clare. Close the fireplace doors. The fireplace insert contains the fire and keeps the house warm, no worries." She glances at her watch. "Mark!" Mark moves the tractor through the arch; and with a louder revving noise, the tractor climbs up the folds of his jacket.

Clare watches Mark. The tractor reverses to navigate the folds. The revving increases and pulses as Mark rocks the tractor back and forth. She reads the next paragraph and without looking up says, "Please, Mom. It's so nice and I'm at a really good part in my book."

Naomi sees Clare's persuasive smile fade slightly. She pats Clare on the shoulder. "Let's go or we'll miss Mass," Naomi zips her jacket and turns to the door. Mark and the tractor continue the treacherous journey. Since Mark has grown too big to hoist into her arms, Naomi experiments with different tactics. She turns, raises her voice slightly and catches Mark's attention, "Oh, I forgot, Mark." Mark turns from the tractor and stops the revving noise. "Didn't you want to show Ben the tractor?"

While she has Mark's attention, she moves to release the jacket from the tractor and inserts Mark's right arm into the sleeve. Mark strains but loses grip of the tractor. As Naomi glances at Clare, she reaches for Mark's left arm, Mark removes his right arm from the jacket and reaches for the tractor. Clare reads another paragraph. Mark laughs, waves his right arm, grasps the tractor again, and wiggles in Naomi's tightening grip. She squeezes harder. Mark squeals, "Mo -om, ow - owa!"

"Stand still, Mark Norton!" Naomi speaks louder. He stops moving. She finishes the left arm and reinserts the right arm.

Clare looks up at the sound of Naomi's sterner voice. "OK, OK. Let me finish this page," she looks down and reads.

"You're finished." She holds Mark's right arm and points to the canvas bag. Mark wiggles free. Naomi's tone has an edge. "If we have one more delay, that tractor's staying home," she grabs Mark's arm and looks into his face. "Do you understand?" Mark puts the tractor in the canvas bag.

Clare closes the book and the fireplace doors. She follows Naomi and Mark out to the car. Naomi takes a breath. As the children buckle themselves in, she runs her fingers along the edges of the cross and adjusts the chain. *Patience*, she says to herself. Another deep breath and she buckles her own seat belt and starts the car.

Naomi parks at the edge of the parking lot. She rubs her hands and reaches in her pocket, no gloves. The first cold snap always catches her off guard. The kids unbuckle and join her. They move quickly among the parked cars catching noisy leaves in their shoes before entering the warm church. They arrive as Linda Arnold lifts her head to the choir and plays the first verse of *Gather Us In* on the piano. Naomi starts to hum as they slip into a pew near the door. She glances around wondering if Zack's flight might have arrived on time. She notices that the church seems more crowded than usual. The congregation stands to join the choir in song. Naomi leaves the day behind and sings. The harmony of many experienced voices surrounds her. How she loves this community, the enthusiasm, the participation, and the way people accept each other even through arguments or differences of opinion. She glances down and sees that Mark and Clare both sing in full voice. She smiles. The thoughtful but tiring visits to find a church where the whole family felt comfortable, seem far in the past. Saint Luke's has become the center of their lives. Sometimes she does wonder if they have overcommitted. Seeing Elizabeth and Father Rogers approaching the altar stops her self-examination. They both embody the concept of commitment to the mission of Saint Luke's. Everything they do inspires Naomi to think of others.

As the piano plays the last measure and people sit, she notices a man with a large TV camera enter the side door of the church and stand quietly against the wall. He bows his head. She wonders if he is on his way to work, though she doesn't recognize him and can't explain why he would carry such a heavy piece of equipment into church. She turns to the altar where Father Rogers says the opening prayer. Father Rogers looks out at the pews. He looks back at the altar servers, at Elizabeth, and at Ben. Ben stands, then sits. Father Rogers turns from the congregation and returns to his seat. Naomi glances at the bulletin and sees that Ben will read from Corinthians 1 -

7:20. Naomi watches him stand and move slowly to the lectern. She closes her eyes. She knows how much Ben loves this passage. His repetition of this reading reminds him of his desire to become a priest.

> *Everyone should remain in the state in which he was called.*
> *Were you a slave when you were called? Do not be concerned but, even if you can gain your freedom, make the most of it.*
> *For the slave called in the Lord is a freed person in the Lord, just as the free person who has been called is a slave of Christ.*
> *You have been purchased at a price. Do not become slaves to human beings.*
> *Brothers, everyone should continue before God in the state in which he was called.*

He reads it thoughtfully. The words remind her of many of the late-night conversations they shared about faith and his calling. She smiles realizing how much of the passage, she remembers. A frown replaces the smile. She watches. Does he still wrestle with his doubts about becoming a priest? His voice carries both meaning and deep feeling. She prays for him to make the final decision to apply and enter the seminary. Why he needs encouragement still puzzles her. He pauses at the end and bows his head before returning to his seat behind Father Rogers and Elizabeth.

Naomi unzips her coat slowly to minimize the noise and touches her cross. She has worn this gift from her confirmation sponsor since the day of her confirmation. Mark sits on the kneeler with his feet resting on his coat and moves the tractor quietly along the pew. Naomi releases his coat and puts it in her lap. She wonders why Elizabeth and Father Rogers both celebrate a Saturday night Mass. Elizabeth delivers the homily and applies Paul's theme to herself. She tells the story of being brought up in a large Catholic family. The discovery in her teens of the many women in the Bible and serving as priests in the early church determined her own future. She speaks about transformation. The stories of these early women paint a picture of a larger more accepting church. She repeats that women served as priests. "Their passion inspired me to learn more, then inspired me to become a priest like many of them." She pauses. She looks over at Father Rogers. Naomi follows her gaze. Father Rogers doesn't smile. Wrinkles fill his forehead. He rubs his forehead. Naomi barely hears the end of Elizabeth's words about looking forward to the Catholic Church, again, accepting women as priests. She hears that sentence as Elizabeth repeats it more slowly. Father Rogers holds his head in his hands. Ben's lips move. Elizabeth reminds the congregation of Paul's gospel "everyone should continue before God in the state in which he was called" and restates speaking each word slowly with a stern expression on her face. "In God's eyes men and women are equal," she says with each syllable cracking her voice. Father Rogers shakes his head. Naomi refolds Mark's jacket and glances at Ben. He bows his head. She can't see his eyes, misses the Prayers of the Faithful, but catches a questioning look on Clare's face. She takes Clare's hand thinking to herself that she must remind Clare that Elizabeth has bad days just like everyone else. These words from Elizabeth, especially the tone, must raise questions for Clare. Her deep admiration for Elizabeth swayed the Norton's decision to attend Saint Luke's.

People shift in the nearby pews. Then, she sees the man with the TV camera. The camera points toward the altar. Father Rogers approaches the microphone instead of proceeding to the altar to continue the Mass. Naomi looks around for a familiar face. She catches a glance from Ben who shakes his head. She sees tears well up in his eyes. She leans to the lady sitting next to her for some explanation. The lady remains staring at Father Rogers. Naomi longs for the Offertory song – any song.

Instead, Father Rogers says "We have an announcement." He hesitates. He looks back at Elizabeth. He turns to the stained-glass window depicting the crucifixion. He takes a breath. His face moves to form his normal smile, but it disappears. The flow of his words seems choppy. He reads from a piece of paper, something Naomi has never seen him do. "The Bishop has reassigned Elizabeth to a new parish -" he tries again to smile, "Queen of Peace." Gasps from the congregation build in volume and pulse from one side of the church to the other. People glance back and forth looking at each other for someone less confused, but they meet the same expressions. "We invite you all to this week's parish meeting on Tuesday," he looks confused, "or Thursday," he sorts through his papers, "this week's parish meeting where we will plan a good-bye party for her." A strained smile ends his announcement.

Naomi happens to look at Elizabeth as Father Rogers speaks and immediately suspects something more wrong than just losing their beloved Elizabeth. She concentrates on the faces of people on the altar. Elizabeth leans forward as if she will stand. At the same time, Ben places a hand on her shoulder. She remains seated. The Mass continues. Naomi wants the missing pieces explained, her uneasy feeling cleared, and the Mass to end. The cameraman disappears. She sees the large 14 on the side of the camera as he hurries out of the church. She wonders if the 10 o'clock news would have more information. Will someone interview Bishop Inman? Thoughts race through her head. *Why would a cameraman cover the everyday reassignments of people within the Catholic diocese? The Catholic Messenger* covered those details somewhere on the back pages. *Who reads what happens at Saint Luke's or Queen of Peace?* Naomi wonders. She only reads the Stanton Diocesan Happenings when she knows someone. Elizabeth's work on women's ordination and her projects to help the homeless certainly have appeared in *The Catholic Messenger*. But TV? As she tries to identify missing pieces that might explain this situation better, consecration continues, and communion follows.

She remembers that Elizabeth encouraged the Homeless Committee and the Committee on Women's Ordination to contact the media. "The way to change things starts with awareness. We must make our message clear. Then, use every means to spread that message." Still it doesn't make sense.

The closing song, *As the Deer Longs*, doesn't reverberate as the opening song did. Many people whisper and shuffle in the pews instead of singing. Even Linda's playing doesn't have the same vibrancy. The choir seems uneven. Naomi tries to sing – her favorite form of prayer. She finds it hard to give the song her full attention as her own questions slip in between the words. "What could have happened? Why?" The confusion wins. When the music stops, people turn to each other and voice the questions raising the noise level throughout the church.

Mark and Clare leave the pew and find Ben as he turns from the procession and places the Mass book back on the altar. A crowd gathers around Elizabeth and Father Rogers. The cameraman reappears with the camera pointing through the crowd. Naomi approaches the sanctuary to talk to Ben. They all stand watching as Father Rogers leans toward Elizabeth and holds her arm. He whispers something in her ear. Elizabeth pulls away and goes toward the cameraman. They can't hear what she says. The cameraman leaves quickly. People move away from Elizabeth. Father Rogers tries to approach her again. She walks away leaving the parishioners and Father Rogers in confusion.

"What happened?" Naomi asks Ben.

"Will you kids go downstairs for snacks?" Ben asks and looks at each with a smile. Mark holds his tractor for Ben's admiration. Clare reaches for Ben's hand.

"We want to stay with you. I can show you how my tractor works." He turns to look around at all the people. Then, he turns back to Ben. "And, and, you said you would tell us the story about your brother and the cat. Please." Mark pleads and smiles at Ben.

"And I certainly will." Ben's worried expression disappears as he admires the tractor and squeezes Clare's hand. "I have to talk to your mother about the parish meeting. It will only take a few minutes and then we will come down." He laughs and touches Mark's hair. "I'll tell you the story about my brother and the dog. Haven't you memorized it by now?" He sees a stern look on Mark's face. "I can tell it all again." Ben leans down as he talks to the children. Naomi looks around the church searching for answers.

"No, no - your brother and the <u>cat</u>! You always get confused. Maybe I <u>will</u> tell it." Mark looks like he feels sorry for Ben. "Oh, all right," Mark pulls on Clare's jacket. "Hot chocolate, for me."

"Me too," replies Clare.

They walk quietly off the altar; and as soon as Naomi turns away, Mark runs. Clare tries to catch him. They run down the aisle dodging the last few parishioners to the basement stairs and disappear.

"Something seems out of whack here. TV cameras for a transfer from one parish to another?" Naomi looks at Ben and sees his somber expression. "Queen of Peace isn't that far away? They have lots of parishioners who work at the homeless shelter? And I'll bet they have people interested in women's ordination?" She shrugs. "And tears? This isn't the whole story, is it?" She reaches for Ben's arm trying to convince herself of her own words.

"What's happening?" Zack interrupts. Naomi and Ben both give Zack blank looks. Ben pulls a handkerchief from his pocket. Zack looks back and forth between the two. "I just saw Elizabeth in the parking lot with a reporter and a camera man?"

"Oh, no!" Naomi looks at Ben and back at Zack. "I –" She tries to find the words and fails. " – Ben?" Naomi kisses Zack. Ben blows his nose. Naomi tries again, "It seems like -, the Bishop – a complicated story?" She watches Ben remove his glasses and wipe his eyes. She turns to Zack. "We missed you." She feels tears welling.

"OK. Let's start with a simple question." Zack looks from Ben to Naomi and watches their worried expressions. He looks again. "Do we still have kids?"

"They went downstairs for hot chocolate." Naomi answers.

Ben puts his handkerchief away. "No, no -" Ben takes a breath and shakes his head. "The Bishop fired Elizabeth without any reassignment."

"But – " Naomi looks at Zack and back at Ben.

Ben puts his glasses on and takes a deep breath. "Apparently Elizabeth got the call this morning. She called

24

Father Rogers. Then, Father Rogers spent the entire afternoon trying to convince the Bishop to consider a compromise. You can imagine the kind of schedule the Bishop has on a Saturday. Father Rogers followed the Bishop from a wedding at the cathedral to a Mass at Saint Mary's Home begging the Bishop every time he got a few minutes with him. Finally, in the parking lot of Saint Mary's, the Bishop agreed to transfer Elizabeth to Queen of Peace."

Ben shakes his head. "Martha kept in touch with Father Rogers all afternoon, feeding him ideas to propose to the Bishop. She found the Bishop's schedule online. She told Father Rogers where to go next and what to suggest. We all arrived for Mass knowing nothing. She gave us vague excuses for why Father Rogers didn't appear early as he usually does for the Mass. The Bishop might fire her too! I didn't know she still had access to that kind of information. She hasn't worked in the Bishop's office for several years."

Ben blinks and a tear forms. "Martha thought about making an announcement that Mass would start soon. Then, Father Rogers appeared. Father Rogers must have found Elizabeth outside the rectory when he finally got here." He takes a breath. "That's why we started so late." Ben looks around, then turns towards Zack and Naomi and lowers his voice. "We all stood there waiting for the procession. But instead of starting Mass, Father Rogers took Elizabeth into her office and closed the door! When do they ever close a door around here?" He shakes his head. "We waited. Martha didn't offer any explanation. At that point she looked as confused as we felt. I only heard Elizabeth." He looks at Zack and then at Naomi. He frowns. "She yelled." Ben rubs his forehead. "I wonder if people in the front pews heard her. 'We must confront them, Father Rogers!' She kept saying that over and over. Father Rogers spoke so softly we couldn't hear what he said. When they came out, she told us. 'The Bishop fired me.'

"Furious! I've never seen her angry and I've never seen anger like that! 'Fired for doing God's work!' She said that almost yelling too and glaring at Father Rogers." Ben shakes his head and looks at the floor. He shakes his head again.

"Then, Linda started playing the opening song and Father Rogers took Elizabeth's arm. The altar servers and I hurried to lead the way. You should have seen her back all during the Mass. I could almost see the outline of each muscle. Talk about tense!" Ben pauses and shakes his head. "I don't think I have ever prayed so hard in my whole life." Ben adjusts his glasses, rubs his eyes, and watches the disappearing clusters of parishioners. He touches Naomi's arm. "But now we must talk to her, Naomi. We want to hear the whole story and figure out what to do." He shakes his head and rubs his forehead. "Good and bad that we have a parish meeting this week. Can you imagine what everyone will say to each other and how the story will change by tomorrow? And what about the Channel 14 cameraman? And a reporter?" He looks at Zack. "Everyone will know something – whatever they put on the news tonight. Right? I don't know. This feels out of control."

"What a day to miss Mass!" Zack waves his hands in the air. His mind races through all the possibilities.

"It seems to me that to decide what to do, we must know why he fired her. People think the worst with information like this. We can't answer questions like: what happened and when does this take effect. The number of questions that spring from those answers will require even more details. Maybe you should talk to her. I could try to ask Father Rogers." She looks at Zack. "Or, what do you think, Zack? You're always logical in crisis." She touches Zack's shoulder watching his face for answers.

"Obviously we have to get more information. Maybe I'll wander around and listen to the last parishioners while you and Ben find Elizabeth and Father Rogers." Zack takes a breath and stretches. He thinks about the comfortable couch at home. Memories of his difficult trip still linger. He wants to talk to Naomi, but he puts work thoughts out of his mind.

Naomi watches the remaining clusters of parishioners. She searches for Father Rogers and Elizabeth without success. "What you say doesn't make sense." She searches the pews of the church again. "We need to talk to Elizabeth!" Her hand touches her cross and feels the edges. She watches Zack circle the pews, greeting some people as he passes. She looks down. The thoughts of how fast information like this travels worry her. Then, she remembers the kids who wait, certainly not patiently, for a fire and a story from Ben.

"Listen, I forgot about the kids. Why not find Elizabeth and come over for some cocoa by the fire? That will give everyone time to consider alternatives in a neutral territory and the fire may calm us down - hopefully. Then, I can put the kids to bed" she smiles "or you can. After telling them your story, we can talk this through and ask all the questions. I've come up with all kinds of things that might cause the Bishop to fire her. I'd prefer to hear Elizabeth's and Father Rogers's sides of the story, and sooner rather than later. Somehow I don't think the Bishop would take my call if I try to get his side of the story." She zips her jacket and smiles, "Zack will give us a sense of what he heard from the parishioners. He always knows the right questions to ask." She shakes her head. "Sometimes Elizabeth blocks questions I've noticed at parish meetings. Zack listens. Hearing the questions people raise will add to our understanding." She smiles at Ben.

"Good idea, Naomi. I'll find Elizabeth. I can stay until she finishes whatever needs finishing." He scratches his head. "Anyway, I can take her home or back to her car afterwards. I'll give you a call if we get tangled up with — what ?" He raises his eyebrows and frowns. "Maybe leave the TV off or set it to record the 10 o'clock news. We want to know what they report. Doesn't it seem like we should understand this better before the kids see something? Especially Clare."

Naomi smiles. "There you go thinking about the kids. Amazing. I imagine the worst disaster and you anticipate how the kids will respond. Thank you!"

Ben smiles. "I've got some pretty scary scenarios forming too. That TV camera frightens me the most. Angry people, especially people in leadership positions, make good news. With our luck, they'll interview Elizabeth but not Father Rogers." Ben searches the church. "We could lose all that Father Rogers worked out as the beginning of a compromise in one newscast. Even if they correct things tomorrow, thousands of people start with what they see and hear tonight. Can you think of a way to stop them?"

Naomi raises her eyebrows, holds her cross, lets her fingers feel the flat edges and moves the cross back and forth. "We probably have to live with what they report and hope we can correct it if necessary. Someone in this parish must know how to manage the media. Not me!" She shakes her head and walks toward the basement stairs. "See you soon."

Elizabeth gave the homily the first time the Nortons visited Saint Luke's, on the Feast of the Holy Family. Naomi sat next to Mark offering quiet toys. Zack and Clare watched people and listened to the service.

When Elizabeth finished reading the Gospel, she invited the children to sit on the altar. Clare left the pew first and Mark followed. They held hands and walked to the altar with the other children. At first, they sat on a step behind the circle of children seated closest to Elizabeth. Elizabeth noticed the distance between them and the other children. She introduced them to Carmela, a tall olive-skinned girl who looked a little older than Clare. Carmela made space and motioned Clare and Mark to join the larger circle. The others made room, turned and greeted them.

Elizabeth addressed the beginning of her homily to the pews while wandering among the children. She described the Holy Family and its simple life style. "I know I should simplify my life. I often look to the Holy Family for inspiration. They certainly didn't have many possessions when Jesus was born – no microwaves or DVD players or electronic toys or computers." The children giggled. She turned toward the children. "It reminds us how important just Mom, Dad, brothers, and sisters are." She extended her hand toward the boy near her. He smiled. Then, Elizabeth took a step and stood by a girl. She giggled and blushed. "We must treasure these people in our lives more than our cars, our houses, our vacation trips, or our toys." She paused as the children gazed up at her. "As we honor and love our family members, we love God. It sounds simple, doesn't it? We are born into a family.

We know the family members well. We should find it easy to love them all our lives. But somehow, instead, we find faults with the familiar people in our lives." She paused and turned toward the pews. "Our wives? Our husbands? Our children? Our parents?" Her gaze seemed to hold her own experiences. Without picking out specific faces in the pews, signs of recognition rippled through the faces.

Caught in her worry about her parents' anticipated rejection of this parish, Naomi looked up to meet Elizabeth's gaze. She smiled nervously wondering if Elizabeth read her mind. Naomi considered how to tell her parents, as she had at every church they visited. She knew her mother wouldn't approve. She could almost hear the first comments. Instead of a feeling of dread anticipating the conversation, she found herself smiling and relieved. She glanced at Zack and saw a smile on his face. She prayed to avoid conflict with her mother.

"Amazing. Yet we have God to remind us how special these people are. We make friends throughout our lives but God has given us our family; and our family -," She stopped and sent her smile across all the pews. "Our family should be just as holy as the holy family. Shouldn't it?" Naomi's apprehension disappeared. Gratefulness to have her parents nearby and involved with Clare and Mark replaced the apprehension. She smiled and glanced at Zack. He nodded and looked at the kids. Her smile broadened and she wondered what thoughts the homily brought to mind for him. She turned her attention back to Elizabeth.

"...It's difficult to step back from our differences and forgive the transgressor, a big word." She paused and sent her smile slowly around the church stopping now and then. She turned toward the children. "I'll have to ask the children to help us with that one." She moved back to the center of the children gathered on the altar. She turned toward them. Some of the younger children had started to fidget and whisper. Elizabeth's timing and sensitivity to attention level amazed Naomi. She knew chaos would erupt if Mark had to stay quiet much longer. She could see many other children younger than Mark who would lead the way if Mark didn't. One little boy quietly climbed up and down the altar steps using his hands to balance himself and tottering until he steadied himself. When he reached the top step for the second time, he moved toward the altar and discovered the fringe on the altar cloth. But Elizabeth's attention turned toward him as he reached up to touch the soft fringe. She took his hand though her back had been towards him and asked the children, "Who knows what a transgressor is?"

Lots of children raised their hands. The first one she chose giggled and put her hand down. The next stood up and smiled but didn't have an answer. Clare had not raised her hand but she fidgeted, looked at Elizabeth and mouthed words. Elizabeth approached her offering her hand, "I'm Elizabeth. I don't think we have met. And you look like you have the answer."

Clare took Elizabeth's hand and stood. Elizabeth held the microphone to capture Clare's voice. "A transgressor is someone who takes something from another when he shouldn't."

Elizabeth smiled at Clare. "What a great definition! And is your sister or brother ever a transgressor?" Elizabeth asked.

"I don't have a sister, but my brother always takes my toys. Oh, and my name is Clare and nice to meet you." Mark folded his arms and grunted. His face flushed with recognition. Naomi prepared for the end of Mark's patience. She wondered if she should approach the altar before something happened. Other parents remained in their seats.

Elizabeth thanked Clare and moved back toward the center of the children. "So, you children can see that brothers and sisters do things that make you angry. Just look at Clare's brother." The children laughed. Elizabeth's kind smile caused Mark to laugh too.

"Now, who can tell me what makes your brother special?" Carmela raised her hand and then stood up. Elizabeth recognized her, "Carmela – you have several brothers! Tell us."

Elizabeth held the microphone toward Carmela and moved it away as Carmela leaned in toward it and spoke with a loud clear voice. "My baby brother, Ricardo." She pointed out toward the pews. "He sleeps in my room and we play in the morning." Carmela smiled and sat down.

"Wonderful. How special to have a baby brother – like the baby Jesus." Elizabeth patted Carmela on the head and asked "And who can tell me something special about your sister?"

Mark raised his hand and stood up. Elizabeth turned toward Clare and asked, "Let's see. Is this your brother?" Clare nodded. "First tell us your name" Mark said his name. "You have only one sister?"

Mark nodded emphatically. "My sister is special because she wants to be a priest when she grows up." Mark hesitated a little, "Just like you." Clare's face flushed red and she shrank back hoping that Elizabeth wouldn't ask her to say anything more. Naomi watched Clare, eyebrows raised and a smile forming.

Elizabeth smiled. "Wonderful!" She looked at Clare and back at Mark. "Your sister wants to be just like Jesus and Mary Magdalene and all the wonderful people we read about in the Bible. It's also wonderful that you see that as special, Mark. Did you know that today women can't become priests?" Mark shook his head. Naomi watched little wrinkles form on his forehead. She glanced at Zack's completely smooth forehead. "Well, today the Catholic Church doesn't allow women to become priests. But many, many years ago women were priests. They led services. They offered sacraments. And we know that many women all over the world: here in Stanton, in the United States, in Ireland, in England, in Germany, in the countries of Africa want to become priests. We all work very hard to convince the Bishops and the Pope to invite women into the priesthood." A smile replaced the wrinkles on Mark's face. Elizabeth turned to include the adults as she looked toward the pews. "And we also work and will work even harder so your sister can achieve her dream. It will take many of us to pray and work for that change and many people like you, Mark, who want that to happen. Thank you. We hope you will both come again to Saint Luke's. We invite you and your family to join us."

Elizabeth found another child to talk about his mother and another to talk about his father. Each child gave her a kernel of insight to expand on and the children remained rapt and attentive through the entire homily – even the little boy who reached for the altar cloth sat quietly with his older brother.

"Now we come to a special part of the Mass. At this time, we must stay very quiet. Remaining quiet allows us to lift up our prayers to God and listen to God's word. Do you think you can stay very quiet and listen to God?" She spoke in a quiet slow voice and knelt down to face the children at eye level. They all nodded. "If you can do that, then you may stay right here, very close to God for the consecration, for this special part of the Mass. OK?" They nodded again and turned toward the altar as she joined Father Rogers and the Eucharistic ministers for the consecration.

Naomi sat in disbelief as the Mass continued and her "enthusiastic" son, as the polite nursery school teacher had described Mark, remained seated, quiet, and attentive. At the Kiss of Peace, they returned to the pew after being greeted, hugged, and introduced to everyone they passed between the altar and the pew. "Mom, Mom," Mark said over the rustle and conversation and beginning of the piano calling everyone to communion. As the voices stopped, Mark's remained loud "we have to go to this church." The people nearby chuckled and then joined in the singing of *Lamb of God*. The music brought the silence again and everyone lined up for communion.

Instead of the choir singing the communion song alone, everyone sang *One Bread, One Body*. The voices strong and weak, on key and off, floated through the church as people walked slowly to the communion stations and took communion. People patted Mark on the head as he walked with the Nortons.

After the Mass, Ben, one of the Eucharistic ministers, introduced himself to Clare and said that he wanted to enter the priesthood too and hoped that when she was old enough, he would be a priest and participate in her ordination.

Naomi overheard the conversation. She worried that Clare, at seven years of age, might have a few more versions of what she wanted to be when she grew up before she reached a final decision. She also imagined the disappointment if her current choice could ever happen with the Church's long history of denying women the possibility to become priests and celebrate the sacraments. But Clare seemed unruffled, introduced herself and introduced Ben to the family. Naomi smiled at the kindness Ben showed her daughter. They chatted while others greeted the Nortons, invited them to the coffee hour downstairs, offered phone numbers, and addresses for future reference.

Naomi watches the glow of the fire fade. She remembers that glow before they left for church, before they knew of Elizabeth's situation, before Zack returned with hints of his difficult trip. She watches Zack sleeping in his father's worn chair. They had agreed she would take the main role in child rearing so he could advance in his job. She wonders about that decision. Did he feel burdened by it? Should she have kept her job? Should they explore ways for them to both work part-time?

Ben returns from story time with the kids and sits on the couch. He sees Zack sleeping and smiles at Naomi. They both stand and move to the table where they can still see the fire.

"Where did he go?" Ben watches Zack and speaks in a whisper. "He looks exhausted."

"When he sleeps like that, I know he's had a difficult meeting. We don't have to whisper." Naomi assures Ben.

Ben whispers. "He works super hard. Is that employee giving him trouble again?"

"I know the employee who has troubled him was supposed to travel with him on this trip. I imagine she contributed to the exhaustion." Naomi shakes her head. "Hopefully having a day off tomorrow will give him time to rest and I'll find out what happened."

"Tomorrow. What will happen at the Masses tomorrow?" Ben grimaces. "Oh, the news. Did you record the 10 o'clock news?"

Naomi sighs. "I certainly forgot. I wonder if Zack remembered." She turns the volume down on the TV and checks for a recording. "He remembered."

"Well, just about the worst coverage we could have expected. Or not really?" Ben shakes his head. "And I'll bet Father Rogers has not seen it. More news stations will send reporters to Mass tomorrow and who knows what Elizabeth will do."

Saint Luke Church Bulletin – Stanton Diocese
23rd Sunday of Ordinary Time

Saint Luke Mission: Serving the poor is the highest priority for Saint Luke's.

Dear Friends,

The geese woke me up this morning and I stood at the window watching them fly across the sky. Some of us don't look forward to fall as much as we look forward to spring. Fall is one of my favorite seasons because God shows us the variety of his love in everything. The beauty of the fall colors and then the simplicity of the bare trees waving against the sky is surely God's work.

Even as you might dread the winter that follows, take time to appreciate the letting go of fall. Perhaps you have things to let go of in your life, someone to forgive, possessions you could give away, or fewer activities to leave more time for prayer.

At Saint Luke's we recognize the most precious of God's creatures, those struggling. Perhaps they lack jobs or addictions dominate their lives or illness has caused financial problems or they have no homes. We started Lombardo House with the help of Bill Lombardo's generous donation. Many poor men use the shelter and enjoy the kind people who volunteer. Parishioners supplement food supplies every month.

We need your help in many ways. Please see the list at the end of the bulletin and find a way that you can help our guests at Lombardo House. Perhaps thinking of someone less fortunate can dull the distaste for winter.

Next Sunday is the feast of our own Saint Luke. The school children have been preparing a play. They will perform at the coffee hour between the two Masses. They will bake cookies in the shape of Saint Luke and sell them at the coffee hour.

I think about Texas weather when the temperatures start to drop. But the Saint Luke's parishioners make up for the cold weather with all their warmth!

Have a blessed week!

Elizabeth Winter, Pastoral Administrator

Notices

- Prayer Line – 453-3344: Call the prayer line with your prayer intentions.
- Lombardo House – Thanks for your generosity. Last year we were able to stock the kitchen for a whole month with those donations! We're also looking for gently used household items: single bed sheets, towels, wash cloths, and new pillows. We serve our guests a warm snack and a hearty breakfast. Bring non-perishable items to the House after Masses: canned soups, crackers, peanut butter, cereals, powdered milk, muffin or cake mixes,
- Women's Committee – The Women's Committee now meets in the parish hall. We've outgrown the living room and welcome all interested in developing proposals to increase women's participation in all things Catholic.
- Tithing – Remember to put your suggestions in our mailbox for organizations serving the poor in the city.
- Peace & Justice Update – Interested in Peace & Justice issues? Join the Peace & Justice Committee. We meet monthly on the third Thursday, keep track of local and global issues, and organize a yearly Peace & Justice Sunday. We'd love to have you join us.

Naomi

Naomi put her apron on a hook. "I shouldn't be too late. I read the list of topics for the meeting. I'm curious to see how they set up for such interactive meetings and how they manage the time." She kissed the kids whose attention remained on the book, *Harry Potter and the Sorcerer's Stone*, Zack had opened. He read the first sentence. Mark wiggled closer. Zack looked up for a kiss.

"Come on, Dad, read the book, read the book," Mark tapped his finger on the book. Naomi leaned over, kissed Zack, and patted Mark on the head.

Zack continued reading. Naomi listened. She questioned her decision to an evening commitment. Slowly she reached for the car keys. Even as she backed the car out of the driveway, she hesitated.

When she arrived at church, she sat in her car wondering if she would enjoy or even have the skills to facilitate after observing the parish meetings. It surprised her that Father Rogers or Elizabeth didn't run the meetings like the parish council at her parents' church.

She remembered the day she decided to join the team. She and Mary had finished stocking the shelter with the latest food delivery, they put on their coats and signed out. Mary's invitation to Naomi to join the facilitation team felt like an honor but scared her. As they passed Jeff's office, Jeff asked, "Are either of you going by the parish office?"

"I have some materials for the next religious education project I want to drop off," Naomi stopped.

"Terrific. Could you take the monthly shelter report to Elizabeth?" Jeff held the report and passed it to Naomi as she nodded. "Just put it on her desk, if you can't find her."

Naomi leafed through a few pages.

"We've had a good month, lots of food distributed, beds occupied every night, and donations cover this month's expenses!" He smiled. "We don't always manage that."

"That is great news!" Naomi showed Mary the report. "I see you featured Lou!"

"Yes, he agreed, though I had some convincing to do. We took it slow. Such a quiet guy." Jeff smiled.

"I know!" Naomi nodded and shrugged. "I bet Elizabeth will find a way to work his story into a homily."

They all smiled. Jeff turned back to his desk. Mary and Naomi continued to the door.

"Have you spent any time with Elizabeth?" Mary asked.

Naomi shrugged her shoulders. "Funny, we've been in the parish for two years and I have not spoken to her myself. I love her homilies. She connects with the guests when she visits here. But I haven't spoken to her alone." They closed the door. Before going to their cars, Naomi said "You know our Clare, our Clare has developed a friendship with Elizabeth. I hope she is in her office! See you next week."

Mary put her hand on Naomi's shoulder. "We all consider Elizabeth one of the parish's treasures." She paused. "I should tell you, she suggested you for the facilitation team."

"Oh," surprise filled Naomi's face. "I wonder why." She drove to the parish office and parked on the street. She grabbed the materials she had collected for Mark's religious education class and the shelter report. Questions filled her mind as she walked to the office.

"Naomi how nice to see you," Elizabeth said as she pulled on her coat. She smiled and left her coat unzipped.

"Jeff asked me to bring you this month's shelter report," she handed it to Elizabeth and turned to find Margaret.

"Do you have a minute?" Elizabeth asked.

Naomi turned back. "Oh, yes, but it looks like you are leaving?"

"I'm not in a hurry and I have looked forward to talking with you. I want to thank you for – Well, I have a list actually. So yes, I do have time."

Naomi blushed. Elizabeth walked back toward her office. As they passed Martha's desk, Martha smiled, nodded, and reached her hand toward Naomi.

"Oh, right. I hope I got the materials you need: big pens, poster board, and tape." Martha took the bag and nodded. "Mark can't wait to make signs for the Children's Food Drive! What a great way to teach children about the poor." Martha placed Naomi's items in a box labeled for the religious education classes as Naomi continued to Elizabeth's office.

Naomi fingered the zipper on her purse as she entered. Elizabeth sat on the worn couch donated by a parishioner. "Have a seat on my mid-century Goodwill couch," Elizabeth invited Naomi to join her. Naomi laughed and sat wondering what Elizabeth could thank her for. She reviewed her own list of benefits the family had experienced since joining Saint Luke's. Two years made for a long list.

As Naomi composed her own list of thank yous, Elizabeth spoke. "Your whole family has added so much to Saint Luke's," Her smile and pause seemed to release Naomi's tension. The feeling she had experienced during Elizabeth's homilies washed over her. While Naomi always felt like Elizabeth spoke directly to her during homilies and she knew others experienced that feeling, she acknowledged the moment. Only she heard these words. She stopped composing her list and listened. Elizabeth watched Naomi and waited before continuing as if she read Naomi's mind. She shook her head. "I don't know where to begin." She smiled and took a few breaths. "I figured you might be the, or at least one of the, reasons we all rave about the Nortons. How would we function without Zack's ability and readiness to fix an ongoing list of things at the school: broken windows, plumbing surprises. I can't even remember how many times he has saved us from closing the school while we search for someone to help. Jeff has told me about your work with Lou." She lifted the shelter report. "He probably doesn't mention your name in this description, but we know."

Naomi nodded and blushed. "We feel like we have found a supportive community. We acknowledge, Zack and I, that you, with your homilies and your work at the shelter, have showed us how to set an example for our children."

"I'm sure Mary has told you what a great facilitator you will be. I hope you plan to join that integral group." Elizabeth watched Naomi's face. "Do I see some doubt there?"

Naomi shrugged her shoulders.

Elizabeth watched Naomi's expression relax from wrinkles of doubt to a faint smile. "Take your time. Ask questions of everyone. You will find all the facilitators bring different skills to the task. And they function as a team. They agree you will be an important addition to that team." Elizabeth's gaze remained on Naomi. "The parish meeting might be new to you. What parish did you attend as a child?"

"Saint Paul of the Cross"

"Ah, yes, a very traditional parish and quite conservative."

Naomi nodded with conviction. "My parents still attend there." She wondered whether to tell Elizabeth about her parents' criticisms.

"I'll bet your parents have questioned your choice to join Saint Luke's."

Naomi sighed.

"We should find a good Sunday to invite your parents and let them see the real Saint Luke's. We all know how rumors distort reality."

"I've thought about that. Maybe you could help us choose a time to invite them."

"I'm sure they love their grandchildren."

"They wish they had grandchildren before they had me. They call, visit, invite, and spoil! I enjoy seeing them with the children." They both laughed.

"So, let's try for the Sunday where the children will introduce the food drive?!"

Naomi agreed and wondered whether to ask about Clare and how to handle her dream of becoming a priest.

"Now my biggest thank you – Clare. What a mature, thoughtful, determined young lady!" She paused. "I plan to spend more concentrated time with her exploring her dream. She will become a future leader, she leads her peers now. I saw

40

that the first day your family attended. But I want to build some reality into those dreams of hers." Elizabeth shook her head. "She helps me to remember my passion. So, I must share my experience in a way that won't dampen her enthusiasm."

"We have struggled with that dream. Zack did not grow up Catholic and has doubts about all things Catholic." Naomi stopped. "Except for Saint Luke's so that gives us some basis to talk about Clare." She smiled. "Still, we'd love the help.

She smiled, removed the keys, and took her purse. She remembered how she told Zack about her meeting with Elizabeth that day. The relief of knowing that Elizabeth would give Clare some reality kept her smiling and a little distracted during dinner that night. After the children finished their bedtime routine that night, Zack questioned Naomi. He could tell she wanted to talk.

"So what's up?" he asked as they cleaned up the dinner dishes.

Naomi rinsed a dish and then put it down. "I – I don't know where to begin."

Zack turned off the water and guided Naomi to the kitchen table.

She took several breaths. Her thoughts from the day settled. "I spoke with Elizabeth today." She sighed and smiled. "And she – she treasures our Clare."

Zack smiled. "Good judgment!"

"I wanted to ask about Clare, about her dream, about – "

"Wow, and she – ?"

"She says she learns from Clare. But she wants to guide her to understand the whole no-women-in-the-Catholic church thing. She didn't say it that way. Sam Bonner would say it that way. Well, he would actually say something laden with less hope."

"Wow, and wow! We have support on one of those tough parenting challenges." Zack reached for Naomi's hand. "Shall we finish up here?"

They both stood. "Oh, and you know the facilitators have been trying to convince me to work with them. It turns out Elizabeth recommended me!"

Doubts still lingered, especially missing story time, even once a month. She pushed her notebook into her purse, locked the car, and entered the church by the side door.

When she opened the door, she heard a single voice singing unaccompanied. She stood on the stairs leading to the parish hall. The voice sounded familiar and came from the basement. She tried to match the voice with a person. She wondered about the physique for such a resonant tenor voice. Did facilitators need to sing too? She remembered Mary had spoken about a lawyer and someone named Ben.

The piano joined the voice. It played softly letting the voice dominate. Maybe a choir practice? She glanced at her watch and sat on a stair not wanting to interrupt. When he sang the psalm from the previous Sunday's readings, she recognized the voice and searched for the face. She could see his radiant smile, the book he sang from and his hand raised to invite participation. She closed her eyes and enjoyed the medley of familiar Mass songs. The piano sounded a little off. His voice remained clear and in tune. Her dependence on instruments and other strong voices made this voice that much more amazing. The slight problem with the piano highlighted its beauty.

The piano stopped. His voice trailed off. She heard him greet someone. She opened her eyes and resumed her path to the basement where Mary introduced Ben Peer to her. She shook his hand with her mouth hanging open.

"Amazing voice, right? Amazing! But wait until you work with him as a facilitator! And this man can't decide if he should enter the priesthood?" Mary threw up her arms. "Anyway –"

"Your voice – " Naomi lost the rest of the sentence as Ben smiled. She remembered the Nortons' first visit to Saint Luke's. " –lovely! And you, you welcomed us all, especially our daughter, Clare, so warmly the first time we attended a Mass."

The first parish meetings flew by. Naomi took notes for several meetings and observed the other facilitators leading meetings and fielding questions. She loved learning about all the activities in the parish, enjoyed the dynamics of the team and left the house with more enthusiasm, except when Zack traveled.

"You know our story. How did you find Saint Luke's?" Naomi turned from the sink. Ben put the dry mug in the cupboard and reached for another. "I – well it's kind of a complicated story." He held the mug without drying.

Naomi pointed at the trays of dirty mugs. "We have time." She smiled. "But only if you want to." She watched his face and turned back to the sink. The other facilitators had finished folding the chairs and said their goodbyes. Though they had become friends, it seemed strange to her that she didn't know this part of his story. Still, she respected his privacy, knew she could ask the question, and didn't have expectations about getting an answer.

Ben dried the next few mugs and Naomi washed. "I guess – " He put a mug down and smiled. "I do want to tell you. Question Five on the application for divinity school asks for my Catholic history. I really think this question keeps the application on my desk instead of in the mail."

Naomi watched his eyes and added another mug to the drainer. She emptied the dirty water and added new water and soap."

"OK, this won't come out in order."

Naomi shrugged her shoulders.

"OK." He took a breath. "I'll just talk. Maybe you can help me create a better order." He took a deeper breath. "Or tell me to rip up the application." He laughed.

Naomi's eyebrows raised and she shook her head no. She turned back to the sink. He talked.

"I was born the middle child in my family. Now, I am the youngest. My younger brother, Ted, died so young, only twelve years old. That made me the youngest." He laughed and held the towel without reaching for a mug. Then he frowned. "I –, have you read theories about birth order?"

43

Naomi shook her head. "Anyway, I seem to have behavior and experiences that don't match those theories." He smiled. Naomi nudged another mug onto the pile. "Three boys: Tim, Ben, and Ted. Our parents grew up Catholic. You'll enjoy this, they attended Saint Paul of the Cross." Naomi smiled and placed another mug on the rack. "We, except for Ted, walked to church, attended Sunday school, and celebrated all the Holy Days." Ben paced back and forth holding the dishtowel and scratching his head. "Tim, -" He paused. "Maybe this part shouldn't go on the application. Or not really?"

"We can always edit later." Naomi stopped washing and watched.

"Right. It seems important. My parents definitely favored Tim. He did everything to make our parents happy, you know, he met their expectations. Ted needed so much. His care wore my parents out. So -" Ben sat at the table. "I took care of Ted, really. I mean, my parents took him to appointments and handled medications; but I talked to him, read to him, listened for his next request, you know. When he felt well enough, I walked with him or, near the end, took him in his wheel chair."

"What did he have?"

"He had MS. After he died, someone told me how unusual it was to contract it so young and to have it move that quickly. But he had a beautiful energy and wanted to do everything he could. My parents just wanted him to stay in bed. I wanted him to have fun, you know, live, and didn't understand why my parents got angry with me."

"Wow, I have a deep fear about how I will fail as a parent. What if we have a child that needs extra attention and second, I worry about favoring one child over another. In the difficult moments of parenting, and your parents must have had many of those, I can't monitor whether I make those errors. I guess someone would classify favoring one child as an error. But how to constantly find the energy to support a sick child?" Naomi put the last mug on the rack and sat with Ben.

"Funny." Ben thought a moment. "Maybe my parents wrestled with those thoughts and feelings? Back then, I only saw how much attention they gave to Tim and how little they gave to Ted. They wouldn't even take him to church!" He shook his head. "You know, my Catholic history begins right there! Ted had a very deep faith and accepted each day as it came. He didn't ever say anything negative about my parents or Tim. He really inspired my faith and my love of children."

Naomi smiled remembering how quickly Ben connected with Mark and Clare. She nodded. "And you didn't think about yourself during all this?"

"What do you mean?"

"It sounds like you provided the emotional support for Ted and got no recognition, reinforcement, even thanks while all the attention went to Tim?"

"I guess you could look at it that way. I just thought about Ted."

"What happened when he died?" Naomi asked shuddering to think of a child's death.

Ben fingered the dishtowel bringing the corners together as if to fold it, looked at the pile of mugs on the drainer, and took a deep breath. "Ted wanted to go to church daily during his last weeks. I took him. After he died, I kept going. Now that I think about it, I guess it became something I still felt I did with him, and maybe for him?" He leaned to stand and then didn't. "I had read about the Jewish traditions after the death of a loved one. I needed some kind of ritual beyond the funeral, when I didn't know what to do. At home, my parents erased Ted from our lives. They cleaned his room. They filled bags to give away his clothes and all his possessions. I had to grab his Bible from a bag and a book the doctor had given him about meditation." Ben looked at his watch.

"Ben, what an amazing story. I can't believe you haven't expressed any bitterness toward your parents."

"I really didn't have room for it and I had the church, even Saint Paul of the Cross. Antonia –"

"No," Naomi's mouth dropped open.

"Yes, what a presence!" Their expressions echoed each other. Naomi's memories of Antonia's compassion balancing her parents' stern interpretation of Catholic doctrine caused a few tears to form.

When Naomi's turn to facilitate came, she hesitated. "Mary knows everyone in the parish. I don't have that advantage and," she turned to Mary, "your ability to respond to everything diplomatically, especially those long-winded parishioners – I can't do that. I'd want to cut them off."

"They might need that. Quite honestly people like Tony Mancuso have two of the most difficult characteristics for facilitating." Everyone smiled. "He acts like a deaf person by preventing any eye contact. That technique alone prevents interruptions and makes you look like the screamer when you do get his attention. The second one works well with the first characteristic; he only uses one sentence which lasts as long as he wants to speak." They all laughed. "Anyway, we have to get you fully trained, now that we lost two of our veteran facilitators." Everyone nodded. Comments overlapped as expressions grew serious. Naomi knew that one former facilitator decided to spend her retirement in Florida instead of remaining in Stanton. Since many of her parents' friends either moved permanently to Florida or spent winters there, she could understand that decision. No one mentioned why the other facilitator left. She wondered and listened. She knew the team would support her. She recalled Ben telling a speaker about the time limit to prevent her from speaking too long. "Let me summarize your point," he had said. The speaker agreed, sat down and the meeting continued. "But – " Naomi started.

"We can do it together," Ben suggested. He glanced down at the agenda. "You should definitely lead the meeting when Lombardo House gives their report. As a matter of fact, why don't we make that the first item?" Everyone nodded. "Then, give me a sign if you want to switch and I will take over. Depending on how it goes, you could take over again at the end. Kind of get your toe in the water." Ben watched Naomi's face. "Or not really?"

Naomi breathed more easily and smiled. "That sounds great!"

Saint Luke Church Bulletin - Stanton Diocese

27rd Sunday of Ordinary Time

Saint Luke Mission: Serving the poor is the highest priority for Saint Luke's.

Dear Friends,

School starts this week and we look forward to seeing our favorite returning students. And we welcome our ten new students to Saint Luke's School! The teachers are ready and we will bless them at the Masses this week. Also, this week's collection will go toward the school.

Beginnings remind us the value of a clean slate and filling it with new learning. It also reminds us to renew our faith. Take time to learn a new prayer or read about a new saint.

Fall is a special time at Saint Luke's. We look forward to celebrating Saint Luke's Feast Day in October and all of the saints in November. Choose a saint or Saint Luke to pray with you as the leaves change and the days get shorter.

When I was growing up, my mother read to us about the saints each evening before we went to sleep. When she became ill and bed ridden, she asked me to tell her those stories. I could remember Saint Luke and tell his story; and I could remember Saint Catherine, my mother's name. But I had trouble remembering the others. I found the book my mother read to us and read it to her each time I visited. We remember as we tell each other these stories.

Spread the love,
Father Rogers

Notices

- Prayer Line – 453-3344: Call the prayer line with your prayer intentions.
- Lombardo House – Our ministry to the homeless has gained quite a reputation. Volunteers are always welcome. Bring your neighbors or your work colleagues to help with the many tasks.

- Women's Committee – Elizabeth will be presenting at this year's Call To Action (CTA) conference in November. At the next Women's Committee meeting she will gather more examples of active women in our diocese. Please bring contact information for the women you'd like to invite.
- Tithing – For those new to Saint Luke's, the Tithing Committee meets quarterly to donate the tithing funds to local non-profits serving the poor. We set aside 1% of all money collected at Mass for this purpose. If you know of organizations that deserve a donation, please leave your suggestion in the Tithing Committee mailbox at the rectory.
- Peace & Justice Update – Interested in Peace & Justice issues? Join the Peace & Justice Committee. We meet monthly on the third Thursday, keep track of local and global issues and organize a yearly Peace & Justice Sunday. We'd love to have you join us.
- Food Collection: This Sunday. Remember to bring your non-perishable food for the poor families in the neighborhood. We'll collect your donations before communion.

Elizabeth

With her divinity degree in hand and a sense of pride for her many awards as the youngest graduate, Elizabeth Winter created a plan to achieve her personal goals quickly. Approaching thirty years old, she matched the goals with a timeline to achieve them. Having achieved the first part of her plan, to present a session at the yearly Call to Action conference, she looked forward to her first job and her ability to establish herself in a parish where she could continue her Call to Action work.

Father Flaherty, the pastor of Our Lady of Providence, had suggested a Best Western near the bus station. The dusty air made her cough as she stepped off the bus onto the road. *A lot different than the Northeast, for sure,* she thought. A shred of doubt entered her mind about leaving Stanton, New York, her family and the diocese she knew so well. Memories of cooler temperatures at this time of year faded as she remembered Stanton winters and focused on getting to the hotel. She lugged her duffel bag across the quiet street. She wondered about the famous Texas hospitality in San Cosmas as she moved her duffel to the other shoulder and walked toward the hotel. At least she wouldn't meet anyone before she changed her wrinkled clothes.

Finding a direct bus from the Houston airport caused her to change her flight. By leaving earlier than originally planned, she could reduce the long trip by several hours. In the hotel room, she lifted clothes trying to avoid unpacking everything. She hoped she would find, quickly, a nightgown, toothpaste, and toothbrush. Piles formed, none containing what she needed to prepare for bed. By the time she found her nightgown, all of her belongings lay in uneven piles on the other bed.

Heading for the bathroom, thoughts of Jay made her frown. His last words puzzled her. She tried to piece them together.

She expected him to show excitement and curiosity about her new position. It wouldn't have surprised her if he had expressed some sadness because she would live far away. As she brushed her teeth, she stopped. *Did he give me advice,* she wondered? She didn't expect advice from her baby brother. Something about baking bread. Yes, he compared her career in the church to preparing and baking bread. She laughed to herself, rinsed her mouth and turned out the bathroom light.

She pulled the covers up and tried to remember his plans for the weekend. Leaving earlier than planned meant she missed his graduation. Jay would wear his cap and gown and march across the green lawn of the university as she attended the first Masses at Our Lady of Providence. At least their other siblings would gather and celebrate graduation with him. She closed her eyes. Sleep didn't come. The more difficult part of their conversation came back to her.

"Elizabeth, congratulations! I'm really excited about your new job. I know you will create excitement for the parishioners and shower them with great ideas. I'm happy for you," he paused, "I just don't understand why you won't stay for my graduation?" She didn't respond to his question. She remembered her impatience and her clenched teeth. She hadn't told him about the change until she called to ask for a ride to the airport. "It really hurts, Elizabeth." The traffic at the airport saved her from losing her temper.

As she closed her eyes again, she said a *Hail Mary* for her baby brother and reminded herself to call him the next day.

Of all the job opportunities Elizabeth received, Our Lady of Providence presented the most challenges and, she had determined after extensive research, the best opportunity to get herself established in the women's ordination movement. Texas didn't have many active women's ordination spokespeople. In fact, she couldn't name one. Texas carried clout in many other venues. She saw her position in Texas as a way to expose and promote her talents. With that base, she would achieve a leadership role in the US movement. Without local competition, she could build a convincing story and lead Texas in this effort. The opportunities outweighed the challenges. She just had to manage the pastor, bring energy to the parishioners and develop vital connections slowly. She assumed the remoteness of the parish would give her the freedom she needed to establish the connections without the kind of oversight a big city parish in the Northeast might include. Slowly, she knew would challenge her most of all. She liked to establish a goal and accomplish it. Jay's advice about the bread and her career would prove valuable. How many things could go wrong before you put the bread in the oven? She pushed that out of her mind and imagined a firm, hard crusted loaf sitting on a board still steaming.

Within a week, Elizabeth met half of the parishioners, attended all the services and functions of the parish and gained respect from the pastor. In the second week, she weighed ideas for taking on more responsibility before suggesting them. Jay's baking advice came back to her. The choice of what to suggest compared with creating the right balance of flours in a multigrain loaf of bread. She sat in the pastor's office planning the weekend Masses for the month and waited for some kind of opening.

When Father paused, she said "Your days seem heavily scheduled. You inspire me with how you handle all these responsibilities." She could feel a rush of excitement. She smiled. "Most people have no idea how much a pastor does!" He looked up from his paper and smiled. "I hope you will let me take more responsibility as time passes." Father Flaherty smiled and nodded. She took a breath and reminded herself to go slowly, but her excitement took over. "I've attended several Preaching Institute Workshops both at Call To Action and my divinity school. Those workshops were the highlight of my studies." She paused. He nodded. She paused. "I know they take a lot of work, but I would love to deliver homilies."

Memories of her homily classes carried her away from Father's lists. "What makes a perfect sermon? What I learned in the classroom didn't answer that question. Even comments on assigned sermons didn't provide a satisfactory answer for me. I try to analyze sermons when I sit in the pews. My personal experience influences my assessments. Though more unconscious for parishioners, they bring their experiences to the pews as I do. I'd love to hear your ideas. Years of experience must create better and better homilies. I read somewhere that crafting a message to touch people both emotionally and intellectually might fail the category of a perfect sermon if the words did not inspire human will, did not give the listener some guidance for major life choices or even day to day decisions. If we don't know our parishioners well enough to touch some of those experiences, a sermon might not keep their attention let alone inspire them."

"An interesting request," he responded, interrupting her musings. "I'll handle the homilies." He turned to the assignment of altar servers.

"Perhaps we can talk about this in the future." Elizabeth felt her heart beat quicken and forced a smile.

"Perhaps," the pastor did not smile.

"I will put some examples in your mailbox. See what you think." She looked back at the list of Mass assignments. He stared at her bright red hair.

A few more breaths and her heartbeat slowed. She checked the items they had accomplished and looked up. He looked away. "Let me know what other tasks I can do." She reached into her bag and pulled out *Spirit & Song*. "Have you used this book? It has most songs in both Spanish and English." She waited. The skin around his mouth and on his forehead relaxed.

"You know we have many Spanish-speaking parishioners?"
She nodded.

He took the book, opened it, and turned pages. Elizabeth watched as he stopped at the introduction and the accreditations. "This looks like it has the right approvals." He smiled. "And - Well, that would add to our services since our Spanish-speaking parishioners love to sing and I don't speak Spanish. Please show this to Maria, the choir director. She will love this." He looked down at his list. He looked up again. "Maria will decide whether to use this book." Elizabeth nodded. Father watched. "She has led the choir for ten years."

She wondered whether to say that she spoke Spanish. Her instincts told her to wait.

As the months passed, Elizabeth noticed that several of the Spanish-speaking parishioners appeared at the office in need of support. One day, Elizabeth heard the pastor sending one to a counseling center in the city. "I speak Spanish, can I help?"

Word passed quickly among the Spanish-speaking parishioners. Her office became the gathering place for that community. She set aside time each week and invited the Spanish-speaking parishioners to gather. Often Elizabeth asked questions and they chatted. She listened to stories of their lives and the community. When one had a private matter to discuss, she spoke to the parishioner after the group left. Father Flaherty didn't thank her verbally, but he often smiled and nodded as he guided a parishioner to Elizabeth's office.

During Elizabeth's last years of study in divinity school, she learned about Call To Action (CTA.) Of course, she shared CTA's goal of including more women and minorities in all aspects of church life. All she learned about CTA's other projects to drive for change, she saw how well they matched her passion. She read announcements about the conferences, checked the web site regularly and found articles and news stories about the Catholics who worked for justice and equality in the church. An energetic group within CTA advocated for women. Attending conferences during her divinity school studies and working on the Women's Ordination Committee, had produced the invitation to speak at the last conference.

Each conference included presentations exploring and advocating for more participation by women in every aspect of Catholic life. After attending her first conference, she joined CTA and communicated with the women most interested in women's ordination throughout the world. Her energy, smile, interest in others, and ready support for CTA goals resulted in an invitation to take a leadership position on the Women's Equality Committee. When she took the job in Texas, she had received Father Flaherty's permission to attend the annual conference that fall. She paid for the conference herself. She returned with more ideas for integrating the Spanish-speaking and English-speaking parishioners. Any free time she had from parish responsibilities went to writing articles and planning conference presentations with others on the CTA Women's Equality Committee.

As liturgies expanded at Our Lady of Providence to include Spanish hymns, she suggested having one or two Prayers of the Faithful delivered in Spanish. Father Flaherty agreed insisting that he choose the readers and she translate their petitions for him. He always chose men despite Elizabeth's recommendations of active women in the parish. She kept suggesting. He kept choosing men.

The parish grew. Many new parishioners spoke only Spanish. They looked to Elizabeth for guidance. They requested services. Her weekly gatherings gave them time to flesh out ideas that appealed to many. Several months after she started these gatherings, Elizabeth moved their meetings to the church hall. The number of people attending each week exceeded even the rectory conference room.

A supper program gathered more and more support among the group members. She encouraged them to present their idea to Father. Elizabeth translated as they presented. His agreement that they could try it for a month, attracted more parishioners. Elizabeth cultivated one of the wealthy members of the Spanish-speaking community who brought his friends to church. As more poor parishioners joined because of the supper program, the wealthier parishioners pledged a large yearly donation that guaranteed the future of the supper program. Father Flaherty's delight and agreement to continue the program still didn't produce a sign of gratitude for Elizabeth's work. He did congratulate the group and thank the donors. Her disappointment at this oversight paled as she recognized how many new parishioners shared her passion for involving more women in all aspects of parish life.

She suggested a note for the weekly bulletin to celebrate the thriving Spanish-speaking activities, the women's committee programs and her own first anniversary with the parish. She failed to notice the editing of her note, both eliminating her anniversary and any mention of the women's committee work. Buoyed by Father's lack of his usual questioning and rewording of her note, she decided to submit a proposal for a presentation about these programs to CTA for the upcoming conference. She knew the parishioners' struggles with immigration issues, family conflict and difficulties finding work would attract CTA audiences, especially because of the strategies she used: inviting wealthy Spanish-speaking parishioners into meetings with poorer parishioners. They heard the stories in person. Then, she solicited their help. As she worked with them, strong friendships developed. Some of the women praised her interpretation of Bible passages that highlighted women. Their praise reminded her of her desire to preach. It surprised her that several of these women even had hopes of following her lead as a pastoral administrator. Elizabeth cultivated these women and met with them to formally launch a women's committee in the parish. They inspired her with their passion for the church and their desire to serve. Though she touched on all the efforts to attract new parishioners, her CTA proposal, "Growing Cross-Cultural Enthusiasm for Women in the Church," emphasized the energy and ideas of the women who shared Elizabeth's passion for more involvement.

When CTA accepted her proposal, she thought about taking at least one of the women with her. She held the letter in her hand as she saw Father Flaherty approaching.

"CTA accepted my proposal for a presentation at the conference next month!" She showed him the letter.

He read it. He handed it back to her. "Did we include this in our budget?"

"Oh -" Elizabeth's excitement remained strong. She hadn't thought about those details. "I will pay for it." Her success at bringing in donations from new and old parishioners kept her smile broad. She looked at the letter. "A wonderful acknowledgement of the -" She looked up at Father Flaherty, "your parish's work with the Spanish-speaking parishioners." Her heartbeat increased. She took a breath and lifted her hair off her neck. Images of bread dough stuck to her hands flashed through her mind. She blinked. The glow of her excitement flickered. She took a breath and spoke of how the parish had benefited. Money, she tried money. "When I wrote this proposal, I looked at the parish attendance over the last year. Did you realize that we are almost 50% Spanish-speaking now?" He didn't respond. "But the most amazing thing is the generosity of these new parishioners. Our collections have increased too! 20%!"

Elizabeth's letter to the CTA committee indicated that a complication, which she hadn't anticipated, would prevent her from attending the conference. She apologized, looked forward to next year's conference and praised the committee for its strong program. She didn't mention Father Flaherty's refusal for her to attend or his establishment of probation for her or the list of new rules she would now follow.

With less enthusiasm, she wrote a letter to the Bishop outlining the programs she had developed to increase the number of Spanish-speaking parishioners as Father Flaherty had directed. The Bishop invited her to a diocesan meeting where she presented the programs without reference to the women's activities. Her CTA proposal had emphasized these activities as a fruit of the community building. Father Flaherty insisted she describe only the other activities and those statistics. She continued to work with the energetic women. When questions moved in the direction of why she would not attend the CTA conference, she changed the subject. It surprised her that none of the women probed further about missing this opportunity. They all worked to increase membership and added women from the non-Spanish-speaking parishioners. The lack of surprise, let alone outrage, that Father Flaherty erased the women's achievements in their parish shocked her. She phrased things diplomatically, but she suspected that her colleagues at the CTA conference knew what had happened. These lovely parish women trusted and withheld, or didn't form, the questions that circled her as she went about her daily tasks.

Not speaking at CTA set her plan back to gain recognition within Texas. That step formed the foundation of achieving

CTA, and eventually, US leadership on the path to women's ordination. She had expected some pushback from the parish women to nudge her plan forward; but still took heart in the support she had. For the moment, next steps eluded her.

During her first months in Texas, Jay called Elizabeth regularly. He tried to replicate the closeness they had experienced previous to her move. When she lived in Stanton, New York, they saw each other weekly. They took walks and hashed out their experiences with each other. Over the years these times had evolved from Jay describing a problem he faced and asking for advice to a free-flowing conversation where they often spoke at the same time. Laughter always punctuated these times. They could say anything to each other.

If Elizabeth returned a call, she rarely had much time. He could hear the keys on her computer clicking as he talked. She answered questions with one or two words and didn't ask him about his new job or their siblings. With all the responsibility to keep the family going after their mother died, Jay wondered if Elizabeth's lack of communication meant she experienced burn out from family responsibilities. She coached him through his own breaking from the family before he left for college and probably his older siblings before him. He tried to understand her lack of communication and caring. None of the explanations he hypothesized gave him comfort. He missed her insight and advice. He longed to know what she did in the new job, he missed the frequent talks; but mostly he wanted to hear about her feelings about the pastor and her role.

Each time he selected her number, he composed the message he would leave as the unanswered rings accumulated. He always mentioned something about bread. He worried that her desire to achieve ordination would drive her to ignore the need to balance her goals with her pastor's and with the character of the diocese. What she had researched before choosing that small town in Texas, might be different than what she found. "Did you read the list of ingredients carefully? It doesn't take much with bread, Elizabeth, to create a sticky mess that doesn't rise."

As the parish continued to grow, so did the choir. Elizabeth and Maria enjoyed choosing music for the Masses and including hymns in both languages. Maria became one of the most active members among the women working to expand opportunities for women in church life. Elizabeth wanted to name the committee the Women's Ordination Exploratory Committee.

"If you put ordination in the title, we'll have the diocese breathing down our necks." Maria shook her head and sipped her Mexican coffee. She added more cinnamon.

"We want that!" Elizabeth felt heat on her neck and tightening of those muscles when she thought about missing the CTA conference, the opportunity to learn about similar activities at other parishes and to gain confidence from others about the potential for change.

"*Claro!*" Maria raised her hands. "*Pero*, but we have to look obedient and find a way to offer alternatives. I know that seems super obvious to us – declining vocations, aging priests, and lack of talented divinity school graduates!" Maria shrugged her shoulders. "If facts like the number of parishes in a diocese going from twenty-six to three doesn't create a major change, we should know how slowly and patiently we have to work to get their attention. We must stay smart enough to lead them step by step on a path with no other destination. If we let them know *el ultimo destino* –"

Elizabeth took a breath and raised her coffee cup. She smiled. "You are a wise woman, Maria. We will name it the Women's Committee." She laughed. "They'll probably think we knit prayer shawls."

"We can do that too!" Maria laughed. "We'll need all the prayers we can get to accomplish even some of the small steps!" She took another sip of coffee. "Have you asked Father about doing the Mother's Day homily?"

"I have not. Some mornings I wake up, know I can ask, and this time he will agree. Other mornings I grab my pad and write down convincing points he couldn't possibly refuse." She shook her head. "Not going to the CTA conference set me back.

I thrive on not only the great ideas I discover, but also the comfort I find in that community, though we live and work far from each other."

"But you can talk to all the people you know who attend and get some of those ideas, no?"

"I can." Her neck muscles tightened again. "I will."

Maria watched the emotions flash across Elizabeth's face. "I had an idea last night." Elizabeth looked up without an inviting expression. "What if we suggest the idea of mothers doing all the Prayers of the Faithful?" Elizabeth didn't respond. "We could write a message that would come out as the last person says her prayer. I mean, you could." Elizabeth's eyes widened. "You've asked Father enough times to allow women to say the Prayers of the Faithful." Her eyes blinked and she smiled. "We know his legs can't reach the step where a mother or any woman, for that matter, gives a homily. Maybe he could let us say a prayer, *un pequeño paso*. He could take a smaller step! He might not think of a good excuse for not allowing women do Prayers of the Faithful, on Mother's Day!" Maria saw Elizabeth's smile and continued with more energy. "We know many who will volunteer to do this. We could even start in Spanish and then the last group would say the same prayers in English." Maria and Elizabeth smiled. "And if we could make him think he had this idea –" They laughed.

Elizabeth pulled out a pen and wrote names on the paper. "Let's use these three for the Spanish version and these for the English."

"We must choose the words very carefully –"

"I know, I know," Elizabeth shook her head and kept writing.

"His idea! He must believe, he had the idea first!!" Maria spoke a little louder.

Jay saw the light on his phone blink, he looked away and back. He saw Elizabeth's number flash off and pushed the button too late to catch the call.

"I arrive on United 234 at 11:13 PM tomorrow night. I'll go out to the curb."

He parked his car at the curb and looked at his phone to see if the flight had further delays. Thunderstorms in Newark had created the first delay. He expected a call from Elizabeth with more details. It seemed a strange time for a visit. But he couldn't remember the last time he had talked to her. Maybe she had a conference in town. She never responded to his suggestion that he spend his vacation in Texas with her. He wondered about flying back with her but suspected that he couldn't afford a ticket bought on such late notice.

The flight screen blinked and a new time showed for her flight. While he watched, the flight's status changed to cancelled. Moments later he received a text: "Delta flight 1241 arriving 1:30 tomorrow. I'll go out to the curb." Jay dialed her number. She didn't answer.

"I won't say this again, listen, listen very carefully, and don't ask any questions. I got fired. Totally unwarranted. I should contest it, file a lawsuit. But I won't. I will need help getting a job quickly." She settled into the passenger seat. "I count on you to help." She glared at Jay.

"Hi, Sis," Jay leaned toward her offering a hug. She kept her eyes focused on the road ahead. Jay sent her a text. "Where to?"

She almost smiled when she retrieved her phone and saw the text from him. She took a deep breath. "Well, I don't know." Another breath and she lifted her hair and loosened her collar. "Warm here for upstate New York."

"Would you like to stay with me?" Jay buckled his seat belt.

"Sure." Elizabeth buckled hers.

Father Rogers

The only son of doting Catholic parents, Father Rogers remained at his father's bedside, as son and newly ordained priest, watching his father wither away. Before taking on his first assignment, he watched his father's casket roll toward him. Words to honor and remember wrinkled on the paper in his hand as he stood on the altar at his first funeral. After his death, he visited his mother weekly and called daily. He didn't share his doubts with anyone. He learned to shepherd parishioners hearing their doubts as he kept his own quiet. He read. He prayed. He listened for God's guidance. One doubt returned over and over.

That doubt, not a new doubt, and the prayers, flowing from memory with words barely distinguishable, followed him through the seminary and into his first parish. Years later, when he became pastor at Saint Luke's, he continued praying. The prayers eventually led him to Call To Action (CTA), a group of Catholic priests and lay people, who looked for ways to "distort Catholicism," its detractors said. Father Rogers read CTA's newsletters and conference programs and saw respectful people urging reform in the Catholic Church. They suggested more inclusive language for the Masses, proposed the ordination of married men, and supported equality for women. The first time Father Rogers read a CTA newsletter, he recognized that others shared his doubt about the celibate priesthood. He noticed many priests' names listed on different committees and as presenters at conferences. Reading the names of several Bishops motivated him to learn more. Before requesting permission to attend a CTA conference, Father Rogers deepened his understanding of CTA and studied articles by those who criticized the organization. He noted the names of other priests in the diocese who attended the national conference and hosted CTA events locally. Though Bishop

Inman did not participate, he supported participation or at least tolerated CTA activities.

The Bishop's permission to attend the upcoming conference surprised Father Rogers when he opened the letter. On an impulse he invited Ben Peer to join him. He looked forward to having a sounding board. Worries about CTA lingered from the criticism he read. Did CTA respect the hundreds of years of Catholic practice and scholarship? Did CTA urge change too quickly or too soon? In addition, he wanted time to understand Ben's plans for the seminary, to probe about his doubts, to give him the ear he lacked during his own seminary years. While he didn't doubt God had given him that path for a reason, he still wanted to ease someone else's way through the seminary. He imagined he might become a better priest by airing his doubts and finding organizations like CTA sooner. He also realized that the future of the Church with the declining number of ordinations depended on people like Ben.

They flew to Milwaukee early on a Thursday morning arriving in time for the opening Mass. During the flight, they reviewed the program and decided which sessions each of them would attend. Bare trees and gray skies greeted them as they landed. The cool fall air reminded them that similar weather would soon arrive in Stanton. Father Rogers zipped his jacket as they boarded the bus to the hotel. He rarely checked weather reports except as winter approached. He always checked places further north, like Milwaukee, first. Seeing how much worse winter treated Milwaukee always gave him comfort when temperatures dropped and weather reports in Stanton claimed lake effect for everything cold and wet.

After checking into the hotel, they followed a crowd to the conference center, picked up the conference materials and found a seat. They glanced at each other as Bishop Gumbleton walked into the conference center auditorium followed by a procession of men and women of all colors and cultures. They felt at home. The whole auditorium joined in each hymn with enthusiasm and reverence. Father Rogers blew his nose and noticed that others wiped their eyes or let tears flow down their cheeks as they sang.

The four days passed quickly. The lunch and afternoon breaks barely gave them enough time to exchange information as they spoke over each other and pondered some of the difficult situations presenters found themselves confronted with when trying to implement change, even a small change like introducing new hymns. Father Rogers, ever the respectful listener, interrupted Ben as he described a session on ordaining married men. He didn't finish before Ben interrupted him to list how many people from Stanton he had met and seen on the attendee list. He couldn't believe the number of men and women contemplating vocations. After lunch on Saturday, they lingered at their table while other attendees left to make phone calls and return to their hotel rooms.

"Father Rogers, I met this woman at the session on women's ordination. Elizabeth Winter, have you heard of her? I can't imagine how she does her job in Texas working on two or maybe even three CTA committees? She presented the work of that committee really powerfully. She has a vision." He paused. "Imagine collaborative leadership with women ordained and participating equally." Father Rogers watched Ben's face fill with a smile. "She spoke beautifully about the work of the committee and honored each of the members and the work they did. Their strategy centers on education. We must tell the stories of early women in the Bible ordained as priests. So positive! The curriculum looks powerful, very respectful of church doctrine, leaders, and policies. The ordination statistics shocked me. Did you know that in 1965 the Church ordained nine hundred ninety-four priests? And in 2005?"

He didn't wait for Father Rogers's answer. "Four hundred and fifty-four! And, that's not all. You might think, no problem, we have fewer Catholics in the world. No! And really interesting, the Church has ordained more, not fewer deacons. Clearly married men and, we know, women want to serve! If we don't ordain them..." He shook his head. "Just imagine what that means in miles traveled and how many churches won't have a Mass every Sunday, let alone daily Masses. We've seen so many new adult converts and many more children at Saint Luke's since you came. Based on the Saint Luke's experience, it looks like the number of Catholics will continue to grow. Without women, without married priests, how can the Catholic churches function or maybe even exist? It makes me wonder if I should enter the seminary. How can one person shepherd so many?" Ben scratched his head and leafed through the program pages.

Father Rogers let the questions rest. He hoped these questions provided an opening. The large hotel ballroom where they ate lunch emptied slowly. They moved to the hallway and continued their conversation.

"When I look at all the things you do at Saint Luke's and in the diocese, I wonder if I could even do part of that. Just thinking about it overwhelms me. Does it ever overwhelm you? Or not really?" Father Rogers nodded. He wondered if Ben would welcome the questions he might ask. Without the clank of dishes and murmur of voices, quiet surrounded them in the long, carpeted hall. Afternoon sessions didn't start for an hour. The conference scheduling allowed for reflection throughout the day. "I could consider a contemplative order, but I like people too much. I'd never last in a small, windowless room devoting my life to prayer and bread making. Mostly, I would miss the children. The children inspire me. Every time I teach a Sunday school class, now we call it religious education, don't we? Anyway, the children give me zillions of ideas for great homilies." They exchanged smiles. "I love the course I'm taking now on writing homilies. Of course, I know priests have many other responsibilities than writing homilies. I have to say that constructing a meaningful homily drove me to the seminary. Does that seem selfish?"

Father Rogers smiled.

"As a matter of fact, I've never asked you, Father Rogers. Do you think I will make a good priest? I've taken all the courses I can take before making the final decision to enter the seminary. I keep hesitating. I don't know why. What do you think? I'd really like your honest opinion. Really."

Father Rogers smiled back. "Very good. Very good." He patted Ben's hand. "Can I ask you a question?" He took a deep breath.

"Of course," Ben replied.

"What has impressed you the most at this conference?" Father Rogers asked. "So far? Your first impressions?"

Ben chuckled nervously. He pondered the unexpected question, then answered in a firm voice, "The loving efforts of people all over the world. We've seen mostly Americans here, but I heard a professor from a university in Germany too. These people want to renew the church. And CTA didn't invent these actions and values. Every generation of priests has worked to renew the church over the decades, most of them in a respectful way. In the fourth century women served as priests in the church. Church doctrine didn't prevent them from serving. Christ never said women couldn't be priests. Let's do it. The enthusiasm, I love that! It seems to come from everyone I meet. The early Church got it, why can't we? The German professor talked about Corinth and the people in Paul's community. She sees the mix of religious influences in the world similar to the factions in Paul's time - declining number of ordinations and vocations, the strengthening of fundamentalists religions, the disdain for religion (in Germany only forty percent of young parents plan to make organized religion part of the children's upbringing). The first thing I will do when I get back, I will read Paul's letters to the Corinthians for inspiration." As Ben spoke, the color in his cheeks rose. He sat forward leaning toward Father Rogers. His hands swept across his body toward his back. Then, he looked back at Father Rogers remembering his question. He chuckled and furrowed his brow.

"Very good, very good!" His smile deepened. He marveled at Ben's energy. "Seeing your eyes and listening to your description inspires me. Very exciting! And your concern for and delight in the children! Ben, you have the love of God, the love of God. And, the recognition that the Church, especially with help of the people who define and redefine the church over the years, can always improve. We never, never complete the job." He closed his eyes and took a deep breath. "If we ever lose that capacity, we lose the church. And we know our history includes corruptness in the Catholic Church. It always takes people like you to identify it and root it out. Today, more than ever, the Catholic Church needs people with the enthusiasm, dedication and spirituality you have. Maybe the more important question for you is why do you hesitate?"

Ben nodded his head and shrugged his shoulders. The animation left his face. His brow wrinkled. But Father Rogers didn't let him answer. "Let me tell you a story about a friend of mine." Ben nodded. Father Rogers continued. "One might say the church marked this friend early in his life for the priesthood. No one who knew him questioned the choice. His parents supported him; his priest recommended him. When the time came to apply to the seminary, his childhood sweetheart gave him willingly to the Church. Despite his love of God and everything that the priesthood meant to him, he had doubts about the church."

Father Rogers took a deep breath. "Serious doubts. Very serious doubts. He never said them to anyone – not his parents, not his pastor, not even his spiritual advisor in the seminary. He prayed about the doubts but never voiced them. Hiding these doubts prevented him from helpful dialogue and, perhaps most important, from working to remove those doubts for others. His story may sound like a common story, but hopefully not your story." He paused. Ben remained still and focused. "Discover those hesitations, reveal them and pray about them before you enter the seminary. If you keep them secret, as my friend did, you support the kind of secrecy that can lead to corruptness." His eyes opened wide. His words surprised him. He scratched his head and smiled. "We've seen such corruption in previous centuries and unfortunately we see it today. How many more children will priests abuse before the church hierarchy admits the crime and removes the criminals from further opportunities? With that situation in the light now, we should wonder about others we may not know about?" He looked up. Before continuing, he watched Ben's face. "We must always challenge the secrecy so that renewal follows." Father Rogers mused about this connection he hadn't recognized before between his secrecy and the culture of secrecy in the church.

Ben let Father Rogers' words register. The muscles wrinkling his forehead relaxed. His thoughts wandered. Of course, the advice sounded simple, simple but not easy. Realizing that the invitation to explore any of his hesitations came with such warmth, Ben smiled and then asked, "Do I know your friend?"

Father Rogers smiled. "Very good, Ben." He chuckled. "Very good. You do." They both smiled. "I told you my story." Father Rogers realized that the openness of the CTA conference, the gentle yet persistent people who worked to make the changes he held in his heart for so many years had opened his own heart and allowed him to shed his own secret. "Yes, and just telling you this has lifted a heavy weight from my shoulders." He laughed and sighed. "This conference seems to have given me new energy to work on these areas of doubt about the church I have hidden since boyhood." He took several breaths. They exchanged smiles. "Think about it. It's an open invitation to tell me about your hesitations. You will enter the seminary older than your classmates. Probing for hesitations might just help others. "He smiled. "And pray for clarification."

They smiled and after a moment hugged.

Ben glanced at his watch. "Hey, I mean," he surprised himself with his informality.

Father Rogers laughed. "Hey, what?" They both laughed.

"That woman I told you about, Elizabeth Winter, speaks at the next session – 'The Tree and the Cross.' Why don't we go together? It means a little less coverage. What did you plan to attend? An amazing speaker and – "

They navigated their way through the conference center to the room where Elizabeth chatted with early attendees at the front of the room. They found a place in the front row of the packed room. A young man gave Elizabeth a short introduction fumbling with his notes and fumbling more as embarrassment flushed his cheeks. Elizabeth shook his hand and thanked him, catching his eye and whisking away the embarrassment with a kind look and extravagant thank you.

"The tree in the Garden of Eden, the tree with its tempting fruit, our subject today." She waited as more people arrived and she pointed out empty seats. "This tree held the fruits of life. God advised Adam and Eve to appreciate the fruit, to learn about the fruit, but not to devour the fruit. What a message!

"I have an apple tree in my back yard. Believe me, in Texas, that it lives deserves attention. And in the spring and summer, I water it constantly so that it will produce a few apples in the fall. I watch the delicate blossoms form in the spring. Behind these blossoms, if all goes well, an apple forms, invisible to us as it forms. In Upstate New York, where I come from, apple trees covered the hills around Lake Ontario. I didn't appreciate the thousands of tiny white flowers so beautiful themselves but transient, so transient. They bloomed on a warm spring day and a few days later we watched a snowstorm of petals. The flowers gave up their place to let the apples grow further. Now I count the blossoms on my apple tree and watch the progress all through the summer until I can harvest the few apples that survive the brutal summer. Can you say harvest when you only have three or four apples?"

The audience chuckled. Father Rogers turned to Ben. "I wonder where she grew up?" Ben shrugged his shoulders and turned to the program where he found her brief bio. He saw Stanton and pointed at it for Father Rogers.

"Those blossoms would look lovely in a vase to decorate a table or counter, to bring spring inside, to savor these early signs. I resisted those early temptations. In the fall when the small fruit buds grow larger, turn red, another temptation arrives; and I can almost taste the first bite. But ripening must finish before a complete apple exists. How many parallels do we have in our lives? We need only look at our children who ache to be older so they can stay up late or gain an adult privilege that tempts them. Of course, a more difficult task is to look inward, look at the temptations in our life to pull the bread from the oven before it has finished baking because we are hungry, to try for the next level of job because of the status or the money before we have the skills, to push the church to the next level. Ah yes – to push the church to the next level – a common goal for CTA members such as you," she looked directly at Father Rogers. "And you" and then at Ben. She looked up and motioned with her hand to include all those in the room, "and you. And" she hesitated, "and me."

She paused and bowed her head. "I planted the apple tree in my back yard to remind me about the ripening process, to remind me to care for the tree so the fruit can ripen, to recognize the effect of not watering and not protecting the tree from the Texas sized bugs that seem to have developed an appetite for apples."

Ben's attention wandered from the talk. He watched Father Rogers, glanced again at his finger pointing to Stanton and noticed the person sitting next to him taking notes. He pulled a pen from his pocket. His thoughts placed Elizabeth back in Stanton, at Saint Luke's, engaged with parishioners, and he wondered. Then, he looked at Father Rogers again. His pen traveled across his open notebook, circles, spirals connected one on top of the other. Then he wrote "Dear Bishop Inman..." Ben looked up, saw Father Rogers watching and they smiled.

Elizabeth concluded her talk. "And what did they make the cross out of that Jesus carried to Calvary, that they nailed him to, that he died on? While we don't know what kind of a tree provided the wood, we do know that even trees that we don't eat fruit from, produce seeds, flowers, and fruits that other creatures live from. Christ was nailed to a tree of life."

The room remained quiet. The young man, recovered from his introduction jitters, stood and invited questions from those assembled. At first people remained silent, then people offered thanks for the insight, asked for copies of her talk, and one person even suggested a particular fertilizer for raising fruit trees in dry climates. Elizabeth thanked the person for the suggestion and relieved the nervous young man of his closing duties as he looked anxiously at his watch.

She caught his gaze and looked at the audience. "A good note to end on. We all treasure those breaks! I hear that lovely guitar music in the hall. Enjoy!" The nervous young man's shoulders relaxed, he stuffed his notes into his pants pocket and rose to shake Elizabeth's hand and thank her.

Ben and Father Rogers stood near Elizabeth as people gathered to ask additional questions. They overheard people talking about Elizabeth and her work in Texas. She worked in a church with many Spanish-speaking parishioners. Her flight that evening would prevent her from attending the closing Mass on Sunday. When the crowd cleared a little, they stepped forward and introduced themselves.

"Oh, I noticed a name from Saint Luke's on the attendance list this year. I haven't been back to Stanton, even to visit family, in two years! Thank you for introducing yourselves. I wanted to find you, but with all these people..." They shook hands. She sat and invited them to do the same.

"We overheard that you have a plane to catch," Ben hesitated.

"Oh, a late flight, I have plenty of time. This was the last session I have any responsibility for. Your timing couldn't be better. Perfect! Since I haven't seen you at other CTA conferences, is this your first time attending?"

They both nodded. She laughed. "I remember my first conference during my seminary studies." She smiled. "In Stanton!"

"Our own seminary?" Ben asked. She nodded. "I am applying there to become a priest."

"Oh, I wish I didn't have that flight tonight." Her smile faded. None of her appeals to Father Flaherty convinced him to let her stay until the end of the conference. She hoped by attending Sunday Mass, his criticisms of her activities would diminish. She took a breath and continued. "Tell me about Stanton, the diocese, Saint Luke's. Has winter arrived? I remember hearing something about your school." she paused "and a homeless shelter?" Elizabeth leaned forward turning from Father Rogers to Ben with a smile.

Ben answered. "Oh, yes. Our school really got the community focused on the poor. Then, we hired a wonderful woman to help us start a homeless shelter. Everyone pitched in to help. She found a parishioner who wanted to donate a house. But she also led the religious education program." Ben looked at Father Rogers suddenly embarrassed that he had answered so quickly. Father Rogers motioned. Ben continued. "As the homeless shelter planning continued, she realized how she had neglected her family. She also felt that her accomplishments at the shelter and the religious education program both suffered. Now, we must find someone else to build the shelter program. We gave both jobs to a busy person and expected her to get all the work done. Rosa! She still attends some of the meetings and tries to help out when she can. With the growth of families in our parish, she added teachers and classes to the religious education program. That means less extra time for Rosa to help with the shelter and have time for her family."

"We must not neglect the children, our future," Father Rogers agreed. "We'll find just the right person, I know." He paused and made sure Ben had finished talking. "We understand that you have worked with Spanish-speaking parishioners and set up a program in the city for homeless people. Did I understand that correctly?" Elizabeth nodded and, uncharacteristically, Father Rogers kept talking, "I dream about Saint Luke's future. Road construction and city development projects have left our church isolated from previous thriving neighborhoods. Poverty and homelessness have increased dramatically among the remaining residents, also isolated. This nearby home a parishioner donated will allow us to reach those people. Many, many possibilities!" Father Rogers smiled and closed his eyes leaving the possibilities to her imagination. "We have such a giving group of parishioners. They thrive on challenges like this. The house symbolizes hope in the community and for the community." His eyes gleamed and he stopped suddenly realizing that he had monopolized the conversation. "Tell us about your shelter."

They traded questions and answers in a gentle game of catch, though a subtle competition between Father Rogers and Elizabeth arose as each competed to ask the next question and turn attention from themselves and their work to the other. Ben watched with amusement. He suspected they would enjoy each other. He didn't predict how strong the connection would become or how closely their goals and ideals matched. He saw a new side of Father Rogers, as if he had stayed a bud on that apple tree for a very long time, longer than anyone would have waited for a blossom to appear. His eyes gleamed, his hands circled and stretched, his voice rose and fell. Ben pondered their earlier conversation about his seminary intentions and hesitations. He appreciated the invitation Father Rogers had offered and vowed to give himself the time to reflect. If he answered now, he would say what he thought he heard Father Rogers say, that the church might not change quickly enough for him. He feared having a collection of parishes to serve where he spent his time driving from church to church and trying to remember how to honor each community as he drove rather than being available in his office and able to visit people in their homes and in the hospital.

"Tell me about you," Elizabeth interrupted Ben's thoughts.

He swallowed and cleared his throat, he began slowly. "Let's see. I grew up in Stanton." He paused. "Oh, and winter has not arrived but Milwaukee usually beats us, until we start to get the lake effect storms and we all move inside." They laughed. "I went to Saint Stephens for high school. I started college at Saint Michaels but dropped out. I didn't know, at least not clearly enough, what I wanted to study and I didn't want my parents to pay for such an expensive education. I couldn't figure out how to get more clarity, especially," he hesitated "especially since my older brother went to such an expensive school and still, even today, seems undecided about his future." Ben chuckled nervously and continued. "My parents didn't need, any more indecision!" He paused. "Now, I take courses at Saint Michael's. I still seek clarity on the objective of entering the seminary." He stopped.

"Marvelous. I watched you at the women's ordination session and hoped I could meet you. What a gift you would be to the priesthood! What a gift!" Elizabeth spoke sincerely and caught Ben in her enthusiasm.

"Truly, God brought me to this conference. Well God and Father Rogers." He smiled at Father Rogers. "I will make a formal application to see if they agree with you." He amazed himself that he said that out loud and turning to Father Rogers he said, "And I plan to make a retreat to offer the final decision up to God."

"Will you go to Piffard? That's where I made a retreat and decided to pray and work for women's ordination and the uplifting of the poor." Elizabeth looked at her watch.

Ben glanced at his watch, "Oh, it is late. We should let you go. I'll look into Piffard. I've heard about it but never visited."

She hugged them both, gathered her papers, and turned back. "Would I insult you by offering some advice about CTA? It took me several years to find the most effective way to participate and it seems like we share many objectives."

They both nodded enthusiastically. Ben took a pen and jotted notes as she suggested people they should meet and committees where they would get lots of ideas for the shelter and other services for the poor. Father Rogers watched and let his mind wander to a new Saint Luke's with Elizabeth as a pastoral assistant. Her presentation and now her valuable advice pushed him to think about the parish finances, a topic he let other people manage. Then, he listed the essential benefits to Saint Luke's by having Elizabeth on the staff he would present to the Bishop. He nodded as Elizabeth disappeared into the crowd filling the halls on the way to dinner.

Ben waited for Father Rogers to talk. They walked slowly by the emptying conference rooms toward the large room where people gathered for meals. People nodded and smiled at them as they passed. Hints of dinner floated toward them. It smelled Italian to Ben. He felt his stomach grumble and imagined large steam tables with pans of lasagna and bowls of grated parmesan cheese. As they entered the room, he could see people carrying plates with collapsing squares of lasagna. They entered the line and followed the example of others choosing small portions of salad, bread, butter, and lasagna. Ben wondered how they might change a similar pattern in the parish and encourage people to eat smaller portions. No one said anything about it at the conference – except, he now realized, the small line on the cover of the program: *Eat Less to Share More. We will transport any leftovers to the local homeless shelters.* Then, at the opening session each morning, they announced how much food the conference attendees had donated and thanked the hotel for providing the transportation free of charge. Normally, Ben filled his plate and went back for seconds. He never saw anyone do that at the conference. If he could change, others could. He hoped he would continue eating more sensibly when he returned home. Fueled by this resolution to eat less, more ideas popped into his mind. Could Saint Luke's encourage something like *Eat Less to Share More* in the parish? Maybe link such a program to the homeless shelter? It seemed like parishioners never ran out of generosity when it came to money and time.

"How soon do you think we could hire Elizabeth?" Father Rogers blurted out. Ben laughed and nodded, then his forehead wrinkled. "She would make the homeless shelter move forward and wouldn't the parish love listening to and working with a woman who speaks so eloquently!" Father Rogers had barely touched his small portion of lasagna. "The Bishop has allowed other parishes to hire pastoral administrators. I have to check, but our parish size may allow us to hire her and having another full-time person would fit in our budget." He took a small bite.

"But what about her work in Texas with the Hispanic community? What would they do without her? I'll bet they would resist losing her. Not to mention her own wishes." Ben shook his head and turned to Father Rogers. "What makes you think she would want to leave?"

"She wants to come home! And if she doesn't know she wants to come home, we'll help her, help her know that!" Father Rogers smiled and finished his lasagna.

While Father Rogers built a rationale for hiring a pastoral administrator, Elizabeth in particular, on the flight home, Ben checked his calendar to find a weekend for a retreat and filled out his seminary application. He always carried it with him.

Occasionally, he pulled it out. Now he finished the last questions during the long delay in Detroit. They asked for a personal statement. He wrote about his love of God, his love of children, his desire to serve and to renew the church. He wrote on about renewal with some trepidation. He wondered if writing too much about it might have a negative effect on his prospects. He looked at the essay. Reading it over he saw that renewal was at the root of his hesitations. He would show the draft to Father Rogers before sending it. Perhaps airing these hesitations with someone else would change his perspective. As he wrote, he realized that Father Rogers hadn't talked about other hesitations, other doubts, other hurdles in his priesthood. He hoped he could ask.

Clare and Mark

"Tell me the story about my name." Mark pulled on Clare's sleeve. Clare moved his hand and turned away. Mark rocked back and forth from one foot to the other keeping his eyes on Clare's.

"You know the story. Mom and Dad told you -" She paused. He placed his hand on her sleeve. She removed it. "A thousand times."

"I like the way you tell it." Mark smiled at Clare. He rocked more slowly. Seeing a slight change in Clare's face, he settled himself on the chair next to her.

Clare frowned and pushed against the table to stand but turned back. "OK, when you were born." Mark smiled and opened his mouth. Clare spoke faster. "Before you made any noise or smiled or cried, you laughed." Clare watched Mark. He laughed and leaned toward her leaving his hand on the table. She smiled.

"Right, not quite like that because babies laugh with tiny voices." She imitated a baby laugh. He laughed louder. She watched Mark's eyes twinkle as he leaned back and then giggled, trying to imitate her. When he giggled, he wiggled. Whenever he laughed, people nearby laughed too. She couldn't help but laugh. "Babies don't laugh until they are maybe two months old or even six months old." He nodded. "Anyway. Mom and Dad had a long list of names they talked about before you arrived. Melinda and Anastasia -" He giggled again. Clare took a breath and raised her voice. "And, of course, they chose names for boys too."

"Frederick and Wolfgang -" he contorted his mouth to pronounce each name and giggled again.

Clare held back her own giggle. "Right. Somehow you didn't look like a Wolfgang. Dad had an uncle named Wolfgang, a very, very serious judge." She made a serious face. He giggled. "He sat on a big chair behind an even bigger desk." She spread her arms to rest on that chair and waited until he paused between giggles. "Mom's grandfather's name was John. Dad's grandfather's name was Mark. So, they thought about John Mark or Mark John. They couldn't decide. When Mom's father –"

"My grandfather!" he clapped and sat forward in his chair.

"Right. Anyway, when he heard about you laughing, he told the story about the apostle Mark, also known as John."

Mark interrupted, "Then he laughed a lot. Don't forget that part."

"Sorry. For the first few years one family called you Mark known as John and the other family called you John known as Mark –"

"and everybody laughed." Mark finished the story.

"and everybody laughed." Clare finished the story. They both laughed. Mark wiggled out of the chair and ran to the door. He turned and ran back. "Can you tell it one more time?" Clare's shoulders slouched. "Please."

The Nortons arrived early for Mark and Clare's baptism. The long search for a religious community caused them to delay baptizing the children. When they approached Father Rogers, he applauded their decision and worked with them to design a service that included the children. Naomi chose a date that would allow Sam Bonner to make the trip from Vermont, aware that he would fill her with his usual questions about organized religion and the Catholic Church, in particular. Once they settled on the date, Naomi's Aunt Patty received her Stage Four ovarian cancer diagnosis. Naomi's parents, who had expressed their own skepticism about Saint Luke's though for reasons diametrically different than Sam's objections, traveled to Florida to help Aunt Patty. Naomi breathed a sigh of relief along with her sigh of concern for her aunt.

People leaving the previous Mass greeted Naomi and patted Clare and Mark on shoulders and head. Naomi guided the family and Sam toward the front pew. "Clare? Mark?' she touched their shoulders to get their attention. "Please introduce Sam Bonner to everyone. He doesn't know anyone." Sam and Naomi exchanged smiles.

"Where am I from, Mark?" Sam tested.

"Mars!" Mark answered.

"Vermont," Clare corrected. Clare turned to introduce Sam to her best friend's family as they passed. Zack and Sam turned to shake hands and exchange greetings.

Naomi left Zack with the family and searched for Ben. Mark and Clare dashed ahead and into the church. *Silly*, she thought, *but it does seem like Ben and Sam would enjoy each other. He said he would sing at this Mass.* She wandered to the piano and looked up at the choir loft but didn't see Ben anywhere.

"We get the special pew today." Clare held Mark's hand and pointed at the ribbon on the front pew. Mark's hand slipped from hers and he ran. "Mark! John!" Clare half yelled and caught herself. People talking stopped to see who spoke. "Sorry." Clare looked for Zack or Naomi. Not seeing them, she walked quickly to catch up with Mark. "Mark." She whispered as loud as she could.

She caught him and they walked back hand in hand. She held his hand until they returned to the pew. Mark put his toys on the kneeler and touched the reserved sign.

"I don't see my name" he said, not making any attempt to whisper. He turned and saw Clare's face. She looked at the sign. He moved his toys and edged along the pew away from her. Then, he stooped down, exited the pew and entered the next pew staying out of sight. He moved quickly along the pew in a crouched position. Clare noticed his absence, saw his head disappear and hurried to catch him without running. Mark moved faster. Clare stopped as she saw his plan. She turned away keeping her eye on his movement. He ran up and down the open pews where people leaving the previous Mass had replaced all the kneelers. As the pews emptied, he picked up speed running down one, exiting, and running back to the center aisle along the next. Mostly he remained stooped over trying to stay out of sight. Clare realized she could walk down the center aisle and catch him on the next circuit. She moved to the pew just ahead of his position. She stood in the aisle. He ran into her and yelped. Clare dragged him back to the pew.

Zack and Sam finished their conversation with friends and walked toward the front pew. Naomi gave up her search for Ben, caught Zack's eye, shrugged, and approached the pew from the front of the church. Then, she saw Ben rushing into the church and heading for their pew.

"Mom, Mark is running in church!" Clare said holding Mark's hand tightly.

"Owww." Mark tried to wiggle free.

Naomi smiled at both children and asked where they would like to sit. Clare moved to the aisle. Mark grabbed his toys and grabbed Ben's hand. They settled into their pew as others entered. Sam sat next to Naomi. They watched as people looked for pews and stopped to shake hands with Mark and Clare before choosing a pew nearby.

Ben

Belief is sure in the way that truth is sure. It rings in our ears like tines on crystal.   Joan Chittister

"Naomi, we must accept it. I don't know. I just don't know." Ben takes a breath. "You invited her to your house to speak with us. I offered to take her to breakfast, lunch, dinner. She chooses not to come." He shakes his head and watches Naomi's face. "She doesn't return calls or answer emails. I don't know what to think or say. I don't know." Ben shakes his head and frowns. Neither speaks. Ben looks at his hands and lifts them. "Can that Channel 14 report really, I mean really, represent anything close to her story? I can't believe it!" He faces Naomi. His eyes drift. "I didn't recognize her, her fist raised and hair streaming out from her face. I've never seen her like that." Ben shrugs his shoulders and shakes his head. A frown covers his face. "I wonder if this is the time to push the issue, as she says, or the way, or the strategy, as she often says, to push the issue. It doesn't feel right, it just doesn't. A more cautious path would have more effect if not for her, at least for other women. The more cautious path she always advocated, I should add. And she constantly talks about the future, about her work. She spoke of it as preparation for what comes later. It just doesn't make sense." Ben gathers his notes for the meeting. "It seems ridiculous to present this without her input, but what can we do?"

"She has changed – hard, so hard, to accept *what* she said." She rubs her forehead. "But you know what scares me even more?" She sighs, "the *way* she said it! I don't know." Naomi frowns and then smiles at Ben. "Of course, I should ask myself, what would I do in a similar situation. Still, it seems like she should trust in God. For heaven's sake. She tells us that in every homily!" Naomi nods her head and turns toward the door, then turns back. "Her actions push the church, and in

80

such an aggressive way. I'm not sure she will get what she wants. And worse, think how these actions will hurt others striving for the same goals." Naomi thinks of Clare and feels the smooth side of her cross against her thumb.

"We'll just have to trust in God ourselves and hope that we can show everyone equal respect the way we agreed to do when we became facilitators. And we must give Father Rogers an opportunity to speak because he will hold back as he usually does. Still – OK, let's stop in the church for a short prayer or they'll start the meeting without us!"

As they walk out of the rectory, Naomi remembers the years working together that created this friendship. She hopes the foundation of that friendship will hold to guide her this disturbing and confusing time.

After meetings, they washed mugs, folded and stored chairs, and sometimes swept the hall. They told each other their stories and shared concerns about parish programs. Ben became a regular guest at their home and joined them for summer weekends at Naomi's parents' house on the lake. She learned about parishioners, causes Saint Luke's espoused, and listened to Ben wrestle with whether or not to enter the seminary. She remembered one of those chats in detail.

"Come to our Cinco de Mayo celebration." He insisted as he washed, rinsed, and placed the cups in the drainer. Naomi dried. "Elizabeth started that celebration." Ben smiled. "Only one or two burners still work on this old restaurant stove, donated by a parishioner; but the Mexican and Salvadoran ladies create smells and food that feed the congregation and many more. You wouldn't believe what this kitchen can produce." He stopped and looked at the stove. "Our version of the loaves and fishes!" They laughed. "And that hall with its long tables housed many Bingo games before Father Rogers became the pastor. You probably saw the paint-chipped score board at the front of the hall."

"I didn't even notice that."

"Father Rogers eliminated the Bingo. Now we use the Bingo tables for religious education classes on the weekend and coats during parish meetings. During the year, the worn linoleum floor holds the feet of those attending coffee hours, baptisms, wedding celebrations, parish meetings, and Christmas bazaars. Tonight's meeting drew a lot of parishioners." He pointed at the pile of mugs in the drainer. Naomi reached for the next cup. "Early on someone suggested the simple hospitality of serving coffee and tea during the meeting. After a few meetings, parishioners started bringing cookies. Maria baked tonight, for sure. She makes those Mexican Wedding Cakes! I ate three!" He looked away.

"Delicious. I saved one for the kids. I wonder if she will share the recipe."

"It might be on the parish web site. Lots of people have asked for it!"

Ben finished washing, cleaned the sink, and turned to Naomi. "Tell me more about your friend Sam. He dropped out of divinity school? Or did I remember that wrong?"

"You remembered Sam Bonner! He taught English at Bucknell, where I studied theater and music. I didn't take a class with him, but I met him when he showed up at the theater." She smiled. "Funny to think about Sam because we had a friendship, Sam and I, like our friendship, at least it feels that way to me." They turned briefly. Naomi hung up the dishtowel. Ben secured the faucets and stored the sponges.

"I feel like I can tell you anything, Naomi, and you always respond in an honest and caring way."

Naomi blushed. "You expressed my feelings exactly and that's the kind of friendship I have with Sam, except that he lives in Vermont and we barely get to see each other." Ben leaned on the sink. Naomi leaned on the refrigerator. "You remembered Sam's story correctly. After Bucknell, he moved back to Boston and taught as a lecturer at Boston University. But, as much as he loves language, I'll have to show you his letters, he just didn't feel passionate about language the way he did at Bucknell. One exploration and another led him to divinity school with the objective of becoming a Unitarian minister. His studies, I should find those letters! His studies raised many questions about organized religion. He finally gave up finding answers and he never finished divinity school."

Ben nodded.

"Funny, I never asked Sam what finally caused him to give up on becoming a minister. We always talk about religion and faith and everything related. But I don't know what closed the door for him."

"I wondered why he attended the kids' baptism. Now I see that others struggle with religion and have doubts. I'd love to hear about his journey. Will he visit any time soon?"

"It surprised me that he came, that seeing our kids again touched him." She shook her head. "I'd love to see him again. But Vermont seems to have its hold on him."

That night they turned out the lights and locked up near midnight, as Ben asked questions about Sam. He looked for parallels that might remove or strengthen his doubts. He wanted to move forward. His questions impressed Naomi. She listened. She imagined what a wonderful priest he could become. Though she wondered why he questioned and doubted, she respected all the discerning. The discerning would allow him to answer similar questions from his parishioners.

Ben and Naomi bow their heads and silently offer up their own prayers. Then, they go downstairs and enter the parish hall. For this meeting, the coffee makers remain silent, the mugs stay on their shelves in the kitchen, and no cookies appear.

People fill the seats they set out earlier. As more people arrive, they retrieve stacked chairs at the back of the room and join the group of seated parishioners. The chatter in the room grows to an unfamiliar level. Other than the volume, the tone seems similar to past meetings – laughter, talk, and a few exclamations. The faces of the crowd look upbeat. Naomi doesn't know what to expect. Did the parish seem like this when difficult issues came to the parish meeting before the Nortons joined the parish? She wants to ask Ben. He knows everyone and chats with people as they arrive. Somehow the faces seem to say, "We can handle this, we'll find a solution."

Ben and Naomi build on the mood with a song instead of a prayer to open the meeting. Ben's voice starts – "Lord you are more precious than silver," he sings softly in his clear voice, "more costly than gold." Less sure, Naomi harmonizes and others join. "Lord you are more beautiful than diamonds and nothing I desire compares with you." After a few rounds, the crowd quiets.

Elizabeth enters and sits on the end of the front row closest to the door. She does not smile and looks down at her papers avoiding Ben and Naomi. Naomi feels a change in the mood as conversations stop. Her neck muscles tighten. Elizabeth says nothing and waits. Ben looks at Naomi and then at Father Rogers searching for a clue. Seeing none, he decides to present the situation as Father Rogers explained it to the facilitators and to those attending the Sunday Masses that followed the original announcement. Naomi opens her computer to take the notes and watches the faces in the hall.

They reviewed the wording so many times striving to present Elizabeth's story fairly. When multiple attempts to reach Elizabeth failed, they sent a copy to her email and left a copy on her desk inviting feedback. None came. Without Elizabeth's comments, they relied on Father Roger's version and emphasized his efforts to keep her in the diocese.

Ben rereads his notes on the events of the past week as late arrivals open and place chairs or Naomi directs them to empty seats in the hall. Ben, Naomi, and Zack watched the news that first night after the children went to bed. The report highlighted a conflict between Saint Luke's and the Bishop resulting in Elizabeth's dismissal and reassignment. The report showed portions of the original Saturday Mass. A reporter interviewed people as they left the church. They quoted Elizabeth "He fired me for doing God's work." The end of the report showed Elizabeth with a fist raised. The microphone caught her shout and the camera lights made her bright red hair almost glow around her face. She looked alien and almost unidentifiable as the Elizabeth he knew. Ben still couldn't erase that bizarre image. The body language said more than the few sentences the reporter used to conclude the report.

The people at the Sunday Masses accepted Father Roger's explanation. The Mass didn't offer parishioners an opportunity to respond. Channel 14 presented those quiet Sunday Masses on the evening news and the clusters of parishioners talking among themselves outside of church after Mass. Elizabeth did not appear at the Sunday Masses. The Bishop had not, to their knowledge, changed his mind about the reassignment despite the Channel 14 coverage. Most news channels and the newspaper also covered the Wednesday night Mass and candlelight walk. A large fire in a city factory shortened the report on Saint Luke's providing footage and photos and little analysis or updates on the stories from the weekend.

When Ben visited the Nortons the following Saturday, they all expressed relief that a large, factory fire had bumped the Saint Luke's story from the headlines in newspapers and television coverage.

"Good evening everyone. Thanks for attending the monthly parish meeting. We have one item on the agenda this evening. We will explain, as best we can, what happened last week, give you an opportunity to ask questions and offer suggestions. We ask, as always, that you respect others who want to speak. This evening we have borrowed the choir microphones. The microphones will allow us to hear everyone. When you have a comment or a question, please line up at a microphone. Naomi will keep track of the order, we will recognize you, and alternate speakers between the microphones." Ben manages a smile. "And please limit your turn at the microphone. It looks like many will choose to speak. As always, we want to hear all. We plan to end at 9 PM as usual. Any questions about how the meeting will flow?"

The room remains silent. Elizabeth fidgets in her seat. Ben wonders if she will approach the microphone before he can give the description they prepared. He glances at Elizabeth and proceeds without receiving eye contact. "OK, let me begin by listing what happened last week. Bishop Inman fired Elizabeth. We haven't read the letter Elizabeth received, but we understand he gave these reasons: sitting on the altar with the priest during Mass, reading the gospel during Mass, and preaching. Father Rogers met with the Bishop several times on Saturday to negotiate an agreement that would allow Elizabeth to stay at Saint Luke's. After multiple refusals, Father Rogers suggested that Queen of Peace in Pittstown lacked a pastoral administrator." Ben glances at Father Rogers who returns a smile and nod. "Father Rogers highlighted Elizabeth's work in expanding our homeless shelter and our Spanish-speaking services. Queen of Peace has a similar mix of parishioners and some of them have volunteered at Lombardo House to explore offering services to the homeless in Pittstown. With Elizabeth as their pastoral administrator, they can accelerate their planned shelter and serve another sector of the city." He looks at Elizabeth. She shows no response. "Ultimately, he convinced the Bishop that Elizabeth could help Queen of Peace." Ben glances at Elizabeth. He strays from the text they prepared. "I can barely imagine how this tested Father Rogers as I know he does not want to lose Elizabeth. And I can't imagine Saint Luke's, without Elizabeth, either." The murmur in the room agrees.

Ben turns a page as Elizabeth stands up and approaches him. She forces a smile. He hesitates. She takes another step toward the microphone. Ben moves away. She speaks with an edge in her voice. "Friends, the Bishop wants to fire me to set an example. Think of it. He says he fired me because I sit on the altar during Mass. I threatened him! He knows that I have the attention, the respect and the admiration of the largest and richest parish in the diocese. What does that mean to him? I control the biggest part of his budget." Naomi and Ben exchange puzzled looks. Elizabeth takes a breath. "He might want to think seriously about the consequences of firing me!" She scans the faces looking back at her. Silence fills the room. "He must face up to what he has done. No one will reassign me." Some jaws drop. Naomi stops typing the notes. "I will sue him. Perhaps that will change his perspective about me and my role in this diocese. He will see what he has gotten himself into." Elizabeth maintains her stern expression and returns to her seat.

Silence spreads over the room. No one moves. No one speaks.

Minny Lord walks quietly from her seat at the back of the hall passing the microphones set up for questions. Murmurs start as she walks. Murmurs build to questions. The unease in the hall throbs. Ben notices a large camera pointed at Elizabeth. As Minny walks, Naomi notices Ellen Scott, the Channel 14 reporter, standing next to the cameraman holding a notebook and writing in it. Ben worries Saint Luke's will appear on the 10 PM news again. Naomi worries about this new Elizabeth matching what they saw on TV, not the person they experienced in the past. She reads what she has typed. She wonders how Scott will transform the story. Then, it hits her that Scott looks for this kind of drama to create her reports. Naomi remembers some of Scott's previous stories and looks for the old Elizabeth but doesn't see her. She wants that engaged face, the ear for every person and sees only her downturned head avoiding everyone's gaze.

Scott stands and walks the aisle toward the back of the hall passing a short woman wearing jeans, a frayed jacket, and a baseball cap, the sports logo unreadable through years of use. The woman continues toward Ben's microphone. Ellen doesn't notice her, just another face in the crowd, a heavyset athletic woman.

The woman reaches the front, touches the logo on her cap, and waits next to Ben. Naomi and Ben remain stunned and silent. Ben moves aside. "My name is Minny Lord. I am an over-the-road truck driver. So -" She scans the faces, waits for quiet. "Many of you don't recognize me, but I have attended this parish for the past eight years." Naomi heaves a sigh. She met Minny at the first parish meeting she attended. Minny read a poem she had written about the homeless shelter after the team reported on the year and before people asked questions. Naomi remembered the thoughtful questions and generous financial commitments made at that meeting to keep the shelter open. It strikes her that Minny's poem influenced people that night.

"I travel all over the country in my truck. Just got back from Arizona. I have visited many churches in my travels and I'll tell you something: this is the best church in the whole country." The murmurs and mutters stop. Those who know Minny Lord clap. Others join in waves. "No, no," Minny raises her hand. The clappers stop. The room becomes silent. Ellen Scott stops and hurries back to her cameraman. He points and films from his seat. "I got back into town and went to Mass yesterday. I talked to Father Rogers for a few minutes. I couldn't find Elizabeth. Then, I read a few articles in the newspaper. A lot going on here during my trip." She glances over at Elizabeth and smiles. Elizabeth's expression doesn't change. "I've written a poem." The cameraman's phone breaks the silence. He silences it quickly. Minny takes two pieces of paper from her back pocket. She unfolds each on the lectern as if she sat in her truck cab, alone and off the road. She removes her baseball cap and hooks it to her belt loop. "Sorry, I guess I rushed in without taking that off." She reads to a now quiet room.

The candles flickered dancing to the song's lyrics
Shoulders touching, we prayed and sang
Hearts touching, we worked and reached out
The poor came
The homeless came
We grew in the light of their needs
God took us there.

The coffee steamed, the cookies disappeared
We celebrated one hundred years
With the young
With the old
With the handicapped
With the poor and the needy
God took us there.

Now we face a challenge
We perform for the camera

We talk for the news reporter
We forget the homeless
We forget the poor
We forget the women
Have we forgotten God?

She bows her head. After a pause, she folds the papers just as carefully as she had unfolded them. She places them in her pocket. The cameraman draws attention as he adjusts the camera position and drops a pen. Ellen Scott positions herself to meet Minny Lord as she walks slowly back down the aisle. Minny keeps her gaze down. One after another, the people in the seats she passes bow their heads. Ellen watches the heads bow and motions to the cameraman. She misses the opportunity to catch Minny and watches Minny return to her seat in silence.

Naomi glances at Ben who walks slowly to the microphone after Minny reaches her seat. Quietly, he sings the opening song again. Naomi joins. Slowly the congregation follows. Linda slips onto the piano bench and plays. Silence follows the Amens.

"Minny Lord has given us the gift of her poem. It's 9 PM but I guess that many of us have questions and/or comments. Shall we agree to continue until 9:30 PM? It won't give everyone a chance to talk. When we get close to 9:30, we'll let Father Rogers -" Ben sees Elizabeth move. "and Elizabeth add whatever they would like to say. We understand if you must leave. Let's see a show of hands for people who would like to extend the meeting until 9:30?" Everyone raises a hand. No one leaves.

Lines form at the microphones. Some plead with Elizabeth to avoid the distress and upheaval a lawsuit would create for her and for the parish. Johnny, the ragged and wrinkled black man who greets everyone at Masses, asks for money "just your loose change." Ben gives him a package of crackers. Others offer other small packages of food. Johnny thanks everyone. Many in the parish carry non-perishable food to give Johnny and others. Naomi remembers hearing that Elizabeth originated the idea of giving food instead of money to homeless people. The substitution removed the temptation to buy alcohol or drugs while helping them survive. She rummages in her purse for her peanut butter crackers. Others speak about the wretched and the oppressed and the unequal treatment of women in the Catholic Church. One woman removes her shoes. "I'll put them back on when the Catholic Church ordains women. I hope you are the first, Elizabeth!" Keeping track of the comments, the speakers and the clock prevents both Naomi and Ben from observing Elizabeth, apparently unmoved by supporting comments. She shows no response to any of the comments.

Ellen Scott and her cameraman leave after the questions and comments start. Naomi winces imagining the story that will appear on the news. Ben reminds people at 9:30 and again at 10 PM, but they have more to say. Finally, when Ben invites Father Rogers to speak, he suggests they schedule another meeting next week.

"Very good. Very good." Father Rogers stands with Ben. His eyes travel over the crowd nodding as eyes touch his. "Very good," he says more slowly. "It's late. We are all tired. We must pray about this. At Saint Luke's, we all have worked to include women in every part of our parish life. I fear the Bishop knows of changes he has not yet communicated to the parishes. Perhaps, the Bishop's action was less about Elizabeth and more about a change in the overall church. Let's pray quietly now."

They bow their heads. Those still standing at the microphones wander back to their seats and join the silent prayer.

"We'll look at the parish calendar and schedule a meeting next week. Check the website to see the day and time or call the office. Thanks everyone. Good night." Ben turns the microphone off and looks at Naomi. He makes a mental note to update the website. "Minny, does anyone see Minny? Can we get a copy of the poem for the notes?" Ben searches the moving crowd.

Minny stands and raises her hand with the poem. She makes her way through the crowd toward the front as groups break up and leave the church. People leave quietly. They touch Minny's arms and shoulders as she passes them. They smile. They reflect.

Ben watches Elizabeth precede the crowd out of the hall barely acknowledging those who move toward her to talk or console or question. He shakes his head and hopes time will bring a different perspective for her.

"You know I have to thank you Ben." Ben looks puzzled. "Remember the first time I facilitated, when I expressed my fears and doubts? You said I should start, and that you could take over if I wanted help." He smiles. "I facilitated the whole meeting. Tony Mancuso wanted the order of the agenda changed. Then, he stood up with a list of questions on two sides of a piece of paper about the expenses for Lombardo House. Every time we seemed to make progress on the agenda, he stood up again with more questions or objections." She shakes her head. "Now, that meeting seems easy compared to tonight's meeting." Mary waves and rushes up the stairs. Fred follows. "Do you think they will quit?"

Ben shrugs his shoulders, stops and smiles. "But remember too, you found a way to get Tony's attention! We all dreaded it when he stood up to speak. You kept track of where he was looking." Ben takes a breath. "Every time I think of the simplicity of that solution, it amazes me." He smiles. "You just raised your hand and even more amazing, when he got used to the technique and didn't stop, other parishioners helped us and raised their hands too. Such a sign of community! It didn't threaten. He didn't take offense. Other people could speak." He takes another breath. His smile disappears.

"We can probably forget that accomplishment," Naomi sits down.

Ben shakes his head and reaches for his papers. He stops. "How do we make sense of everything?" He sits down. "I guess we had signs. We just didn't pay attention." He scratches his head. "And boy do I miss Fred's participation. He always steps back and uses his unemotional mind to analyze the facts, a gift we need now. He would raise questions. I sure hope we don't lose him or Mary." Naomi nods. Ben takes a breath. "You know I remember an old friend at Saint Paul of the Cross telling me a story about Antonia, she must have been an amazing pastoral administrator. Did she get fired? Or did she leave?"

"She left. My parents go to that parish. That parish has become even more conservative than when I attended. Very conservative." Naomi touches her cross. "Your mention of Antonia makes me wonder how the parish changed. Or was it conservative when you grew up?" She doesn't wait for an answer. "She, Antonia, gave me this as a confirmation present. She sponsored me. Funny we each include her in our Catholic stories." She shows Ben the cross and takes a breath. "She answered my questions without ever making me feel embarrassed to ask. I know she did that for many others, too."

"Didn't Father Rogers talk to her about joining Saint Luke's?" Ben looks up at the ceiling. "Oh, you didn't attend at that time? Or?"

"From what Mom and Dad say, and we don't talk religion in any depth, Antonia 'misinterpreted the idea of being inclusive.' I wonder if my parents helped pressure her to resign. I never wanted to ask either her or my parents. As a matter of fact, I haven't seen her recently." Naomi holds her cross and sighs. "You know, my parents did all they could to prevent us from joining Saint Luke's."

Naomi looks at her watch. Zack will wonder why she hasn't returned. She caught the last sleepy nods after previous meetings, but tonight the kids won't budge when she kisses them. "Ben you know everyone here and their histories. What can we do? Who can help us?" She looks at her watch again.

"You should get home. Let me sleep on all this. I'll try to summarize in the morning before I go to work. I'll send it to Mary and Fred too. Maybe their response will give us an idea whether they still think of quitting or better what we can do." He pauses. "We can't quit now!"

"I keep thinking about what Mary said about our objectivity. That summary will help us. Maybe we have to meet before we send out the minutes? How do we strike the balance of remaining open and not fueling more controversy? Standing for or against Elizabeth doesn't seem to lead to any solutions."

Ben nods. They gather their materials, turn out the lights, and go to their cars.

Naomi puts plates on the table reviewing the details of the last parish meeting. She has spent the afternoon reading the agenda, trying to anticipate questions, and searching for ways to guide the meeting to avoid surprises.

"Parish meeting night, tonight?" Clare asks.

"I don't like broccoli!" Mark pushes his plate away.

"Not a late one, I hope." Zack checks email on his phone.

"Let's say grace," Naomi puts her plate on the table and sits down. "Mark, your turn."

Mark folds his arms and clenches his teeth.

"I can say it." Clare offers.

"My turn!" Mark bows his head speaking quickly. "Bless-us-oh-Lord-and-these-thy-gifts-which-we-are-about-to receivefromthybountythroughChristourLord. Amen. I still don't like broccoli!"

Naomi pushes his plate toward him. Zack straightens his chair.

"Tell us about school!" Zack intervenes putting his phone in his pocket. Not expecting an answer, he continues imitating Mark's mood. "I don't like work, boring, boring, boring. I don't like my computer, slower than a broken-down truck. My boss wants me to visit another customer on Mars."

Mark tries not to laugh.

"Not Mars again!" Naomi feigns exhaustion.

Clare puts a piece of her broccoli on Mark's plate. Naomi raises her eyebrows and Clare takes it back before Mark notices.

After several negotiating rounds about the broccoli result in a bite eaten and he swallows, Naomi asks, "Do you have another trip?"

"Just a day trip but I have to catch that early flight." Zack watches Mark attempt to move a piece of broccoli to Clare's plate, intercepts and returns the broccoli to Mark's plate.

"I wish I knew how long the meeting will last. I don't know what to tell you. Elizabeth doesn't seem to communicate with anyone. So, we don't know if she has agreed to take the job at Queen of Peace. Lawsuit! She only talks, when she does talk, about a lawsuit." She puts her fork on her plate. She looks at Zack. Her expression changes from confusion to sadness. "Now, Ben does not return calls. I'm really concerned about that." Clare and Mark each eat a piece of broccoli. Zack confirms that he has his boarding pass. Naomi sighs. "I'll try to leave right after the meeting."

"Where's Ben?" Mary shuffles papers and glances at the piano. "He usually arrives first. I missed hearing him practicing as I walked down the stairs."

Naomi looks at her watch, the piano, and the stairs. She shrugs her shoulders.

"Quite honestly, I'm glad he hasn't arrived. What's going on Naomi?" She leans across the table toward Naomi.

"And Fred?" Naomi asks.

"He said he would arrive about fifteen minutes late. I think he wanted to check some precedents again. He keeps thinking he will convince Elizabeth to drop this lawsuit. But no one has reached her, let alone gotten a response." Mary pauses and waits for Naomi to look up. "Naomi, you and Ben have become best friends working together. Have you spoken with him? How does he see the situation now?"

"I wish, Mary. I wish I could answer your questions." She shakes her head. "Ben doesn't seem like the Ben with the mesmerizing voice or the Ben with the even-handed temper and perspective." She rests her head on her hand. "I don't –" She looks away. "I don't know. I haven't spoken to Ben for over a month. I'm just reporting what you and I have both seen at parish meetings."

Mary places her hand on Naomi's elbow.

Naomi removes her head from her hand and places her hand on Mary's. She shakes her head and continues. "And he, of all of us, really knows Elizabeth. Can't he see how she has changed? She has put the whole parish at risk! Fred will tell us the details of that risk." She closes her eyes. "We spoke last after the parish meeting where Tony Mancuso ranted about Saint Luke's straying from Catholic law and he had a whole list of other women employed by Saint Luke's he wanted fired. As usual, Ben offered to summarize that meeting. He wanted to sleep on things. Did we ever get the minutes from that meeting, let alone the summary?"

Mary shakes her head.

Naomi continues. "Ben, the old Ben, understood Elizabeth's concern about things happening in the diocese and even anticipated that the Bishop would have to make some tough decisions. They both predicted he would reduce women's participation in some way. Funny how things happening at other parishes take on more meaning in a situation like this."

Mary's shoulder slumps. Naomi doesn't notice. "Did you know that Ben grew up at Saint Paul of the Cross?" Mary nods. "And I grew up in that parish too. We both knew Antonia, my confirmation sponsor." Mary looks surprised. "You know her too? Ben and I talked about Antonia when he told me parish meeting stories from the past. When the Bishop fired Elizabeth, I knew Ben's ideas would help Elizabeth see another path. I wondered if he might try to contact Antonia. It seems like her experiences might guide Elizabeth. Did you know her?"

Mary shakes her head. "I certainly heard about her. Mostly rumors, though."

"Rumors! That's what we are living now." Naomi glances at the agenda. "And Ben cares for this cause too. He wants to preserve the women's ordination work, expand services to the poor, include more people in the community as much as she does. She paid attention to the diocese and what the Catholic church did in the US and the world. I remember sitting in on one of those women's ordination committee meetings and hearing Elizabeth repeat 'anticipate change.' Her explanations were so reasoned. Ben showed me some of the ideas he planned to give Elizabeth after the Bishop fired her. I saw Antonia's name on that paper. Each suggestion built on all the work Elizabeth had done in the diocese and the parish –" Naomi looks away. "Obviously Elizabeth didn't give those ideas a chance. Though, who knows, maybe Ben never suggested them. No one seems to reach her. If she could step back and look at her actions, she would advise a different course, for herself."

"She can't step back now," Mary shakes her head. "Maybe I should say, she won't step back now."

In the silence that follows, the church basement remains quiet. They hear no approaching footsteps on the stairs. They both gaze at the piano remembering Ben's pre-meeting practice sessions. Naomi reviews all her attempts to reach Ben without success. The gravity of the situation overwhelms Mary.

"Quite honestly, I feel out of my element these days when it comes to parish meetings." Mary watches Naomi's face. "I'm not objective. The lack of civility among parishioners astounds me. Each time an interrupting shout erupts, I want to walk out. Or worse, yell back!" Naomi watches Mary twist her pen. "I hoped we would bring in new people, but now – Now, I don't want new people exposed to us. Showing someone our meeting guidelines, a travesty! I can just see the response of someone who has attended these meetings since the firing to reading those guidelines." Mary rubs her forehead. "And I feel bad convincing you to join us."

Naomi shakes her head. "Mary you can't leave!"

"Maybe we all should?"

"Huh? I – Maybe we should talk to Father Rogers. I know we always used Elizabeth for guidance in the past. Father Rogers relies on her for things like that. But – "

"Poor, Father Rogers. He has to do everything now that Elizabeth devotes all her time to the lawsuit." Mary shakes her head. "But this has gotten to, honestly, to a dangerous point. I see the factions sitting on opposite sides of the room and – "

Naomi watches Mary's face. They both look at the clock wondering when Fred might show up.

Sam

Dear Naomi,

Another one of our marathon talks last night. I tried to talk some sense into you! As you know, I've seen and studied organized religions theoretically and practically. Not one of all of those religions escapes from some deep contradictory flaw: narcissistic preachers, caring Christian communities who exclude their neighbors, pastors who run off with the funds or someone's spouse... Bet you didn't think I had more to say after last night! Take it for what it's worth and know that it comes with deep care and concern for you and the family.

What are you really looking for in a church? There are plenty of wonderful causes like your homeless shelter that you could volunteer for and they are not connected with a church. As a matter of fact, knowing you, you could probably run something like the shelter your church has started. But that's another conversation. You said that many of the volunteers come from outside the parish. Others do it. You see, even without the church, you can work for a worthy cause.

I know I won't insult you as a Catholic when I remind you about Catholics and women. You may have a woman pastoral administrator now; but if you see what is happening around the world in Catholic congregations, in Rome and, by the way, in the conservative Christian communities, you will realize that the Pope and his cronies have no plans to include moving women into positions of power – certainly not the priesthood. And even the next Pope, whoever he may be, will not move quickly to restore, remember that, restore women to the priesthood.

Why, you ask? Well, we have the scandal with the priests who abused young boys, a scandal that the church covered up for decades, a scandal that certainly persists even now. How many times did Cardinal Law in Boston deny that anything was wrong in his diocese and look what happened there. I just heard that Father Cuenin has been removed from Our Lady Faith of Christians in Newton, Massachusetts. A man who enjoyed his martinis, invited full participation AND walked the line in the diocese to keep his work going with the poor, with women, with the Voice of the Faithful, and with the hierarchy in the diocese. It was probably the martinis! What does that tell you? And Saint Luke's has a reputation in the liberal Catholic community. As long as we have Popes and the Vatican machine, they will find reasons to clamp down on Saint Luke's. Don't kid yourself. Oh, and if you haven't seen that movie about the Boston scandal that the Globe uncovered, <u>Spotlight</u>, watch it right away! If I can't convince you, that might help.

And don't kid yourself that the community will be able to stay together through whatever happens. Have you talked to people from the Church of the Most Precious Blood, there in your own city? They have stories to tell about what happened to their church, for sure. It was a woman, as I recall. I read lots about that parish while I was in divinity school, and she had a devoted community who worked with her in the inner city and ... Well if you don't know the story, I'll attach the collection of news clippings I used for my paper – "Zero Chance of Women's Ordination in the Catholic Church". I know I sent you a copy of that when I finally finished it.

Anyway, keep your eyes open, girl!

I love Vermont. The peace up here is beyond what I might have imagined. I am in touch with God in a whole new way. Your Sam!!

Sam Bonner,

You were right! I don't have time to explain now. She, Elizabeth, our female pastoral administrator got fired. How did you know?

I'm off to a meeting at the church. We're trying to discern what we should do as a community. I am a little apprehensive because some people seem very angry and I asked several people to stand guard throughout the church, just in case. I can't believe how people are acting!

Then, my friend, Ben, the kids' god father - of course you remember, Ben - anyway he is also a facilitator with me for the parish meetings. He just called to say that the conservative Catholics in the diocese have planned a protest outside Saint Luke's in favor of firing Elizabeth. We will be out of our league here. We know how to facilitate meetings and make sure everyone has a chance to speak, but there will be extra tension if these other people show up. I have always been amazed at how many people attend these meetings, nothing like my parents' parish when I was growing up. Now I am frightened that too many people will be there tonight.

More later. Hugs.
Naomi

Naomi

Naomi wakes up before the alarm and slips out of bed. She loves Thanksgiving more than any other holiday. Her dream follows her into the bathroom – a packing dream. She smiles. This time she packed suitcases with books. *What trip would we want books for? And why did Clare have such a big suitcase?* she wonders. She pulls on her sweat suit and runs a brush through her hair. Packing dreams remind her that they occur when an aspect of her life troubles her. She concentrates on the details looking for the cause this time. In last night's dream, someone unpacked the suitcase after she finished packing it. Looking at the clock told her she had missed something. *Picking up the kids somewhere? A meeting? Why did I pack kitchen utensils with the books? I don't see the connection.*

Then she remembers the family in *The Poisonwood Bible*. The missionary father restricted each family member to one piece of luggage when they traveled to the Congo. She loved the way Barbara Kingsolver created such unique characters. The mother in that story tried to prepare her children for their adventure in Africa. She dressed them in shirts and slacks under several dresses. When the suitcases overflowed, she created a bag out of string to tie cake mix boxes around their necks. Then, Naomi remembers the father. The details of the chapters where the father abused his family and his congregation make her tremble. He ignored their basic needs, natural disasters, and the surrounding war in the Congo. *What a situation for a young family!*

"Not a pretty picture of a church," she mutters as she walks downstairs. *Did the dream also remind me to pay more attention to my family?* She thinks about the kids and how much she looks forward to spending the whole day with them. The large suitcase Clare dragged from the house in the dream sends a shudder through her body.

Picking up toys as she walks through the family room, she mutters, frowns, and stops. A memory of the angry expression on Elizabeth's face at the parish meeting merges with the missionary father's heartless demands. She paces dropping toys into baskets without looking. She stops and breathes deeply. An image of Sam Bonner nodding knowingly after one of their late-night religious conversations joins the jumble of memories and dream scenes. Switching back and forth among the dream, memories, and *The Poisonwood Bible*, she smiles at the clean kitchen counters. Turning to find an apron, she instead reaches for the phone, frowns thinking of Elizabeth's face and voice, and calls her mother. She winces away thoughts and greets her mother speaking quickly. "I miss you, Mom. How will I do the chestnut dressing without you?"

"I just started peeling the chestnuts." Her mother chuckles. "I can't tell you how many grocery stores I have visited in this area of Florida. We wouldn't have the chestnut stuffing from scratch if I hadn't brought those nuts from New York! I miss you too, sweetie. How are my kids?"

Naomi smiles, pulls a chestnut from the warm water and peels. "Fine." Naomi listens to her mother's voice muffled by tucking the phone between her shoulder and chin. "Excited," she stops and sits taking the phone back in her hand. "Excited about Thanksgiving, though they have asked about you and Dad and Aunt Patty several times. They insist and I agree, it's not Thanksgiving without you and Dad. I promised we'd call, but I couldn't wait. I wanted to start Thanksgiving with you - like we usually do. By the way, how is Aunt Patty doing?"

"Thanks. She seems stable for the moment. We'll probably eat around 2 today, but you will too?" She listens for sounds from Patty's room. "Really well when you consider... Not her old self, but this chestnut stuffing should do the trick. Just a few days of keeping food down has put a little color in her cheeks. We'll see what Thanksgiving does. She should have her test results next week. I look forward to coming home and sleeping in my own bed. I forgot to ask, any guests this year?"

"Yes, we invited Ben, as usual, and Father Rogers. And we invited Lou." Naomi hesitates. Should she explain Lou and listen to the cautions about exposing her children to "such people"? She opens the refrigerator and decides not to explain. She remembers the first time she met Lou and wishes she could describe his journey. She can't figure out how to tell his story without causing her mother to start her litany about Saint Luke's. "Yup, we will eat around 2, also. Shall we call later in the afternoon?" Naomi remembers her dream again and hurries to hang up before her mother asks something about the church.

"Patty doesn't last too long. Please don't call too late, if you can manage." She drops a chestnut and tips over the salt shaker on the table. "Remember not too much salt in the stuffing."

"Thanks, I won't, especially now since everyone is on this healthy eating kick. Love you."

"Love you too, sweetie. Good-bye."

Naomi heaves a sigh and sets the table for breakfast with more enthusiasm. Then, she takes the turkey out of the refrigerator and puts it in the sink. As she finishes washing it, Clare appears in her nightgown.

"Mom I want to help. You said you would wait!" Clare sits at the table with her arms crossed over her chest and a pout on her face.

"Good morning," she replies smiling, watching, and waiting. The sides of Clare's mouth move a little but return to a determined pout. Naomi turns back to the sink. "In this first step, we wash, Clare." She motions Clare over to the sink. "We wash the turkey and all the areas the turkey touched before doing anything else. This avoids food spoilage and contamination. I want to finish that part before we eat breakfast. Tom can rest right here in the roasting pan until we finish and then you can help with the next step." She lifts the turkey from the sink to the roasting pan on top of the stove. Clare watches. "When you develop a little more strength, you can help with the washing too. Twenty-three pounds challenges even me." Naomi washes the sink, counter, and her hands.

Clare returns to the table. She fills her cereal bowl and takes milk from the refrigerator. "Will Ben come early to help too?"

"Yes, he will bring the vegetables and we can all peel onions and potatoes together. I want to get that big plastic tablecloth for the table so we can work here. And he will eat his breakfast first," Naomi fills her bowl and cuts a banana into pieces for both bowls. They eat quietly.

Zack and Mark appear as they finish. Mark carries a box of markers and a package of construction paper. "Daddy and I have the best idea ever for place cards. But," he pauses, looks at Zack, and continues, "it's a secret." He hugs his supplies. "We will make them in my room so nobody can see them until we set the table. And don't try to peek." He looks at Clare. "We just need a few things, but we can't tell you what things, right Dad?" Zack nods and winks.

"Well, I'm helping with the turkey," Clare says and winks at Naomi.

"So, we all have special things to do today. Who remembers what we are thankful for?" Zack sits and fills his cereal bowl.

"Oh, Daddy. We know," Clare frowns, finishes her cereal, and takes her bowl to the sink. She looks for an apron.

"And?" Zack replies. Clare purses her lips. Zack looks at Mark. The spoon leaves his mouth and collects a new pile partially spilling back into the bowl. He holds it in the air and hurries it into his mouth. The amount of cereal it delivered prevents answers. He chews.

"I'm thankful for my children," Naomi prompts. Clare finds an apron and ties it around her waist. She looks at Mark. He keeps chewing and avoiding his father's glance. "And my husband and my parents" Naomi hesitates. She didn't say Saint Luke's. She marvels at how things change. Then, she adds "and Saint Luke's and Father Rogers and Ben" she hesitates again.

"And Elizabeth," Clare adds.

"And turkey and pumpkin pie," Mark adds finishing his cereal and closing his eyes. Then he opens them again, "And Gramma and Grampa."

"And Aunt Patty", Clare adds.

Mark and Zack ask Clare and Naomi to leave the kitchen for a few minutes while they gather additional supplies for the place cards. Zack reaches the package of noodles on the high shelf and Mark finds the glue in the bottom drawer. "What about the toothpicks?" Mark whispers. Zack pulls open several drawers and cupboard doors. Mark paces by the kitchen door to make sure no one comes back. Zack finds the toothpicks, gives a thumbs up to Mark, and puts them in his pocket.

"OK, you can come back now," Mark calls. He holds his supplies close to his chest and runs to his room. He avoids looking at his sister and mother. Zack follows with a serious look on his face for Clare and Naomi.

Clare stands beside Naomi with the hum of the warming oven accompanying their tasks. Her own bright yellow apron shows signs of the last kitchen project. She pushes her sweatshirt sleeves up and mixes the herbs into the chunks of bread they cut the night before and left to dry. She hates getting dirty and frowns at the spots on her apron, but she loves helping more. She adds the chopped herbs and dips her hands into the deep bowl to mix the stuffing. She adds the melted butter and stock. It takes her a while to notice the new stains on the apron and the sleeves of her sweatshirt.

"Oh, yuck," she comments as she finishes.

"That's why we wear our old clothes for this? Right!" Naomi wipes her hands across the faded map of Stanton on her apron and turns the turkey on the rack. She hands Clare a large spoon. Clare shovels stuffing, Naomi packs. Before the oven beeps, Naomi fills the smaller cavity with the chestnut stuffing and places skewers through the skin. Clare dips the basting brush into the melted butter. After basting the turkey liberally, Naomi slides it in the oven. Clare stands over the sink washing her hands. She adds soap to the already bubbly water and washes again swiping at her apron and sleeves. Naomi sets the timer and uses Clare's suds to wash her own hands.

"Now what?" Clare asks drying her hands, apron and sweat shirt with the hand towel.

"Let's see." Naomi pops a soap bubble on the jumble of curls on Clare's forehead. "Look at you!" She adds a chunk of butter to the melting pan and places it near the oven vent for the next basting. "We could set the table. Gramma usually helps with that, but we'll have to do it today." They smile at

104

each other. She glances at the timer. "When the timer buzzes, we will turn the oven down and set it for another half hour. We baste every half hour for the first few hours to keep it moist."

"I can turn the oven down and I can do the basting!" Clare insists. Naomi nods.

"Good. Remember to tell Gramma what you did when we call them later!" Naomi hangs her apron on the hook.

"Look, a toothpick on the floor. I'll bet they will use toothpicks for the place cards!" Clare holds it up for Naomi to see.

"I wonder what they will make?" Naomi takes the toothpick and they laugh as they go to the dining room. Clare tries to fold her sleeves to hide the spots. Naomi kneels at the cupboard searching for the tablecloth and napkins. Memories of Thanksgiving at her grandmother's house come with the tablecloth as she pulls it out of the drawer. "I just wonder what my grandmother would say about all the happenings at our church. She always had an opinion."

"What?" Clare removes her sweatshirt and places it on a chair.

"You don't remember Grandmother Bessie, do you? She died before you could walk!"

Clare shakes her head. "But I look just like her." She points toward Grandmother Bessie's picture on the living room wall of family photographs. "Grandmother Bessie, right?" Clare frowns.

"Right, I miss her today." Seeing the frown, brings the large suitcase from her dream to the surface. Naomi worries about Clare and her ability to understand what Naomi can't explain or understand herself. Naomi pushes Saint Luke's out of her mind and places the tablecloths and napkins on top of the chest. "She always used these linens for Thanksgiving." Naomi smiles at Clare and runs her hand across the bleached white tablecloth with its worn woven pattern. "We'll have to add an extra leaf in the table so we can fit everyone." Clare reaches for the oak board leaning against the wall. "Careful, it's heavy." Naomi takes one end and they carry it to the table. "Can you find the latch?"

Clare nods, kneels down, crawls under the table, and opens the latch. "Mommy, I want to sit next to Father Rogers." She stands back up and looks at Naomi. "Please?"

Naomi motions for Clare to take the other end of the leaf and they steer it into place. "You'll have to ask Mark and Daddy." Clare turns toward the family room. "Better wait until they finish, though?" Clare stops. "Can you close the latch now? I heard it click into place." Clare climbs back under the table and closes the latch.

"Now, let's set the table! We need room for the plates and the serving dishes. Let's think. We'll have two gravy pitchers one at each end and," Naomi places dishes on the table as she speaks, "a dish for the beans,"

"And two cranberry sauce dishes, one for the jelly and one for the whole cranberries," Clare adds.

"Right," she pulls the cranberry sauce dishes from the cupboard and hands them one by one to Clare. Clare places one at each end near the gravy pitchers, "and –" she looks to Clare for help.

"Sweet potatoes – yum, mashed potatoes – yum, creamed onions and brussel sprouts – yuck, beans – yum, yum, and two dishes for Gramma's chestnut dressing." Naomi nods. "I wish Gramma and Grampa could come." They place the serving dishes in the center. "Wow, we do need all this space." Naomi finds the newly polished silver salt and pepper shakers and hands them to Clare.

"Now, we'll count the people to make sure we have a place for everyone." Naomi hands the dinner plates to Clare as she says the names. The extended dining room table extends from the dining room into their living room. They add candles and napkins before returning to the kitchen to continue with the other preparations. Clare bastes the turkey while Naomi holds the pan of melted butter.

When the doorbell rings, both kids race to the front door. Naomi captures the dripping basting brush before Clare dashes away. Ben hands the beans to Mark and the sweet potatoes to Clare. He returns to the car to gather the other vegetables. While the others chop vegetables, Naomi sets the ingredients out for the mushroom gravy. Lou only eats vegetables and she wants him to have gravy for his mashed potatoes. She found a recipe that included several kinds of mushrooms and more herbs than she had ever used in one recipe. With the vegetables in process, she can concentrate on learning a new recipe.

"That looks like gravy, Mom? I thought you made the gravy after the turkey came out of the oven?" Clare asks.

"It's a special vegetarian gravy. Lou doesn't eat meat. The recipe makes a large portion. I hope everyone will try it." Naomi replies as she adds the herbs to the simmering mushrooms.

"It smells good," Ben added.

As the kids, Ben and Zack finish the vegetable preparations, pots stand ready on the stove for cooking. Removing the turkey from the oven sets off the final flurry of preparations. Ben goes with Mark to see his latest construction. Clare curls up on the couch with a book. Zack goes outside to collect wood for a fire.

Naomi watches the activity as she stirs. She loves the chaos of activity, smells, and joint projects. Friends and family dominate the celebration of Thanksgiving, and of course food. This year Ben insisted on more vegetables as he tries to simplify and reduce the amount he eats. He also asked Lou what vegetables he liked the most and added a green salad and steamed carrots to the usual list of dishes. She makes a final check of recipes, adds another serving dish, and cleans the counters. They all look forward to having Lou at the dinner. His frost-bitten fingers have almost healed and the manager of the Delta Sonic Car Wash has welcomed him back to his old job. She watches the birds flitting around the yard before going off to change her clothes.

"Probably time for you to get dressed, kids." Naomi suggests as she finishes the gravy, dries the last utensils, and sets out serving spoons.

"What about Dad?" Mark looks at the pile of wood and Zack's smudged pants and shirt.

Zack piles the last wood and sweeps the debris into the fireplace. He looks at Mark and shrugs his shoulders.

"Oh, wait," Mark motions to his mother to turn around. He whispers to Zack, "Wait, we didn't do the place cards. Dad?" They disappear into Mark's room and return with the miniature toothpick structures balanced on cardboard bases covered with construction paper. "Now you can look, Mom. I made this one! Daddy works here." Mark holds the delicate structure up and places it at the head of the table without any mishaps. "And," he takes the next one from Zack, "and this is the car wash where Lou works." He points. "The hoses for the water and for drying when the car is all clean." Mark explains each piece and most of them make it to the table without losing too many of the toothpicks.

"Which is mine?" Clare asks. Mark points. "It looks like a church."

Mark gleams and nods his head. "See, just like the one for Father Rogers!"

Naomi checks the timer and gets the potholders off the hook. Ben reads the newspaper. When the timer sounds, Ben moves the turkey to the serving platter as Clare steadies it. Naomi starts the vegetable dishes. The kids made pilgrim hats in school and they both appear wearing their hats along with the new outfits Gramma gave them before she left for Florida. The doorbell rings. Naomi anticipates Mark and Clare racing to open the door. She smiles as the predictable collision at the door doesn't happen.

"Mom it's Father Rogers!" Mark jumps up and down and hugs Father Rogers's arm.

Zack comes down the stairs and Naomi removes her apron to meet Father Rogers at the door. They all hug. Naomi looks beyond Father Rogers. "Did Lou come?"

"Lou said to thank you very much but he couldn't join us today." Father Rogers smiles and holds Naomi's hand. "Don't be disappointed. He got in the car. Then, he started to shake and asked me to drop him off at the shelter." He looks from Naomi to Zack and then to the children. "Very good, very good... he comes to Mass almost every day now." He smiles and pats first Mark on the head and then Clare on her shoulder. "We know his story and – ? Who knows? Perhaps he has some kind of phobia about people? He always sits alone in church far from others. But we know, he loves us, and he will continue to make progress in his life. We should all thank God for that. No?" He looks at the kids and decides against further explanations. "Well, well look at our two pilgrims. You've come a long way, too. Did you come over with Columbus?"

The kids giggle. "Father Rogers, women settlers didn't come until <u>after</u> Columbus," Clare corrects. Zack offers wine to the adults and gives the kids ginger ale in wine glasses guiding their hands to hold the stem with one hand and the bowl with the other. They toast a Happy Thanksgiving and chat in the kitchen while the last parts of dinner come together. The serving bowls come from the table to the kitchen, receive their contents and return to the table. All hands pitch in and soon they find their place cards and take their seats around the table. Father Rogers offers grace.

"Can we still pray for Elizabeth?" Mark wonders as they say Amen.

"Of course, we can. It doesn't matter what people do or what happens to people, prayers go for everyone all the time." Clare answers.

"Very good, very good..." Father Rogers nods and smiles. "What a lovely way to think of prayer." He turns to Ben, "I see what you mean about children." Then, he turns back to the table and bows his head. He says an extra prayer for Elizabeth and then he says, "Since this is Thanksgiving, let's tell God what we are thankful for. We'll take a few minutes of silence and then we'll go around the table." Mark glances at Clare but her head doesn't move.

The list that forms in Clare's head overflows even without putting Elizabeth's name on it several times. She speaks first and the others follow. Naomi concludes with, "We'd better take a pause from thanking and start eating this food before it gets cold. Did we thank the place card artists?"

Mark blushes and giggles.

"You didn't tell me about mine." Ben asks.

"It's - " Mark looks at the structure. "Oh, Dad did that one. I forget."

Zack explains. "A special lectern for parish meetings with a control panel for all the microphones." Zack points at the components.

"Oh, I'll have to share this, Naomi!" he holds it up.

"Oh, I forgot to say thanks for the Call To Action conference and all I learned there. Especially about eating," Ben puts his place card down and takes a small portion of sweet potatoes before passing the bowl to Mark. "The shelter guests have a Thanksgiving Dinner tonight too, don't they?" Father Rogers nods.

"I sent one of our pumpkin pies to the shelter," Naomi adds as she takes a spoonful of cranberry sauce. She notices that everyone follows Ben's example. "You really started a trend with the small portions, Ben. Did you know someone suggested a fundraiser for the shelter where all the leftover food will go to the shelter as well as the money we collect? Good for the attendees and good for the shelter."

After dinner, Ben and the kids play *Monopoly* while Father Rogers cheers them on with a dish towel in hand. Zack and Naomi wash and sort the dishes. Father Rogers dries the dishes that Zack doesn't put in the dishwasher. Then, Naomi puts the leftover vegetables and gravies in the refrigerator. She cleans the turkey and makes packages for Ben and Father Rogers. She saves the carcass in a large plastic bag for a turkey soup she will make later and places it in a cooler in the garage. When she returns to the kitchen, she hears Zack saying, "I just hope we can get this resolved quickly. It takes a toll on everyone."

Father Rogers agrees. "It does for sure. Elizabeth still seems very upset, from what I can tell; but I believe she will avoid the lawsuit and take the job at Queen of Peace. I studied under Father O'Malley and he will renew her spirit. He told me he wants to send her on a retreat as soon as she arrives. Time without immediate responsibilities will do her some good. As much as we will miss her, having distance from Saint Luke's will also benefit her. We can regroup as a parish and talk about how to get her back. Of course, the longer she stays at Queen of Peace, the harder that will be. But at least we'll still have her in the diocese." He laughs and turns from the sink. "Very good, very good… Looks like we finished!"

"Thanks, Father, for all your help." Zack closes the dishwasher and turns it on. They join the others in the living room where they all sit on the floor around the coffee table playing *Old Maid*. After Ben reveals his identity as the Old Maid and the kids exclaim that they knew it, Father Rogers thanks everyone and says good bye.

Ben helps clean up the game and then goes to the closet for his coat. "Did Father Rogers have any clue what Elizabeth will do?" he asks as he puts his hat on.

"He seems to think she will take the Queen of Peace job. I hope he's right." Naomi replies.

"Well, she called me last night and wants to meet. At last, we might get some insight on her thinking instead of all this guessing." Ben says.

"Wow, great! Maybe she wants to tell you first. We need more direct information before we do that meeting in December, and, I might add, before we have our planning meeting." She shakes her head. "Parishioners want the truth and we haven't given it so far."

"I agree. She didn't say when she wanted to meet. I will ask if we can do it before the planning meeting. I'll put my listening hat on." Ben pulls his baseball hat on and smiles. "Hopefully, I can give back to her what she has given to me all the times I have talked about the seminary. She never tells me what to do. Amazing. She listens and then just by saying it out loud, I understand better what I should do. Father Rogers had suggested I talk about this more in depth with someone when we attended the CTA conference. It just turned out I found her in her office the day I finally decided to talk. She's probably tired of all my indecision. But this time I conquered it, and I sent the application. I warned my boss that I will quit if they accept me. I finally feel totally comfortable with my decision. I want to tell her personally; but well you know, no one sees her at the church or if they do, she avoids talking to people."

"Ben, terrific! The last time we talked you listed more doubts. I have to admit, it seems obvious to me that you should do it. Great! I'm excited. Elizabeth will share in that excitement too. Maybe good news like this will brighten her day."

"Thanks. I should remember that I have also bent your ear a number of times and I do appreciate your unquestioning support. I probably don't tell you that. But I do."

"You may not tell me explicitly, but I know. Oh, this really makes a perfect Thanksgiving!"

Expectations

As Naomi sees the school bus disappear around the corner, she sets the Christmas cookie recipes on the ledge above the counter and gathers the ingredients. Baking serves as a form of meditation or even prayer for her. Grandmother Bessie said each ingredient reminded her of a special person in her life. Naomi tries to build on that tradition. As she names her family members, neighbors, church friends, she matches each to the sugar, flour, nuts. She lingers when she thinks of Elizabeth. She tries to remember last year's list. Did she match Elizabeth with the yeast? She looks at that recipe, one of Zack's from his German grandmother. Yeast doesn't fit Elizabeth this year. The sticks of butter, cups of flour and sugar line up alongside the nuts, sprinkles, and flavorings. She thinks about Ben and doesn't find an ingredient to match him either.

She bakes the thumb print cookies and the chocolate chip cookies. As she reviews the recipes, she wonders if the kids will remember this tradition. Clare will certainly have an ingredient for Elizabeth. She tries to guess their special people when they return from school to bake the cut-out cookies. Though Christmas preparations often overwhelm her, she never eliminates cookie baking. The bright sun reflecting on the snow adds to the kitchen's light. She marvels at the crystal-clear sky and twinkling snow as she walks back and forth naming, measuring, mixing, baking, and decorating throughout the day.

She misses her mother. Usually they spend this day together early in December. Each year they share recipes and tell Grandmother Bessie stories in between naming their special people. Her mother didn't return from Florida after Thanksgiving as she had hoped. The test results showed cancer throughout Aunt Patty's lymph nodes. The doctor recommended hospice. Naomi's mother struggled with the choice of missing another holiday with her children and grandchildren. In the end, she stayed. With careful attention to dosage and timing, Aunt Patty retains her faculties. Naomi understands. The kids still ask many questions. Answers, though thoughtfully given, don't hold back the flood of questions they ask.

Flour covers the counters and floor. She will have a major clean up job. She wipes her hands on her apron and assesses her work - two recipes baked and cooling, two recipes ready for her helpers. She saves the cut-out cookies for last knowing that the kids will want to choose the cookie cutters and decorate the cookies. She grabs the sponge and then hesitates. It won't pay to clean up before sprinkles, colored sugar, tiny stars, raisins, and nuts join the flour covered surfaces. Her mother would clean up after each batch, but today she cooks without her mother. After they have sampled the last batch, she will package a box for Aunt Patty and mail it to arrive before Christmas.

In the evening, the facilitators arrive for the planning meeting and find Naomi's counters clear and her face smudged with flour. Smells of chocolate, sugar, and cinnamon mingle with the hot dog soup, Mark's name for the pea soup recipe Naomi makes often in the winter. It feeds the family quickly and the bowls disappear into the dishwasher as Ben arrives.

They all chat and sample the cookies Naomi set on a plate decorated with small Christmas trees. She adds red mugs with snow flake decorations and a pot of tea. They stop talking as she sits down, say a brief prayer and Ben reports on his meeting with Elizabeth. "Elizabeth wants us to devote the entire agenda to her at this meeting." Ben's eyes focus on his notes. Mary's jaw drops. Naomi shakes her head, raises her eyebrows, opens her mouth, and looks at Fred who listens and writes. Ben continues without pausing. "The lawyer has developed a plan for the lawsuit and described approximately how it will proceed. He wants her to sue the diocese for $1 million." Naomi swallows the words she had readied and her jaw drops. She expects details, lots of details. "Elizabeth can tell you all the reasoning. To win the suit, and the lawyer assures her she has a great chance, really depends on getting the right amount and kind of support from parishioners. She thinks we can put together a group of parishioners who will serve various functions during the trial and –"

Mary interrupts. "But we haven't all agreed that she should sue the diocese?"

"Did she talk about the decision? This doesn't sound like the kind of parish meeting she has encouraged in the past. Where or how do we invite the parish to deliberate on this? This looks like a process issue." Fred adds quietly, pausing to let each question register. As a lawyer, himself, he spoke privately with Elizabeth offering advice about the options she might pursue. He offered his own services for free, a generous offer from someone who devotes his practice to the poor and disenfranchised in the community. Instead, and ignoring all of his advice, she chose another lawyer from one of the large law firms in Stanton. Fred waits quietly as facial expressions around the table register shock, except for Ben. Fred continues, "Dixon, Grossmann, and Peak command the highest fees of all law firms in town." He pauses. "Who will pay for those services?" Ben looks at his notes. Fred clears his throat. "An even more important question: how does this look for a parish that states in its mission," Fred pulls a previous agenda from his folder. Saint Luke's mission appears at the top of the agenda as it does at the top of every document the church distributes. "Serving the poor is the highest priority for Saint Luke's."

"Quite honestly - those questions barely scratch the surface. You can bet on that. This community doesn't hold back. People will want to know everything." Mary adds. She gazes into her tea cup.

Naomi looks from face to face ending with Ben who continues to shuffle his papers. Then, she remembers the shelter. She gasps. "Also, we want to review the shelter and its budget for next year at this meeting. We must save time for that." Naomi leans towards Ben.

"Elizabeth wants us to concentrate on one thing." Ben looks up from his notes and then at Naomi. "Don't you think we will avoid dragging this out if we concentrate?" Ben asks.

"Then, that means waiting until January to look at the shelter budget, and we know that they will end the year in the red. We have to find someone to work on grants. Now we have Lou as a success story – which we almost didn't have, by the way because some of us..." Naomi grimaces and points her finger at herself. "I don't have to look far!" She looks at Ben who looks away. Fred nods his head in agreement. "Well, anyway, as a parish we turned away from our shelter responsibilities during the last two months." Naomi ignores her tea. She turns from her embarrassment and guilt to action. "It's the perfect time to apply for grants. We even talked about a special Christmas Eve collection for the shelter." Naomi reminds them as if the cookies and the candles and the decorations around the family room didn't already remind them about Christmas.

"It looks like the time has come for me to resign," Fred says quietly. "Elizabeth knows that I recommended not going forward with this lawsuit. She will see me as biased if I facilitate a meeting and that wouldn't benefit her or the parish." He looks around at each person.

"No - No, Fred." Naomi reaches for Fred's hand. "We all – Elizabeth, the parish, and the facilitators – need your quiet perspective, your patience – not to mention your legal expertise at a time like this." Naomi pleads.

"I don't know." Fred shakes his head.

Mary hesitates but then adds, "Quite honestly, I have thought very seriously about resigning myself."

"No," Naomi gasps and looks at Ben. "You two anchor the facilitators' group." She gulps her tea. She looks at Ben for agreement, a comment of support, a nod; she sees no expression on his usually expressive face.

"Yes." Mary speaks more confidently. "This lawsuit makes me nervous. Church and lawsuit don't belong in the same sentence! Nothing personal Fred, but my policy on life in general doesn't include contact with lawyers. They blow things out of proportion, at least some of them. Maybe I read too many newspapers!" She smiles at Fred. "It seems like the more expensive ones have the worst records for high fees, whether or not they win. A million dollars! Where did that come from? We are a church community not a business, aren't we?"

Mary shakes her head, breaks a cookie into small pieces, and looks around at the others. "It's become very difficult to maintain our objectivity in this situation. People count on us for that. I admire you both," she motions toward Naomi and Ben. "You do a terrific job." The responsibility she feels for the Saint Luke's community mixes with her fears about the lawsuit and where it might lead. She wavers. "Maybe Fred and I could take notes all the time instead of rotating the responsibilities. Naomi and Ben could facilitate. That way we still have a team, but we don't bias the outcome."

She pauses trying to make sense of her feelings and thoughts. "Quite honestly, the more I think about it, I'd rather sit with the parishioners in the chairs and make sure someone asks these important questions and insists on answers. As facilitators, we can't raise the questions without seeming to drive decisions in a certain direction. Fred is right, we agreed at the last meeting we would bring the parish in on that decision – to sue or not to sue. We committed to define a process for that. How can we present a done deal?!" She stops for a minute. Hearing her own words pushes her to a deeper understanding. "Maybe I just talked myself back into resigning."

"Elizabeth has done so much for Saint Luke's. We must support her." Ben counters.

"Fred and Mary raise a process question. We did agree to have the parish involved in the decision. Let's step back a minute. It seems like a bigger issue remains hidden? I never worked as a pastoral administrator, no one ever fired me, still I have sympathy with how dramatically this could affect me. I do sympathize." She looks directly at Ben whose head remained turned away. "We all sympathize. But I don't hear Elizabeth talking about anything but herself these days. What happened to women's ordination and relating this struggle to the struggle of all women in the church? Is it just me? I can support the more inclusive version of this issue. Can we help her reframe?" Naomi wants to say more but the look on Ben's face alarms her.

Ben cuts in without acknowledging Naomi's questions. "We face a time constraint here. The lawyer insists that for maximum exposure, we must file the lawsuit this month. He believes the timing of the lawsuit coming soon after the settlement by the diocese about the abusive priests will benefit Elizabeth. We don't have time to think of the larger issue." Ben leans forward and raises his voice. "And Fred and Mary we really need you. I can facilitate all the time. Let's not get into a disagreement here. Mary can you help us this week and then make a final decision? OK?" He looks at Mary and then at Fred. Fred nods.

Mary agrees reluctantly, "OK, I'll do the notes this meeting. We travel during the Christmas break, maybe that will give me time to think in between all the Christmas activities."

"Thanks, Mary. OK with that Fred? And Naomi?" Ben asks.

They both nod. They each take another cookie for the road and thank Naomi for baking and hosting. They forget their final prayer. Ben leaves before the others without saying goodbye to Naomi or extending his visit as he usually does. Naomi wants to ask him more about his unquestioning support for Elizabeth. And then, she realizes they didn't resolve the lawsuit issue: would the parish participate in the decision about the lawsuit, or would they present as Ben had outlined? She gathers cups from the table and gasps as she remembers the shelter budget.

Since hundreds of people now attend the parish meetings, they dispense with the refreshments and concentrate on having enough chairs, borrowing the microphones from the choir, and setting them up so people seated at the back don't have to walk the length of the hall to speak. Naomi counts the people as they drift in and take seats. Her tally shows fewer people than at the last two meetings. She checks all the microphones. If Fred and Mary quit, she doesn't know how they will manage these large meetings. She wonders how they can find a way to replace the hospitality of the old coffee maker, the odd collection of mugs, and the cookies. She notices several parents of the large families in the parish entering the hall and wonders how large families manage to maintain their family rituals with more and more children. She vows to ask them for suggestions after the meeting. People greet the facilitators as they move further into the hall to find seats. The season for Christmas sweaters, mittens, and scarves has arrived. People unbundle themselves and place coats on the cold, metal folding chairs. Ben opens the meeting with a prayer. He states the agenda. Naomi notices several surprised looks. Ben does not offer an opportunity for the community to discuss the lawsuit decision or indicate Open Forum at the end of the meeting. Instead, he starts to outline Elizabeth's plan. Elizabeth stands up and replaces Ben at the microphone. When she says, "one million dollars," noise in the hall builds. Naomi can hear many exclamations and see many puzzled looks.

Elizabeth's smile stiffens, "I know this sounds difficult, and" she gazes around the room.

Naomi watches as instead of engaging people with her smile, a trait Naomi has always admired in Elizabeth, her smile sears those whose eyes meet hers. Many turn away. This tight, unfriendly face makes Naomi gasp. She can't see Ben's face. She glances around the hall as Elizabeth continues and meets startled expressions from the parishioners.

"I know I can depend on you to support me." Elizabeth looks across the room not meeting anyone's gaze. "I deserve justice. You can make it. We will make history!" She looks down at her papers. "Now, I will describe what I want you to do. I need character witnesses to appear in court. Ben" she turns to Ben and smiles, "has already agreed to do this. Don't worry, the lawyer will explain what to do. I need at least a hundred people to volunteer for this." She looks up from her notes. "This parish always rises to challenges like this. The more people, the greater the impression." She pauses. Her smile relaxes. "I know you can do this for me." Now she clenches her fist and grins with anticipated success. "The greater the impression, the more chance I have to attract the attention of the TV stations and the newspaper." She pauses, "here and around the country!" She looks around expecting to see nods of agreement, if not enthusiastic clapping. The room remains silent. Questions appear in the crowd. A few people stand and move toward the nearest microphone. "Then, I need specific people to testify. I haven't broken any church rules. I haven't defied the Bishop. My lawyer will help you say this in your own words. The lawsuit hangs on the enthusiastic, loyal parishioners I know so well. For this category, I have a list of who I consider key witnesses and will contact you directly. I depend on your participation and support during this lawsuit. I know you can do this." She turns to Ben. He steps forward and invites questions and comments.

A few people whisper. No one speaks. Ben waits. Elizabeth's expression becomes more serious. Ben encourages and repeats the standard opening for people to comment, "We have a reputation here at Saint Luke's for tackling difficult challenges." Naomi still can't make eye contact with Ben. "I know we can do this. Please ask questions and step forward for Elizabeth. Elizabeth can't do this alone. She really needs our help." He nods toward Elizabeth. "I know we can do that for her." His smile invites more than Elizabeth's. Still no one steps forward. People hover around the microphones. Elizabeth folds her arms across her chest and clenches her teeth.

Then, Bob Harrington, the city fire chief, without a signal from Ben giving him permission to speak, pulls the nearby microphone to his mouth and asks, "Everyone hear me OK?" Heads turn toward him and nod. "My first reaction - whew!!" He stands and wipes his forehead. "A million dollars!" A little nervous laughter erupts. "I know Saint Luke's has earned a gold medal for begging. And we have a great record for collecting money. But I've never heard us ask for money for ourselves." He looks around the room and sees recognition on the faces. "Since you expect to win the lawsuit, you probably have a plan for that money, Elizabeth, and you just haven't told us."

Elizabeth's look says she doesn't have a plan and doesn't consider it relevant.

"Can you give us an idea?" Bob asks with a note of surprise.

The stiff smile reappears. Quiet extends as people wait for the familiar smile to appear on Elizabeth's face. Her face does

120

not change. "Bob we're talking about bigger issues here. I need to meet with the people, character witnesses, who will help me win this case!" she pauses and glares. Then she manages a stiff smile and softens her voice, "I'll go upstairs to the church. I know you will follow me." She glances at Ben as she goes through the door.

Bob replies to her back shrugging his shoulders as she disappears, "Bigger than the poor or the homeless? Bigger than appearing to be a money hungry parish rather than one that gives everything away? Did someone change Saint Luke's values without notifying us?" He returns to his seat shaking his head.

Silence blankets the hall. Ben stands and urges, "Let's show our support for Elizabeth. I know I'm with her." Ben follows Elizabeth up to the church.

Naomi sits stunned for a moment then approaches the microphone, "Perhaps people need time to think about this." She pauses realizing she certainly needs time. "Take time to – to consider. There are many ways to support Elizabeth, many ways." She knows, she hopes there are many ways. She can see lack of agreement as she scans the faces. She fears the sour looks on faces in the crowd and her inability to guide the crowd. "After reflection, give the rectory a call with your ideas. This is important to Elizabeth and to Saint Luke's. Remember we value everyone's opinion." She doesn't see Martha in the audience and doesn't want to clog the phone lines without Martha's agreement. "Perhaps rather than flooding the office with phone calls, those with web access can add thoughts/comments/ideas to the suggestion box on the website." She hesitates a little. "You can also call any of the facilitators, well, I'll make that offer for myself." Naomi glances at Mary and Fred for a suggestion of what to do next. The crowd remains in their seats though many groups talk among themselves. A few more people leave the hall.

Minny Lord stands up at the back of the hall and walks toward the front touching, as she passes, the shoulders of people standing to leave and those still seated. Naomi smiles and hopes that Minny's poem will at least bring closure to the evening if not to the issue. Naomi says, "Minny Lord, welcome home!" She scans the room quickly. "It looks like we're done with questions and comments for tonight. Let's close with a poem. Hopefully, I'm not jumping to conclusions?" Minny holds her hand up showing her notebook pages and nods agreement.

She turns toward the mumbling crowd of parishioners and smooths the wrinkled hand-written pages. She smiles at everyone and then reads.

My roads are long
The nights dark
The time lonely
But God is here.

Saint Luke's road is long
We walk together
The journey will be hard
But God is here.

Alone with a flat tire
The skies dark and cloudy
The road empty
But God is here.

This crisis is only a flat tire
It can be fixed
I feel God's breath
God is here.

The load is already late
The customer will grumble
The repair takes too long
But God is here.

Patience to find the tools
Time to make the repair
Wisdom to make it right
And God is here.

A cloud hangs over us
The lightning divides us
The wind turns us away
But God is here.

Patience to find each other
Time to pray
Wisdom to stay together
And God is here.

The tires hum again
Miles fade away
The sun sets again
And God is here.

We walk with God
The path is unclear
God is here.
Remember, God is here.

Naomi

The dishwasher hums with the dishes Naomi inherited from Grandmother Bessie. They make a lighter sound than the everyday dishes. Naomi listens. She thinks about traditions. These dishes have become part of the Norton holiday traditions. She passes on to Clare and Mark the care for the dishes as she teaches the handling techniques she learned from her mother. Memories of her own childhood Christmases include both these lessons and the stories her mother and grandmother told about Christmases past. The kids can now tell the story about how Naomi broke the pickle dish at age five. Now, Mark tells it as he carries another pickle dish very slowly with two hands held high to the sink. Holidays hold many stories and the kids love stories. They each take a red snow flake mug of cocoa and gather around the Christmas tree near the crackling fire. New snow floats quietly down and decorates the bare trees piling flake upon flake. Snow, cold, the tree, most of the family – they have all the ingredients for a lovely holiday.

Zack's grandparents came from Wilhelmsdorf, a small town in the southern part of Germany. He visited the town during his junior year in college and spent Christmas with his grandparents. All he remembers about the visit holds a special place for Zack. His grandparents moved the year after his visit. They spent their final years living with Zack's family. Zack especially loves the Christmas tree traditions. Tonight, they will light candles on the tree and open gifts from family members. He places a large bucket of water near the tree and waits until everyone sits quietly. Clare looks forward to being ten years old. Then, she can light candles, too.

"Look, the fire. What happened? It keeps going out." Naomi remarks.

Zack opens the grate and stirs the coals. Then, he adds rolled newspaper and places another log over the glowing embers. "There, it just ran out of wood. Too much going on tonight."

"Mommy, how can we have Christmas without Gramma and Grampa?" Mark pouts and wiggles closer to Naomi.

"Gramma and Grampa want to sit right here with us tonight." She pats the empty seat next to Mark. "We have added that tradition to your father's Christmas traditions. But you know that Aunt Patty is very sick." Naomi places her hand on Mark's shoulder. "She is Gramma's only sister and she doesn't have anyone else to take care of her. Though Gramma would prefer to celebrate with us, she and Aunt Patty love each other." She watches the childrens' faces. "Maybe they are remembering all their Christmases around the tree when they were children and what gifts they made for each other and all the surprises. We hope they can return in time for New Year's Eve! Let's look forward to that."

Mark accepts the explanation but adds, "I still miss them." Naomi smiles. He returns his attention to the pile of Legos balancing between his legs and builds a tower.

"And without Ben?" Clare sits forward and leans toward Naomi.

Naomi takes a breath and then another. Clare watches her face. Smile wrinkles fade. She opens her mouth and closes it. "Ben has a cousin," She pauses remembering past Christmases full of the silliness Ben stirred up, including stories about his own traditions. She smiles as Mark's tower reaches tipsy heights. "his cousin," her brow wrinkles, "he hasn't seen his cousin in several years." *Why now?* She wonders. Naomi watches the flames build and wonders about this visiting cousin. Though he expressed it as a family obligation, doubts bother her. His response, an email, to her phone call inviting him to Christmas fueled her doubts. They have not spoken alone since the last parish meeting and she feels a strange distance. "His cousin came to town for Christmas," she says glancing at Zack.

Zack interrupts to avoid further explanation. "What do you think?" he turns back to the tree and takes a long wooden

125

match from the box. "We'll have to go to Germany soon to buy these special matches."

"Me too." Mark chimes in. "I want to go with you."

"Me too." Clare says almost in unison.

"We should do that!" Naomi agrees. "Well, not just to get the matches." They all laugh. "The kids should visit Wilhelmsdorf. Did I pronounce it correctly?" Zack nods. "We could see your grandparent's house and meet those distant cousins, like Wolfgang." Mark smiles. She watches the tiny flames as Zack lights the candles. "We should go at Christmastime. You have told us about the Christmas markets with the cookies in star shapes."

"To visit the Weihnachtsmarkt, Christmas market, we must visit before Christmas. They close the day before Christmas Eve. In almost all the towns they have little wagons that sell food and crafts and, of course, all kinds of decorations. I've always wanted to go to the one in Nurnberg. Oma collected angels from that market. She lived near there as a child. Those angels." He points to the line of little wooden angels that surround the crèche on the table. Naomi puts them among the greens that surround the Holy Family, the shepherds, Wise Men and the wooden animals her parents brought back from Africa. Each tiny angel plays a different instrument. On each round head two small dots defined the cheeks.

"And those too," Mark jumps up and points at the small choir that circles the top branches of the tree. "Now we have to light those candles so they can see their music and sing. And this one so my car can see where to drive." Mark points at the ornament near the center of the tree.

"Right. Can you turn the lights off?" Zack motions to Clare; and she reaches above the couch where she sits, turns the light switch off, slides back into her place, and reaches for her cocoa cup. Zack checks each candle to make sure they stand straight up and away from the branches. Then, he lights the match and the candles. They all watch as the tree's candles replace the electric light in the room.

Then, Naomi places the presents on the table for the kids to distribute. For presents, they follow Naomi's tradition. Each family member draws a name from a hat on the first Sunday of Advent and makes a present for that person. This tradition fits nicely with the tree lighting tradition as they concentrate on opening one present while the candles burn and flicker.

This year Mark is old enough to participate. In previous years, they drew names among the three of them and all made small presents for Mark. Mark drew Clare's name. He wanted to make a car for Clare's doll house but settled for a table after several conferences with Zack. Mark loves secrets. He spent more time camouflaging the work bench in the basement, making signs for the basement door so no one would interrupt his work, and whispering about his progress to Naomi than he did making the table, "all by himself." First, he chose the wood from Zack's collection of leftover pieces and then the color of paint. Of course, he knew Clare loved purple; but he had to find the right purple which required several shopping trips to different stores. Even though Zack's travel delayed the project several weeks, Mark set up his sign and went to the basement every afternoon and covered his work when he finished. When he didn't work on the gift or shop for supplies, Mark asked Clare's advice about making a gift for Naomi and told Naomi how he had fooled Clare in loud whispers. "This is worse than the Catholic Church," Naomi remarked to Zack after the kids were asleep that night.

"A bunch of little boys making and keeping secrets. And you just figured that out!" Zack replied. The scandal over the priests abusing young boys tested Zack's faith. Though he respected the Saint Luke's community because of its positions on the edge of Catholicism, the abuse made him question. "Oh, you meant Mark and his present caper!" They laughed at the mistake and grimaced at the recent news of more priests abusing young boys.

They open their presents in age order. Mark can barely sit still until Clare opens the tiny package wrapped in comics from the Sunday newspaper. The purple yarn ties the package together. "Oh, it's beautiful. Should I guess my secret Santa?"

"Me, me," Mark bounces on the couch.

They hug and Mark almost forgets to open his own present – a small garage that matches Clare's dollhouse and has enough room for Mark's tractor. Mark jumps up and down on the sofa, then runs to get his tractor. Zack moves the garage away from the tree and the dripping candles. They sing "Oh Christmas Tree" alternating verses in German and English. Zack takes the candle snuffer from the mantle. Each person snuffs a candle. As Naomi puts her candle out, she notices that the fire has died mysteriously again. Seeing that the new log did not catch fire, makes her wonder why. The kids put out a plate of cookies for Santa Claus and hurry off to bed without nudges, threats, or stories.

"Too bad we can't think of a more regular motivation to get them to bed on their own." Naomi muses as she and Zack monitor the tree. Thin wisps of smoke swirl from the last candles and disappear. "I saw a teenager at the mall yesterday, with her pierced belly button and half her stomach showing. When does something go beyond being a style or a whim and predict the downfall of a culture? What happened in Rome that suddenly the exuberant celebrations of life, fertility, harvest, and accomplishments become orgies? Do I sound like Grandmother Bessie? Or, I don't know, I sound like the men who blame women for rape because the women them tempt with their actions and skimpy clothing?"

"You lost me?" Zack replies.

"Oh, Saint Luke's again. A topic I can't stop from invading my thoughts even on a lovely night like this."

"I should have known. It's Christmas you know."

"I know but – look the fire –?" Naomi finishes her cocoa and puts her cup with others on the matching snowflake tray. She wonders what stories her precious Christmas things will create when she passes them down to the kids.

Zack gets up and moves the log. He sees no signs of the glow the fire makes when it eats into a log. "I checked to make sure I chose a dry log. I remember the markings. I know I put this one inside at beginning of November?" He pushes the log back, tests another for dampness and places it on the fire with more newspaper. The newspaper creates bright flames which surround both logs. "That should catch now."

"How do we know whether we should support Elizabeth in this lawsuit? We can see the firing in the context of more conservative actions in the church against women. We should resist. Yet, will this lawsuit improve the condition for women in the Catholic Church? Or will it just bring publicity focused on Elizabeth? Which may be bad publicity for Saint Luke's and prevent us from continuing our work? She doesn't talk about women in the church anymore. As a matter of fact, she hardly says *we* – not *we* women, not *we* – Saint Luke's parishioners. She's so angry too. The anger that has burnt all her graciousness and selflessness away. We have many examples inside and outside the church of people who stick their neck out for a principle, and the result affects many people. The family who hid Anne Frank's family during the war shows such bravery for a cause that benefited other people. This just doesn't feel like a battle with that kind of cause burning behind it. From everything she has said in the past about the need to make women more central to the church, it should be. She doesn't talk that way. It makes me wonder if she has a personal vendetta against Bishop Inman. If so, what a horrible position to put the parish in!"

"Can Ben shed any light on this new Elizabeth? What does he say?" Zack asks.

"I don't even know how to answer that. The way he spoke at the parish meeting, he will do whatever Elizabeth asks. That doesn't sound like Ben, does it?" She shakes her head. "His closeness to Elizabeth, suddenly, puzzles me. Now that I think about it, does it seem strange that after all these years of friendship, Ben suddenly has an out-of-town cousin, who he has never mentioned. Ben doesn't return phone calls."

"It does seem strange."

"I haven't spoken to him since the parish meeting. I guess he expected me to follow him and fully support Elizabeth. I didn't follow him upstairs. I didn't encourage others to follow them. That behavior, and we know Ben well, tells me that something is not right about this whole thing."

"I guess I didn't realize Ben had changed that drastically." Zack struggles to keep his eyes open.

"Elizabeth takes no criticism, no advice – unless it matches her plan or her ideas. She criticizes the Catholic hierarchy for that kind of behavior, exactly. Does she see the contradiction – the Church's unwillingness to recognize the place of women in the church and her unwillingness to accept anything that diverges from her view? She always had such an eloquent way of differentiating human decisions from Christ's teachings, to eliminate women priests for instance. You remember how she listened? And I say *remember* on purpose." Zack nods. "Before this all happened, if I walked into her office, she put everything down and gave me complete attention. Now, for one thing, I haven't seen her door open any time I've visited the rectory since this all happened. And, for another, she doesn't stand at the door after Mass until the last person leaves. When she does stand there, she smiles and chats with one person and ignores the next. It's like Dr. Jekyll and Mr. Hyde."

"Now, Naomi, maybe an exaggeration?" Zack asks. "Maybe Santa Claus should do his work before somebody wakes up and finds no presents under the tree."

They both get up and go to locate the presents and bring them from their hiding places. Zack takes several bites from the cookies. Naomi writes a note from Santa thanking the kids. "Did you close the grate? Look that log didn't catch either. Strange how the fire keeps going out tonight."

Tony

Tony Mancuso looks at his watch, paces to the window, shrugs, and mutters. "This is it. I can't believe it! I tell people, how many times have I told people, especially these annoying liberals, women don't belong in the Catholic Church. They belong at home! Mother o God, they can't run anything let alone the Catholic Church. Now, maybe everyone will get it. Pope Benedict doesn't want women on the altar. God doesn't want them there."

He paces and begins to smile. "This is it; this is it!" he sits by the window as the importance of eliminating Elizabeth Winter seems within reach. "First, I will write to Pope Benedict." He smiles. "He will take action. Maybe Father Rogers has to go too!" He nods and smiles again. "Times favor my point of view. With Benedict we might even get the Latin Mass back!"

He frowns. Memories swarm. He paces. He stops. Those memories grab his attention. As often as he has pushed aside previous efforts to confront the local, liberal Catholic idiocy, his past attempts distract him from Elizabeth. His passion loses to the memories. His eyes land on the cross on the living room wall. As that first defeat a long time ago takes his attention, memories of his grandfather, who left that cross to Tony in his will, crowd his thoughts. "What would Nonno have done? I need you Nonno, now!"

That original confrontation abruptly interrupts thoughts of Nonno. In his first year at Stanton's only Catholic school for young men, Saint Charles Jesuit, he tried to drum up support for a showdown with the local Bishop when news came from Rome, prohibiting Masses in Latin. Hearing the consecration in English still sets him off. His grandfather's rants come back clearly: *Our traditions! We must preserve sacred traditions! Do not touch our Latin Mass! Not now! Not ever!* Tony hears his grandfather's loud voice and passionate opinions. His death shortly before Tony started middle school caused more anger than sadness, an anger that surfaces now.

As he started at Saint Charles Jesuit, he felt his grandfather's spirit with him. He set to work trying to remember what his grandfather had said about Latin and the foundations of the church. He made a plan. He told whoever would listen how they should want to preserve the Latin Mass. Tony's insistent monologues drew more laughter than advocates. As the youngest of six, he had gained experience speaking out and speaking loudly. Gio, who started at Saint Charles Jesuit the same year, admired his stamina, especially as they both experienced life in the new school. Gio tagged along passing out flyers. Instead of the crowd Tony hoped to assemble, Tony and Gio stood alone on the school steps. Instead of a march on the diocesan offices to confront the Bishop, they had a meeting with the principal of Saint Charles Jesuit. He offered the Bishop's regrets, listened to their proposal, praised them for their work, explained the Vatican Council's decision, offered suggestions on how to approach the next Vatican Council with their proposal, and sent them off to their next class.

That experience formed the basis of a lifelong friendship between Tony and Gio. Over the school years they gathered more friends, mostly Italian, from the neighborhood. Many attended Saint Prasseda Church in the Italian section of the city and served as altar boys. In addition, Tony nurtured a festering anger fed over the years by the diocese loosening policies that defined the Catholic Church for him. Each affront added to that anger. Tony, whose older brothers also served as altar boys, spent his free time at the church helping the pastor with chores. The pastor appreciated the help. Tony enjoyed the kind of attention he didn't get at home as the youngest. By the time he reached middle school, the pastor relied on Tony to distribute the altar servers' schedules and fill in when someone called in sick.

The second confrontation formed when he saw a girl's name on the altar server schedule. The anger that drove him to fight to restore the Latin Mass reappeared. The first time he saw a girl's name on the list, he crossed it out and wrote his own name in her place. It took a few months and many ignored phone calls, for the pastor to notice. Finally, repeated calls from the girls' parents sunk in and caused the pastor to investigate. He spoke to Tony who responded with a passionate monologue. The pastor praised his logic and encouraged him to become a priest where he could have influence in situations like this. "Work from within the system, Tony. Create respectful change."

Tony considered his advice briefly. In defeat, he took his own name off the list when the pastor scheduled him with a girl and substituted another name. Meeting his future wife around that time, might have influenced the choice not to enter the priesthood. Marrying a woman with the same interpretation of Catholicism, especially when it applied to a woman's place, strengthened his opinion about women in the church and all women, for that matter. They joined her parish, Saint Luke's, after their wedding. Elizabeth Winter's appearance at Saint Luke's ignited and then deepened Tony's festering anger.

He watches Gio park his car across the street. The others pull their cars into spaces ahead of and behind Gio's. They all gather in the kitchen talking quietly to each other and watching Tony as he paces back and forth.

He speaks as the conversation winds down, "What the hell is going on here?" He watches their faces. He takes a deep breath. His adoring audience waits and smiles. "I told you no good would come of hiring a woman. It's not Catholic." They nod in agreement. Tony paces the floor of his kitchen between the table and the sink. "Mother o God!" He shakes his head, clenches his fists, and takes another breath. "Now look what she's done. This demands action, action – " He stops and looks at his buddies seated at the table. Sal opens his mouth, "before she bankrupts the parish. She's already done it to us at the Masses, funerals, baptisms, you name it. A woman! What does she know about anything?" The men nod. "We let her in the door. We put up with her. Now, we're done. No money for that lawyer!" Sal and Gio start to speak at the same time. The others nod, make fists and watch. Tony continues. "Lawyers! I see lots of zeros with these legal fees. Lots of <u>our</u> money!!!"

"Troublemaker." Sal thumbs his fingers on the table. "I – "

"I never liked her anyway. I don't think she really is Catholic. Something about her? Maybe she wasn't born Catholic. What do you think?" Gio scratches his head.

"Come on guys we have to come up with a plan!" Tony paces.

"Troublemaker." Sal shakes his head. He looks at Gio and watches Tony pacing. He shrugs his shoulders. He looks from one to another, expecting someone to speak. "What can eight guys do? Gio tried to talk to Father Rogers and can't get an appointment until next week." Sal waves his arms as he speaks. Gio nods his head. Sal frowns, "But why is it our money?"

Tony slaps his hand on the table. Everyone flinches. Elbows leave the table. "What do you think, Sal? She sues the diocese, right?" Sal nods. "Do you think she has the money to pay those thousands of dollars?" Sal shrugs. "Of course she doesn't. Who does she work for?" Sal's eyebrows lift. "No more stupid questions!" He sits at the table, puts his head in his hands, and mutters, "Mother o God." His friends watch and wait. They look at each other and shrug their shoulders. These sixteen elbows have visited Tony's kitchen table many times over their years of friendship. The friends wait. They watch. They look at each other. Questioning looks pass from friend to friend.

They smile when Tony stands and resumes pacing. "Hmm." He pulls out his phone and scrolls through his contacts. "Our buddy, Kevin! Why didn't we think of Kevin?" Tony stops pacing and holds his phone out to his buddies with a picture of Kevin in his contact list. Their smiles don't communicate what Tony expects. "Where did our buddy Kevin go when he left Saint Luke's?"

The buddies look at each other. "I think he still lives in Stanton. I haven't seen Kevin in – ?" Gio scratches his head.

Tony looks at Sal and waits. Sal wrinkles his brow. "Troublemaker that's what she is." Tony waves his arms. Sal watches and slowly his eyes widen. "Saint Elizabeth's!"

"Saint Elizabeth's! Our buddy, Kevin," Tony waves the phone. "Our buddy, Kevin went to Saint Elizabeth's." They laugh.

"Saint Elizabeth's," Gio chimes in. The others nod and agree.

"You know —" Sal scratches his head. "Funny, but somehow that doesn't sound right? Saint Elizabeth's?" Sal's smile turns to a frown.

Tony touches Kevin's entry in the phonebook. He stops pacing. "My notes say, right here - Saint Elizabeth's." He shows Sal his phone and points at the note. "He keeps telling me to switch parishes. They don't have any women on the staff at Saint Elizabeth's."

"Ha, funny, but -" Sal laughs but goes back to frowning.

"Right, Saint Elizabeth's!" Tony smiles. "Saint Elizabeth's wouldn't hire Elizabeth Winter!" He scratches his head. "I'll bet I could get Kevin to help us out. Kevin knows people. Kevin knows, Kevin -"

"But – I somehow -," Sal can see Tony figuring what to say to Kevin. He tries to remember why Saint Elizabeth's doesn't sound like the right parish for Kevin. Then it hits him. "Hey." Tony and Gio exchange Kevin's information and ignore Sal. "His kid, Patrick, his oldest kid? Right? Patrick will go to Saint Charles Jesuit following his Dad, that Patrick -" Tony and Gio turn to Sal. Without getting any affirmation, he clears his throat and takes a breath. "Patrick had his confirmation at Saint Paul of the Cross." Sal beams.

"Right. So, let's see. Maybe - When is the next parish meeting?" Tony asks.

"Why would he go to Saint Elizabeth's and have his kid confirmed at Saint Paul of the Cross?" Sal waves his arms to get their attention.

Tony and Gio conclude neither of them know the date of the next parish meeting. Neither of them has a bulletin.

"Call the parish line. They put stuff like that on the recording." Tony points at Gio. "We'll bring a few friends to the meeting." He looks at the faces around the room everyone signals agreement. He paces, scratches his head, and thinks.

"Kevin will have ideas; he always has ideas." He paces a complete circuit of the kitchen and stops as Gio ends the call. "We'll send our proposal in ahead of the meeting. Then, they have to listen to us."

"What should we propose?" Gio hangs up his phone and reports. "The next meeting is on Tuesday."

"Better correct your phone there." Sal points at Tony's phone.

"What do you mean?" Tony turns abruptly toward Sal.

"Saint Paul of the Cross." Sal speaks clearly looking directly at Tony. "I went to his confirmation!" Tony frowns. Sal speaks faster. "Might even be better that he goes to Saint Paul's, a very conservative parish." Tony waits. Sal pauses and then continues, almost crushing his words together. "Probably Kevin knows even more people there." The frown leaves. Sal doesn't smile. Then, he pauses and gushes: "Great idea Tony!" Tony smiles.

Lou

Lou heard stories on the street about shelters and tried the Mission Shelter. He begged for the money, imagining warmth, food, and quiet. He paid for a bed and food. Soon after he arrived, he found that the other men frightened him. Fights broke out. The smell of alcohol permeated the sheets. Volunteers ignored the bizarre behavior even when arguments occurred or fights trapped innocent bystanders. He lost his appetite. He felt safer on the streets. Then, he followed someone to Lombardo House during a bitter winter storm and walked into a warm room with tables, chairs, and a pot of steaming soup. The volunteer gave him a bed with clean sheets. No one asked for payment. He slept the night through for the first time in months. His eyes devoured the breakfast plate filled with toast, bacon, and eggs. He stared at the plate. The steam evaporated before he picked up a knife and fork. The next storm brought him back.

"Lou, welcome back," Naomi Norton watched him sign the register.

Lou nodded. He took a towel and found a seat in the corner where he waited for his turn to use the shower. Naomi brought bowls of soup from the kitchen and offered them to the guests. She brought the last bowl to Lou. He nodded and smiled.

"I haven't seen you in a while." Lou shook his head and took a spoonful of soup. "Have you been coming, just not on the days I volunteer?" He shook his head again. Naomi didn't recall much of the conversations she had with him previously. She did remember how little he said. She sat down and glanced at the other guests. She wondered if anyone had reviewed the shelter rules with him. She observed that he hadn't joined in the lively conversations about sports with the other guests, and he didn't say much to the volunteers. "Did we give you an overview of the Lombardo House shelter and explain the rules here?" Lou shook his head.

Naomi smiled and spoke quietly. "Bill Lombardo, a parishioner at Saint Luke's," Naomi pointed out the window to the church, "gave this house to the church when he moved in with his son. If you'd been in the neighborhood five of six years ago, you might remember Sam." Lou shook his head. "I didn't know him either, but he sounds like a wonderful man. We offer this shelter program and a food program to help the poor neighbors. At the shelter, you can have a bed every night during the winter months." She saw a look of surprise on Lou's face. "We ask you to arrive before 9:30 PM, avoid all use of drugs or alcohol, and leave the room clean each day." He put his spoon down and smiled at her.

"Thank you." He paused. He smiled. "I think I can do that." He looked at the clock on the wall and his bare wrist.

"Great. When you finish your soup, we'll sign you up for the rest of the winter." Naomi stood and moved to the door. She pointed at the closed door. "Just outside this front door to the right, you can see a big clock above the gas station's garage door." They both smiled. Lou went to the window and saw the clock.

He liked Naomi. Her soft voice and long pauses left time for him to think and speak. Hunger, confusion, and daily survival erased the pre-homeless years from Lou's memory. He returned to Lombardo House through the remainder of the winter. In the spring after the overnight shelter closed, he came to help the volunteers distribute food and gratefully took the snacks they offered. Instead of just a building to walk by, Lombardo House became his destination each day. Years of walking the streets, collapsing wherever he landed, eating what he scavenged, and waking when the weather, danger or help dragged him from sleep had transformed his body mentally and physically. At Naomi's suggestion, he ventured into Mass at Saint Luke's and eventually attended every Sunday.

Though Naomi enjoyed volunteering at Lombardo House and sometimes took Clare, she felt frustrated that the men returned to the streets at the end of the winter. She didn't voice her frustration. Helping those less fortunate gave her children an opportunity to see poverty first hand. She tried to answer questions and give Clare background on the guests without invading their privacy. The more Naomi volunteered, the more she wondered if she belittled the men who came to the shelter by using them as a teaching opportunity for her children. Clare's question during one visit nudged Naomi.

"Mom, will Lou ever have a house or an apartment that belongs to him?" She dried the soup spoons and placed each piece back in the drawer. The last guest brought his spoon and bowl to the sink. "Thanks." She took the bowl and her brow wrinkled as she watched the man gather his towel and head for the shower. "I guess he would need a job."

Naomi nodded. "Yes." She realized that Clare's question put her own frustration in perspective. They finished the cleanup, put on their coats and turned toward the door. The overnight volunteer unlocked the door, and said "Good night," and locked the door behind them.

As they drove home, Naomi found herself mulling over Clare's question. "Clare, you asked a very good question. The question makes me think. Saint Luke's can do more for the poor." She remembered the history she had pieced together from parish meetings and working as a volunteer at Lombardo House. "Saint Luke's opened Lombardo House to address poverty in the neighborhood and pay tribute to the Lombardo family. First, they collected food from parishioners and opened the food cupboard. We still bring food on the last Sunday of the month for the poor neighbors. Because more neighbors use this service now, Jeff, the director, searched for more sources of food. Now we partner with restaurants and grocery stores to increase supplies." Clare listened though her eyelids drooped. Naomi kept talking. "Then, I don't know when, Saint Luke's opened the homeless shelter, available only during the winter months." As she spoke, Naomi saw the pattern of starting new projects, inspiring people's enthusiasm, seeing a project go beyond its original intent, and watching the parishioners and staff adjust to how a project had changed. She smiled. Clare's head slipped sideways. "Now we rely on other parishes to provide volunteers for all the Lombardo House programs."

139

Naomi looked over at Clare and saw her eyelids, heard her slow breathing. Clare's question and potential answers kept her thinking on the drive home.

Clare repeated her question the next night at the dinner table.

Zack smiled. "Your mother woke me up last night to tell me about that question, Clare. It looks like you have hatched an idea for a new program at Lombardo House. I have some ideas too. Shall we do a little poking around and see what we can find?" Before bedtime, Zack and Clare had a list of web sites from other cities where organizations ran homeless shelters and a list of services for the homeless in Stanton.

The next morning Zack read about a state funded program called Housing First in the newspaper. He showed Naomi and winked. "Clare, didn't we find an example like this when we were doing our research last night?"

"Housing First, I think we saw something like that." Clare reached for the paper. Zack helped her read through the article. Her eyes widened and she clapped her hands as they finished reading.

Later that morning Zack called Jeff, the part-time director of Lombardo House. Jeff confirmed that he had spoken to Elizabeth about applying for a Housing First grant. "Who knows maybe Elizabeth planted the idea with someone in Albany. She had a way of convincing people to do things! This program has our name written all over it!" Jeff paused and Zack could hear a change in his voice. "Many ideas these days sit on Elizabeth's desk or in her voice or email. I can't tell you how many messages I have left for her." Jeff drew a breath. "We have a few days before the deadline for that grant application passes. Based on the number of homeless people and poor people Lombardo House has served, we fit the qualifications the grant targets. With the grant, we could take the next step." He sighed. "If we still have a Lombardo House."

"Wouldn't we need a lot of renovations to make the upstairs livable?" Zack asked.

"One of the parishioners who runs an engineering company looked at the upstairs. He said we could make two of the bedrooms and a bathroom livable for about $10,000, maybe less. We could even do a trial run using the two rooms that need less renovation. But -" Zack took notes as Jeff talked. "You know how many projects Elizabeth initiated. That application probably sits under lots of other worthy projects." Jeff took a breath. "We would qualify for this grant. If I understand the requirements of the grant correctly, we could include another part-time staff person. We'll need more coverage if we have people living here year-round. But it all looked like it would work." Jeff's enthusiasm burst through. "Everything fits perfectly for us, timing, size of grant, capacity."

"Have people talked about it at the Homeless Council? Would Mission Shelter apply?" Zack wondered.

"Good question." Jeff paused. "I can't imagine that they could create two living spaces for less than $50,000. It looks like the city should condemn that building. I'll bet Jack, the Mission Shelter director, doesn't have the time or the energy to think about things like grants. Having a person like Elizabeth, who always thinks about the future combined with the committed volunteers, like your wife, who keep finding new volunteers, gave me the time to prepare that application and write the proposal." He paused. "Maybe wishful thinking, but Lombardo House should get this grant."

"Holding down two jobs must fill more than any normal person's week." Zack looked at his calendar. "Maybe we could finish it together." Elizabeth's lack of involvement in day-to-day parish activities brought a frown to his face. "If we can't get Elizabeth's approval, maybe we can ask Father Rogers."

"Wow, would you have time?"

"I'll make time." He looked at the family picture on his desk. "Clare got this started. I'll tell you about that later." He saw his cell phone blink a message. "Send me possible times you have available and let's see if we can wrap it up this week. Would that give us time to take it to Elizabeth?" Elizabeth's name flowed so easily. Zack wondered again how and why she seemed to abandon everything she started at Saint Luke's. "Let's take it to Father Rogers. We can leave a copy for Elizabeth."

"Just enough time. Zack great idea! I'll send those days and times after I hang up. Evenings work the best for me. Probably for you too?"

With renewed energy, Jeff invited Lou to move into the larger bedroom upstairs. He stayed with Lou the first few nights. The shelter volunteers learned the extra task of checking on Lou. Jeff knew the Housing First grant expected outcomes. Lou could provide outcomes. The grant looked for indications that residents would develop self-sufficiency. Employment for the initial residents would allow Lombardo House to apply for more funds and support additional residents. With the stability of knowing where he would sleep and a little encouragement from Naomi, he looked for a job. Naomi went with him on his first interview. She spoke for him.

"Lou has shown his reliability at Lombardo House. He volunteers every week and always arrives on time. He became our first full-time resident recently and has an admirable record." She smiled. "We could bring other people to vouch for him too." She watched the owner's face relax. "You have us as a reference and we'll support Lou."

Several days later, a volunteer at Lombardo House took a message for Lou. Lou waved it at Naomi when she arrived at for her shelter shift. She took the paper and read. "Lou," she hugged him. He blushed. "Terrific!" She read the note again. "This means you will clean the facility after it closes!" She turned to those gathered around. "Lou has a job at the Delta Sonic Car Wash!" Everyone gathered to pat him on the shoulder and shake his hand.

During the first months, he accomplished the job easily and on time. He finished with enough time to arrive at the shelter before the curfew. When the cold set in and the first winter storm hit, he didn't finish cleaning until 10 PM. The accumulated salt took more time to clean and the cold building made the job harder. When he saw the time on the gas station clock, he walked back and forth nearby to keep warm. He could see movement in Lombardo House through the windows. He considered ringing the bell. He approached the door and turned away. He wouldn't break the 9:30 PM check-in rule. He knew how others abused the rules. He couldn't, especially with his new responsibilities and the privilege of having his own room.

When Naomi arrived at Lombardo House the next morning, she saw Lou walking on the side street. She delivered several bags of food.

"That neighbor of yours, I should have kept a total of all the food she has donated." Jeff took the bags and set them on the table. "Be sure to thank her."

"I will." Naomi turned to leave.

"Lou didn't show up last night?" Jeff saw the surprise on Naomi's face.

"I just saw him walking along the street. Not a night to stay outside in that weather!" She moved toward the door. "Maybe he is still there. I will find out what happened."

She scanned the streets, the gas station, and the parking lot. When she reached her car, she saw him walking away. "Lou."

He walked looking only at the ground and moving quickly to stay warm. "Lou," she called again. "Lou, Jeff said you didn't sleep here last night. What happened?" He didn't answer. She got in her car and followed him until he came to a cross street and stopped in his path as he tried to cross the street. "Lou." He looked up. "Where were you?" He didn't answer the questions. Eventually, he offered some nods. She figured out that he had finished too late to go to the shelter. She scolded him. He only had the space to say "but" she filled in the rest. She said she would call the next night's volunteers and tell them that his schedule might cause him to arrive late. She went with him to the Delta Sonic Car Wash manager to make sure Lou met the manager's expectations. The manager praised Lou's work and said they wanted him to stay.

Naomi took him back to the shelter, gave him some food and explained the situation to Jeff. "Can he come in late? He has worked hard to get this job." Jeff didn't hesitate and went to the logbook to write special instructions for the night volunteers. "Lou, see he's written down that you have a job and can come in late." Naomi pointed at the logbook. Lou read the words. He nodded.

After he had worked for a few more months, Naomi helped him open a savings account at the neighborhood bank. She wrote down an amount on a sticky note attached to his savings book. When he reached that amount in his account, he could look for an apartment. She offered to help him find an apartment.

He works and he sleeps and he eats at the shelter; but he doesn't see Naomi. He doesn't ask for her. He understands that something happened at the church. He hears things at the shelter, but they don't explain her absence. He only attends the early morning Mass on Sunday – a quiet Mass and he prays. He prays for Naomi. He thanks God for his job and for Naomi, he doesn't listen to announcements. As days pass, he imagines an accident. He doesn't attend other church functions, and he doesn't know other people in the parish. He fears breaking the other shelter rule to never sleep in the church. He avoids the church despite its warmth and quiet. He only knows that he misses his friend and he wonders why she doesn't return. He considers going to a later Mass where he might see Naomi. He doesn't like having people stare at him. Eventually he assumes she left the shelter because of him. He asked too much. He crossed a line.

One night, he turns the pages of his rumpled savings account booklet over and over. The bottom number matches the number Naomi wrote on a pink sticky note and attached to the front cover of the book. He sees that he has enough money now to look for his own apartment. He can't look for an apartment alone. He places the book back in the zipper pocket of his shirt and glances at the clock - 9:30 PM. He walks the three blocks to the shelter. His hand touches the zipper pocket. His head nods back and forth. He knocks. A new volunteer comes to the door, but only speaks to him through the window. She won't open the door and he can't explain through the window – can't make his voice work in the cold night air. Finally, she turns the outside light off and leaves him there alone. His warm jacket hangs in his room behind the locked door.

He finds his way to the emergency room that night through the empty streets. The nurse bandages and treats his frost-bitten fingers and gives him hot coffee. The policeman on duty offers to take him to the Mission Shelter. Lou grimaces and says "No, thank you."

The policeman doesn't hear him and asks again. He shakes his head and the policeman replies, "Your choice, buddy. Warmer than the streets these days! Looks like those fingers could use some warmth."

Balancing a pen carefully in his bandaged hand, Lou slowly writes the address of Lombardo House on a piece of paper. "Oh," the policeman smiles. He looks down at Lou's hands, "One of the Saint Luke's gang! Sure, I'll take you over there, buddy." Then, in a lower voice, he adds, "better choice than the Mission Shelter." He points at the small booklet in his hand. "Our instructions list the Mission Shelter. I guess you are more of a Cadillac kind of guy. Let's go, buddy." Lou smiles, nods at the nurse, follows the policeman to his car, and climbs into the front seat. He gazes at all the buttons, lights and switches. The policeman uses his phone to notify the base office of his next stop. Lou watches and holds his hands gingerly to avoid the pain.

As the policeman drives away, Lou rings the bell cringing from a shot of pain and apprehension. He closes his eyes and hopes Naomi will answer the door or at least one of the volunteers who recognizes him. Instead, another unfamiliar face peers out of the window, shakes her head "No" and flicks off the light. He slumps against the door into the icy snow bank.

A neighborhood police captain finds him the next morning at the end of his shift. "Another one, what a night!"

A young newspaper reporter accompanying the police captain leaps out of the car with his camera. While the captain completes paperwork and calls the hospital, the reporter shoots photos from every angle of Lou slumped in the snow. *This could clinch the series*, he thinks. *Or maybe this one.* The nightly rides with the captain have provided volumes of material for the paper's recent series on homelessness. He steps over a dirty snow bank and leans back to capture both Lou and the hand-painted sign: *Lombardo House – Saint Luke's Ministry to the Poor.* He urges the captain to call in his report before they carry Lou to the car. *A little more time, a few more photos, I have to get the right one*, he thinks. By the time, Lou rests in the back seat, the reporter has hundreds of photos. As they drive toward the hospital, the reporter reviews the first photo. The faint predawn light gives the photo an eerie quality – a quality that fits the series perfectly. In other shots, he notes the angle and light – Lou in the lower corner of the photo, the large sign for the shelter in the upper corner. He doesn't know which photos the editor will choose but smiles and bets on this one.

"I've got my story!"

"Right, we see lots like this especially with the temperatures dipping." The captain looks back at Lou.

"And what a story!" the reporter clicks through more photos.

When the policeman stops at the emergency room door, the reporter rushes to his office. As Lou wakes up and eats a warm meal, the reporter finishes the concluding story in the five-part series. As Lou dozes throughout the day, the editor decides to run a page of the reporter's photos and considers submitting the story to a competition. As he sleeps, the paper goes to press with the last article in the homeless series including the photo of Lou and the Lombardo House sign on the front page of the paper next to an article about the Saint Luke's parish meeting.

Naomi moves slowly through her morning tasks. The long meeting, the conversations after and her anxiety once in bed prevented her from rising before the family. The arguments kept playing over again as she tried to sleep. Even repetition of how the meeting went reveals nothing new, as she stumbles into the new day.

The people who supported Elizabeth's dismissal replay as she washes, dresses, and combs her hair. Holding pieces of paper as they spoke, the never-ending sentences left little room for interruptions. Tony Mancuso must have taught all of them, maybe even prepared scripts for them. People who supported Elizabeth seemed confused about an Elizabeth they didn't recognize and listened for the old values they didn't hear in her voice.

Naomi takes a brief look in the mirror. Elizabeth, when Naomi thinks again, dominated. She only listened to her supporters and interrupted everyone else, managing as Naomi didn't to break through those sentences with an unfamiliar loud voice.

What really kept her awake and makes her neck muscles tense and her stomach feel empty but not hungry, is her part as a facilitator. Objectivity – she knows she lost that. Honoring all voices – she failed on that too. She hurries through the morning routine without any awareness of the family. She packs lunches while they eat breakfast. Tears form in her eyes. As she reaches to brush her eyes before they fall, she recognizes a familiar feeling of imbalance. She finishes the lunches and turns her attention to the table.

Mark with his usual enthusiasm jabbers about the indoor soccer game Naomi missed because of the parish meeting. He lists the goals his team made, the saves by their goalie, his stumble and fall. He points to the evidence. "Look Mom, - a bad one." He holds his knee up and touches the large bandage the coach placed on the cut. "Mom, look! You're not looking." Mark rests his foot on the kitchen table. "Mom!"

Naomi places the lunches on the counter and glances at Mark. "Oh my. How about taking your foot off the table?"

Mark removes his foot, touches the bandage and notices blood. "Yuck, more blood. I need a new bandage!"

Returning unused lunch fixings to the refrigerator, Naomi says, "It looks like you can last the day. We can change it when you get home."

Mark doesn't agree. He starts to cry. He points at the blood, puts his foot back on the table. Tears pour down his cheeks.

Naomi knows the sign; knows she should sit down and recognize the wound and Mark's accomplishments at the game. She knows but doesn't sit. Soon Mark tears transform into sobs.

"Isn't this Lou?" Zack asks. He reads the headlines on the front page of the newspaper while sipping his orange juice. He holds the paper up for Naomi to see.

Mark's sobs become wails. Naomi leaves the mess in the sink and sits at the table with Mark. "My, just look at that cut! Maybe we *should* put a new bandage on it. Do we have big enough bandages to cover that?" She touches his knee gently. "What would you like – car bandages or airplane bandages? Oh, yes, we'll need more than one with that cut!" Naomi leaves one hand on Mark's shoulder and touches the bandage gently. She feels another tear and brushes it away. Then, she brushes Mark's tear away. "Would you like me to choose a bandage and surprise you?" Mark nods.

"Check it out," Zack leaves the paper spread in the center of the table with Lou's picture commanding a third of the page. He takes his bowl to the sink, rinses it and places it in the dishwasher. He turns toward Naomi's back. "Another late night, tonight." He says this a little louder trying to get a little attention.

"Mom, your friend from the shelter! Lou! The one that you helped. Look Mom." Clare holds the paper up and waves it in front of Naomi as she leaves the table.

Naomi finds car bandages but no airplane bandages. Mark's face tells her the surprise doesn't please him. She points out the BMWs and the Corvettes, his favorite cars. She keeps her attention on Mark until Mark accepts the cars. She removes the old bandage carefully and applies two car bandages. Mark resumes his lively morning chatter. "Mom, today we go to the Norton Country Museum, remember? And you come too! I want to go to the print shop. Then, I want to go to the old kitchen because the teacher said we get to taste old-fashioned food – like they ate at the first Thanksgiving!" Mark drains the milk from his cereal bowl spilling on the table and his shirt.

Naomi forgot she volunteered to chaperone his class field trip. She stands up to make another lunch for herself. She senses Zack standing in the doorway and hands him his lunch, forgetting to add a sandwich. He doesn't pick up his lunch, but she doesn't notice.

Clare leaves the table and the newspaper. "Come on Mark, we'll miss the bus," Clare urges.

"OK, I'll see you at school, Mark. Have a good day, Clare." Naomi kisses them both before they run out the door.

Zack waits until the door closes behind the children. "Did you look at the paper? Did you hear that I will work late?"

"Oh, no. I didn't. And, no?" Naomi focuses on Zack's face. "Something about Saint Luke's?" Naomi sighs, picks up the paper and sees Lou slumped on the snow bank outside the shelter. "Oh, no!" She grabs her mouth. "Lou! Horrible!" She gasps and looks at Zack. She tries to remember the last time she saw Lou. Her eyes pass to the next column – "Parishioners' Fight Over Dismissal Continues." Her hand falls to her side. "Oh, no and they did have a reporter there last night! Zack look at this!" Zack nods as the impact sinks in and she voices what he thought. "It looks like we have abandoned Lou to argue about whether or not to fire Elizabeth. Horrible, just horrible. And I haven't been to the shelter in two weeks." She frowns. "Probably more than two weeks! Lou had almost enough money to rent his own apartment. I know what happened. Oh, Zack. I don't know what to do?" Naomi slumps in a chair.

"Take it easy today, Naomi. You didn't get much sleep last night and things might look different with some rest." Zack sits down beside her.

"Of course, of course." She can't take her eyes off the photograph. "But Lou is in the hospital. What will happen?" Naomi looks at Zack hoping he has the answer. Her mind races. "Look it says he has frostbite! Now, he probably can't do his job." She looks at her own hands. "My fingers hurt just thinking about him. How can I think about sleep?" She shakes her head. "He might die? What will a new perspective do?" Naomi straightens a little and begins to calculate what she can do in the time she has before the field trip. Then, she thinks about the long trip to the outdoor museum. After all the snow they had been having, she lists other outings much closer and not requiring extra clothing for the children.

Zack puts his arm on her shoulder. It doesn't stay there long as he remembers what faces him at work. "Well, at least give yourself a break before picking up that phone. I can see those plans piling up in that sweet little head." He turns her head to face him. "A late night for me tonight. We have a client coming in today and we must take him out to dinner. And if I don't get this situation settled with Melissa, we might not have the client." Zack takes his brief case from the chair, kisses Naomi on the cheek and turns to walk out the door.

Naomi gets up from the table and looks back at the photograph. She manages to ask, "Oh, I forgot. How are things going with Melissa? I thought you found a new way to motivate her."

"Apparently not. She went to Human Resources and filed a formal complaint against me. They will present me with the complaint today. Such a waste of time. I gave her the promotion to recognize her accomplishments. That seemed to motivate her to stop producing and start complaining about lack of recognition. The only female lead engineer on the largest project the company has landed in recent memory seems like recognition. Doesn't it?" Zack shakes his head and looks at his watch.

"Ask for help, Zack. You've spent the last three months guiding Melissa into this promotion. Maybe she can't handle it. Promoted beyond her competence?"

"She can handle it. She got that promotion based on competence, work ethic, and communication. No. No. It's a grudge. A grudge? I don't understand?" Wrinkles fill his forehead.

"But can you really take the time to sort this out with the project deadline approaching? Next week?" Naomi holds Zack's hand.

"Maybe you're right. She worked for Ed for a while. I'll talk to him and see if he has any ideas before I talk to Human Resources." He smiles. She nods. "I hope Lou is OK. Give me a call after you see him and let me know."

"I will and let me know what happens with Ed." They kiss.

She watches his car disappear around the corner. The options swim around in her head – call the Delta Sonic Car Wash manager and explain what happened, call the shelter to see who worked last night and what the log said, go to visit Lou in the hospital to make sure they don't release him without a place to go. She paces and walks by the statue of Saint Theresa that her mother gave her as a confirmation present. She stops and prays the simple prayer she memorized for her confirmation – "remember God is with me, remember my special gifts, remember to share them with others, find joy in each day." She has simplified it over the years, but the meaning remains and it always comforts her.

She looks at the clock, forgets her lunch and drives to the hospital to visit Lou before the field trip. Though the morning started with sun, clouds increased as they ate breakfast and snow began to fall. She imagines the kids joy as they watch snowflakes outside the school windows and hope for a snow day. The small flakes accumulate creating a slippery layer on the city streets. Even with the recent cold snap, she can't believe this snow will amount to anything. Winter shouldn't start for another month. She takes her foot off the gas and lets the car slow down. "Not a bad idea. Zack is right, I should slow down and not rush into all these things," she thinks as she passes the church and the shelter and drives farther into the city. The snow falls more quickly and soon she can barely see the car in front of her even at such a slow speed. The temperature causes the snow to stick to the windshield wipers. Clumps of snow ride back and forth on the wipers. She glances in the rear-view mirror. Snow collects quickly on all the windows. She stops at a gas station to fill up and cleans snow from the windows and headlights. Several blocks later, she stops again to clear the windshield. When she reaches the hospital, she searches for a parking place in the garage. After parking, she clears the all the windows hoping to save time when she leaves.

Lou greets her with a big smile and she finds out that the hospital will keep him for another day. Though grateful for the snow forcing her to slow down, she still checks her watch as they visit. She decides not to ask Lou how he happened to be outside the shelter in a snow bank instead of inside in his bed. Finally, she tells Lou she will call his boss and gives the nurse her cell phone number in case they decide to release him earlier. "I don't think we'll have to worry about that, dear." The nurse assures her as she points out the window.

Naomi reaches her car, confirms that she has plenty of time to reach the school. Her cell phone rings. The crackly reception prevents her from hearing the caller. She sees the number. Finally, she recognizes the school number and hears Mark's teacher's voice telling her that they cancelled the field trip and have closed school because of the snow. She offers God thanks and drives home even more slowly reaching the driveway before the school bus returns with the kids. She absorbs their unbridled joy and the jumbled exclamations: "...Snow Day!... snow fort... snow man..." Mark's challenge for a snowball fight after the fort argues with Clare's plan for sledding on the neighbor's hill. They run into the kitchen both talking at once and tossing their backpacks and jackets on the floor.

The search for snow gear keeps the noise level high. Naomi picks up backpacks and locates missing mittens and hats. Neighbor children appear outside their houses. Once outfitted, the kids join in snow fort and snow ball activities. Naomi marvels at how persuasive Mark can be with his older sister. She positions herself at the kitchen table where she can see them, anticipating the disagreements that might follow.

Turning from the snow activities, she reads through the notes Ben emailed for the extra parish meeting to talk about Elizabeth and what to do. The time on the email indicates he sent them at 5 AM. She wonders how much sleep he got. She notes that over eight hundred people attended and they finished at 11 PM. While she ran the meeting and attended to who wanted to speak and who had already spoken, she noticed how far they wandered from the agenda. She took a breath as she remembered the emotions giving way to insults and accusations. She had never seen anyone at Saint Luke's treat each other like that. She also noted the names of the two or three people who didn't belong to the parish. Ben obviously caught them as they left the microphone because they had not identified themselves when they spoke – despite the repeated invitations she made in between speakers. Ben listed the parish too - Saint Paul of the Cross. The Nortons had visited that parish, she remembered. Mark spoke first in a loud whisper, "they don't like us here" when they had taken a seat in a back pew. Naomi had shushed him and moments later realized the same feeling. People looked at them without smiling. No one shook their hands at the Kiss of Peace. No one sang with the choir. And the priest had turned away from them when they approached him after the Mass. At every church they visited, they tried to meet a parishioner after Mass or at a coffee hour and always stopped to talk with the priest or pastor at the end of the service. Funny how quickly they reached a unanimous opinion of Saint Paul of the Cross when they drove home that day.

She still doesn't understand why people from a parish they treasure, and the Saint Paul's parishioners treasure and protect their own church, would pay attention to what went on in other churches in the diocese. Of course, she suspects now that jealousy must exist between Saint Luke's and other parishes because of Saint Luke's growth and the parishioners' generosity. She knows Saint Luke's collects more money each Sunday than other parishes which could motivate jealousy. Do outsiders know how much Saint Luke's give away? She helps with the shelter budget and sees the shelter director receives a salary that is less than what Naomi spends on groceries each week. Without Jeff's second job, he couldn't afford to stay. Most of the money in the budget feeds the men during the shelter months, assists them with welfare services, heats the house, and keeps it in repair. Though a parishioner donated the house to the parish, the donation came with surprises. Repairs accumulated until a crisis required immediate attention. They planned to reinsulate the house to reduce the heating bill, but the roof leaked after they had accumulated enough money to buy the insulation. They couldn't find parishioners with roofing expertise so they had to pay for the roof replacement and the roofing materials. The insulation money went toward the roof and the collections for the shelter then focused on finishing roof payments and beginning the insulation savings all over again.

She questions the Saint Luke's custom that anyone may attend parish meetings. "What about people from outside the parish? Perhaps, they can attend but not speak," she suggested as they went over the agenda before the meeting.

"Not a good precedent to set. We want to treat everyone respectfully. People from other parishes have joined our parish because they see that we hold that value, we walk the talk. We just have to find a way to respect their opinions without acting toward them the way they act toward us." Ben reminded her.

"Right, probably one of the reasons we stayed here ourselves," she remembered hearing herself say. "*But*," she now thinks, "*where had it gotten them?*" It seems, as she reads over the notes, that the Saint Paul's parishioners had set a negative and more argumentative tone to the meeting. She hadn't noticed that during the meeting. Reading the notes makes her realize that she hadn't posed questions along the way to balance the tensions. Where was Minny Lord when they needed her? Since the firing had been announced, Minny appeared out of nowhere it seemed, read her latest poem and calmed the tensions that had built to that point during meetings. Minny's work took her away frequently. What state had she traveled to this week?

Saint Luke Church Bulletin – Stanton Diocese
3rd Sunday of Advent

Saint Luke Mission: Serving the poor is the highest priority for Saint Luke's.

Dear Friends,

As we anticipate the joyous celebration of Christ's birth, Advent offers us the time to reflect and renew. Apostle Luke is our guide for readings during this season. His message in the gospel for the 3rd Sunday made me think about happenings in the parish. I'm praying that we won't become a "brood of vipers" as John describes the crowds. Let's take time to reflect on our own actions and let Apostle Luke guide us to the joyous feast.

We know that you have many questions about Elizabeth and her future assignment. We will always give you updates in the bulletin. Right now, we are waiting for word from the Bishop. Parish meetings are a time to ask questions and make comments. The meetings will resume in February.

Finally remember the poor families in our neighborhood with your donations to Lombardo House on the Sunday before Christmas. Well-preserved Christmas cookies and cakes will give them an extra treat at this time of year!

Spread the love!

Father Rogers

Notices

- Check the website for Notices
- Prayer Line – 453-3344: Call the prayer line with your prayer intentions.

Father Rogers

"Very good, very good," he hesitates. "And – " Doubts overwhelm him. His smile of admiration for Martha's efficiency and seeming lack of doubts replaces his frown momentarily. He shakes his head. The worry wrinkles reappear.

"Father Rogers A – O - K, go!" He listens to her calm confident voice. He nods. "We have a priest for each Mass. No meetings. The Bishop knows your schedule. He wants you to go. We have four backup priests for emergencies. And we won't need any of them, but we have your cell phone number and the number of the retreat center. Go."

Though his smile does not reappear, she assumes agreement, pats his shoulder and points to his suitcase. The admiration returns and the sides of his mouth move in the smile direction. *How could we function without her? Especially now*, he wonders. "Very good, very good. And thank you. Thank you, dear Martha."

She nods toward the airport door. "Now go or you will miss your flight!" She closes the trunk.

He turns toward the door. Thoughts about the trial freeze him. Visions of the piles of paper on his desk prevent his movement. Questions about Elizabeth tense his muscles. *Did she answer my last voicemail? Should I have signed something? The shelter insurance policy?* He turns back to ask and sees the car pulling away from the curb and into the traffic. The back of Martha's hand waves above the car roof. *I shouldn't go. I really shouldn't go on retreat with so many unanswered questions and loose ends in the parish.* The taillights of her car disappear among the cars, taxis and buses. He turns to enter the airport, puts his bag down to search for his boarding pass. He knows she put it someplace obvious, but where? As he searches inside, through files and books he realizes he will miss his flight. Ready to give up, he zips his suitcase and notices the boarding pass sticking out of the side pocket on the bag.

He manages a brisk walk and a kind security agent who waves him through security check to reach the gate just as the attendant pushes the door to close it, but she lets him board.

"Bless you, dear. So sorry, so sorry. I hope I haven't held the flight up." She smiles and motions for him to board. He reaches his seat and falls asleep during takeoff.

The flight, sleep and the quiet of the retreat house and grounds at the Center for Action and Contemplation push his worries into the background. He falls easily into the retreat schedule and discipline. Prayer, quiet and the expansive sky and landscape make him realize how little prayer, deep reflective prayer, he has experienced in the last few months. Here it comes effortlessly, continuous prayers flow. A strong wave of gratitude for his Mother hits him as he walks in the nearby woods. He feels her praying with him! Each dry branch, distant mountain, wandering cloud contributes to a sense of joy. Then a doubt forms to interrupt the joyful memories of her. He returns to the chapel and paces the aisles slowly.

After several circuits around the pews, by the altar and back to the choir loft, scenes from his youth stop his movement. Stories his mother told him emerge from his memory. He remembers his response, to brush them off, to discredit what she said. Now, as the times she tried to get his attention emerge one by one, those stories sound all too familiar. He realizes she described the parish priest attempting to abuse her. He tries to pull back more of those instances. He doesn't think she used that word, *abuse*. But standing in the shaft of light in that chapel, he understands what she meant. He understands that he, a young seminarian, believed the church's denial of something that now has reached around the world damaging how many women and children. *And children!*

He sits down in a pew. He believed the church, a church his parents revered. He didn't believe his mother. With all the recent revelations about abusive priests becoming public, he realizes how much he didn't want to believe her. He realizes how easily he ignored her pain. Wondering how he could have ignored his own Mother forces painful acknowledgements

157

beyond her. Knowing what she might have experienced makes him marvel that she continued to her dying day to attend church, to put money in the collection, to support him in the seminary. Christ is the only answer for her unwavering faith. She knew Christ would not condone that behavior or the greater church's denial. His raising her to sainthood without understanding the abuse possibility makes his assumption stronger. He also realizes that she must have had doubts. To support his calling to become a priest having experienced something that no one would acknowledge brings a smile and a frown. He never had a conversation about doubts with her. He wonders if he could reach that level of dedication where doubts fall away. His renewed admiration for his mother humbles him, but also sets a new sense of resolve. He hopes the retreat will help clarify how to act on that resolve.

Everything comes through prayer. Mother knew. Prayer strengthens faith, allows the details of the world to release their hold. Here he feels his strength building with each prayer, with each quiet moment. Even no longer living, she sets an example. God provides these examples to inspire us. Pushing away the regret that she no longer lives to hear his new resolve, to give him some guidance, he gains strength by this new perspective, this revelation. He feels the value of prayer renewing his life.

Near the end of the week, the parish enters his prayers. He prays for everyone as he says their names, as many as he can remember, thanks God, and seeks support for each parishioner and staff member. He says a few extra prayers for the staff members. When he hears the dinner bell, he has not named everyone.

During evening prayers, the doubts reappear. *If I don't support Elizabeth, does it mean I don't support the ordination of women?* Elizabeth believes this. For weeks, her sharp and critical words have plagued him. Mother stands up there with all the inspiring women of the Bible. For her, he will continue to remind the church to acknowledge those sins. He hired Elizabeth as a way to force himself to pursue that goal with more energy! However, he sees clearly that he has not convinced Elizabeth. She claims he does not support her. His many messages and voicemails encouraging prayer as a path to a better resolution for this situation have gone unheeded from what he has heard and not heard. He ponders other ways to reach her.

On the last full day before his retreat ends, he wakes before dawn. He sees the obvious answer and, with the benefit of some reflection, Elizabeth would answer the same way. Though his messages have recommended prayer, he recognizes a more inviting way to encourage her. The doubt melts. He sits down gathering the words for a letter to Elizabeth. He hurries to finish so he can walk by the river as the sun rises. It seems simple, so simple. She will see the simplicity. First, she must take time to reflect. In the end, his note says only that and breaking retreat rules, he calls and leaves that message on her phone – *Dear, dear Elizabeth - make a retreat, take time to reflect.* With the prayer that flows, she will see a different path forward. Once she returns from the retreat, they can talk about specifics and get help where needed. If ordaining women was easy, every diocese would include women priests. He wishes some of those early women leaders remained alive! Following that thought he acknowledges that people like Elizabeth shine as today's leaders. The approaching sunrise helps complete the short letter without advice other than prayer. He drops the note in the mailbox and leaves by the back door. Sunrise over this small trickle of a river fills the sky. He pauses to appreciate. The shadows of the bare trees cross the uneven path.

Thoughts of Mother appear as he watches birds lift up together toward the brightening sky. A solitary cloud disappears behind a mountain peak. As the last wisp goes, he feels a weight lifted. He stops and without noticing thought emerging as words, he whispers: *I accept that a priest did horrible things to my mother. I also accept a new role for myself to stand by victims now, as I didn't with Mother.* The sun pales the blue sky. The first rays beam from the mountains. He raises his arms to God, to the sun. Not only does he notice a strength to take on new challenges himself, he recognizes his responsibility to encourage that in others. Somehow, this hope replaces the urge to find out what happened to Mother. The sun almost blinds him. Instead of wondering and worrying about the past, he renews a conviction to stand up for women's ordination and to push the church to take care of their people by eliminating abusive priests. Turning toward this controversy feels as easy as turning away felt yesterday. His next steps appear as clear as this worn river path. The sun seems to pop above the mountain top. With the brightness comes the understanding that this experience, whatever happens to Elizabeth, whatever happens to the parish, will bring opportunities to build strength. He can speak out and will to remove the injustice his mother suffered. The walk back to the retreat center fills him with renewed energy. Each leaf, each shadow, every ray of sun, every sound of the trickling river, and the wind adds lightness to his steps.

While waiting in the living room for the airport van, he sees Edwina Gateley. Memories of the inspired talk she gave at the last Call To Action conference start him thinking. She described the work with women prostitutes. Women prostitutes! He remembers how that word shocked him. He thinks of Elizabeth. Both her quiet purpose and attention to women seem much like Elizabeth. He wonders if she knows Elizabeth.

"Father Rogers. How are you?" She takes both his hands and looks deeply into his eyes. "And how fares your Saint Luke's through all this controversy?" She doesn't let go. She squeezes.

Overwhelmed with surprise and gratitude that she knows his parish, has heard about Elizabeth's situation, and expresses such deep concern, leaves his jaw dropped. Words don't come.

"Your parish travels a very challenging path. I pray for you daily. I pray for the future of your good work with the poor and in promoting women."

Still he doesn't find words. The van arrives and they climb into the middle seat. Before he manages to respond, she offers to visit Saint Luke's, meet with Elizabeth, and learn from the parishioners. "And we'll find a way to pay for it. I have a talk in Boston. That's not far from you."

"Speechless. I'm speechless." He can't imagine anything better for Saint Luke's than someone who shares the values and commands so much respect throughout the country. "Very good, very good. Of course." He takes her hands and squeezes back.

At the airport, they exchange dates and contact information before finding their flights. He leaves a message for Martha to reserve the hall and put information in the bulletin. *Prayer, thank you God for the perfect timing.* Before boarding he leaves a message on Elizabeth's phone suggesting that she invite Edwina to stay with her while at Saint Luke's.

Efficient Martha waits at the curb even though his flight arrives almost a half hour early. "Very good, very good, my Martha what would we do without you." I hug her and note the surprise on her face. "Right again, as always, my Martha. What a gift the time, the prayers – and, and to meet Edwina Gateley in New Mexico! Her visit will give everyone an inspiring launch into Lent. And I left a message for Elizabeth suggesting that she invite Edwina to stay with her!"

Martha's expression changes as she buckles her seatbelt and starts the car. He pulls out a pad and reads the date of Edwina's presentation and Martha turns her head from the road. "The next parish meeting will use the hall that evening."

"Very good, very good so we can lead off with Edwina or reschedule the parish meeting. I remember the first time I heard Edwina speak. She spoke at the same Call To Action conference where we met Elizabeth." He looks out the window to see the surroundings transformed by a fresh snowfall. "Ben also attended. Elizabeth heard Edwina's talk that day. Or? No, she had to leave early. She will gain so much by meeting Edwina! Though it does seem like she must know Edwina. They both have spoken and written for Call To Action causes. Imagine what a gift from God, that I should meet Edwina at this time!" He smiles and shakes his head. "Very good, very good."

Martha parks the car and takes his suitcase. He looks around and follows her into the rectory. "You know Martha, Edwina's sense of humor combined with her spirituality will boost everyone's spirits. Don't you think?" Martha leaves his suitcase by the stairs and heads toward the office. "And, you'll be proud of me, Martha. Because she speaks in Boston before she comes to Saint Luke's, we can save on travel costs." He smiles. Martha heads into his office with a large stack of papers. "Now that I think of it, Zack Norton often has business in Boston. Maybe he could drive her! No travel cost!"

"We'd have to get her home afterwards." Martha doesn't smile.

"Right. Not very expensive, though." He smiles but wonders why she doesn't smile. "Do we have a parishioner with connections in Chicago?" Martha's expression doesn't change. "And, have you spoken with Elizabeth? I suggested that Edwina stay with her." Even this obviously great idea doesn't move Martha.

Martha taps her pencil on the desk.

He stops talking hoping to see any recognition on Martha's face. Her serious expression makes him pause but he presses on. "Very good, very good," He sits next to her. "What do you think? Having Edwina stay with Elizabeth will give her a sounding board, kind of bring the retreat to her, help her get a new perspective." Martha raises an eyebrow. "Yes, and another idea, to have Elizabeth go on retreat." He begins to think he hasn't convinced Martha about this idea, either. He makes another attempt. "Did she schedule that?" Martha shakes her head. "So, a backup plan! No retreat but more time with Edwina! Great idea! Probably more doable than asking Elizabeth to leave on a retreat. She always feels committed to her causes and never even wants to take a vacation." He looks out the window, slightly convinced that Martha now agrees with him. "I do think she went on retreat last year, didn't she?" Martha's shaking head tells him she didn't. "All the more reason for Edwina to stay with her!" He remembers the quiet ride to the airport when they didn't talk and how comforting it felt. "Who better to spend time with than an inspired woman who shares Elizabeth's passions about women and the church, about the poor?" And has more patience by far than Elizabeth, he acknowledges, hoping some of it will wear off on Elizabeth and willing his smile to change Martha's mood.

A phone call takes Martha to her desk.

Though Martha hasn't acknowledged the wisdom of any of his proposals, he hopes the phone call will change her perspective. This pile of papers on his desk probably contains calls and emails from parishioners about the trial and all the controversy created in the parish. He hopes the news coverage has stopped. Edwina can show Elizabeth how sticking with the day-to-day responsibilities exemplifies a commitment to her causes. Edwina never forgets or lowers the priority of the house she founded in Chicago to help prostitutes. She puts the house activities first. She wouldn't take any speaking engagement if it conflicted with the house and the many women who depend on the services. She embodies the idea of a shepherd. She tends the sheep, never herself.

Martha appears at the door. "Father," He invites her to sit. She remains standing and still doesn't smile. "Father, since Elizabeth hasn't responded to one message during the whole time you were on retreat, I can't imagine her responding let alone inviting anyone, even Edwina, to stay with her." She folds her arms across her chest and shakes her head. "I don't know, maybe you can reach her where we have failed." She shrugs her shoulders and waits.

"Very good, very good, I'll try again and we'll think of alternatives, won't we?"

"As long as you don't put a hotel on your alternatives list!" She barely takes a breath. "And don't even consider offering a stay at the rectory. We haven't fixed the pipes in the extra bathroom and –"

"Right, right, probably too expensive for us. And right, not the rectory." He remembers the rectory repair list, his promise to find a parishioner to make repairs, and wonders where he put that piece of paper. He feels the weight, shed at the retreat, returning.

She nods. He gives her the schedule Edwina suggested before they parted at the airport. "Those gaps will allow Elizabeth and Edwina time together. If she doesn't stay with Elizabeth, we'll think of other ways to have them spend time together. Does Elizabeth have any meetings during that time?"

"Considering that Elizabeth has not attended a meeting in the last month, it probably doesn't matter that she usually has at least three meetings a week with the shelter and several with the women's group and – but who knows?"

He wonders about asking Martha to host Edwina, but something about Martha seems not like Martha. He calls and leaves a message for Elizabeth about Edwina's visit and writes a note to put on her desk. The pile of messages and unopened mail almost falls over as his request joins the pile. He moves the letter he sent from New Mexico to the top of the pile.

"Elizabeth you reconsidered! Very good, very good." He stands and reaches for her hands. She doesn't extend hers. He drops his hands and fidgets. He smiles. "Of course, the parish will cover the costs. The shelter certainly dug itself out of a hole with that collection! We have such generous parishioners. We can count on them to replenish the funds. Very good, very good." He pushes aside the pile of papers on his desk. "When did you want to go on retreat?" He tries to find the parish calendar among the scattered papers.

"I'd like to go next week! I plan to go to Piffard. Less expensive – " she doesn't finish the sentence. "I haven't visited there in years. Just far enough away to," she hesitates, "to leave everything here." He watches her face. "And the smell of bread baking every morning!" She notices his stunned expression and smiles.

Without finding the calendar, he shudders. "Very - Oh, next week. But ...next week, Edwina comes. You received that schedule, didn't you?" He smiles and pauses briefly to find a convincing reason. "Why not choose the week after. I'm sure you and Edwina will – Edwina looks forward – It's such an opportunity – for the whole parish – and." He looks for the flyers Martha created for Edwina's schedule. He finds one and hands it to her. He sees Elizabeth's smile disappear and a stern look replaces it. The expression on her face stuns him. He waits. It doesn't change. A frown appears. Suddenly, that open, welcoming smile covers her face. He smiles recognizing her again.

"It took me a while to realize how much I need this." She pauses and sighs. "I'm afraid if I don't do it now, I won't do it. You know?"

He sees acceptance of her need to pray and have solitude. He encouraged that in his letter and messages. He sees that he can't force this on her.

"Very, good," he sees relief on her face. He nods, "Very good." He says a quick prayer for her and delivers her troubles to God.

"Thank you for understanding Father Rogers," she smiles again but doesn't reach out to hug as they usually do. He knows something is missing. Unable to identify the something, he convinces himself that she will find the missing piece and much more during the retreat. She leaves his office without stopping in her office. He doesn't hear anyone speak to her. She doesn't greet anyone as she leaves.

He prays. He hopes and prays that she will see things differently after her retreat. He tempers his disappointment knowing that Edwina will bring light, inspiration, and new perspectives to the parish with her humor and deep interest in Saint Luke's. Everyone must feel a loss where Elizabeth touched their lives. He sees that God has brought Edwina to lift the parish out of disappointment and sadness. He knows many parishioners feel a loss and hope they have not lost Elizabeth forever. Trying to summon the strength built during his retreat, he sees possibilities. Without Elizabeth, perhaps parishioners can turn their attention to their own spiritual needs. As Edwina visits the shelter and the school and joins in daily Masses, she will touch many parishioners with her insight. She shares this gift with Elizabeth to connect deeply with every person she meets and fill each one with her glow. He sees a parallel between lighting candles during prayer and her effect as she touches or talks with people. Surely with this shared glow, everyone will see the situation in a new way. Edwina will inspire many suggestions. Elizabeth will return with her glow more visible. He realizes even in the difficult conversation, some of the Elizabeth who inspires and who they have all have missed remains. He feels hopeful. He trusts God. She will too, soon.

He starts each day with prayers for Elizabeth, especially today, her last day on retreat. If he could send her the opening he felt in New Mexico, an opening available only with prayer, he would. Each day his prayers ask God to provide that opening so the parish can have Elizabeth back.

He remembers how Edwina laughed and loved the idea of a person having a glow. Though she believed her glow originated with God. "That glow exists in all of us!" She thanked him for the idea. They talked about how a person shares glow, perhaps without knowing. They invented glow-sharing. Of course, she took the idea another step and described how a glow brightens when one shares it, knowingly or not. She also found scripture passages to augment these ideas. He never laughed so much preparing a homily.

He had a difficult time saying goodbye to Edwina. With the insight and energy from his retreat and her visit, he felt the energy to face, maybe even enjoy, whatever challenge arrives at the door. He regrets that Elizabeth won't experience Edwina as intimately. Her talk put smiles on people's faces, even Martha's. Addressing the endless piles of paper on his desk, he vows to finish everything before Martha arrives. He imagines an even bigger smile. He hopes this glow that drives him through this dreaded task will transfer to her. After ignoring these piles for so long, she must recognize the accomplishment. He admires the dwindling height of the piles. He has signed all the reports and the thank you notes to the priests who replaced him during his retreat. He turns to the smallest pile of phone messages to return phone calls from the diocese. He hears Martha drop her keys on her desk.

"You can stop praying for Elizabeth," she looks angry.

"Very good, very good. Has she returned? Full of God's wisdom?"

"She didn't make a retreat!" He wonders what Martha can mean and moves the smallest pile off the chair so she can sit, but she doesn't sit. "My neighbor went on retreat at Piffard and returned last night. He said Elizabeth showed up at the monastery at the beginning of the week when the retreat began. My neighbor saw her arrive. He saw a person taking photographs of her. Then, he watched her get into her car, drive away, and didn't see her the rest of the week!" Martha puts the papers down in the piles where they belong. She opens the newspaper on the top of the last pile. She holds the paper to show him Elizabeth at the door to the chapel at Piffard surrounded by a headline, *Winter Seeks Wisdom for her Trial.* She lays the newspaper carefully on the trial pile.

He wants to question then wonders what happened. "Perhaps a sick family member or someone from the parish needed her?"

"Maybe her lawyer," Martha shakes her head. "Have you looked at any of the messages, emails, and documents about the trial?" She sees the piles. She must see that they are smaller.

"No, looks like you haven't touched that one."

He sees the largest pile she stares at and he missed. The glow fades as he realizes he has not addressed the trial letters, notes and messages, again.

Zack

Zack returns from reading stories with the kids. His smile disappears as concerns about work collide with concerns about Naomi. He paces in the hall searching for explanations. A smile passes across his face as he remembers how Naomi always relies on him to see his way through difficult situations. The big picture, she wants him to tell her the big picture. He wonders how to reach that picture, how to access that amazing talent.

She uses the word *amazing* a lot. He attributes that adjective to her as he realizes that he stands inside that picture both with work and family. He can build a big picture for others as long as that picture doesn't include him. He thought he had done that for his employees at work. Now he questions. The whole Saint Luke's situation has left him without a big picture he can describe for Naomi. He needs Naomi to listen and each day a new crisis arises that drags her further away from the family. He knows he should reach out to her, offer to listen. Her lack of listening lately makes him less enthusiastic about offering. He feels that every time he listens and then tries to put the facts into logical order, they don't cooperate. He finds her so distracted that he doubts she listens. He wonders if he should get a babysitter so he can attend a parish meeting. He would probably understand better and make some headway at reaching that big picture she keeps asking for. Then, discouragement stops him.

He is pretty sure she doesn't even realize that she lets things go that he could never imagine her ignoring. He stops pacing. Lists form as he accumulates the many things she usually keeps track of at the same time. He smiles and labels that an amazing talent. The memory of Lou's photo on the front page of the morning paper next to a dirty pile of snow turns him toward the family room. As he walks that way, he remembers that she used to contact him almost every day. Now that photo shocks him into the reality of how this upheaval at the church spills over to the family, and surely to other families and

168

relationships. Everything that drew them to this community has disappeared. Wow! *Does she see that?*

He sees the big picture! He sees her at the table immersed in her papers. Perhaps, he has found a way to talk about this and get some of her insight on his work situation.

"You look very serious, Zack." Naomi moves papers around and writes something on the top page.

He wonders if now is the right time. "This whole mess –," He tries to find words that won't set her off. He watches her but can't tell if he has her attention. The familiar lists run through his mind. If he has gotten her attention, he needs the right words to describe what she won't want to hear. Criticism of his own less than ade4quate communication makes him wonder if he has remained objective about her involvement with the Saint Luke's chaos. He wonders if he has helped her. As he questions his attempts to point out what he sees and she doesn't, he can't explain her responses and assumes she doesn't want to hear.

Finding this community gave her so much joy. He admits sharing that joy. He admits how easily doubts slid away and how he used to look forward to both the Masses and the projects. Used to. What happened to Lou should serve as a warning that bigger problems exist, problems they don't see. He discards using phrases like *the tip of an iceberg* as words that won't work. He knows that words, in a situation like this, can light a fire. Then, the kids, he decides she will listen if he starts with the kids. "How about you, Nay?"

That smile looks like a Naomi he knows. He takes that as a good sign. "How are you doing?" She listens. He accepts that smile and returns a hug.

"OK, yes OK." He will try this.

"OK, I like that." They both smile. "What did you mean? You mentioned a mess." She joins him on the couch.

"Well – " he watches and tries to predict her ability and willingness to listen. He recalls the times when they don't listen to each other. Similarities with Saint Luke's these days strike him. He searches for starting words. "How can I start?" She doesn't offer any help. "Lately, I feel puzzled about work, about Saint Luke's, about –" They lean on each other shoulder to shoulder. he puts my feet on the coffee table. She curls hers up on the couch. "I don't know what my next step should be in relation to Saint Luke's, or yours, or Father Rogers or – or anybody's, for that matter. I don't want to abandon you, especially; but we need a little more of you at home." He avoids looking at her face. "And, unfortunately, I must pay more attention to work."

She sits up and turns toward him. "Not Melissa?"

"Melissa is on the list. For sure. But – " he hesitates and then work consumes his thoughts, "I guess she filed a harassment claim. The client I thought would highlight her talents, a perfect match, or so I thought, complains about her. I haven't paid enough attention to either of them lately. You know it's bad when your boss finds out about the unhappy client and a disgruntled employee. You can guess that consequences will follow. I know where I'd go in his situation." He swallows. "He wants to talk to me."

Her face tenses. He wants to take the words back. "But what I wanted to say – I'm still here for you and Saint Luke's. I just might have to limit the Saint Luke's time." His confidence fades, not the right time.

He arrives home late. No lights in the children's rooms remind him how long he worked. He pays the babysitter and reads Naomi's note, another meeting. Thoughts of last night's talk lead him to what he should have said, *Naomi, I need you. I need your intense listening and honest judgements. These days, many things seem unsolvable without you. We both need a center. Let's figure this out, together. I can't function without you. Please.*

He wanders around the kitchen. The long day piles up on him and feelings of anger surge forward. Work nags. He cites other bosses who clearly deserve harassment claims. But Melissa has chosen him and she has worked for at least two other bosses who, in his judgment anyway, seem much more obvious harassment candidates. *She can't possibly lump sexual intimidation in her claim, can she?* As he thinks about assignments, reviews and progress reports where he

170

highlighted her work, he concludes that nothing he has done shows her that he values her work. The Human Resources representative told him that they must take her claim seriously. That means he must document every assignment, every review, every email, everything he can find to contest her claims. He shrugs his shoulders unable to remember anything negative he has written about her. *What did I do that led her to this place?* He knows Naomi would give him honest feedback. He pulls the files from his brief case. He wants to show her all this. He hopes she can find a way to present it truthfully and respectfully.

"Another trip?" Clare asks him at breakfast.

"Not such good timing, sorry. My return flight arrives late Saturday night." He sits next to Clare. The disappointment in her face stabs and he can't think what to say.

Naomi, finally, had the energy to sit with him after her meeting and help develop a plan to handle the disgruntled client. Even though she hates the weekend travel, especially with the extra time she spends at Saint Luke's these days, she suggested it. She definitely predicted the client's response to the suggestion that they visit him immediately. His quick response and offer to book a hotel gave Zack hope that they could save the client after all.

When he turns to look at Mark, he sees more disappointment, He tries to lighten the mood. "What will I miss?"

"Everything!" Mark pouts.

"Wow, so we'll just sleep all day Sunday?" He touches Mark's shoulder. He pouts harder.

"His religious education class will say the Prayers of the Faithful at Mass on Sunday, like our class did last week." Clare smiles.

He looks at Mark. Mark tries to hide a smile of pride.

"Well, I can't miss that, can I?" Mark holds the smile back. "What prayer will you say?"

"He's praying for Elizabeth, just like I did last week." Clare scowls at Mark. "But he will not say the same thing and he won't tell you what he will say!"

Mark punches Clare's arm. Clare recoils. Zack touches Mark's shoulder. "Quite a responsibility, Mark. Do you want any help?"

"No," he looks at Clare, "I'm not telling." Mark pounds his hand on the table.

"Then, we'll just have to go to Mass to hear you." Now, Mark lets out a half smile and folds his arms.

"You have to get up, Dad," he hears Mark's voice. Even half-awake he knows Mark's voice. "Come on Dad." His little hand pounds Zack's shoulder. "Da – ad." He opens his eyes after two hours of sleep and rolls Mark into a hug. "You have to get up!" He pushes in rhythm with his words, "Up! Up! Up!"

"Umm" Zack rolls over and closes his eyes. Mark rolls Zack back and drags him into the bathroom. "OK, right. To work? Time to go to work?"

"Mo – om. Dad won't get up and get ready for church!" He turns back and puts his hands on his hips. "Hurry up or no breakfast."

Zack shakes himself, stands up straight and reaches for clothes. He dresses quickly. Mark keeps his hands on his hips until Zack turns to go to the kitchen.

"He doesn't listen, Mom." Mark sinks into his chair. Zack winks. Mark won't take a morning kiss, but Clare and Naomi accept his offer. Hands still on hips, Mark points at Zack's chair.

As a silent breakfast proceeds, Zack remembers when the family first arrived at Saint Luke's. After suggesting every church, avoiding all Catholic churches, Naomi's description of Saint Luke's caught him by surprise. He wanted a church where the whole family could connect. With two different backgrounds growing up, they looked for some kind of bridge between her Catholic upbringing and his Protestant experience. A strong sense of community kept coming up as they reviewed churches they visited and considered others. Despite his lack of respect for the whole Catholic hierarchy, he fell in love with Saint Luke's. It didn't feel like a typical Catholic church, no matter how you looked at it. Every aspect of Saint Luke's put the poor and the disadvantaged first. Many churches claim this kind of value; but many of those who say the words, don't act on those words. His first shock happened the day they decided to add a handicap ramp. He had nothing against a handicap ramp, but the roof leaked. The roof seemed urgent. But not to these people who wanted to make sure the folks in wheelchairs and with disabilities felt welcome.

But now, now he doesn't sense community at masses or when he participates in volunteer projects. He feels the tension when they walk through the doors. He looks around to convince himself they didn't take a wrong turn. He knows these people. He worked with many of them on that ramp, on the roof, on the old furnace at the school. He played with them at all those celebrations when they finished a project. No one smiles or nods. The Prayers of the Faithful break some of the tension. But tension builds back up again as soon as the Mass ends. Instead of the burst of laughter infused conversations, people cluster in small groups and whisper. Naomi and a few of the facilitators huddle by the door. Tony Mancuso looks ready to start a physical fight. He understands why Naomi worries when Tony attends the parish meetings. He can't figure out how those bonds between such different people shattered and expressions like Tony's that would have seemed out of place months ago, appear on too many faces.

"Nice job on those prayers, Mark." Mark nods to Zack briefly and heads out the door to play. "Any homework?" Mark closes the door and disappears out into the yard.

"We'll call them in before dinner and ask that again." Naomi pulls out her facilitator folder and looks up. "So how did it go with the client?"

"Boy did you get the in-person visit right!" Naomi smiles. Her hands move up and down the folder. "I let Melissa lead the meeting. She showed all the qualities I love about her work.

She went down the client's list of concerns and addressed them one by one." He chuckles. "It brought back memories of working with the old Melissa. Her technical strengths enhanced every meeting and all the casual conversations I heard. People skills, she excelled in everything. I could see the client's expression change during the two days of work and meetings." He glances out the window as he remembers the beginning of the meeting. "Though it didn't seem that we would be successful when we sat down the first day. He had a long list, even longer than the list he sent last week. I prepared myself to step in, but I held back. Melissa acknowledged his concerns and then addressed them. She worked with his staff to add a feature they wanted, not on his list or in the original design. She saw the benefit of addressing that quickly."

"Great, Zack." Naomi sits back in her chair. "And how did you and she get along outside of the client's office?"

"She met a friend for dinner and I took the client out. That avoided the main social situation. At dinner, the client expressed his concern about her capabilities before we arrived and thanked me for taking such quick action." Zack smiles. Naomi nods. "I probed to make sure the client's confidence had returned. I'll have to check in with him regularly." He scratches his head. "I guess she changed her seats on the flights. I looked at the tickets when they arrived from the travel agent, she had assigned adjacent seats, as she usually does. She knows we like to work on the flight. Not this time! We had a brief chat to plan the meetings at the airport, but she kept to herself pretty much." Naomi opens her mouth ready to ask another question, but Zack continues. "I made sure to compliment her at the end of each day for the work she did. Really, I didn't have any criticism. 'Constant criticism,' appeared on the harassment claim multiple times, so I kept that in mind. During this meeting, I saw the Melissa I hired who impressed me with her potential. Maybe she'll withdraw her claim?"

"Wouldn't that be nice."

His frown competes with his nod. He sees Naomi's hand handling the facilitator folder. He wonders again about Saint Luke's, whether to question her. She seems relaxed. "How about you?" She shifts in her chair. "I mean Saint Luke's, anything new? Anything resolved?"

She looks up and then away. She watches the kids playing outside. One hand moves over the facilitator folder. The other clicks a pen slowly.

"I haven't given you much support lately." He follows her gaze to the kids. He can't remember the last time, he joined them in play. "I can't blame work for everything. "

Her face wrinkles as she finally talks. "The whole mess at Saint Luke's has gotten out of hand."

He sees tears in her eyes and takes her hand as he sits.

"I don't know, Zack. I feel like everything that brought us to Saint Luke's has disappeared. The community, the collaboration, the attention to the poor, -" Tears take over. He puts his hand on her shoulder. Her breathing becomes uneven. He reaches for a tissue and hands it to her. He resists agreeing with her, wondering what pushed her to this state. "And – "she drops her head in her hands. "I feel responsible." Now the tears shake her.

He holds her. Questions about Lou, about the facilitators who threatened to quit, about Elizabeth and Father Rogers accumulate. He doesn't ask.

Mark bursts into the kitchen crying.

When he walks into the meeting called by the Human Resources representative, he knows Melissa has not dropped her claim. He recognizes his boss. The number of other Human Resources staff members including the Vice President and several other people who he does not recognize cause him to remain standing.

"Mr. Norton –" the Vice President begins motioning him to a chair at the head of the conference table.

He takes a breath and doesn't move. Both the travesty of the situation and the extreme danger confront him. He doesn't focus on the travesty. Fear of lawyers, especially with details from Naomi about Elizabeth and her fancy, threatening lawyer so recent, recedes. An unfamiliar face at the table causes him to assume by his tie and suit that someone has invited a lawyer.

This recognition makes him assume the balance of attendees tilts toward Melissa. Many possibilities exist for the outcome of this meeting, none of them favorable to him. His folders contain strong and detailed accounts of job responsibilities, performance reviews, improvement suggestions, and Melissa's behavior as documented by him, coworkers and clients. However, this situation now requires additional materials. The word ammunition pops to mind. Naomi's suggestions about getting other perspectives, while a good suggestion, will hold no value in this venue. He interrupts the Vice President having heard bits of his formal jargon about the proceedings and nothing of the participants. "Excuse me." He stops talking. "I received an agenda addressed to three attendees." He places the agenda on the table. "I see more than three attendees. Perhaps the agenda has also changed?" He looks at each of the attendees inviting a response.

No one speaks. His breath remains calm. He smiles. A reservoir of professionalism gives him strength. He has no idea where this strength comes from. Saint Luke's!?

"Let's not waste this many people's time. If the agenda has changed, perhaps you can revise and resend it?" He looks directly at the Vice President. No one responds. "Might the new agenda indicate that other material and perhaps other people, like my lawyer, should attend?" The man he assumes is a lawyer takes notes without looking up. Zack places his folder under his arm. "I have a pretty open schedule today but if I do require a lawyer, I'll need more time before rescheduling."

The lawyer doesn't look up. The Vice President hides a frown aimed at the lawyer. His boss remains expressionless. Zack leaves the room.

On the walk back to his office, He passes Melissa who says nothing and looks surprised. The walk lifts some of the shock from his mind. Though, his aversion to confrontation returns. Questions form about Melissa's expression and her potential knowledge of the agenda he did not receive. The message light on his phone blinks.

He sees Naomi's number, "Zack did you hear me say that your old boss called yesterday? I hope the meeting went well and that you have solved the harassment mess. Oh, and he called again this morning. He has a project with your name on it, he says. I saved the message; you can listen yourself."

Zack turns first to the task of finding a lawyer to advise him, someone who can review his folder in light of harassment laws. The presence of the Vice President and a lawyer implies that the company doesn't believe him, guilty without all the facts. Names of lawyer friends send him to his phone to begin the search.

Hearing Naomi's message lightens his mood. He calls and listens to the message from his old boss. He knows he can't walk away from this situation, but just listening to the message gives him a sense that he has options. After deleting Naomi's message, the light on his phone blinks. He listens to a message from a vendor, looks at the pile on his desk, calls the disgruntled client to make sure he remains satisfied and listens to another message from Naomi.

"Do give your old boss a call, Zack, despite all the other things clouding our judgement these days." His mind drifts to those things and he hears the end of the message. "We both need some perspective. Saint Luke's used to expand our perspective on so many aspects of life. We both have noticed more gaps and deficits created by this upheaval at Saint Luke's." He can hear her breath and her voice catch as she continues. "After you make that call, I have another idea. We could get perspective tonight. Edwina Gately came to the shelter today. You must meet her. I found a babysitter. Meet me at church if you can't get home for dinner."

"Sorry I didn't make it home for dinner." He slips into a seat next to Naomi. He looks around surprised to hear the familiar buzz of Saint Luke's gatherings and sees smiles on people's faces. Naomi smiles and points at the lady talking with Father Rogers.

"You should have seen her in action at the shelter today. What a model! She treated the men like guests. We call them guests, but she showed us how to treat them like guests. We learned a lot from her, watching the way she addressed the men. I think Lou might even have said a few words to her! You know how long it takes him to talk to other people, amazing." She took a breath. "I do miss Elizabeth. Since all this happened, nothing attracts her to anything at Saint Luke's." They watch people entering and look around the room. She shakes her head. "Again, no Elizabeth! The two of them together!? You'll see. I might take notes. She says things so clearly. I hope the retreat improves Elizabeth's mood. Martha says it is impossible to work with her, and she certainly doesn't respond to anyone I've talked to." Naomi reaches for his hand.

Bob Harrington leans over and greets them. "I've been looking forward to this." Bob points towards Edwina. "I have heard she really holds a crowd when she talks, even the likes of us! Wish we could get her ministry here. Many of the worst fires we see involve prostitutes. You wouldn't believe the situations they live in. Have you read *There Was No Path So I Trod One?*" Bob holds up a copy, its spine loose, its cover stained. "I want to ask for an autograph. I hope she has time for autographs." They all watch the hall fill up with familiar and unfamiliar faces.

More people enter the hall until few seats remain. Bob and Zack get up to find more chairs and add them to the rows already set up. When they return to their seats, Naomi hands Bob his book. He sits down. "This looks fascinating. I haven't read any of her books. But Ben told me he heard her speak at the Call To Action conference. His description made her sound so funny and sane. I can't imagine working with prostitutes. She treats our shelter guests the same way she treats the volunteers. It sounds simple, so simple. I want to buy *A Warm Moist Salty God: Women Journeying Toward Wisdom*. I like the title." They laugh and Father Rogers draws attention toward the front of the room.

"I haven't seen Father Rogers' eyes twinkle like that for too long." Naomi whispers as Father Rogers begins.

He relates meeting Edwina during his retreat in New Mexico. His soft voice and humble carriage end conversations throughout the room. "Imagine finding yourself sharing a taxi with Edwina Gateley!" Father Rogers chuckles. "Very good, very good but you don't have to imagine. She came to Saint Luke's. Many of you have met her at the Masses or the shelter or the school. Thank you, Edwina!" They give full attention to his description of her story. Leaning back in his chair, Zack lets Father Rogers' words push thoughts of work aside. She started working with the poor in England. Her work in Chicago as an HIV counselor led her to create a house for female prostitutes. Zack wonders how dedicating your whole life to the poor and disadvantaged works. He suspects she doesn't earn much and must beg for her guests. "We have many of her books available for you tonight. My favorite is *A Mystical Heart* which describes the journey in solitude with God. Solitude provides us with an opportunity to bring God closer to us, to invite God to look inside our hearts, and to give our troubles to God. We welcome you to Saint Luke's." They all clap as she walks to the microphone.

Edwina nods to Father Rogers and adjusts the microphone. "The thanks go to you" she looks directly at Jeff sitting with shelter guests and volunteers. "and you" she faces, names, and smiles at each of the shelter guests. Lou smiles as she names him last. "You have given me blessed days here in Stanton just the way my sisters at our house do. Your difficult journey reminds me of God's goodness and of her presence in every moment of every day. I learn from you to recognize that presence and respect it in my thoughts and actions. Thank you. And I understand you claim some of the worst winter weather here in Upstate New York? Come visit me in windy Chicago in January and see what you think!" She continues with thanks to the school principal and the teachers who she finds with some difficulty further back in the hall.

"I wonder if she'll have time to talk about her work with all this thanking?" Naomi whispers.

"At Boston College, Sister Callista Roy, a nurse on the faculty – though that barely describes the feisty, loving person who both teaches and does research in spirituality and justice, introduced my talk – 'Spirituality and Justice: The Demands of a Lived Faith.' Father asked me to repeat the talk here. Well, I can't do it." She smiles, shrugs her shoulders and lifts her hands. "No, I can't give the same talk I gave in Boston because I've learned so much here at Saint Luke's. You have nourished my soul and shown me many examples of your spirituality and your commitment to the poor children of your neighborhood and the homeless. You define the word, justice, with every meal you serve, every bed you offer, every child who arrives at the school each day. That's a mound of justice as we say in England." She chuckles and draws laughter from the audience. Though her talk centers on women and ways for them to attain more rights and responsibilities, she uses language gracefully without belittling others or deemphasizing her points. Zack thinks about Elizabeth and how strident she has become. He wonders of they spoken during this visit? He sees Naomi's face full of attention and then a frown appears. He looks around the audience but doesn't see Elizabeth. He agrees that a meeting between Edwina and Elizabeth seems timely and doubts that it will happen.

"So, I thank you for reminding me that we who have received the gift of faith must share that love. We cannot contain it." Clapping comes slowly and then builds to an enthusiastic clatter. She nods, thanks, and moves to the book table. The clapping stops.

Zack watches thoughtful faces absorb her message and shares the feelings he sees on their faces. He wants to ask her how to fix Saint Luke's. He wonders if anyone asked her that? He thinks of this ability to treat the shelter men as guests that Naomi described in her voice message.

Work intrudes. His jaw drops and slowly he sees Melissa's perspective more clearly. He knows he worked hard to find the best project for her; but what she feels or understands has nothing to do with what he intended. She sees the project he gave her on a different level, inferior to other projects, especially, projects he gave to the men on the team.

Reaching for her arm as she begins to stand, he blurts quietly to Naomi. "I have given the best projects to the men on the team." He watches the crowd surround Edwina. Naomi's face questions. "Melissa thinks that. And –" It all seems so clear. "I could have just asked her what project she wanted! Perspective, I have a new perspective!"

They stand and follow the crowd. Naomi shakes her head. "Perspective." They smile at each other. "Edwina gives us the perspective that we all keep missing." Naomi stops. "What would Clare think about this?"

Zack responds immediately riding on his work revelation. "Right. I have the younger version of Melissa living in my house!" He shakes his head and remembers similar friction with Clare. He tried to anticipate what Clare would want, just as he did with Melissa. Every example he can think of has the same pattern. He presented his great idea, Clare dismissed it with her idea. He countered with reasons her idea couldn't work. Remembering these interactions brings a smile to his face.

"I wonder. I wonder about talking to Melissa? How simple if it worked? Let her choose the project she wants!" Naomi smiles.

"It just goes to show how you can have many reminders but still miss the point – at least in some parts of your life." They move toward the front of the hall. He looks at his watch. "Look at the line, pretty long. Should we just pick it up at the bookstore?"

"If we buy it here, a portion of the money goes toward paying Edwina's expenses; and we can use any leftover money for other speakers. Did you see the sign on the table when we came in?" They move slowly as Edwina engages each person while she autographs. "Do you see Ben anywhere?" Naomi scans the crowd without success.

Not seeing Ben reminds him of another gap in their lives. He can't remember the last time Ben dropped by. He had become such a fixture in their home playing with the children and working with Naomi on parish meetings. He marvels at how much this change impacts their life. "No wonder we feel lost," he mutters. He looks at his watch and the autograph line. Naomi catches his expression as she pays for her book. They shrug our shoulders and head for the car.

Naomi

Dear Sam Bonner,

Oh, I might have to call you just to hear your calm voice. Can I just transport myself to Vermont?

I feel like we're losing everything – the community seems to be coming apart at the seams. Get this - Elizabeth took over the parish meeting the other night and demanded.... That's right, demanded people decide whether they were for her or against her. And Ben! I don't know how to say this but he acts like someone brainwashed him. His phrases are her phrases. I called him after the meeting, but he never called me back. That's not like Ben. It makes me wonder how objective I am. Oh, and the other two facilitators want to quit! Other than that, everything is fine.

I'm probably not making much sense. Zack always says I assume that he understands more than he does and - well I'll try to do this chronologically or at least logically. We had another parish meeting. I'm sure I told you Saint Luke's attracted us, at least in part, because of the way the parish makes decisions, more like one of your Vermont town meetings I imagine than a Catholic parish. Elizabeth pushed for this format. She wanted parishioners involved in decisions as equals with the staff. You know about liberation theology very popular in Latin America. Though strange to my parents' generation, it does have some Catholic grounding.

But things have changed, I just didn't realize how much. After she, Elizabeth, got up and gave a detailed list of what she needed, no demanded, the way she said it that made it a demand, at first no one spoke, or even moved. Since I have facilitated these meetings, I have never, and I mean never, heard silence after someone presents an idea or a proposal. They didn't know what she meant or maybe they couldn't believe she demanded and didn't invite people to offer alternatives. Dialogue grounds this community. Demand? It must be hard to run a parish when you invite so much dialogue, but the dialogue allows people to support things they might not otherwise support because they have had a voice in the decision. Things happen quite differently than originally presented or planned. Originators, those who suggest change, even those who speak against a proposal end up supporting the final version. We listen. Anyway, she was definitely not looking for anything but agreement. Listen to this! She didn't ask for agreement in principle, she asked for agreement to follow a script. Sign here. I'll tell you what you signed later!

Then, she explained that by refusing to let the Bishop fire her, we could save her. (Oh, I forgot to say that Father Rogers, behind the scenes worked out a compromise - a transfer to another parish. She would keep her benefits. She wouldn't be far away. It just doesn't make sense!) She insisted that the lawsuit would save her! You should have seen the faces in the hall. It was like she was speaking another language and they were waiting for the translation. The silence started to scare me. I was lost, trapped in the respect for her and astonished at what she was saying and how she said it.

I don't know how much you remember about her. She has this red hair that fluctuates between being dark like the inner flame of a fire and almost the color of a rose. It frames a delicate face with bright blue eyes and an exuberant smile. Well, she wasn't smiling that night. I know I'm exaggerating, but I almost expected flames to come out of her mouth she looked so angry. And her hair! All flame color. I've never noticed before how her hair looks different at different times. Finally, she said anyone who was with her could meet in the church. Can you imagine that? Meet in the

183

church? Without saying anything else or acknowledging any kind of meeting process, she left the microphone, and walked out of the hall.

Before she left, the only parishioner brave enough to speak stood and asked the ultimate question. Oh, I forgot to mention, the lawsuit sues the diocese for $1 million. The ultimate question was: "what did she plan to do with the money?" Bob, the fire chief, asked it. He wasn't angry, he's the ultimate negotiator. He was thinking the way we do at Saint Luke's - if it has to do with money, who can we give it to? The Saint Luke's answer, one that Elizabeth in all previous situations would have given immediately included options: totally to the poor or toward the CTA women's ordination committee - she is a founder of this committee and has done a lot locally. If everyone wasn't so stunned both by her demand and her lack of an answer, someone would have started the ideas flowing. Any of the suggestions would have played well with the press - even the jury! How do I know? She didn't answer. Instead, I only got the last phrase she said, "bigger issues." He asked what could be bigger than poverty, trying to pull her back and crack the silence. She didn't turn back or acknowledge him. And then, Ben followed – without a nod or recognition of his responsibility to finish the meeting. Several people followed after that.

So, there I am. I had no idea what to do and then Minny Lord came walking toward the microphone. She didn't hurry. She might have been the only person in the hall smiling. Have I told you about Minny Lord? She emerged from nowhere at the first meeting after we found out that the Bishop fired Elizabeth. She drives one of those big 16 wheelers or is it 18 wheelers – huge trucks - pulled by this cab that looks like you need a ladder to get to the driver's seat! Not the typical poet! Not the typical person who can communicate faith eloquently! Imagine using the word eloquent and truck driver in the same sentence! The expressions on people's faces scared me. She walked up to the front of the room and read a poem. Basically, it was about remembering that God was in charge and implying that more prayer might be in order, though because it was a poem, she didn't really direct everyone to pray. But we did.

And Father Rogers wasn't there. As I write this, it was really a perfect storm situation. The hospital called just before the meeting started; and while everything crumbled, he sat and held Earl's (a longtime parishioner) hand in his last moments. Father wouldn't have made a different choice, but I can't imagine how it feels to be torn like that. He convinced Elizabeth to come here from Texas and he worked closely with her to encourage their shared goal of having women more involved in the church, in the liturgy, and in decision making. He looks like he has aged twenty years in the last few months. He would have spoken against the lawsuit and his voice would have given, at least a sense of, balance to the meeting. Everyone knows he wants more for women and for Elizabeth. He doesn't see the lawsuit as the way to achieve those goals. His calm voice and his words would have balanced, at least, Elizabeth's message.

Luckily, we don't have another meeting until February. On the other hand, it seems like Elizabeth won't respect the parish meeting process she worked hard to develop. Up until this incident, everyone held the process sacred. She reminded us when we strayed. February will give the facilitators time to put the issue in balance and attend to all the other things we have let go – like the shelter review we do every year. But it sounds like Elizabeth will proceed with the lawsuit no matter what anyone says.

Facilitators! I might be the only one left. Ben? Mary and Fred?

I'm sure you have wise words for me about all this because I don't. It still takes my breath away to think how hard Elizabeth worked to establish the participative decision making and how quickly she abandoned it.

Maybe worst of all, I've lost my friend Ben. It doesn't make sense. I wish we took notes at the facilitator planning meetings. I do remember that he said Elizabeth agreed to meet with him when he was here for Thanksgiving. That meeting must have happened after the planning meeting because he didn't say anything about her plans and, most shocking, his intention to support her. He agreed with me, I do remember that, that she would take the Queen of Peace job and she obviously has no intention of doing that. I can't figure out what happened to change him so dramatically.

Hope I haven't rattled on too long. How is my favorite Vermont spiritual mentor doing?

Hugs,
Naomi

Dear Naomi,

Sounds like you need a break. How about a weekend in quaint Vermont with the knee-deep snow refreshed every evening? We can walk in the woods and chat, roast hot dogs in the fireplace. Bring the family!

Open invitation!

So, do you have spiritual mentors in other states? Sounds like you could use a few more than me...

Your,
Sam Bonner

Saint Luke Church Bulletin – Stanton Diocese
3rd Sunday of Ordinary Time
Saint Luke Mission: Serving the poor is the highest priority for Saint Luke's.

Dear Friends,

When I don't hear God's voice clearly, I often go for a walk. Being in a park or near the river allows me to hear God's voice more clearly. Recently, God has been telling me to listen more and more deeply. We know that God often asks difficult things of us and we also know that following God's path is sometimes disheartening and confusing. Still we listen and walk.

My retreat took me to a river in New Mexico where many other retreatants walked by the river, prayed, and reflected on their lives. As we approach Lent, it is a time to pray more.

Recent events have created confusion at Saint Luke's. We have had some surprises that might make us question God's wishes. When we are tempted to question God, that's the best time to stop and listen.

We must also remember our mission to help the poor even in this confusing time for the parish. Let's not forget the poor during this confusion. Lombardo House will need many food supplies to feed our neighborhood families for the rest of the winter and to address emergencies in the neighborhood. God reminds us to care for those who need help. We collect food supplies on the last Sunday of the month.

Spread the love and support each other,
Father Rogers

Notices
- Notices – online
- Prayer Line – 453-3344: Call the prayer line with your prayer intentions.
- Peace & Justice Update – The Sisters of Saint Joseph are holding an all-day retreat next month. See their web site for details – www.ssjreneva.org

Martha

"Father Rogers, you must talk to the Bishop in person. Must! Make an appointment. I can make it for you as long as you promise me that you will go." Martha paces the floor in front of Father Roger's desk. Father Rogers turns papers over from one pile to another. "Don't mess that up! You're putting Urgent in the Later pile." She stops pacing. Her sigh gets his attention. She lowers her voice. "I want to simplify your work, especially the work you like to avoid. Without Elizabeth, you don't have the advantage of losing a note in that Urgent pile. You, of all people, would not want anyone to die without a visit! I have already removed the other requests, complaints, and tasks from your daily deluge." She shakes her head as he smiles and shrugs his shoulders. She tries not to smile but fails.

"I'm sorry." He puts the papers back in the right piles. "Very good, very good. You keep me organized and you know I appreciate it." His smile broadens. "I – I –"

She remembers her reason for standing in his office. She doesn't wait for the rest of his sentence. "I know you appreciate it." She smiles and sighs. "And, I will appreciate it, if you will talk to the Bishop." She waits. He nods. "We don't want this situation with Elizabeth to get worse. Can we agree on that?" He doesn't respond. "Knowing what the Bishop thinks will help." He looks puzzled. "Listen, having worked there all those years, I know that the Bishop gets a lot of information from the people around him. Will they support us? Will someone propose a different plan for Elizabeth? What does he say about the lawsuit? We need to know!" Father Rogers nods. "But even more important, you must show that you respect the Bishop. After all the press coverage, don't let him assume all the absurd things that rumors can create. Stopping rumors must happen quickly, absolutely essential. Absolutely! If you don't want to make an appointment, just show up in the Bishop's office. Chat with whoever you see. If the Bishop won't see you, ask for an appointment or just wait." She laughs. "What would they do if you sat down and waited? Sit just outside his office. Then, he will walk by no matter where he goes."

Father Rogers nods and listens.

"So, when will you go? Do you want a ride?" Martha paces again. "This meeting will help Elizabeth too!"

Father Rogers looks for his calendar.

"Now, how about now? You don't have anything until noon."

Waves of admiration and doubt exchange places on his tired face. Not knowing what to say and knowing what Martha will suggest, if asked, competes with his shame about creating a problem for the Bishop and his frustration at not having any communication with Elizabeth. Still he admires Martha's tenacity and can see her point, if only someone else could go. He takes a deep breath and wishes for the tenth or eleventh time that day that he could walk to Elizabeth's office. She could advise him or – but he has to remember his new strength. Elizabeth will not take on this task. Martha stands at the desk with her hands on her hips. "Very good, very good. I'll go now."

Instead of going to Saint Luke's the next day, Martha drives to the diocesan office muttering and complaining the whole way. "I'll have to get this out of my system before I walk through that door." She drums her fingers on the steering wheel. "See that green light Mr. Chevy Volt. Move it! Now! Why people get behind the wheel when their brains remain anywhere else but here on the road, I'll never know." She enters the highway and merges with the traffic as she did daily during those years when she worked at the diocesan office. "I wonder if I will know anyone in the office, anyone who will speak openly, share rumors or anything." Spending most of the night wondering why Father Rogers didn't, and finally deciding, couldn't, talk to the Bishop when the parish, a parish he had nurtured for so many years, demands his attention, put her on the highway to do it herself.

She remembers the flow of information that seethed through the diocesan offices during those years. Stories developed either into short-lived and quickly forgotten tales or long complicated, everchanging epics. The epics lasted, often boiled down to inaccurate myths that acquired a life of their own. Accuracy rarely held anyone's attention. With accuracy and someone to clarify, the stories disappeared. Martha wants the Saint Luke's story to disappear. She knows that every day allows the Bishop and all his staff to elaborate and exaggerate the story. They hear the news reports and listen to people who pass stories on without questioning and even add their own opinions along the way. The Saint Luke's story grows darker without intervention. She practices the introduction Father Rogers should have said to the Bishop so that Saint Luke's emerges from this mess and the story disappears: *Your Most Reverend Excellency Bishop Inman, you know Elizabeth Winter, a passionate Catholic, so active throughout the diocese. Talking to her directly can clarify and cut through a lot of inaccuracies. We've seen this before with the news media. Do we want to keep the diocese out of the news?* Asking questions always gives the Bishop a way out. It shows respect. She takes the exit and shakes her head talking to the empty car. "Oh, he probably couldn't say things that way even if he believed them. He's too nice and doesn't want to make trouble. *God, any chance that you could speak a little louder on this one?* Can't he see how much trouble he could avoid? Maybe the parishioners would calm down and talk to each other instead of calling him multiple times a day. Facts, they want facts. The news people want the same thing. Without those facts they make assumptions and guess.

She pulls into the diocesan parking lot and notices a few familiar cars. As she enters the building, she realizes that she should stop in the Ladies Room before entering the main offices. She needs time to compose herself and think of a credible reason to justify her visit. As she hangs her purse on the hook and prepares to use the toilet, she hears two people enter the room.

"Why did Father Head ask you to do that?" Martha doesn't recognize the voice.

"He said they needed evidence of problems to use at the trial." She recognizes this voice.

"Problems?"

"You know, that, that woman, I don't remember her name, is neglecting her duties or breaking some rule, I guess."

"So, what did you do?"

Martha remains motionless in the stall as the two voices move out of the room.

Luckily, she remembers baptismal forms she asked the diocese to find. In all the confusion, she forgot to collect them last month. She takes a deep breath and leaves the Ladies Room. She stops at a few desks to greet friends only exchanging family updates and health concerns of other acquaintances they share. She does check the calendar, telling the clerk, she needs some possible confirmation dates on the Bishop's calendar. "Father Head will do your confirmations this year." The clerk hands her Father Head's calendar. Martha doesn't ask why. She knows this year Saint Luke's should have the Bishop. The clerk doesn't offer any explanation. Like the others in the office, even people she knows, they offer only the shortest responses and claim work to dismiss her.

She leaves.

Elizabeth

Traditionally meetings stopped at Saint Luke's from the fourth Sunday of Advent until before Lent. Martha made sure to add announcements in November about the meeting hiatus and encouraged attention to posted schedules. Elizabeth or Father Rogers added the spiritual reasons for the hiatus when they wrote the weekly bulletin. The shelter volunteers followed their schedule juggling family holiday plans to keep the shelter open. The school didn't open until just before the Feast of the Holy family. The Masses and confessions kept the same schedule and all altar servers and Eucharistic ministers received their assignments late in November for December and January. As always, Martha posted schedules on every bulletin board and the web site.

Elizabeth, without a second thought, ignores the tradition and calls meetings with the people who volunteered as character witnesses in the trial against the Bishop. The lawyer, Monty Forsyth, attends and briefs the parishioners. He describes how he anticipates the trial will proceed and when he might call them to testify. He indicates that the case will probably come to trial in March. The diocese might make a counter offer between December and March. He puts a low probability on that chance and urges people to schedule travel before March or in the summer to ensure that everyone they require for the trial's success can testify. Forsyth coaches people on their testimonies. He gives them lists of questions the diocesan lawyers might ask. They practice answers together. He takes notes at every meeting. He maintains a list of witnesses. The numbers beside each name, written in pencil, indicate who he would choose first and last to create the most positive impression of Elizabeth for the jury. He doesn't share the order with the witnesses, or Elizabeth. In private meetings, he questions Elizabeth about the people to formulate his own questions with an eye to showing Elizabeth's dedication, strong faith, and work ethic.

At the start of the meetings for these potential witnesses, he takes attendance, repeats details about probable trial dates and stages, discourages travel, and emphasizes the importance of their role in making the trial reach a successful verdict. He describes his own objectives in selecting jury members. He will try to eliminate conservative Catholics from the jury. He hopes to include members of the other more liberal church communities in Stanton. He chuckles along with the parishioners about the difficulty of eliminating unsympathetic jury members and identifying jury members who will understand Elizabeth's value. Staff members in his office will collect lists of parishioners from those churches so that he can recognize names during the jury selection.

Elizabeth holds the meetings at her house to avoid criticism from Father Rogers and other parishioners. Ben attends. Forsyth decides early in the process that Father Rogers will not fall in line with his objectives and anything but falling in line will create a danger they can't risk. No support from him will avoid the risk of a misinterpreted statement in response to the diocesan lawyers. He knows many of these lawyers. They spot holes when a witness hesitates. One hesitation, one mistake will cause a lawyer to twist the witness in another direction. Soon such tactics could lead to a witness seeming to support the diocese rather than Elizabeth. He tells Elizabeth stories to illustrate how witnesses can make or break a case. Elizabeth agrees. He determines the chances of the diocesan lawyers calling Father Rogers as a witness low. Father Rogers doesn't receive notice of their meetings. They assume they have his support. Elizabeth wonders, to herself, if the diocese might try to shake that. She doesn't know how that might happen. She puts it out of her mind.

Forsyth encourages Elizabeth to maintain communication with Father Rogers. "Any information we can collect about diocesan plans for this trial allows us to anticipate. Anticipating gives us the upper hand. We need to know that kind of information every week. We also need his support to remain strong and constant. You should make sure we have that."

Elizabeth knows Forsyth's advice will benefit her, but she finds herself avoiding Father Rogers' calls, the church office, other parishioners, the school, and the shelter. All her attention focuses on the trial. She has nothing else to talk about. Yet, she knows Father Rogers, and everyone else for that matter, will ask about it. She has little energy left and no patience to chat informally or work on parish projects. No matter how many times Forsyth repeats what Elizabeth knows she should do, she can't. Parishioners leave messages she doesn't listen to and notes pile up on her desk. Father Rogers seems to call every day. No energy remains even to contact her Call To Action colleagues across the country. Forsyth suggests that too. She knows they would help. Again, she understands his logic, again she doesn't call. *Hadn't she put in enough hours in the last year to count for something?*

Since they agree they won't ask Father Rogers, Forsyth suggests she ask Ben or one of the other facilitators to pledge support. He suspects that a facilitator's support would influence others in the parish. On the first evening as Ben enters followed by others, he declares himself right. While facilitators don't have as much influence as Father Rogers would have, perhaps they will respond positively to Forsyth's suggestions about what to say.

Once she saw a lawsuit as her only option; but before she asked for support in public at the parish meeting, Elizabeth presented the request to Ben. She found thoughts flowing easily and genuine smiles accompanied her words. She offered tea. They met at La Tea Da in the afternoon on a weekend when few people visited in the restaurant and tea room. She sat back as if nothing else in the world mattered but him. She invited him to talk. He told her that he had sent his application to the seminary.

She clapped, stood, crossed to his chair and hugged him. "Ben, Ben, Ben. Finally, others will see and experience the insight of your caring soul!" She burst into the exuberant smile

194

that endeared her to so many people and she offered her total support. Though she added that she didn't know how much good it would do him to have support from the black sheep in the diocese. She laughed easily at herself. She asked about his plans. She asked how he felt. She left time for him to share his resolve and his doubts. She didn't interrupt. She listened.

Ben relaxed. One subject flowed into another. He didn't notice the change in her expression or the tension.

She paused. Her smile faded. It took Ben a few minutes to understand the change. Instead of asking more questions she had started to present her plan. "...You'll like Monty. He's efficient and to the point. He wants to win this case as much as I do. We both agree that you will be the center of my case." Her smile bloomed again. "You radiate your spirituality like no one else I have ever met. And communicating! Name a difficult audience, you can explain, listen, even convince." She elaborated with examples of the things she praised. She smiled. She paused and waited for his response. She saw acceptance of her praise and continued.

Ben buoyed by her praise and grateful for her support, saw the opportunity to support her as a way of thanking her. He concentrated on what she said. His doubts faded.

"It might sound odd but standing for this cause will be good preparation for the seminary." She saw that she had touched him. Then, she described how the lawsuit would proceed and emphasized how winning this lawsuit would become a major step forward for women's ordination. By the time she brought up the lawsuit, she had his cooperation guaranteed. She invited Ben to meet Monty Forsyth.

The next day, they met with Forsyth at his office. Forsyth had urged Elizabeth to choose Ben based on what Elizabeth told him. He wanted to meet Ben and question him to see for himself.

Forsyth shook Ben's hand, "I've heard a lot about you." He watched embarrassment fill Ben's face.

"All good I hope?" he looked at Elizabeth.

Elizabeth smiled. Forsyth invited them to sit. "Tell me about yourself, Ben. I understand your family comes from Stanton? Stanton Short on Sunshine echoed in my house growing up." Ben smiled. Forsyth listened to Ben answer and took notes.

The interview revealed the components Forsyth looked for: his strong Catholic upbringing, his intention to enter the seminary, and his ability to speak with enthusiasm. Meeting with Ben confirmed his hunch. Then, Forsyth proceeded to outline what Ben would do during the trial. Elizabeth added additional praise as she listened to the questions the lawyers would ask Ben when he sat in the witness chair. Finally, Forsyth suggested that Ben declare his support for Elizabeth at the next parish meeting. Forsyth emphasized the importance of that unwavering support. Not only would that kind of support attract other witnesses, but it would also simplify the process of screening and preparing them for the trial. Ben hesitated at the parish meeting suggestion. Elizabeth remained calm and persuasive, listened to his indecision, and eventually convinced him to follow by praising his work in the parish, writing a note to herself to finish her letter to the seminary, and ending with her warm smile. When she saw a nod, she gathered her papers, repeated how the meeting with potential witnesses would flow, saw approval on Forsyth's face, and concluded their meeting.

Elizabeth responds to Father Rogers' plea to go on retreat with a grateful voicemail on his phone. She leaves the message late at night when she knows no one will answer his office phone. Elizabeth doesn't stay at Piffard to join the quiet monks in their simple monastery and follow the monastery schedule of prayer, contemplation, and simple work as her message states. After a short visit to the monastery with Monty and his reporter friend, she disappears into her townhouse and ignores her phone for the week. Organizing her notes on the trial and reviewing the many answers she has practiced with Monty alternates with assessing her wardrobe. She chooses three simple outfits to wear on the trial days. Setting Monty's suggestions about black and primary colors aside, she selects shades of pink and red to emphasize her red hair and pearl white complexion. Each outfit projects simplicity and professionalism as Monty suggested. She practices walking in the outfits, sitting, and holding an expression that will prevent, she hopes, people from guessing her thoughts.

Elizabeth always looked up to the women in the Catholic Church past and present who spoke out, who stood for justice, and who promoted women's place in the church. She learned their words and quoted them often in her homilies. She recognized their accomplishments. They inspired her. During her retreat week, she finds herself looking at examples of women outside the church for ways to present herself to the public. The admiration and imitation she used throughout her career transform to outright copying of ways to sit, stand, and walk. She practices in front of a mirror. She watches old newsreels of Eva Peron and tries to strike the posture, expression, even the extended arms. As she holds her hands high her fingers stretched, she imagines the completion of the trial, the announcement of the verdict, and all that becomes possible at that moment. She stands before a mirror arranges her hair to fall in its simple waves on her shoulders, then thrusts her arms above her head and opens her mouth as she saw Eva Peron do on the newsreels. She practices walking down the stairs in her entryway imagining the stairs outside the courthouse and thrusting her arms high as she reaches the crowd of people waiting for her. She doesn't see individual faces; she sees a smiling throng. She sees herself approaching a microphone or, no, shouting without one. As the week progresses, the details of that speech take form. Ordination of women comes toward the end of the speech. Details about her next steps, she must hint at that without letting those details detract from the victory. The speech will capture the moment as Martin Luther King's speeches always did. The moment of winning the trial launches the worldwide campaign to ordain women in the Catholic Church. She will lead that effort. She paid her dues with Call To Action and parish work. *My work now starts, in the world.*

As she savors that thought, she lists her many qualifications and recognizes how they will impress the jury, the lawyers, and eventually the world. Then, she recognizes a parallel between the dwindling of support in the Saint Luke's community and Christ in the Garden of Gethsemane. She works from her memories of the old newsreels and composes her own simple not smiling, not frowning expression that she remembers Peron had. It carries her message. She imagines Peron saw what no one else saw.

"Edwina Gateley can't fathom the breadth of the message only I can deliver," she says to herself.

Jeff calls Naomi the week after he realizes the parish did not review the budget and other financial requests at the last parish meeting. He asks for guidance on the financial situation at the shelter. Normally, the parish devoted all fundraising activities in March to the shelter. They held a Diet for the Homeless dinner and twenty percent of all the collections in March went toward the shelter. Jeff indicates that they can't wait until March for more funds.

He adds, "Based on the last time I saw the numbers for the whole parish, not a surprise, the parish can't cover the extra costs either." The insurance costs weigh heavily on his mind since the diocese has demanded that the parish carry enough liability insurance to avoid any vulnerability the diocese would inherit. That obligation requires him to send the paid receipt for the insurance to the diocese.

"Late payments to insurance companies could cancel our policy." They exchange several ideas and decide on a special collection. With Father Rogers in New Mexico on retreat, getting Elizabeth's permission, the most logical option, they no longer can depend on. Neither one wants to ask Elizabeth. "The year-end report still sits on her desk. I put it there three weeks ago. She doesn't return calls. Martha says she doesn't come into to the office. She doesn't come to the shelter either." Jeff sounds discouraged. "Martha told me she has a fulltime job finding the message someone asks about, moving it to the top of the pile, and then running to answer the next call. She says she spends the day running back and forth because she gets so many calls! Elizabeth's church voicemail filled the first week. Martha answers calls from the same people about the same issues!"

Naomi suggests that they take responsibility. She will call Elizabeth and leave a note for her. But she won't wait for a response. She will try to get Lou to speak at the Mass and then request a second collection for the shelter. Jeff wishes her luck with their quiet friend. Naomi finds new energy in turning her attention to the shelter again. She knows Lou has saved enough money to get his apartment. She also knows that he wants to help the shelter and doesn't know how or what to do.

She meets him before he starts work one sunny afternoon during a January thaw. She explains the situation. His eyes show concern. He scratches his beard. She waits while he thinks. She watches the cars line up for car washes and the ones emerging from the spray gleaming in the afternoon sun. When his breathing slows, she suggests in more detail what he might do. She explains how the Mass flows and when they would talk to the parishioners. She points out how much more credibility he has as a guest at the shelter than she does as a volunteer. She reminds him that he wants to do something for the shelter. "This is a great opportunity." She watches signs of doubt flicker across his face. His body starts to shake and his head turns back and forth. "I'll stand there with you!" She describes what she will say. "Listen, you don't even have to speak. Just standing there with me will emphasize my points." He stops shaking. A small smile forms and he nods. She marvels at how much that nod says about his progress over the year.

The substitute priest says a quiet Mass. Martha included the extra collection in the notes she gave the priest. His homily relates to the poor and homeless. He invites Jeff, Naomi, and Lou to the altar. Naomi introduces her "friend" Lou. He smiles and his face flushes red. He makes a small bow. Jeff tells Lou's story. He ends with the news that Lou will soon live on his own, thanks to Lombardo House. He pauses and acknowledges Lou. Then, he describes the financial situation at the shelter and the immediate need to pay the insurance bill. He turns to Naomi.

"Jeff came to me when he realized the timing of the insurance payment. Unfortunately, we don't have a parish meeting," She remembers that they should have presented this information at the December parish meeting. "And, I apologize we should have handled this at the December parish meeting." She hears grumbles and fears someone will shout. She laughs. "We didn't want to interrupt Father Rogers' retreat. Martha will inform him when he returns." She thanks Elizabeth for her understanding. She doesn't elaborate.

As she completes the explanation, she calls attention to the ushers standing in the aisles. "The ushers will pass the empty soup cans that fed people at the shelter for the collection" Lou nudges his way to the microphone and says, "Please help," in a meek voice then steps away.

The collection more than covers the insurance payment giving the shelter the cushion it needs to offer services until March. In fact, it exceeds any previous collection Saint Luke's ever gathered.

Martha bears the brunt of Elizabeth's absence and lack of response to anyone. "I'm telling you, the only change in her office happens when someone, usually you, Father Rogers, moves the note they put on the desk to the top of the pile." She doesn't try to be diplomatic. "She doesn't work here."

Father Rogers leaves notes on her desk asking questions, different on each note. He hopes some topic will bring her back. With Martha's reminders, he gradually takes on her responsibilities overseeing the school and the shelter. He also visits all parishioners in Stanton's hospitals. He finds the energy he accumulated on retreat ebbing away each time someone mentions the trial. He rarely turns on the television. Channel 14 reports on the trial frequently and parishioners become more and more uneasy about the trial's effect on the parish. He tries to remain positive in his messages to Elizabeth urging her to set aside time for prayer and to remember the activities that refresh her. He avoids asking the many questions that plague him. Many versions of these notes pile up in his wastebasket as he rethinks, rephrases, and revises what he wants to say. He struggles to suggest that she drop by the shelter where she always enjoys talking with the men and hearing their stories. He decides against the suggestion afraid that it would draw attention to her absence.

Then, he reminds himself of his resolve to be more forthright in his communication and clearer about his leadership in the parish. He wants to maintain the respect he has for Elizabeth. Having to hold her responsible for her duties in the parish challenges him. She always surprised him with her efficiency. He worries about the Bishop. He hasn't rescinded the agreement to transfer Elizabeth but he hasn't put it in writing either. Any hint that she shirks her parish duties, and worse, has shirked the duties since the original announcement, may eliminate the possibility of the transfer. He writes down what he wants to say, "Take time for a visit to the shelter, Elizabeth. The Lord speaks to us through the poor. Listen. Also give us an indication of your intentions. This will allow us to respond to the diocese about your work and to cover your responsibilities." This time he decides to call her instead of leaving the note on the growing pile on her desk. He reads it through several times, then calls. When she doesn't answer, he leaves the message on her answering machine.

Elizabeth picks up the message when she returns from court that night. The number of witnesses has dwindled to five. She knows the five have many doubts and will join the other deserters the next time the diocese cross-examines one of them and she doesn't know what to do. She hasn't prayed in days. Something about Father Rogers's tone and directness catches her off guard. She kneels in her bedroom and attempts a prayer. She paces the room when nothing comes. She considers leaving a message for Father Rogers and rejects the idea. If she can't pray, she will eat and try to pray again. After eating a can of soup, she kneels again and tears come.

"Mom, I don't get this part - 'Lent is for wanderings'" Clare holds the sheet of paper up for Naomi to read. "You know how our religious ed teacher always tries to relate our class to the homily." Naomi opens the car door and looks for Mark and Zack surprised not to see them crossing the parking lot. Zack comes from the church basement looking toward the car. Not seeing Mark with Naomi, he shrugs his shoulders and goes back into the church.

"Mom? Why is Lent about wanderings?" She looks at Naomi as Zack goes into the church. Clare reads the prayer again stopping at the phrase coming after 'Lent is for wanderings'. "All I can think of when I read that part is how Mark is always getting lost?" Naomi turns to Clare and stands where she can read the prayer too. "He does it on purpose don't you think?" Clare glances at Naomi but doesn't wait for an answer. "Maybe he should give up getting lost for Lent? Wouldn't that be nice? And every time we didn't have to look for Mark, we could say an extra prayer." She smiles at the great idea and the smile grows larger as another, even better, idea forms. "We could say this prayer and we could say it all together. That's part of Lent too! Praying. Right? We can give up candy and treat each other nicely, even Mark. And we should pray. Our religious ed teacher said the Sisters of Saint Joseph wrote this prayer; do they know Mark?"

Expectations

"Welcome everyone to our parish meeting." Naomi pauses as people take their seats and become quiet. "This evening we begin the celebration of Saint Luke's School month. Father Rogers, the principal, and teachers will give us the yearly report on the school and describe plans for the future. Remember Saint Luke's School in the second collection this month at each Mass. We will have a short report on Shelter Month. Jeff will thank you for your generosity in December during the special collection and remind you about the Diet for the Homeless dinner in March. We can support many more homeless people. And we'll end with Open Forum as always. Any questions on the agenda?" Naomi scans the crowd for Fred. Mary called earlier with a sick child and won't attend the meeting. As she considers asking someone to take notes, Ben walks in and joins her at the front. He opens his laptop and sits. Naomi looks at Ben for an explanation, but he keeps his head down and his gaze on the computer screen.

Someone at the back stands up. Naomi points toward the microphone nearby. "I don't need a microphone." A soft chuckle agrees with his statement. "I don't see anything on the agenda about the trial?" He doesn't wait for an explanation. "We," he turns to point at the group and raises his arm for them to stand. They stand in unison. "We want answers about the trial." Naomi recognizes Tony Mancuso. She glances at Ben. He raises his eyebrows.

She takes a deep breath and remembers all the questions raised at the facilitator meeting. Ben did not attend. Naomi, Fred, and Mary feared that parishioners would have questions about the trial. "What if Tony Mancuso shows up?" they all wondered. Tony's name sent Naomi off to find answers. But when she couldn't find anyone with answers, they didn't put the trial on the agenda.

Naomi doesn't know what to do. Ben rises and stands beside her. "I can give an update on the trial during Open

Forum. I'll try to answer your questions and Father Rogers can probably answer any questions I can't. Would that be OK for all of you? Or we can adjust the agenda?" Tony says a quiet OK, frowns as he looks at the standing group, and then sits.

A rush of feelings overwhelms Naomi. Relief, shock, and apprehension make facing the kind of conflict Tony incites more daunting. She doesn't know what to think with Ben functioning as if he helped plan this meeting, as if they had spoken weekly as they used to. She smiles at him as he takes his seat. His smile seems like her old friend. She takes breath and proceeds.

The principal gives the first part of the school report. The school remains in debt, but they reduced the amount of debt with a grant from a local congressman. The grant covered the remainder of the large rewiring job they did after an inspection by the Fire Department found problems. The principal thanks the long list of electricians from the parish. Then, Father Rogers reads the letter the congressman will receive from the parish. He places the letter on a table near the door and several blank sheets of paper for parishioners to sign as they leave the meeting. He urges everyone to put their address when they sign so that the congressman will see how many of his constituents this grant serves. At the end of the report, they show a film. One of the parishioners on the school committee created the film to start fundraising for the purchase of computers. People seated around Tony Mancuso whisper and frown.

"Why would we spend money? You just said the school has a debt of over $15,000?" His loud voice interrupts. "$15,000!" He repeats.

Father Rogers stands and responds thoughtfully. "Very good, very good." He nods at Tony and nods to draw everyone's attention. The whispering ceases. He chuckles. "I'm learning. We're learning. And this very serious school committee," he points to the committee sitting in the front row of the hall, "decided that plans like this would not happen if we don't raise the money. So, raise the money and then spend it." He smiles. "We haven't always done things this way. But - we

204

will always repair the school and keep it safe for the children, even if we don't have the repair money in the bank. Of course, we'll take any donations of computers, but we will not buy new ones until we have raised the funds." He nods toward Tony and scans the room to see how people respond to his comments.

Several parents of children who could not attend without scholarships make statements. Naomi hates to cut these people short as they remind everyone about the importance of the school. *It takes courage for them to stand in front of a crowd*, she thinks.

She also anticipates a long Open Forum and wants to allow enough time for all opinions and questions. Balancing the naturally talkative and the quieter people in the meetings, requires patience, time, and tact. She thanks the single mother who leaves the microphone in tears of thanks, touching her shoulder as she walks by. "We've run over our time for this topic. Shall we proceed to the results of Shelter Month? Or do we want to devote more time to the school." She receives a 'yes' that doesn't come in unison but seems to represent the sentiment in the room. Amid that 'yes' she hears louder whispering from the group sitting near Tony Mancuso. Jeff outlines the results of Shelter Month. He provides the details of the budget. He highlights the positive balance and thanks everyone for their generosity.

Only one person from the group with Tony asks a question. "Does this mean that the shelter can cover its yearly budget?" Before Jeff responds, the questioner adds, "All year?" Naomi cringes at the sarcastic tone. Jeff answers with a definite 'yes'. Naomi offers a leg stretch break and comments to Ben, "I'm scared, Ben. What do you think they will ask? Can we head off a long monologue?"

Ben responds with a sigh, "Stay prepared. When they hear the amount of the lawyer's bill, the topic will explode." He pauses. "But I won't desert you this time." He smiles and bows his head slightly.

Naomi doesn't know what to say and jokes, "So we might not end on time?"

"That's right. And we might not end in one piece," Ben looks apologetic.

Father Rogers raises his hand first at Open Forum. Other hands fall from the group at the back of the church and Naomi invites Father Rogers to speak. She shrugs her shoulders in Ben's direction as she sits down. He wrinkles his brow.

"Our parish renewed itself based on a commitment to serve the poor. We gained parishioners. We helped many. Tonight's reports on the school and the shelter remind us both of the importance of the mission and the difficulty." He nods at the school representatives and the shelter representatives and smiles. "Now we must consider additional ways for Saint Luke's to serve the poor. Edwina Gateley's visit gave us an example and we know our Elizabeth's work here in our parish." The group at the back of the hall shift in their chairs and whisper among themselves at the mention of Elizabeth's name. Father Rogers still composing how to make his proposal doesn't notice the group. Naomi does. "I propose this idea in Open Forum. Let's consider it at a future parish meeting and consider other ideas as well before choosing a new focus of our goal to serve the poor. I propose that we create a Saint Luke's Women's Pastoral Committee. We can think together about what the committee does. It might represent the parish in larger interfaith forums here in Stanton or help us connect with more national groups that we can collaborate with and learn from. The existing women's committee here at Saint Luke's has initiated many educational activities both here in the parish and with other churches in the diocese. This new committee would more formally state our support of women in the Catholic Church. Perhaps we could devote a month to women as we do to the school and the shelter. In this new century, we must increase our attention on women in the church again."

"What kind of an example does Elizabeth represent now?" someone shouts from the back of the church.

"Please stand and state your question." Naomi takes a deep breath. She doesn't like the tone of the question or the disregard for their meeting process. "Did I hear a question?"

She tries to control the emotion in her voice. The questioner remains anonymous.

Other parishioners ask questions about the idea, about the failed pastoral committee and the wisdom of using the same name, about the timing. "We might need to poll people in the parish on women's issues. Is this what we want now?", Naomi keeps expecting the trial to surface again. She wonders why Father Rogers hadn't waited to present this idea, especially when Tony started the meeting with so much anger. Other parishioners suggest finding out what other parishes around the country and the diocese have chosen to emphasize. Naomi reminds everyone about the time. They allow Open Forum suggestions and questions ten minutes before moving on to the next topic. Naomi can see Tony Mancuso whispering with others and becoming more agitated. Seeing no objection to moving to a new topic, she addresses Tony. "Sir, you had a question for Open Forum. Please state it again so we all can hear."

He stands. Tony's small frame holds a resonant baritone voice. He clears his throat. The facilitators had contrasted the meeting-of-all-meetings stories with his choir voice resonating above others in the room. Naomi realizes that the choir has sounded different without his voice lately. Heads turn as he speaks. "Did someone say tired of women? You bet! Women's issues? We want a Catholic Church. Women, especially Elizabeth Winter, don't belong here! You bet we are sick and tired of women and their issues. More than sick and tired!" Naomi pulls away from the microphone, tries to keep a blank expression, and takes a deep breath. She looks at Ben but before she can say anything, Tony continues without a breath.

"Listen I said this the day Father Rogers hired her. Women belong at home. Marry her off, I said. And let's forget this idea of women on the altar. They cook, they raise children, they do what a husband commands. End of story. We've run the church for over 2000 years. We did just fine until this woman infestation." He holds everyone's attention. Naomi scans the shocked, stunned, and cheering faces of spellbound parishioners.

"No place for women, no place. No place for women in the Catholic Church." He looks around nearby parishioners. He stares at Father Rogers. "Should I say that again? I warned you all. And now I will tell you what I have done." Ben's fingers fly over the keys. Naomi glances at her watch, grips her pen.

"I've written to the Pope and to the Congregation for the Doctrine of the Faith to report every infraction since the day she arrived." He turns and Gio hands him a large box. He holds the box up. He pulls a paper out. "I wrote this last letter about Elizabeth Winter." He looks to his cronies and sneers. "Finally," he smiles, "finally, someone listened. I got her fired. Done. Done!" He smiles and looks at his buddies. "Doesn't anyone else pay attention around here?" He doesn't wait for an answer. "No! No, you listened to her again and this enormous debt, not anything like the school or even the shelter, would bury us if we didn't act. Because you didn't!" He points at people one by one starting with Father Rogers and moving his finger to point at each person he identifies as a sympathizer. "Why? Her debt! Not our debt." He pauses. He looks directly at Father Rogers. He pulls a paper from his pocket. "I will send this letter tomorrow. It lists all the things you have done." His finger points at Father Rogers and he pauses. Gasps come from the parishioners. Both the words and delivery have frozen Naomi and Ben. What parts of what he said are true? Has he gone too far? "You'll be following her out the door soon. None too soon." He smiles and continues untouched by the wounded expression on Father Rogers' face or Naomi's barely audible attempts to interrupt.

"Before we think of another way to spend money. We demand to know who is paying for this trial? The lawyers at Dixon, Grossmann, and Peak charge exorbitant fees. Just look at the front page of the newspaper any week of the year and you see what they charge. Lots of zeros!" The group around him mutters agreement. The other parishioners listen. Tony waits for quiet. "And - we have information about parishioner meetings, more hours to increase those zeros! At one thousand dollars per hour can you imagine the amount on the current bill? And the final bill?" Parishioners gasp.

Ben stands to answer the question and Naomi sits to take the notes. She takes a deep breath and turns to the computer. She wants accuracy and exact amounts for every question. Someone will have to check each detail before any kind of dissemination to parishioners. "The diocese will pay all the legal fees" Ben pauses "if we win the case."

Before he can continue, Tony, who remains standing, asks, "and if you <u>lose</u> the case?"

"If we don't win the case, it's probably the parish - Saint Luke's will receive the bill for the fees." Ben looks at Father Rogers for clarity. Naomi searches the crowd for Fred and doesn't see him. She looks around the hall for other lawyer parishioners but sees none.

Father Rogers stands and turns to the group. "Very good, yes, yes. I believe that Ben is right. Saint Luke's must pay the lawyer if we lose the case." He squeezes one hand with the other.

The chairs squeak and scrape the floor as the group at the back murmurs and nods. They lean forward ready to talk. Tony takes a piece of paper from Gio, seated behind him. "Well, let us tell you what we figure Saint Luke's will owe, because - " Tony scans the room stopping to gaze at the parishioners with the largest expressions of disbelief. He smiles and nods recognizing many of the faces with the most shocked expressions and continues in a softer but still audible voice. He stares at Father Rogers. "By the way, all of this will go in my letter tomorrow." He puts the paper back in the box Gio holds. He turns back and continues. "She will lose this case." Naomi sees the heads of some parishioners whose attention wandered turn. She types, bent on capturing all of Tony's words. "We never see her in the parish," he pauses to allow each person to search their own memories of the last time they might have seen Elizabeth and continues speaking with pauses between each word, "which - raises - another – question, – about her salary?" Another pause increases the number of frowns and questioning expressions. He increases the pace of his words. "We have had our people in the court room. We have contacts in the diocese. We talk to them. They know about our letters.

So, believe us when we say, she will lose. The news stories we read and see clearly predict a win for the Bishop." He turns and takes a handful of newspaper articles from Gio. He waves them above his head. Then, he turns and passes them to the person in front of him. "We hear nothing from the altar. We see nothing in the bulletin. And if she loses this case," He pauses again and looks behind him. Gio and Sal nod their heads. "we figure the parish will owe close to five hundred thousand dollars!" He listens to the murmurs. He waits for the shock to settle in. "And that's not all. Losing means Saint Luke's pays the legal costs of the diocese," he pauses. Naomi hears some questions near the front of the room with the words *cost* and *diocese* repeated. "when she loses, that half million is just the beginning. The diocese didn't choose a cheap law firm either!" Jaws drop and mumbling increases as people look back and forth to find confirmation or denial.

Father Rogers cringes at the numbers and realizes that Martha tried to tell him something similar. With his usual dislike for the business affairs of the parish, he put her notes in the towering pile of papers related to the trial that he should have addressed but didn't. He remembers that day she appeared in his office insisting that he listen to her. He begged a time later in the day and then forgot. These were things that Elizabeth handled smoothly always willing to relieve him of the tasks she did well and he disliked. He let that detail slip and he wonders how many other important details slipped as he tried to cover more in her absence. Father Rogers stands and walks toward Ben. Ben steps aside and lets Father Rogers speak. Father Rogers looks first at Tony and then at Ben. "Could you see me after the meeting and give me the details you have gathered?" Tony has more to say but Father's soft voice and discouraged expression causes him to agree and sit down. A pause quiets the room. "We will check this out thoroughly and provide a full explanation in next week's bulletin. You raise very, very serious questions."

Ben reminds them they have exceeded the topic time limit. Then, he summarizes the questions and the promised responses. Father Rogers nods his agreement of the summary.

Ben asks and receives Tony's agreement with the summary. Naomi checks over her version grateful for the repetition. Seeing no further hands raised, Ben offers a brief closing prayer.

Ben and Naomi put the last chairs away in silence and gather their belongings. Naomi asks Ben if he wants to stop at the house on the way home as they often did after meetings. She questions herself but Ben agrees quickly. They drive separately to her house. One light remains on in the kitchen. Zack's note saying he has an early flight the next morning and would leave without breakfast sits on the counter. The kids both left notes. Clare needs money for the school trip. Mark drew a picture of a driveway full of cars and trucks and flowers blooming in the garden. Naomi realizes she hadn't noticed the start of her perennial flower garden outside the kitchen window. She switches on the outside light as Ben enters the family room. "Look, the crocuses have almost finished blooming and I haven't even noticed them."

"A lot has gone unnoticed lately," Ben sits on the couch by the fireplace shaking his head and looking at Naomi. "Naomi will you ever forgive me? Will I ever forgive myself?" He watches her and mumbles, "or not really?"

"It feels strange to hear you ask questions like that." Naomi shakes her head. "Though maybe this is a time in our friendship to ask questions." She frowns. "It certainly seems like a time in the parish to ask questions." Naomi sits across from him in the Shaker rocking chair.

"Like why haven't I returned your phone calls?" Ben chuckles looking down.

Naomi chuckles and nods. She sees the old smile and the honesty she loves about Ben.

"Oh Naomi, I don't know. I've taken a detour in my life that God must have lots of questions about." Tears form in his eyes. "Speaking of questions." He brushes them away. "I haven't told you that the seminary sent an acceptance letter," he pauses, "to me."

"You certainly haven't. And yet I don't see the exuberant smile, an expression that I saw the last time when you told me you finally applied?" Naomi frowns.

"No. Perhaps they won't want me when they know what part I have played in this whole fiasco."

Naomi asks, interrupting, "Fiasco?"

"Fiasco, not only the right word to describe this, perhaps the only word," Ben looks down and closes his eyes.

"I need more details here?" Naomi speaks softly and without blame or accusation.

"Naomi, Elizabeth" he inhales, " - I don't know Elizabeth anymore. We met a different person at the Call To Action conference. Someone has taken her place. She isn't the person who always seemed in lock step with God. She might not even pray anymore. When I went with her that first evening and others joined us upstairs in the church, I went with conviction. I went to support her as she supported me in my discerning about the priesthood. I couldn't understand why you didn't join us after the meeting ended. I looked forward to planning a strategy for getting parish participation with you. I, well you remember that I had hesitations about the lawsuit at the very beginning." Naomi nods. "It didn't seem right. I should have followed my intuition. That came from within. Now, I see how following her wishes" he shakes his head, "no orders! She gives orders now – she makes no effort to gain consensus, consider other options. She doesn't smile." He looks down, shakes his head and then looks directly at Naomi. "But -, Well – she doesn't see how she has changed. This woman who championed women's ordination for all women, who found ways to invite and encourage more women to participate in and take charge of all aspects of church life, who celebrated all women for their efforts and accomplishments, no matter how big, thinks about, speaks of, and promotes only herself. It's like a demon took over her mind. It finally hit me at the last meeting we had with the witnesses. But I guess it didn't hit me hard enough?" He scratches his head. "Now I think of all the signs I missed along the way. I couldn't believe how she treated Mary's friend. When she stood up and asked Elizabeth why she couldn't trust people who had volunteered their time in support of her, Elizabeth called her a deserter." He takes a deep breath. "called her a deserter in answer to a sincerely asked, straightforward question. I have to admit, I tried to ask questions like that several times. With me, Elizabeth wasn't so direct. She changed the subject or deferred my question. Still, I didn't speak up and note that others might have questions, and expect the thoughtful answers from one they respected. I didn't encourage Elizabeth to answer the question." Ben holds his head in his hands.

Zack's observations echo as Naomi sees the extent of the trial's damage on the parish. Though not seeing Elizabeth or interacting with her made it hard to know how she might have changed, what Ben said made her wonder and question even more. "So, what do you think will happen? I mean not just with the case, but with Elizabeth. Wow, one question piles on top of another. In either outcome, win or lose, which Elizabeth will remain? We want the inclusive, outward looking, spiritually inspired person we hired. After all our searching for a church, you know why we stayed at Saint Luke's?" They both nod. "Elizabeth Winter, right." She frowns. "I don't want to think about the Clare questions." She hesitates. "Or will she stay centered on herself, her own goals, and her own well-being? If she wins the trial, she could take the money, pay all the legal fees for the parish, and go back to her ministry work or she could take the money and go on a speaking tour never looking back and never thanking the parish for the support." Naomi's mouth drops. "If she loses, who knows? She could sue the Bishop directly; you never know what the lawyers will suggest next? And what about all the legal fees? I never thought about fees of that magnitude!" Zack's work situation stops her.

"If I were a betting man, I would say that we won't see Elizabeth again after the trial. It would surprise me if the Bishop still keeps the offer open at Queen of Peace. It would surprise me even more if she takes the Queen of Peace job." Ben shakes his head.

Naomi's face remains frozen. Then, she looks at Ben. "I want to know what you will do, now and about that letter of acceptance? Have you voiced your doubts to Elizabeth? What commitment have you made to her?"

"I've tried," he looks down at his phone. He lifts it to show Naomi, "but I haven't managed to talk to her without other people around. After the first time I tried, she avoids speaking to me alone. If I request time with her, she never gets back to me. 'I'll give you a call,' she'll say and then she doesn't. Does this sound familiar?" Ben shakes his head and puts his phone in his pocket. Then, he looks at Naomi. "I'm so sorry Naomi. I don't know why I didn't return your calls."

"It sounds like you did what she did." Naomi relies on their honest former relationship. "She didn't accept criticism. You suspected that I would criticize. I can't remember what messages I left? I was very confused and a little hurt. I probably didn't sound too inviting. So, you didn't call back."

"You're right," Ben says sadly. He smiles.

She nods and rocks back and forth. Hearing Ben's description and remembering the cauldron of feelings at the meeting gives her another perspective. "So many contradictions, we live in a parish where we invite participation, questions, and disagreement. We have our rituals that signify we want to function that way – Open Forum, open office doors, everyone on the altar, inclusive language in the liturgy. Then, someone closes a door – literally and figuratively. A part of the culture changes. We don't ask questions. We don't disagree; but we still act as if we invite participation, questions, and disagreement. We've done it as facilitators. We didn't question the breach of the process when Elizabeth decided to sue." Naomi sees Ben frown. "We did, but we didn't act on it. By not acting on the questions when no one answered us, we changed the culture. By not inviting parish into the sue or not decision, Elizabeth changed the culture. And now we may have huge debts and responsibilities at a time when factions have been built within the parish." She shakes her head. "Or maybe judging by Tony's comments tonight, existing factions have gained strength in their outrage." She remembers the group with Tony and shudders. "I'll bet most people in the parish have completely different
214

ideas than their pew mates. Different ideas depending on so many influences about: the trial, the Bishop, the parish meetings. We saw that tonight!" –" She stops. Tears form in her eyes. "You all, Elizabeth leading the way," She takes a breath. "spent all that time building trust in the parish meeting process specifically so that parishioners would know their opinions and ideas meant something. Tony's group doesn't trust anymore. Have we broken everything?" Ben nods looking away. "Now that I think of it - another example: Father Rogers wanted me to put the idea about a women's month on the agenda and have us vote on it tonight. I asked if he didn't want to allow the parish time to think it through – not that anyone would vote against it." She stops herself and realizes that people grumbled when Father Rogers presented the idea.

"Right – a good example both because you assumed everyone would agree and kind of forgot how the woman, we've been admiring for so long has disappointed us." He shakes his head. "And, further evidence of the breakdown, Father Rogers didn't plan to follow the process. He followed Elizabeth's example – just ram it through. It requires a delicate balance to invite participation, listen, and adjust. Who knows if we achieved it when we designed it, tested it and developed what we thought would preserve it? If we had it, we've lost that balance now!" He glances at his watch. "Wow, I should go."

Naomi looks at the clock, "I should be tired." She remarks. "But, maybe our friendship," she hesitates, "we can trust each other and build our friendship again?"

"Of course, if you can trust me again after all I have done," Ben replies.

"OK, we won't take this for granted. We will talk more. But not tonight." Naomi stands. They hug and she opens the door.

The trial started and stopped so many times that Elizabeth's desire to have it done transformed quickly to anger with each new delay. The diocese rejected many of the potential jurors. The court sent new letters to the next batch. Elizabeth's lawyer found many to reject in that group. During each stage of the trial, Elizabeth sat in the courtroom and listened. She conferred with Forsyth during the breaks or paced the floor in the lawyer's room. At night, she collapsed though she slept little. She kept a list of things Forsyth asked her to do and prepared for her own testimony. As the number of delays accumulated, the newspaper and TV stations lost interest in the trial and turned their attention to other stories. She continued to prepare for questions from the press but had few opportunities to use her prepared statements.

One morning after they completed jury selection, she arrives at the courthouse and finds herself in a long line at the security checkpoint. She waves at one of the guards she sees every day and asks if she can use the judge's line. She points to her watch. "My trial resumes at 9 AM." She smiles and waits for permission to change lines.

The guard nods yes. She leaves the line and approaches the judge's line. The guard's supervisor sends her to the back of the line, increasing her delay as she stands behind a group of students taking a tour of the court house. They jostle back and forth and follow the guard's instructions slowly. Ellen Scott appears in the line behind Elizabeth with her notebook in hand. At first Elizabeth doesn't see Ellen. Ellen recognizes Elizabeth right away and flips to a blank page in her notebook. Her cameraman stands outside. Ellen expects the jury in the criminal case she reports on to reach a verdict and wants to interview the lawyers when they leave the courthouse. Seeing Elizabeth reminds her to check on that case while she is at the courthouse. Elizabeth reminds herself of her practiced statements. Ellen writes notes. The clock moves past the hour. Elizabeth turns away from Ellen, takes a deep breath and waits.

Naomi

Naomi glances at her calendar when she hears the doorbell ring. Nothing. Seeing Ben on the porch, she takes a deep breath before opening and misses most of what he says as she takes his coat and they move to the family room.

"Listen Naomi, you know if <u>you</u> say no to her, that will just feed her resolve. She doesn't see any change in the bond she has with Elizabeth. For Clare, it remains and remains strong, maybe even stronger." He pauses before continuing. Boundaries, he wonders what boundaries to respect. Not finding an obvious answer, he presses on. "In fact, seeing your lack of support, it looks like that to her, she tightens her bond to Elizabeth, for sure." He barely looks at her for a reaction. "You're the mother. Right? The mother says, even suggests, the child rejects. Or not really?" Now, he watches Naomi wring her hands. He hesitates. Repairing their friendship scares him. He wonders if he has gone too far. She rubs her forehead. He wants this friendship back as much as he can remember wanting anything. He speaks more quietly. "Let me talk to her." She doesn't respond. She stops rubbing and wringing. She looks at him. "Just let me listen to her. I won't give her advice. I won't suggest, ask, reject, discourage, encourage, -" He takes a long breath. He smiles.

"Ben," she turns away and turns back, "you -" She shakes her head. "How is it that you seem to know how to communicate with my daughter better than I do?" She laughs. He laughs. "Wow, I've missed having you as a sounding board." She looks away and then back again. So many thoughts crowd in. "With Zack's problems at work, I'll have to catch you up on his work! You won't believe… Zack…Melissa… " Naomi feels torn. She sees evidence of their old friendship. It touches her. A tear forms. She remembers many long talks about Clare and Mark, before everything started to fall apart. Ben's words and sentiment always touched her, opened her eyes. Still she hesitates. Clare demands such detailed explanations and can't

217

understand why Naomi doesn't defend Elizabeth. She feels tired and challenged by all these problems without solutions. How to respond to Ben?

Ben's arrival at her door surprised Naomi. She greeted him with a hug and then felt the doubt that hovered over her since he disappeared. These accumulated doubts of the intervening weeks confused and plagued her. Juggling the emotions puts the brakes on her responses. She wavers between feeling glad to see him and comfortable in his presence and worrying about the pieces of her life that lack foundation she can depend on. In the old days, she would have poured out her worries to Ben. Yet, she doesn't know why he stopped communicating. She has more questions than she can count.

Ben remains quiet. Though he wants to help Naomi and do something to regain the friendship, he decides not to push. Elizabeth pushed him. The push caused him to forget his own priorities. He can't do that to Naomi. He tries to think of ways to express how he can help Clare. He sees that his support of Elizabeth and how she changed through the crisis allows him to speak more genuinely to Clare. He wonders how much to tell Naomi about this transformation in Elizabeth. He still doesn't quite understand it himself. He longs to blurt it out to Naomi. He waits.

He won't tell Clare things that will shock her. He knows he must edit the experience to find the highlights that Clare can understand. As he considers appropriate examples, he remembers the last witness meeting. He winces. Before all this, he would just tell Naomi everything. She would help him digest, find the highlights, and then trust him to convey caution to Clare. Trust, he decides, emphasizing trust as a foundation would help Clare understand. As he waits, the details start to surface more clearly. He remembers Elizabeth's insulting and dictator-like behavior in the meetings. Now the memories shock him. Why didn't he respond with shock then? Not having Naomi to talk with during that time resulted in choices that embarrass him. What he did, he realizes may have destroyed their friendship. He ignores the shards of the friendship with Elizabeth. Seeing the anguish on Naomi's face, makes him want that friendship back more than anything else. In the past, he wouldn't have hesitated to tell her about every insult of people Elizabeth supposedly respected. Naomi would have helped him find insight and wouldn't question his offer to speak with Clare now. He knows this is such a pivotal time for Clare. He sighs.

Ben, Naomi and Zack had observed the transformation in Clare during her time at Saint Luke's. Though Clare previously expressed interest in serving others when she grew up, meeting Elizabeth solidified those thoughts into following Elizabeth's path. Clare wants to become a priest. The Catholic Church doesn't ordain women. With all the upheaval at Saint Luke's, instead of turning away from her dream, she holds it tighter and can't understand why her mother expresses doubts about Elizabeth.

Naomi wants Clare to understand the impossibility of her goal without draining her of the enthusiasm that has transformed Clare over the Saint Luke's years. Elizabeth fed the enthusiasm. Now, Elizabeth sits in the middle of a controversy rooted in her quest for ordination. The controversy transformed Elizabeth into a person Naomi no longer recognizes. How can she explain something to her daughter she doesn't entirely understand herself?

Ben watches the emotions flow across Naomi's face. He sees doubt, fear, and anxiety. He reaches for her shoulder. "I don't see belief, comfort, or acceptance. Or not really?" He waits. "Maybe it would help if I told you more about Elizabeth as she acts today, in mostly unpleasant detail. If you get an idea of what I have seen, it might make sense to you. You might see, and hopefully believe, my current perspective. You know I have great respect for her. And I know your wisdom will guide me in what to say, how to say it. Then, maybe – " He waits. He wants to say *trust*. "Maybe you will agree to let me talk to her. Don't you see? Or?" He keeps his gaze on her face and waits.

She shrugs her shoulders. "I have this experience you don't have. And remember your role, one you put a high priority on, mother, including all the baggage you accepted on the day she emerged from your body and grew into this dynamic young lady. There will be things she doesn't want to say to you just because of your role as her mother!" Naomi nods. She looks at him. "And you have raised doubts about Elizabeth. What does Clare think about that? Because of the bright daughter you have raised, even at eight years old, we all know experiences like this can cause children to break from their parents. Part of growing up but..." Ben keeps his hand still. Naomi listens. "Some of the courses I took at the seminary teach us to just listen. It sounds easy but it's not. An emotional connection like a mother has makes conversations like this harder. Mother and daughter, talk about emotional connection!" She smiles. "Let me tell you, at eight years old, for goodness sakes, she has a long list of things she doesn't want to admit she doesn't know or knows and thinks you don't know or who knows what else!" He watches her warm to the idea. "I need this kind of practice." He chuckles. "Maybe it will even help me write a letter to the seminary to explain this journey to them." He shakes his head. "Unless they just decide to rescind my acceptance."

Naomi shakes her head. "Not likely." She takes a deep breath. "They've probably never seen such a long list of preparations or recommendations and with Saint Luke's only one part of all your qualifications." She wrestles with her doubts about her responsibilities as a mother. She smiles. "I don't know. It's a lot to ask of a friend." She watches his smile. "I know I don't want to hear all the details about Elizabeth. What I have heard shocks me enough. You imply that what I have heard leaves a lot out." Ben nods.

She sighs. "Yes, " she hesitates, "and no conditions. I trust you to talk to Clare. You can communicate what you know without the heavy hand of a mother. She needs that. And we agree on a private talk, a talk that you don't report back to me. Good practice for the seminary!" They nod and laugh. "Even though I believe it takes a village to raise a child, I forget at times like this and think I must solve, decide, and direct every detail of all the aspects of her life." They hug.

Sam

Dear Naomi,

The letters you wrote to me, do you have copies? Read what you have written, dearest friend!

I, you've rendered me wordless. I know, not a familiar aspect of the Sam Bonner you know. I started to analyze the path you have taken over this last year of church shenanigans. You still have my letters. I probably covered the points I would make again here about the dangers of religious organizations, especially hierarchal religious organizations.

And Clare, precious Clare, with so many more positive paths to follow in our world, steer her away from this one... Wake up Naomi Bowring Norton!

In the past, we had some rich exchanges on Buddhism, not without its own religious organization problems for sure. But, try to tap into something that quiets you so you can see better. I've rediscovered T. S. Eliot, a very spiritual man. Find a quiet moment, let go of all this drama.

Get The Four Quartets and read the whole thing. If you don't have time for the whole thing, which you really need, read the second one, Burnt Norton. Don't worry, nothing to do with your married name. Time!

Nough from,
Sam Bonner

Naomi

Naomi's dream shakes her awake. Windows without lights in neighboring houses tell her midnight has come and gone. She stands. Instead of the dream, Jeff's call relating what he found online confronts her. Hearing Jeff's voice, she expected him to ask about the shelter. But no, he described a blog he found with entries about the church in Texas where Elizabeth worked before she came to Saint Luke's.

Questions come to mind, questions she had not asked when he called. Her concerns about Lou and the Lombardo House guests distracted her, she remembers and wonders where her ability to concentrate has gone. Then, a phrase hits her from his story, "Forgotten is not forgiven." Slowly as she paces the halls and walks quietly downstairs, the details of the story emerge describing Elizabeth's departure from the Texas parish. Each new detail discards a detail she understood from Elizabeth's version of the story. The story's author, a parishioner in the Texas parish, published entries in a blog ending with Elizabeth's removal from her job. Now Naomi wished she had listened more closely. *Had Elizabeth read the blog? Did Elizabeth know the parishioner?* Jeff raised those questions and others without providing any answers.

The blog writer seemed to chronicle Elizabeth's entire time in Texas, "so many parallels to Saint Luke's", Jeff kept saying. Remembering the sound of his voice and more of the unanswered questions, she finds her computer to search for the blog. She combines Elizabeth's name and Texas to search for the blog. After several attempts, she finds the entries with Elizabeth's name. Scrolling through the entries, she reads oldest to most recent entries with amazement. The parallels with Saint Luke's accumulate as she follows the parishioner's experience from Elizabeth's arrival to her departure. Parishioners, especially the Spanish-speaking, applauded her arrival. "She brings new life to our parish. We even sing some of the songs in Spanish!" "Activities, both targeted at Spanish speakers and women, attract more parishioners." Naomi remembers their first visit to Saint Luke's. "Her energy, dedication, and insight inspire everyone. We attend Masses, meetings, and celebrations as never before." She feels tears form and leans back before reading more.

By the time dawn light streaks through the windows and touches her shoulder, she reaches the final entry. Things seemed to unravel in Texas when Elizabeth began preaching. An entry near the end of the blog encapsulates what Naomi has not yet found the words for:

> As parishioners lined up for or against Elizabeth, communication broke down among parishioners. Those who lost respect for Elizabeth led efforts against her. Those who supported her fought for her. People fought mostly with words creating disastrous effects. It took me a while to see that using *disastrous* to describe what happened to us fits the situation as much as it shocks me seeing that word on the page. Basic beliefs and values our community held have disappeared. Friends doubt each other as they find themselves on different sides. For and against Elizabeth turns out to be the tip of the iceberg. Old, not forgotten it turns out, affronts cloud the issue with Elizabeth and deepen disagreements. Some days I can't tell who believes what. Trust, an unspoken expectation for everything we did, has dissolved. It seems as if we live on a different planet – same language, different definitions!

The final entry, dated several years after the events, said simply: *Forgotten is not forgiven.*

After Naomi drags herself through breakfast, cleanup, and departures, she calls her best friend from college who invites her to visit.

"You're kidding?" Nancy turns from the stove. "I mean –" Expressions ripple across her face. The smile that gave Naomi relief when she arrived disappears. Naomi doesn't interrupt.

224

She waits for the familiar rhythm of their long friendship. Nancy starts to speak. Instead, she turns away. Then, words pour out with the tea water, "The last time I saw you? When? I don't remember. You talked non-stop, as usual, about that woman, about your homeless friend, about problems in the community... Did you talk about anything other than that church?" she hesitates, "I, well, I, frankly I stopped calling because I feared, I feared" she shakes her head "fundamentalists had kidnapped you! You talked about nothing else, not even your kids." She stops pouring before the cup overflows. "Not even your kids! I mean when do we not talk about our kids? Before we had them, we guessed their personalities, eye color, even the shape of their noses!" She sighs and stands looking down at Naomi trying to smile. She fails. "That did it for me!" She throws her hands up as high as the kettle in her hand allows and shrugs. "But really, Naomi, I would call you to have coffee or even go grocery shopping, even fundamentalists must go grocery shopping! Don't they?" Naomi can't find the words to respond. "And you, not only never had the time, didn't say a word about Clare or Mark, you also wouldn't stop talking about this situation with the Bishop and something or other with that woman, who I have to admit sounded like a self-absorbed, power-hungry, narcissist!" Nancy returns the kettle to the stove. The water splashes onto the burner.

Naomi's head drops to meet her hands. Nancy's words reverberate. *Is Elizabeth a power-hungry narcissist?* What seemed so obvious to Nancy months ago, now hits Naomi. Words from the Texas blog join Nancy's description. Naomi wonders how she missed what happened, whether Zack missed it, and lifts her head again with difficulty. Feelings of shock, embarrassment, and disbelief take turns consuming her attention.

"Now look what I have done?!" Nancy finds a sponge. Without turning back, she carefully wipes the area and dries it before trying to light the burner. Then, she dries the kettle and places it on the burner.

Finally, she returns to the table takes a sip of tea, and sighs. Still, she doesn't continue talking. Naomi scans Nancy's expression and body language and despairs that she may have lost a friend. They stir and sip.

"Speak to me Naomi," Nancy pleads. Without a pause, she continues talking. "We've hardly seen each other over the past year and I haven't, I couldn't – " She looks away. "but I couldn't stand all the talk about your church. Instead of looking forward to your calls, I only thought about avoiding you." She looks back and looks away again as Naomi's expression stops her. She smiles. "I did see you on the news now and then." A laugh that might have followed acknowledging their common distaste for public appearances disappears. She gets up and paces back and forth.

"Honestly, do you and your friends think only Saint Luke's helps the poor? Do you read the papers? And women! Remember where we live. You have visited Seneca Falls, right? Do other Catholic churches support women? Expand their roles? How about other churches in other denominations? It seemed like you, at least from what I saw on the news, and the other parishioners thought only your Saint Luke's helps the poor, only your Saint Luke's respects women?" She shakes her head and takes a deep breath. "Really, I didn't think I knew you anymore." Now she looks sad. "I felt like I lost my best friend."

Naomi stirs and regulates her breathing to avoid a surge she feels rising from her chest. Words of explanation accumulate. She remembers the family's desperate search for a church they could all agree on, the comfort of becoming part of the open community, the maturing of the children to recognize and respect people of all colors and income levels, and the conversations they all had at home exploring differences of all kinds. She wonders about the future, about helping the poor, about acquainting her children with the kind of diversity she missed as a child. She despairs that they will restart their search to replace what seems to have disappeared from Saint Luke's.

The potential loss of a best friend of so many years stops her robotic stirring. She wants to defend herself. Explanations arise but no words follow. The need to apologize consumes her. The longer Nancy rails on about the last year, the loss she only begins to recognize grows. She stops listening after each new example. She shuts the next words out. Stunned and shocked, her thoughts turn to Zack. *What did he say and not say? Or what did I not hear?* She can't think of anyone who knows her better than Zack and Nancy. She realizes how true it sounds, shockingly true. She looks at her hands, feels her face, and wonders if she looks different. The memory of seeing Elizabeth angry reminds her how different she looked in that mood. *Am I still Naomi Bowring Norton? Maybe Zack tried to tell me something like this?*

Her mind wanders back to college where they shared a room freshman year in college and formed a friendship that deepened during college and gained new dimensions as they worked, married and had children. Lots of adversity helped establish those ties. They both disliked, even hated, college social life dominated by drinking and drugs and all the variations fraternities could devise for becoming mindless. They went through the motions of the first few parties and found ourselves back in the dorm before everyone else. She remembers sitting on her bed looking at Nancy saying something like, *we could do better than this!* Nancy started to sing an *Alleluia*. After they recovered from a bout of laughter, they discovered their shared love of music.

They competed with each other to find every activity that involved singing - chorus, choir, and the theater productions. Studying consumed the rest of the time. They both attended church on Sundays, Naomi went to the local Catholic church and Nancy attended the Presbyterian church. The small-town congregations welcomed them, especially when they joined the choirs. As they walked to and from church, they listed all the problems with religion, giving equal time to all denominations.

"...and the TV? I know the news people, especially Ellen Scott, go for the jugular, paint everything in black and white, and create conflict if they can't find it. Your community comes out looking like blind, loyal fundamentalists on those broadcasts. My best friend, a fundamentalist?" Nancy dips a cookie into the tea. She shakes her head and continues. "You know," She throws her hands up, "of course you don't, because we haven't seen each other in a year! We've stopped going to church, completely." She shakes her head. "I wonder about the kids. We look to the church to help them learn ethics and morals and how to treat other people with respect. But then I look at the extra-curricular activities of some of these ministers. Why would I take my kids to church and then have to explain to them why a minister or priest abuses children or steals from the parish or whatever else they do while standing in the pulpit chastising us for doing what they do. Kids don't take long to see the contradictions! When they asked why we stopped going to church, I wanted to tell them we go to church to remind ourselves not to do things like the ministers we read about on the front page of the newspapers." She gets the kettle and pours more water in the cups. "Well, I didn't explain it to them exactly like that." She smiles. "If I were God, I would make religion a sin!"

Naomi smiles remembering those college evenings filling the teapot over and over as they relived the horrible fraternity parties, the disgusting forms of entertainment, the discovery of each other's shared resolve, the search for fun found in singing activities, and those walks ranting about religion. She wonders how she got to this point.

By senior year they had achieved a great balance. They didn't attend even a perfunctory fraternity party as they had in previous years. They sang together in the Catholic choir at the 5 PM Mass on Saturday and at the 10 AM service at the Presbyterian church on Sunday mornings. Luckily, each church held choir practice on different evenings. When the Easter season arrived and both churches added services, they faced some challenges. Luckily only a block separated the two churches. They could sing in one church, standing in the back row, slip out, and run the block to sing in the other. Weekday evenings they sang in the college chorus and the chapel choir on campus. Solos consumed the other evenings. She doesn't remember much about classes and studying, though they both graduated near the top of the class.

The memories of the roots of the friendship stir Naomi to listen to Nancy more intently. Examining the year and the church events fades. Nancy's perspective, while shocking, provides information she ignored. She knows she must talk to Zack to incorporate what Nancy has said and figure out how to function. She takes a deep breath and notices Nancy still has more to say. Nancy puts the kettle back on the stove and raises her voice. "And that Elizabeth Winter sounds like the perfect example you would never want your kids to see in action! And what about Clare? Such an impressionable age and such an admirer of Elizabeth, if I remember when you first joined the church? What about that precious daughter of yours?"

Naomi's neck muscles tense when Nancy says Clare's name. *I have kept my family the highest priority of my life. How can she even think that, let alone say it? Haven't I? I paid attention to the effect of all the turmoil on them. Zack and I took time to talk to the kids, make sure they understood. Zack wouldn't let me forget the family.*

She stops herself. She sees the new perspective in danger of leaking away. Another breath and some resolve forms to repair their friendship and figure out what to do about Saint Luke's. Clare must take her full attention. Ben's offer to talk with Clare becomes all the more urgent. She wonders if he has spoken to her yet. Then, she reminds herself to make sure she hasn't missed any fallout from all the turmoil that might affect Mark?

She feels the tears welling in her eyes. She manages a smile and a nod. While confusion and resolve change places in her thoughts, she knows she holds the sole responsibility to figure it out. Nancy sips her tea and changes the subject. She drifts in and out. She hears Nancy mention her kids, husband and parents. She forces herself to concentrate and listen but her thoughts overwhelm her. Again she reviews their reasons for joining Saint Luke's and tries to explain how so many cracks in the loving community appeared in the wake of Elizabeth's transfer and rejection of that change.

She still hopes that the community can find its way back to the trust and values that drew them to join. But she also wonders if it is too late.

Forsyth

Forsyth notices the last of the employees walking toward the elevator. He widens his pacing from his office to the hallway. Seeing the elevator door close, he continues to the reception area and stops at the bank of windows. His gaze lingers on the distant hills south of Stanton. He weighs the situation. *If she backs down this time, I drop the case. I need the exposure of a case like this for my career and I must win. If I don't get the kind of cooperation that allows me to build a strong case, I can't win.* He tries to list the missing conditions to achieve his goal. He considers sitting down with her to explain how these things work, again. She sees the end, but the end as if they could beam themselves there. He wonders if she has already planned her ordination. He knows long term goals work to motivate people like her and winning this case moves her in that direction. He hasn't convinced her to focus on the many steps required to reach that long term goal. He despairs at the number of steps that lie ahead, a number he avoids counting as he nudges her toward the first step. These steps require that same laser focus she applies to ordination. He turns back toward his office, sits at his desk and wonders if a list would get her attention. He picks up his pen to start the list. *She's such a brilliant woman with an astute appreciation for strategy, why can't she understand this?*

His pen hovers as he wonders how many lawyers the Catholic Church employs worldwide. He suspects a good number of them already know about this case, at least those working for the New York dioceses. The Stanton diocesan lawyers probably have received counsel especially from those involved in cases like this. He drops his pen and turns to his computer to research similar cases. An institution like the Catholic Church hasn't existed this long without legions of experienced protectors of their heritage and wealth. He counts on some over confidence gained from all their past successes to work in their favor.

Winning a case against even a small diocese of the Catholic Church presents a significant career opportunity for him. A little world attention of a positive nature will surely influence his move to Manhattan. First, he wins this little case. Next, word of the win spreads. At the point someone advises the diocese to appeal, word of Dixon, Grossmann, and Peak's work, accomplished by him, should reach headquarters in Manhattan. Then, he requests that transfer. But he has to win before all that can happen for him. He thinks about his personal goals. An aggressive, savvy person like her might even give him some advice. All strategies, now, point toward understanding the importance of this first step. With understanding should come responsive, unquestioning actions on her part.

He has his own experience of misjudging absolute power at DGP. Looking back, he sees he should have seen the big picture from the first interview. He wonders if he missed a Law Firm Politics course in law school. When you have the power, you can do anything. He didn't need a course to know that, but he thought he had it. He had the cards to play. However, he didn't think about, guess or even try to find out what cards the partners, especially the Stanton partners, had. A colossal misjudgment! Now it seems so clear, he didn't factor the objectives of the partner without the prestigious degree he had worked so hard to secure. In addition, he dismissed him, his current boss, as a threat because of his University of Stanton law degree. Light only dawned when he opened his assignment letter sending him not to Manhattan, but to Stanton. His first political lesson! He thought his work with the Harvard and Yale partners during law school created an ironclad advantage. But his boss didn't play the alma matter cards. Or he did, but his boss played poker while Forsyth thought he had a bridge partner to give him the advantage.

Now his goals align more closely with his boss who hopefully wants major successes from this office to bank what power he has for the future. At the current level of press coverage, the case could benefit DGP, the boss and hopefully him. He stops and sees another possibility. Winning the case could motivate his boss to keep him in Stanton. He gives himself the advice he has tried to give Elizabeth: *first the case. Win the case.*

If she doesn't respond now, what do I do? If he doesn't win this case, he has no basis to request a transfer. Now he considers that train of thought. He can't waste time on this case without a high probability of winning. At the rate she seems to lose idol status among the parishioners, dropping the case would give him more time to reassess his options. He guesses, "I'm getting another lawyer," might come sooner than he expects. Then, he could make a comfortable exit without too much of a loss professionally. Still, she impresses him with her stamina and determination, but the dwindling support certainly raises questions. So far, he hasn't seen the magnetism people describe when they talk about her. He thinks about her diaries hoping they will give him a more rounded assessment. He will look for life-long goals and characteristics like her determination. On the other hand, he has the homilies which impressed him. No, he convinces himself, he needs both. He can't misjudge the challenge facing him.

The jury must conclude the diocese chose to fire a loyal, hardworking, and inspired pastoral administrator. She has exceeded the diocesan job description. They have those facts in the folder he has on his desk. Glowing reviews by her pastor, diocesan leaders, and the Bishop describe her as not only doing her job, but also inspiring others (volunteers, staff, priests) to stretch themselves to new levels. Some of those people express a willingness to testify on her behalf. Unfortunately, no one from the diocese returns his phone calls. Just one person would strengthen the case. He jots a note to try them again.

He leaves his office to circle through the dark corridors and thinks about her family, none of whom he has met. People always write about other family members in their diaries. Questions pile up: why won't her youngest brother testify in her favor? Jay, she has mentioned him numerous times. She said she raised him after their mother died, encouraged, guided, and felt support from him about pursuing ordination. Her father, in sharp contrast, spoke against her ideas, especially the idea of becoming an ordained priest in the Catholic Church. Without any first-hand confirmation of what she has told him, it makes him wonder. He needs a family member. He returns to his desk.

He sees the light blink on his phone. He presses the button hoping she has left a message. *Will you deliver for me Elizabeth Winter?*

His pen hovers as he hears that she will deliver <u>some</u> of the diaries, not this evening but tomorrow morning. *OK, she does not understand.*

He sits down to spell it out, step by step. He will create that list, maybe a table. He will place the steps in the first column. The other column answers the question Why? He considers a third column with the consequences of skipping a step. For everything, especially this diary, he must choose which entries and which parts of an entry will support the case. While he might choose the same selections she makes, he will need the background which she might deem unnecessary. The background allows him to overcome the diocesan lawyer's accusations with facts! He has to guide her to see the importance of the information he seeks and she seems to hold back, to achieve their common goal of winning the case. Again, he wonders what makes her tick. He loses confidence that he can prevent some unanticipated outburst that might blow the case apart.

Leaving the chart at the hand-drawn stage, he wonders about her first job. She didn't give him any reviews from that job. He types an email to a partner law firm requesting information about the Texas parish. Texas raises questions as he types. He can't ask why she took a job in Texas when she grew up in New York. The local law firm can find out more local history and perhaps he can ask her in person at their next meeting, at least see her facial expression if she stalls. All her siblings live here, a supportive family or so she says. She knows the churches. Perhaps she didn't choose Texas. He doesn't know how people get jobs in the church. Maybe she applied to churches here and they didn't hire her. He would never have chosen Stanton when all the plum assignments and potential for big salaries happen in Manhattan. He has connections and could use them in every aspect of the job. The who-has-the-power question haunts him. He needs more information to help assess their chances.

Maybe parishes in this diocese saw her as too outspoken. The local parishes might have categorized her efforts in divinity school as training to become a potential trouble maker. The diaries will help with that. He considers researching diocesan policies and communications as well as looking into the legal databases. Since the diocese would also have access to that same information, he sees the importance of pursuing this research. If he doesn't find anything, the diocese couldn't surprise him. If he finds evidence that the real Elizabeth Winter differs from the stories she tells, he can prepare responses that contradict whatever the diocese claims. A person who goes to school, participates in national organizations, strives for a goal which requires lots of like minds must have left evidence of her early endeavors. One thing in her favor, she understands the importance of the press. He hopes she sent all those press releases.

Forsyth parks his car near the divinity school chapel. As he locks the car door, he imagines his mother's response if she witnessed this visit. Fainting crosses his mind. The quiet and the simple lines of the chapel's architecture impress him, such a contrast to his office in the city or the courthouse bustling with people and security guards where he spends so much time. Since he has arrived early, he lingers outside and then enters the chapel. The cool silence surrounds him as he enters through the main door. He stands under the entry arch. He feels no impetus to go farther. The silence seems to envelop him. He senses a nudge to move, but his feet remain planted. He hears organ notes coming from above. He lingers until the organist stops.

Before he notices, his appointment time with the head librarian has come and gone. He turns and finishes a slow walk around the chapel and heads for the library. Uncharacteristically, he doesn't compose a list of excuses for his lateness but simply apologizes. The librarian accepts the apology efficiently, asks what information he wants. After he explains, she, points him to the area of the library containing school publications. She recognizes Elizabeth's name, "quite an energetic student, as I recall." She doesn't offer any additional information or indicate reading about the current Elizabeth and her struggle with the diocese. She also doesn't ask for any identification or the reason for the search. He wonders if his lateness made her forget. She disappears into her office to take a call and he goes to the publications she recommends – the divinity school newsletter and the diocesan weekly newspaper. He checks with the reference librarian to find Elizabeth's final paper later published by Notre Dame Press. She also indicates that the bookstore may have copies for sale. "Very few of our students have their work published by Notre Dame. The bookstore features publications of former students and faculty."

News articles about her participation in Call To Action at national conferences, divinity school newsletter blurbs about her work with the homeless in the city, and announcements of her high grades all support the stories Elizabeth told him. He reads the title of her final paper on the rise of the Spanish-speaking populations across the country and decides not to buy it or even thumb through the pages. As he closes his notebook, he sees a list of short pieces on seminary graduates. The entry announcing Elizabeth's job in Texas ends with a quote from two pastors in Stanton who had hoped to hire Elizabeth.

The library trip kills the theory of sharing the distinction of an unwanted first job with her. It also makes the initial question of why she started in Texas more urgent. A woman like her with such clear goals and studied understanding, or at least attempts at understanding, this complex structure of a diocese within the Catholic Church would not choose Texas randomly. So, he asks himself, again, why Texas?

The chapel lures him in again and he listens to starts and stops as an organist practices. The small chapel holds and molds the organ music in a way he has never experienced. He pulls out his phone considering whether to take a selfie for his mother or record the sound. His phone rings.

He sees an unfamiliar number on the screen, "Monteith Forsyth here."

"Hi, this is Jay Winter. Did you call me?" He hesitates and reaches for his notebook. "Who are you? Maybe a wrong number?"

He takes a breath and wonders which question to ask Jay knowing that he might shut down when he makes a connection to the case. He wants to gain his confidence and find someone, especially a family member, to speak openly about Elizabeth. He decides on honesty, "Jay thank you for returning the call." He looks up at the small stained-glass window above the altar. Light carries the colors to the simple stone floor at his feet.

"So, you meant to call me. Who are you?"

"Sorry Jay. I'm standing in the chapel here at the divinity school mesmerized by the light when I should not waste your time." The light holds his attention. "I'm sure you've visited here. I haven't, please excuse my distraction." He returns his attention to this opportunity. "Jay I'm representing your sister in the upcoming trial against the diocese."

"Oh" he hears sadness in Jay's soft voice.

"I know she asked you to testify on her behalf. I'm calling to ask you questions that will help me understand her better." Jay doesn't respond. "She says you have expressed hesitations. I'm not calling to convince you to testify." He hears Jay's breath exhale. "Your sister seems like an amazing woman. I just need another first-hand perspective to help me formulate a good case."

Elizabeth

On the ride in the elevator, Elizabeth adjusts her jacket and hair. She rehearses her words to Forsyth avoiding any kind of apology. She skips the receptionist and walks directly to his office. "I have the materials you requested."

Without looking at his face or waiting for his response she spreads the papers out on his desk and points to the labels for each pile. "In addition, I wrote descriptions of all the witnesses including how I have worked with them and their strengths." She points to the description of Ben. "Knowing a little more about each one will give you some ideas of how to approach them and where to place them in the trial. Ben will provide the best perspective, maybe our lead witness. He plans to enter the seminary soon, a good inside kind of witness. But he has attended and belongs to Call To Action (CTA), the Catholic group of parishioners, priests, and nuns who espouse more roles for women in the church." She sees Forsyth reach for the witness list and glances at his face. She matches his smile with hers.

"Good and did we get any press coverage this week?" Forsyth hands her his monthly invoice and opens his press folder.

"I don't think we did." She stuffs the invoice in her purse, opens her press folder and turns over several pages.

"Did you send any releases out?" Forsyth turns to his computer.

She sees the faxes she prepared to send and realizes she didn't send them. "Oversight on my part. Sorry. Should I send these this week or –?"

"Let's review them when we finish and see what we might want to revise."

She looks through other papers and sees the letter from Father Rogers.

"Looks like an important letter?" Forsyth sees the parish letterhead.

"Father Rogers sent it. He wants me to go on retreat." She holds the letter, moves to place it in her folder, and shakes her head. A frown forms as she imagines how Father Rogers probably pays little attention to day-to-day parish activities, evidence of which she saw on her desk the last time she visited the office. His dependence on her to keep him up to date should result in criticism of her. Instead, he suggests a retreat. She smiles, "I do appreciate the thought, sweet really. Also, he offers to have the parish pay for it. We never do that." Forsyth takes the letter and reads. She watches resting her hand on his table ready to receive it back. "We have always agreed that we won't spend parish money on ourselves." She smiles and reaches for the letter. He holds the letter and scratches his forehead. "He just returned from a retreat in New Mexico. Looks like he sent it from there." She points at the date on the letter. "Have you ever done a retreat?" He puts the letter down. She picks it up and reads, or pretends to read. As he talks, she slides it toward the folder. He retrieves it and puts it on his folder.

"No. No, I haven't. I remember hearing my mother talk about trying to convince my father to join her on a retreat. I don't think she ever convinced him. He grew up without any religious connections. Am I right to assume it involves a lot of prayer and quiet?" He turns his full attention to her. She admires that direct style of communication.

"Retreats sew your spiritual life together." They laugh. "You let go of daily life and invite God in. Really you remind yourself that God is in charge." He doesn't respond. He hides his thoughts well.

"It sounds like something my mother would have loved." He looks out the window. "Have you responded to Father Rogers?"

"No, but I don't see how I can go now." Her jaw drops as she wonders what he is thinking.

"Let's see those press releases." He skims through the pile of unsent releases and pushes them aside. "Let's not send any of those." He takes a clean sheet of paper and reaches for a pen. "A retreat might put some of those wobbling parishioners' back on our list of committed witnesses." He smiles. "We require more people on that list. We know situations will arise that remove witnesses as the trial progresses. The more names on that list, the more our confidence builds." He nods. She nods in response. He speaks as he writes, "Try this: a headline like – dedicated church worker prepares for trial through prayer – what do you think?"

"Elizabeth. Wow great to hear your voice and – Well I'm not sure I can help you. Could we get together? I need more information. I haven't talked with you since I picked you up at the airport. When did you return? Are we talking years?" She slams the delete button on the answering machine.

She opens the shade in the living room. Somehow the apartment feels darker hearing that brother who she brought up, listened to, encouraged – that brother! That brother not saying the simplest thing. The only thing. *Yes. Yes, I will help you. Yes, I owe it to you. Yes - unconditionally.* But no. He wants some background. She can't believe he could have missed background from the newspaper, the television, and the rumors! Though she admits if he relies on rumors, he certainly does not know the true story.

The panic of the last days in Texas increases her pacing. She knows she must eliminate panic. Breath after deep breath she reassures herself that only she can elevate this issue to exact a solution, the only solution. Panic hovers. With renewed effort to push the panic away, she counts accomplishments. A ripple of anger threatens as she remembers how she taught Jay to quell anger, step back and consider the positive aspect of a difficult situation. She begins her list: conference organizers invite her to present at prestigious conferences, she convinced the Bishop to allow women on the altar as readers, she helped grow two parishes by emphasizing causes vital to the parishioners served, like inclusion of the largest population of Spanish speakers in every aspect of parish life. She notes her work with advocates around the world on many projects aimed at solving these global Catholic issues. She has vision that no one else has. Jay, of all people, knows this about her.

Despair creeps back. She turns on more lights. She can't fathom Jay refusing support! They both support this cause. Raising the level of women in the Catholic Church, Jay always encouraged her. *Doesn't he see this opportunity will make this cause a reality?* Win this lawsuit. Not complicated to figure out. And who better to verify her capabilities, her honest attention to the cause, her careful acknowledgement of boundaries? Who better?

She paces again slowly: hall, living room, bedroom, kitchen, bathroom, and one more time. She turns on more lights. She can't give up. She needs a hook. She hasn't kept regular contact with Jay since she returned to Stanton but their relationship has deep roots.

She stops. Guilt! She hasn't tried guilt. It worked in the past. She knows she can work on Jay, but it strikes her that a better result might happen if Forsyth took charge laying guilt on Jay. She takes a few breaths. She smiles. A glance at her watch tells her, as she dials his number, that he probably sits busy at his computer within reach of his phone.

"Forsyth here. Elizabeth?" he has such an efficient manner. She loves it.

"So, Jay hasn't returned my call." She must persuade him that only he, with the ultimate tool (though she won't name it), can secure Jay as a key witness. "He knows me the best. With all his education, he can articulate my qualities so anyone can understand. As I told you, I brought him up after my mother died. He needed a lot of emotional support and encouragement. I did all that." She doesn't hear the keyboard. A good sign. "He shares my conviction that women should have a larger role in the Catholic Church: leadership, responsibility and, of course, ordination. Jay supports that. Jay belongs to Call To Action. Jay knows the issues. Just appeal to him with all your authority!" She smiles expecting his agreement. She wonders if he recognizes that his operative technique should employ guilt.

"We're not in a good place if you, his sister, can't convince him to support you."

"But –" she can't believe, maybe he didn't get the whole guilt thing from his Catholic mother? He has more to say.

"Why? I'm asking myself, why?" She can hear a frown in his voice. "Lots of whys: because he doesn't attend Saint Luke's? Lacks the details?" A pause and he continues, "Because he has questions? What questions? Have you answered them?" Her mind wanders searching for alternatives. Persuading him to deliver guilt fades as a strategy. "These questions trouble me. Elizabeth?" She hears his chair squeak. "Perhaps you can see how I might doubt your story." He pauses. She remains expressionless while options disappear from her mind. "I can't doubt. Doubts jeopardize my ability to represent you well. And win this case." Another pause. "An objective I thought we shared?"

She feels larger waves of despair surging up and finds no words to answer him.

"In my experience, this kind of witness tends to present unwelcome surprises when placed on the stand to testify. We can't afford that, especially with the turmoil I hear among the parishioners. The family witness must show unwavering support and, in your case, we need blindingly energetic enthusiasm from a family member. We want that from your parishioners. Now, I have my doubts about them. A hesitant family member?"

Her despair builds to rage. She freezes.

"Have you considered asking one of your sisters?"

Eyebrows, which luckily he can's see, arch up at the thought of her sisters who follow every single rule the Catholic Church creates without a question. She remembers uncomfortable conversations with them together and individually when she asked about their views on priests abusing children. That conversation ended when they responded with concern about how the church treated the poor priests. They said nothing about the children! They have children! Blind loyalty? Yes. The Catholic Church demands, they obey. She can't see how they could become candidates to support her or her causes.

"Oh, and what happened about the retreat? Did you schedule it?" He pauses. "Don't send that press release until the day you return."

The thought of finding another lawyer, a woman, crosses her mind. She questions why she didn't find a woman lawyer originally. It seems so obvious that would make a difference though DGP had the reputation, they didn't employ any women lawyers. He suggests her sisters! She writes a note to look for a woman lawyer. She writes CTA next to the note and her spirit lifts. She takes a breath. "We will have no surprises with my sisters on the stand." She wonders if getting one of them to agree, might prove easier. They have expressed some admiration for her achievements in the past. "I hadn't thought about them. But they may have just what I need." She brushes aside her disdain for their unblinking dedication to the Catholic Church. "Any one would consider them to be very good Catholics. Let me see what I can do." And they have consistently criticized everything she does behind those always-find-something-nice-to-say compliments. She resolves to call Jay.

She paces another round in the apartment. The phone rings. She sees Father Rogers number. She goes to the bathroom and closes the door while he leaves his message. She admires her hair, brushes it through and adds a little conditioner to control the frizz. When she hears the beep indicate the end of a message, she decides to change her blouse. She reminds herself that she should only wear pale colors. She checks herself in the hall mirror and approves. She reaches the phone and dials Jay's number.

"Elizabeth."

"Jay."

"I – good, great to hear your voice. I have a thousand questions. I – "

"I have one."

"I got your message. I – Can you come over? Can we meet some place? I haven't talked to you in so long. I need to see you, Elizabeth." He speaks quickly.

She feels her teeth clench. She takes several breaths

"I – Well, I've seen a lot in the newspaper, on television. I don't understand. I –"

She can't hold it any longer. "Stop Jay! Jay Winter, you owe me this. You owe me this! Remember who stood behind you every step of the way through school. Who convinced that scholarship committee at Boston College to give you the money you needed?" She feels the heat on her neck. "I've never asked you for anything. Never! The Catholic Church won't fire me again!" Her throat aches. She resists an urge to hang up. She barely hears his reply.

She hears something about *consideration of others*. He asks several times what she wants him to do. And *examining patterns*, she catches that. *What did I learn after getting fired in Texas?* Oh, and *blind loyalty*, He questions her asking him for blind loyalty. She thinks of family and the unique bonds of their relationship, an appropriate place for blind loyalty. She wants to say these things. He leaves no pauses. She can't concentrate on that quiet, tempered voice. She doesn't hear her sweet, logical Jay. She wonders what happened to him. She hangs up. She sees Forsyth's point. She doesn't need that at the trial, the youngest, ungrateful brother taking out stored aggression in the courtroom. She gives Forsyth credit for anticipating that possibility.

She reconsiders her sisters. She thinks she can handle Susie. If she can follow Catholic Church rules, she can follow what Forsyth tells her to say. Elizabeth can't remember her saying a critical word about anyone in public. Sitting in the witness chair will bring out her good side. Forsyth can build on her hollow compliments. She leaves a message and invites Susie to lunch at The Country Table. Susie always liked that restaurant, a good location outside the city, where fewer parishioners tend to visit.

"Give me everything you have." She deletes Forsyth's message and paces to the kitchen and back to the phone. She gathers her hair, pulls it up and pushes it into a knot leaving strands dangling. She thinks back to what she told him about the diaries and remembers her emphatic rejection of his idea to

244

use the diaries. She gave him all her homilies, except the one that pushed Father Flaherty to fire her. Forsyth doesn't understand enough about Catholic liturgy, let alone Flaherty's crazy preaching schedule, to notice a gap. And, Flaherty never kept copies of his own homilies let alone anyone else's. She gave him all the letters of praise from Call To Action officers, even the very reserved letter from Father Flaherty after the first year.

She tucks strands of hair behind her ear, paces the whole apartment conscious of magazines out of place, towels hung without folds, and the overflowing laundry basket. She stops. Something in the tone of his voice on that voicemail sounds desperate. She hasn't heard him sound desperate. She knows they can't take that tone into the courtroom. He knows that. Thoughts tumble into words: *I need this trial to make my ordination more, much more, than just a Catholic cause. Only I can do this. Though merely a start, nothing for women's ordination will happen without me. That's one point I can't seem to pound into his head!*

Diaries! Again she asks how the diaries can help. She made several attempts to get those diaries, at least mentally. Something always prevented her from getting into the car and driving to the storage facility. She dreads the task of reading through and editing which ones to give him and which ones to withhold. Not only does it require time but weighing the impact of what she will find on a jury presents the biggest barrier. Just thinking about that task always stops her before she even looks for the keys to the storage locker. She can't have her image tarnished by random musings from the past. This campaign can't have a single loophole, certainly not now, not when everything hangs on the right outcome of this trial.

She vows not to answer the ringing phone or stand close enough to see who calls. She considers unplugging the phone but fears that will prevent callers from leaving messages. Forsyth again? Or Jay? She approaches the phone and sees Forsyth's number. She turns from the phone, looks at the clock and calculates options. She could stay up all night and read the diaries. Since she doesn't sleep, she might get through most of them. The only way to ensure Forsyth gets the right information boils down to reading and choosing. She knows only she can make those choices. She tries to remember the life events Forsyth suggested would paint a picture of her for the jury. He mentioned teenage romances. She grabs her trial folder to see if she took notes about other life events. She didn't. She writes down teenage romances and calculates though she had few, finding them will require reading every diary.

Seeing the late hour, she knows Forsyth will have left the office. She plans her call without listening to his latest message. Then, she retrieves his voicemail, takes another breath, and smiles as she leaves him a message "I'm on my way to the storage facility right now. I'll drop those diaries off at your office tomorrow."

After weeks of no sleep, she drifted off and stayed asleep the whole night! She wakes up surrounded by the diaries on the living room couch. The clock tells her Forsyth has already arrived at the office. He won't expect the diaries now, but she might only have a few hours before he starts calling.

She reaches for the open diary on her lap wondering what might have bored her to sleep and sees the entry describing John, her first boyfriend. Fifth grade John loved her red hair. She reads the entry and tags it. She remembers seventh grade Tom but can't find anything about him in the diary except the day she broke up with him. She guesses that counts as a romance entry. She can't remember what ever attracted her to Tom. He never showed as much interest in her as she did in him. It seemed like an accomplishment to break up with him before he did it to her. She realizes this aspect of romance sounds a little harsh and cold-hearted. Then, she thinks if she doesn't include that last page, it reads like a normal teenage breakup. She tags that and writes a note on the tag about the last page.

She hadn't calculated the editing time and she wants it to look like sampling not editing which takes more time. Surely, he will see the wisdom of not giving him three boxes of diaries covering fifteen or twenty years. He won't have the time to sift through them. He will appreciate all the work this culling will save him.

She reaches age fourteen and finds the day of Mother's death.

> Today Mother died. Father B called and asked about funeral arrangements. Our father couldn't, No, he wouldn't take the phone call. He just stared at me and walked out of the room. Jay, sitting nearby in the kitchen, heard me plead with Father. Jay started crying. I told Father B we would call back. I sat with Jay. I don't remember anything he said. I have to forget my own sadness. I have to forget. I just remember saying to him, we will plan Mother's funeral. I asked him if he remembered her favorite readings and what songs she liked. He calmed down gradually. I took a pad of paper. I knew how much the church meant to Mother and thought how I'd like to have her remembered. As Jay wiped his tears, he named songs – *On Eagles Wings, Amazing Grace.* I found the program for our grandmother's funeral tucked in the back of the pad Mother used for grocery lists. Its worn edges reminded me how often, Mother pulled it out and brought her own mother back by rereading it. With a glass of milk and cookies to fortify us, we listed all the songs, readings and who would do them on the pad. Instead of calling Father B, we walked over to the church and gave Father B our plan. He thought our Father wrote it. We just smiled. Something told me that if we told him we did it, he might not have believed us, and worse, he would have rejected our suggestions. We had a laugh on the walk home.

She chooses earlier years to look for more romances. Finding none, she places the first diaries back in the box and moves forward in her life. Lots of entries about taking care of her siblings show her dedication to family. She finds many entries where she wrote about Jay and remembers how close they became as they struggled through those first years after their Mother's death. The entries where she tries to set an example for Susie and Mary show the beginnings of her passion for guiding young people through challenges in their lives. They also floundered after Mother died and missed the patience Mother had for their silliness, something she could never quite tolerate. She tags those and leaves out the complaining entries about Father as he turned more inward and left family responsibilities to her. Reviewing the entries, she has tagged for Forsyth, she removes the tags for the entries expressing impatience with Susie and Mary.

When Forsyth calls, she realizes afternoon has replaced morning. He has an evening function and can't wait for her to deliver the diaries today but would appreciate having them first thing in the morning. She assures him, not knowing how or where she can copy the sections, he will have them first thing in the morning. He defines that as 7 AM; and she agrees, smiling through the unanswered copying questions.

The afternoon disappears as she ignores more phone calls from Saint Luke's and reads on deciding to include the entry on college graduation and her valedictorian address. Father's comment at the reception: "Women will never be ordained" stays along with her quest to convince him about the importance of women's ordination. Knowing how many other Catholics held, and still hold, views like his in some form or another, still motivates her to find convincing arguments. That marked a turning point for her. If she could convince Father, she could convince anyone.

Though she knows Forsyth will question her choices from the diaries, she stops with the entry on the day Father died.

Father died today. We all struggled in the last months because he suffered so much pain and nothing the doctors prescribed seemed to touch it. Jay and I shared the care duties and heard many stories of his life, some repeated. Jay didn't know Father almost became a priest or that the article Jay left for him last year inspired Father to enroll in the program for becoming a deacon. He wanted to keep it secret, until he assured himself he could do it. And he had lots of questions about whether he measured up to all the requirements. If he had lived, the diocese would have tapped him to train future deacons. He just glowed with passion this last year even through all the health struggles. He would have made a great deacon. In his last moments Jay and I heard him encourage us both to follow our dreams. Those words meant a lot to me because I realized a part of him didn't want me to be disappointed. Even though in his mind no possibility existed for my ordination, he, in some way, acknowledged my dream. Through much of my life I read his negativity as criticism. I fought to do the things he objected to or criticized not realizing the protective part of those warnings. Just hearing him say, follow your dreams, inspired me in a whole new way.

First challenge on this quest: convince Father B that I will deliver the homily at the funeral. I'll rely on Jay to help me with that.

He will miss Susie's wedding and his first chance for grandchildren. When things settle down, Mary will surely announce her engagement.

She looks at the clock and thinks about copying.

The church! She can count on an empty office and no one using the copier. She gathers the tagged diaries and puts them in two canvas bags, hardly a full representation of her life but the right one. She goes to the church office, ignores the pile of messages and papers on her desk and turns on the copier. An hour of copying accomplishes the task and she finds used envelopes to label for Forsyth's copies.

Forsyth

People amble back into the courtroom fanning themselves. The jury members returning from their air-conditioned jury room look refreshed. Heat penetrates every other room in the court house. Observers walk to their seats muttering about the heat and wiping sweat from their faces. Elizabeth and Forsyth sit erect at their table, suit jackets on, and faces dry. The diocesan lawyers nod to each other, consult papers, and take notes. Murmurs float from some observers, but everyone else remains quiet.

Conversations halt abruptly when the judge returns from the lunch break. He walks briskly from his chambers and takes his seat. In the respectful silence, he requests a meeting with the lawyers in his chambers. He indicates that the meeting will be brief and directs the jury to remain in place. Elizabeth stands to accompany Forsyth. He indicates she should remain in her seat. She frowns, sits down, and looks at her papers. The lawyers follow the judge to his chambers. Murmurs resume. People fan themselves and remove scarves, hats, and sweaters. Some stand, walk, and seek a cooler corner waving papers to create a breeze. Murmurs become longer conversations. Elizabeth fidgets, turns papers over, and moves her pen randomly underlining witness names in Forsyth's notes. The short time extends to half an hour and then forty-five minutes. The court guard assigned to the jury invites the jury to return to their room. He remains at the door and checks on them frequently to monitor their conversations. His presence prevents conversation about the trial. Their exit produces a few mumbles about tax dollars and air conditioning. More people pace. Other people leave the court room. Elizabeth fidgets. She finds it difficult to sit quietly with a blank expression on her face as Forsyth instructed. The noise and movement give her some ability to shift her position and straighten her jacket. Her suit makes her look professional. Hiding the discomfort of the heat and the weight of the jacket becomes more challenging.

After an hour of waiting, she begins to pray the rosary. It comes easily to her - she chooses the Sorrowful Mysteries. She uses her fingers to count the *Hail Marys* and pauses to reflect on each mystery. The familiarity and repetition help her to stop fidgeting and maintain a neutral expression. Time passes. She doesn't look at her watch. The prayers consume all of her attention with the familiar rhythm of the words and the sequence of mysteries nudging the courtroom and the trial out of the way. Eventually even the whispers and additional chatter, fade from her awareness.

When the clock on the city tower strikes the hour, an observer approaches a guard and questions him. Two hours have passed. The guard shrugs his shoulders in response. Then a clerk enters from the judge's chambers and whispers to the guard. The guard opens the jury room door and summons the jury members. Slowly, they return to the courtroom and take their seats.

The chatter disappears. Elizabeth stops in the middle of a *Hail Mary*. The judge enters, takes his place, and remains standing. When the lawyers reach their places, he reads a short statement. Then, he adds several comments while he looks directly at Elizabeth. Elizabeth remains expressionless. She waits for the next witness and further interrogation. She doesn't process the judge's words though she meets his gaze and nods. People mutter and stand.

Forsyth repeats the judge's words quietly to Elizabeth through the rustling of papers and movement in the courtroom. "The trial has concluded." He waits to see those words register. "We agreed with the diocese to drop the case."

As Forsyth's words sink in, the judge thanks the jury and the clerks. The sound of his hammer meeting the desk closes the case. People shuffle from the courtroom questioning each other. "What happened?" "Why would the diocese drop the case?" "Why would she drop the case?" They glance at Elizabeth who sits frozen. She still holds the finger that counted the last *Hail Mary*. She remains sitting, stunned. Anger and confusion increase her heartbeat causing the skin on her neck to redden. The color moves up her chin to her cheeks. Forsyth moves quickly to take her arm. He leads her from the courtroom to the lawyer's room avoiding the questioning crowd and the press who will soon have the same information everyone in the courtroom heard.

After closing the door, he begins to explain slowly. She hears the part about the witnesses for the diocese. She hears something similar about her witnesses. Then, she hears, "I told them that you will accept the diocese's offer. The judge graciously praised our decision. To confirm this decision, he only requires your signature. You can write the statement. The diocesan lawyers have already given their statement and provided signatures in the judge's chambers. We must bring your signed statement to the judge."

She can barely contain her fury and begins her reply yelling. Forsyth interrupts quietly, points to the door, and indicates that the press might have already positioned themselves outside. He reminds her to maintain an even temper, to remain calm, and preserve her dignity. She blows up at the word dignity, a word he drummed into her, a word he repeated too often. "What dignity? How dare you make such a decision when you know why I started this case and you know I won't accept the job the diocese offered. I hired you. I make the decisions." Her whisper comes out raspy. "I may not stay at Saint Luke's once I win the case and my more important work begins. But I will NEVER accept a transfer to a suburban parish. Never!" She takes a deep breath. Her whisper wavers. "I will stay at Saint Luke's. I will appeal this decision AND" she glares at Forsyth, "I will get a new lawyer."

Forsyth gives her time to clear her throat and take a breath. "You certainly have that choice," he tries to make eye contact with her. She avoids him. He chooses his words carefully speaking in a soft, even voice, "but, in this case and situation, not a wise choice. The diocese made this offer under pressure. Did you understand that?" He waits for a sign of recognition. She folds her arms and holds her mouth tightly closed. He leans towards her and continues to whisper. "Someone in the

Bishop's office approached the judge and told him that the diocese had pressured witnesses. The judge spoke to the witnesses personally yesterday. The diocese wants to avoid negative publicity at this point." He speaks even more slowly. "You will absolutely not get this opportunity again. They need to cover up. They make the offer, we accept. The judge seals the information about the discovery forever. No one knows." He stops talking as he sees her unexpected response.

Elizabeth's frown disappears. She leans forward. Her hands form fists. Her voice restrained and exploding makes him cringe. "But why, why on earth would we want to keep that information sealed? Secrets, pressure applied privately while speaking otherwise publicly. All this must stop!" She laughs. "Great! Terrific!" She throws her hands up in the air approaching but not quite reaching the Eva Perone position. "I wish I had planned this myself. We don't accept the offer. I don't accept the offer. No way. What do I care about a job? Perfect! Don't you see? Everyone finds out that the diocese doesn't operate honestly. Everyone knows more about all these secret dealings. A step, and a significant one, toward making the church more open. Don't you understand? We did it! Even with our few witnesses. We did it!" Elizabeth throws her hands up in the air reaching full extension and laughs out loud.

"Apparently, you didn't hear the other part of the agreement?" Forsyth frowns and hesitates. "You didn't hear -" he pauses and then turns. The soft voice disappears. He speaks more forcefully, "If the case remains unsealed, if you choose to appeal, you will experience consequences worse than you can imagine." Not waiting for her response, he stands and crosses to the window. He looks out on the river. He wonders whose career will suffer the most. He turns back to her. "One of your parishioners, also went to the judge. She took a recording of one of our earlier meetings with witness volunteers. She recorded the whole meeting." He pauses. "She recorded the night you called that woman a deserter. The judge played part of the tape for us. The lawyers for the diocese heard everything." He takes a breath and continues with less speed and assurance. "I shouldn't have recommended that tact. I have been successful and avoided scrutiny in the past with this method of coaching witnesses. I guess I went too far. I won't use this technique again." He hesitates, then adds "if I maintain my license after all this." He shakes his head and wipes a bead of sweat from his nose with his handkerchief. "The tape gives the judge enough evidence to open a new trial against us for pressuring witnesses. The person from the Bishop's office didn't have a tape, didn't have concrete evidence. So, you see, we have limited options at this point." He shrugs his shoulders. "The diocese has a little more experience at keeping their secrets a secret."

Her own defiant words, another uncontrolled fit of anger, echo in her brain, and she cries. The bright red of her cheeks and neck fade gradually. Waves of disbelief and rage evaporate as she sees that she has lost. Through the tears, rage returns. The reasons to deny meet a reality she can barely face. She went too far. She sees her goal evaporate. Her mind fills with alternate scenarios too late to pursue. And again, she can't believe it. Back and forth the reasoning and the questioning change places. She sobs and gasps, denies and regrets in waves over and over. Forsyth stands and looks out the window without a strategy for himself. It hits him that few paths forward exist for him. This realization makes his strategy for her look strong. She uses the last of her tissues. The clerk knocks on the door. Forsyth opens the door and blocks the clerk's view of Elizabeth. Forsyth asks for paper. The clerk reminds them that the judge waits for her signature, a signature that requires witnesses. Elizabeth hears that she must sign in the presence of the lawyers and the judge. Forsyth requests more time and closes the door.

He sits beside her and waits for the sobs to subside. He offers his handkerchief and relates what the clerk said. She listens and nods. He stands up and walks to the window again. Cars leave the court garage in a steady line below as the evening rush hour begins. Juries, judges, lawyers, observers, clerks, and guards all navigate their way through the waves of heat rising from the asphalt streets to find refuge in their homes. He considers his options. Dixon, Grossmann, and Peak will fire him. Information like this travels quickly, though his boss has barely paid attention to his weekly reports about the case. He wonders how long it will take and how it will happen. Sealing a case does not stop the flow of information. How many neighbors or friends had the people who spoke to the judge already talked to before they received the advice to remain silent? How many employees in the Bishop's office might find their job gone tomorrow? News like this would travel quickly in the legal circles. He enjoys his sports car, his town house, and the European vacations; but without a job, he can't afford those. Somehow, he doesn't feel as distraught as Elizabeth looks. He admires her stamina and single-minded energy. He doesn't have faith, at least that he recognizes as faith. He sees some benefits to living without faith as her sobs lessen. That thought floats off as he imagines himself visiting her in her new church. He will certainly have time to explore the idea of faith or even consider representing the poor and immigrants or finding a totally new profession. He discards the thoughts quickly and turns back toward her.

"How are you doing?" he asks looking at his watch and repeating, "It's past 5 PM, they wait in the judge's chamber for us. A timely response will avoid too many theories reaching the news people. We must prepare a brief statement for you in response to the judge. Their lawyers will review the statement. I doubt they will make any changes if we keep it simple. Next, you sign the paper in front of the judge and the lawyers. Then, we leave. As we leave, the press will want a statement. Care in phrasing the statement will influence where this story falls both today and tomorrow. General statements that avoid blame work best. Sometimes that kind of statement tempers the folks crafting headlines. We favor headlines that won't place this story on the front page. No guarantee, but no one expected the case to end today. Whatever we give them they will use. So, we can take advantage of this timing. You may not agree with this, but it must _appear_ that we agree with the diocese. The diocese prefers very neutral statements that say nothing. That will work to your advantage too. If we frame it, they will edit; but we'll get what we want." Elizabeth regains some composure as he speaks with a confidence she lacks. He clearly describes the next steps and repeats. He continues to talk to give her time to breathe normally. Then, he suggests that she use the rest room while he drafts the two statements.

Elizabeth enters the marble-floored ladies' room. The clicks from her shoes echo against the marble walls. The whole building gives off a steady, solid feeling. She feels the cold metal on the toilet handle and holds it hoping it will spread further into her warm, wilted body. She removes her jacket and fans herself with the jacket. She rests her cheek on the cool walls. The water splashed on her face and arms help. When she finally looks in the mirror, the relative composure surprises her and gives her energy to work on the details. She arranges her hair, reapplies lipstick, and adjusts the collar on her jacket. A memory of the women from the Texas parish who gave her the turquoise pin surfaces as she adjusts the pin. They welcomed her with the pin, a small turquoise Christ which matches her blouse. She straightens her blouse and adjusts her skirt. She feels the urgency to put herself back together and erase any signs of despair. She checks buttons, smooths wrinkles, and wipes her shoes with a paper towel before wiping the sink and throwing it away. She touches her hair. A frown crosses her face. She takes a breath, replaces the frown with a smile and assures herself that she can do whatever it takes to survive the next hour.

She did not lose. She did not win, but best of all she did not lose. She can take the first steps to reconnect with the parishioners and family members. She knows how to apologize. Somehow, she can summon sincerity. She will find a way to make the Queen of Peace job work. Most of all, she will plan the next steps to expose the diocese, and all of the Catholic hierarchy. She knows they won't abolish their old ways. A quick confession and they will resume their secret activities. Now, she has more experience with secrets. But the next time she will plan more carefully and build a broader base of support. Her eyes twinkle as she contemplates the possibilities. She brushes her hair back to uncover the rosier shades. Another breath and she acknowledges that the diocese will move quickly, and secretly, to find a way to fire her. Anticipating, paying attention, watching her back will guide her in her quest.

Forsyth has prepared the two simple statements. Elizabeth rewords the public statement slightly. Forsyth takes that as a sign that she can survive this last test. She looks strong. The makeup restored her color. She stands straight and smiles. He smiles back as he accepts her edits. He leaves the room to give her time to memorize the statements. He summons the clerk.

Brief evening news reports announce that the case concluded. Channel 14's report includes Ellen Scott standing in front of the courthouse explaining the surprise announcement by the judge. She promises that Channel 14 reporters in the courtroom will pass information to her as soon as they can talk to the judge and the lawyers. She repeats the recent edict from the state court that TV equipment must remain where she stands outside the courthouse. The camera moves to show the courthouse guard standing nearby his hands folded behind his back. She interviews a few parishioners who attended the trial and a priest participating as a witness at another trial that day. "Though I lack familiarity with this trial, our diocese takes care of its parishes." He smiles at the camera. "Bishop Inman considers himself a shepherd much as Christ did in his time. He cares deeply for all the sheep in his flock. Whatever the outcome of this trial – " He continues to talk before realizing she has removed the microphone and returned control to the studio.

Naomi doesn't usually watch the evening news. Dinner time demands her full attention, but she heard a report on the radio as she drove the kids home from swimming lessons. She sits watching the news in the family room. The kids play outside. Zack joins her. He heard a similar report when he reached his car and decided to skip the gym and see if the TV reported more information, at least to fill in answers to so many questions. They try different stations but all reports contain only headlines. The reports indicate that the lawyers have not left the judge's room, promising more details as they become available. The phone rings during dinner as neighbors call to tell and ask the Nortons about the trial outcome. Parishioners expect that Naomi has more information than the brief reports on the early evening news. Ben drops by while they clear the table. He brings ice cream and cones. The kids go outside after devouring their cones and the adults turn on the radio.

"Father Rogers has probably left the phone off the hook! I just can't imagine what happened." Ben muses.

The phone rings again. Naomi recognizes Mary's phone number. No one speaks. She hears only crying in the background. She waits. Finally, after Naomi hears Mary comforting someone, the crying quiets. Mary speaks and explains what her neighbor told her between the sobs. Naomi turns on the speaker phone so Ben and Zack can hear and urges Mary to start again. Mary gives her neighbor's summary. When the neighbor recovers, she takes the phone and says that she went to the judge and explained what Elizabeth did at the meeting when Elizabeth called her a deserter.

"I didn't mean to, but I recorded the meeting on my phone." Shock and surprise hit Ben, Naomi, and Zack. The neighbor takes another breath. "Before the meeting, I recorded a call from our grandchildren." She sobs and gasps. "I must have left it on when I went to the meeting." She gradually recovers and breathes more normally. "When I realized what happened, I didn't know what to do. Then, I became more and more worried that we might lose Saint Luke's. So, I called the judge. When I listened to the recording with him, I couldn't believe all the things Elizabeth said." No one speaks. "The judge told me, -- I can't remember everything he told me." She pauses. "I think he told me not to tell anyone that I had spoken to him. Then, he said something about, if the case concluded today! I don't think he said the case would conclude today?"

She explained to the judge that she already told Mary. The judge interrupted her and cautioned her, "This ruling takes effect when the case concludes, it applies to what you say after that. Though I do advise you to say nothing when you leave this office to anyone."

When she arrived home from the grocery store, she saw her answering machine full of messages. TV stations, radio stations, and newspaper reporters, she guessed. Some of them didn't identify themselves. They all wanted a statement from her. "How did they find out? What should I do? I'm so, so s-scared."

Mary takes the phone. "We can't let her face this alone after all she's been through with Elizabeth. What do you think?" The lack of a response scares Mary. "I can't do this. You know I have had my doubts about this whole lawsuit but I can't speak calmly or deflect stupid questions. Please."

Ben looks at Zack. "You meet with people all over the world and have a sense of what to say in situations like this. And your size, big, and imposing presence might help in a situation like this." Ben urges.

Zack shrugs. "What a brave thing to do! Now, you probably wish you had kept your mouth shut. Of course, now we know why people don't testify or bring forward information because of the fear of retaliation, and the press can retaliate. They have no concern for people. They chase the story." He looks at Naomi and Ben and sees encouragement. "I'll do it. It sounds like she should only say: "I have no statement." If she says more than that, she admits she went to the judge. Then, they will just barrage her with questions. What do you think?"

"Perfect, perfect. That will also make it easier on her. And just leave your suit on. A first impression might make the press less aggressive? Maybe? We can hope anyway." Naomi tells Mary that Zack will leave to join them. Mary suggests he come to the back door.

When weather permits, Father Rogers usually spends his day off walking the high trails above Cachaqua Lake. He takes his cell phone but mutes the sound during the hikes, reserving it for emergencies. He hears Martha's voice, "Leave it in the car. Check it when you finish the hike. We can't schedule deaths or emergencies. Take a little time for yourself. With the addition of all of Elizabeth's responsibilities, you need it now more than ever. If someone dies during that short hike, I'll get another priest to come. You do it for them. You deserve a break." But he takes the phone anyway. Even with it the sound turned off, he usually feels the vibration in his pocket. It seems like a good compromise.

As a child growing up in Massachusetts, he walked the Presidential Range of the Appalachian Mountains in New Hampshire. He always dreamed that he would hike the entire Appalachian Trail one day or at least the rest of the trail in pieces. The first few years after he moved to New York, he took vacations in Maine and started the process walking south from Mt. Katahdin. Then, his parents consumed his vacation time as they grew older and required more care and attention. After arriving in Stanton, a parishioner took him to Overlook Park above Cachaqua Lake one winter afternoon; and he discovered the gentle rolling hills only a short distance from Stanton. He took on the lake trails with equal enthusiasm keeping track of his progress and devoting days off and vacations when he could to create more checkmarks on his maps.

He chooses a short hike to leave time for a swim before returning home. The heat of the previous days caused him to start his hike earlier to escape the city's heat. He looks forward to the cool forest trails that wind through the hills surrounding the lake. He parks his car at the beach and sets off to walk around the small lake. While this doesn't take him up into the hills, he will have pleasant views of the lake and the activities on the lake. He hopes to surprise a deer on a more secluded section of the trail. He checks his backpack for supplies anticipating a pause to eat a snack and listen to the wildlife.

Returning to his car, he considers checking his cell phone before the swim, but decides against it and dives in, leaving his clothes on the car seat. He floats in the swimming area as most bathers pack up their equipment and picnics and head home. The sun slips behind the hills and he feels a change in the air. He watches the ripples from his steps as he walks from the lake to his car. He feels refreshed. He smiles thinking of Martha and resolves to thank her for nudging him. He puts a towel on the car seat and a shirt on before starting the car. As he ponders which route to take back and whether to stop for a bite to eat, he checks his cell phone.

He expected messages. He doesn't expect twenty-five messages. He turns off the engine and retrieves the messages one by one. Martha called shortly after 4 PM, leaving a message that the trial ended. In her usual efficient way, she said she would call back when she had more information. Four parishioners each more upset than the previous one want to know about the court costs. The last wants to sue Elizabeth for the costs. He recognizes Tony's voice. Martha left another message apologizing for the volunteer in the office who gave Father Rogers' cell phone number to someone. She doesn't remember which volunteer gave the number. He hears the frustration in her voice as she promises to answer all the calls and find a way to get him a new number for his cell phone. "At no cost to the church!" In another message, she indicates that news of the end of the trial has spread to all the radio and TV stations. "They all seem to extend their reports with general Catholic blather because they can't find anyone: judge, lawyers, clerks, window washers or Elizabeth to interview." By the end of the messages, he knows nothing more about the trial and all that he feared about the disgruntled parishioners. Martha's patience disappeared by the last message.

He stops in the village to buy a fish sandwich. Instead of driving right home, he drives up to Overlook Park and watches the lake as the sun sinks deeper behind the hills and sunset colors appear. He feels closer to God in the mountains or the hills. He thanks God for the day by the lake and gives himself to God as he anticipates the coming hours and days. Then, he thanks God for the challenges he faces when he returns to the parish. He anticipates many difficulties. He knows he will falter, but he also knows that God walks with him. Here on this hill surrounded by the quiet pine trees with lights flickering below, he knows it. He holds on to that knowledge, that faith, hoping to take it with him through the next days and months.

By morning, the case still remains the lead story. One station interviews Mary's friend. Zack's shoulder appears in the corner of the screen. His presence calmed her and allowed her to repeat that she has no statement. The reporters hypothesize that she approached the judge. Someone saw her near the court house. They guess what she might have said. But she adds nothing to their hunches. Ellen Scott, who claims this as her story since she caught the beginning when the Bishop fired Elizabeth, speaks to more people. She discovers the unrest that Father Rogers heard in his cell phone messages. But her producer wants information about the trial outcome. She finds one or two parishioners who heard something about witnesses. They speak to her. The footage doesn't satisfy her producer. Though Ellen calls the parish office frequently throughout the day and drops in late in the day hoping to find Father Rogers, Martha refuses to give her any information or to tell her when she might reach Father Rogers. She refuses to have the camera on while Ellen interviews her. Ellen offers strongly stated refusals for the story with Martha's name, position in the parish, and former position in the diocese. The producer finally uses Martha's statements at the end of the story. Martha's characteristic directness adds a little punch or differentiation to the story, even without seeing her on camera. The producer urges Ellen to dig deeper.

Elizabeth makes a simple statement to interviewers, "I am pleased with the outcome of the case. We have reached a satisfactory agreement." She says the same thing to each interviewer. When asked what she will do next, she thanks the diocese for providing a transfer to Queen of Peace. In every interview, she smiles and speaks calmly. Elizabeth manages each interview calmly and politely. With a smile and a turn to the next person, the interviews last only two or three minutes. Deeper questions on everyone's minds, remain unasked and unanswered. Not capturing an outburst as Elizabeth provided in the weeks leading up to the trial, reporters lack the drama their unanswered questions might have revealed.

Father Rogers returns to the rectory after midnight. The reporters' and parishioners' messages have piled up on his desk and office voicemail. Some waited outside the rectory but gave up before he returned. The next day he appears in the church early for the morning Mass. Martha gives him a short version of what she knows and notes that she has no direct information from Elizabeth as he prepares for Mass. People fill the pews. TV trucks surround the church. Father Rogers says the Mass in a slower pace. Without answers to the questions, accusations and threats he anticipates, he adds extra prayers to God for those encounters.

After Mass, Father Rogers listens politely to all the questions and explains that he has not spoken with Elizabeth and would prefer to answer questions when he understands everything. He praises her work and knows that Queen of Peace and Father O'Malley will benefit as Saint Luke's has with her participation in their parish. Tony Mancuso shouts above the others and demands answers. "Now tell us, who pays all these legal bills!" The TV cameras focus on Tony Mancuso. Father Rogers reiterates that he must have all the information before he answers. He acknowledges the many calls from parishioners and states that he doesn't want to upset people more by answering incorrectly. "You know the answer," Tony Mancuso shouts. Father Rogers excuses himself and returns to the rectory. He asks Martha to find Elizabeth and arrange for them to meet somewhere.

"If she doesn't answer the phone, please go there and find her. I want to quell this unrest before people start to make up information. I haven't been sensitive enough to the parishioners during this trial." Martha nods and leaves.

Elizabeth chooses a park on the other side of the city to meet Father Rogers. She provides an even-tempered explanation, smiling but lacking her former warmth and openness to him. He asks questions.

She answers. "We must understand the outcome benefits us all." Her smile flattens. She shakes her head, nods, and adds nothing more.

Father Rogers waits for more details. Hearing none, he asks, "And the Queen of Peace job?"

"Yes, I will take the job."

Again, Father Rogers expects more. He looks for a gesture or word. She provides nothing. "Very good, very good. You will remain nearby." He smiles. She doesn't smile. "And, and, the legal costs, fees…"

Elizabeth doesn't hesitate, "The Bishop will, if I know him, raise the goal for this year's Thanksgiving Appeal to cover the diocesan legal costs." Without a sign of concern or apology, she continues, "Saint Luke's must pay our part."

Taking a deep breath, he asks, "And, your responsibility for our part of the costs? The total amount?"

She admits the magnitude of the legal costs, saying she doesn't have the final bill and continues to distance herself from her responsibilities on this topic and from Father Rogers. He frowns at her answer. Elizabeth questions his support of women. She pauses. Father Rogers asks about her responsibility to the parish. He misses her warmth and collaboration. She fears the consequences of paying the legal costs herself and hopes he won't push her. He sincerely wants her to have a new start. He doesn't know how the parish can survive this financial burden. She wonders if she can confront Forsyth to reduce the costs. Finally, he both accepts the heavy financial burden as a signal of his commitment and support to her. After a pause, he urges her to use her creativity to help in whatever way to cover the costs. "Set a goal for yourself - half the costs or more would go a long way to show your respect and commitment." As he watches a wrinkle form on her forehead, he nods. He trusts that God will show him a way to find the rest or talk the law firm out of the fee. They both nod. He asks her to provide all the final information by afternoon. Elizabeth agrees. They part formally each relieved to have finished the conversation. Father Rogers regrets his demand but recognizes his commitment to hold people more accountable. Elizabeth steels herself for the coming months.

Once he receives Elizabeth's account of the trial expenses, Father Rogers invites Tony Mancuso specifically to receive answers to his questions and to bring anyone he wants with him. He plans to speak privately with the most boisterous members of the parish, try to address their concerns, and then invite others to question at the next parish meeting. He leaves several messages with Tony Mancuso and receives no return call. He asks Martha to keep trying Tony and locate the parishioners she remembered being the most outspoken. He calls Naomi to have her check parish meeting notes. He doesn't locate anyone.

Clare

"Mommy, I want to come with you tonight," Clare carries her dinner plate to the sink and waits for Naomi's reply.

Naomi continues rinsing the dishes in the sink and placing them in the dishwasher. She senses an unfamiliar resolve in Clare that restrains her from the usual motherly list of questions.

"Don't worry, Mommy, I've done my homework, I took the trash out, and I take my bath tomorrow night." Clare takes care of the list and remains standing by the sink close to Naomi.

Naomi catches the "no" look in Zack's eyes. She agrees with that look though she wants to understand this new resolve in Clare, this new firmness. She turns toward Clare. "Mommy I'm old enough to stay up. And I want to become a priest when I grow up. And I want to see what happens at these meetings. You said I could go someday. How about today?" She stares at her mother.

Zack turns toward them. "My, that sounds like a grown-up young lady!" Clare turns toward her father without moving away from her mother. "You know Clare, these meetings often last until well after your weekend bedtime. And you have school tomorrow."

Naomi finds herself thinking of ways to bring Clare to the meeting, and feels relieved when Zack speaks first. Then, without getting the benefit of the relief, she says "I wonder if Daddy could come and pick you up at bedtime? That way you can get a sense of what happens in the parish meetings and still get to bed on time. A fair compromise?" She looks at Clare and then at Zack.

Clare nods and runs to get her coat. Zack shrugs his shoulders in acquiescence. "How about quarter of nine? Hopefully things will remain calm until then."

"Thanks. I have my doubts about this. I can see you do too. But she should know what she's getting into, I suppose. I don't

266

know, Zack? Should we change our minds on this? She's only eight years old."

"Mom, nine, almost nine. Come on you always arrive on time! I want to see the before part, especially since I can't see the end of the meeting." Clare calls from the hallway. She stands at the door waiting with a notebook tucked under her arm as Naomi gathers her papers.

"Maybe you can count the people tonight. That would really help."

Naomi wonders what to say to prepare her without frightening her. The months of meetings seem like years. Sometimes they reach resolution but more often the conflict and disagreement persist or spring up again unexpectedly. She still can't understand why people say such unsubstantiated things which always set off a furor before they can determine the facts. She hopes with the lawsuit out of the way things will calm down. She and Ben placed a bet, though they both bet Elizabeth won't accept the position at Queen of Peace. Now Father Rogers says she will take the job. Naomi hopes for some form of normal in her life. Elizabeth taking the job would help. These options consume her thoughts, mixed in with concern about the legal fees.

She asks a question. "I know you hear me talking about the parish meetings with Daddy. You probably hear us when we have facilitator meetings in the kitchen, tell me what you expect tonight."

"Not like church!" Clare swings her head back and forth. "You always talk about getting people to talk or stopping people from talking. In church, only the priest talks and the people who do the readings and give the homily. In school only the teacher talks. Well mostly. But it sounds more like school than like a party where everyone talks?" Clare watches for the houses of her friends. She sees a light on and stretches to see if she can see anyone. Her friend closed the curtains too tightly. She feels grown up going out on a school night to a meeting where no other children will attend.

Naomi worries that Elizabeth, as she has changed, will frighten Clare. She has only Ben's stories about Elizabeth and wishes, now, that she had asked Ben about his meeting with Clare. She expects that losing the lawsuit, or not winning, won't restore the smiles from Elizabeth that warmed so many people. Since the Bishop fired her, she hasn't made an effort at the few Masses she attends; and she hasn't shown anything but anger at the parish meetings, when she attends. Still if she accepted the new job, maybe that gives reason for hope. Since their first visit to Saint Luke's, Clare idolized Elizabeth. They always greeted each other enthusiastically and Elizabeth spent a little extra time with Clare. Though it seems unlikely Elizabeth will attend the meeting, she still anticipates Clare's shock at seeing her again. She broaches the subject carefully, "You understand all that has happened has upset Elizabeth?"

"I'd be upset too, if someone fired me. I don't understand why he fired her anyway. And what is a lawsuit?" Clare has more questions.

"Of course, you would. We can all understand, a least a little, how losing your job could really mess up your life, though luckily she has another job." She discards the idea of mentioning Zack's problems at work and a possible job change. "We can go and visit her at her new church. We can even go to Mass there now and then." Naomi waits at the traffic light and glances at Clare. Clare seems calm. "So, don't expect a cheery Elizabeth when you see her. In fact, she might not even come to the meeting tonight."

"What do you mean? I thought she went to all the parish meetings." Clare turns to Naomi.

Naomi takes a breath and wishes she had asked a few more questions before leaving home when Zack could help with this conversation. She suspects that Clare anticipates seeing Elizabeth. "Well, she seems to concentrate all her attention on other things lately. She doesn't spend as much time chatting with people and asking them questions. I've noticed that a little at church too. Have you noticed?" She waits.

"Noticed what?" Clare's attention has wandered.

Naomi pulls the car into a parking space near the door and she tries one more time. "Clare, Elizabeth loves you. You two have a special friendship. But she might not give you that big

268

hug as she usually does." Naomi has Clare's attention now. She adds softly, "She might not talk to you. You'll understand, won't you?" She watches disappointment fill Clare's face. "And with all that's going on with Elizabeth, she might not attend this meeting." Naomi hopes she won't.

Clare nods her head. They go into the church hall. Ben gives Clare an enthusiastic hug and a questioning look to Naomi. Elizabeth arrives just as the meeting starts. Clare waves. Elizabeth ignores her. Naomi turns to Clare and sees the look she feared. "Have you got that count yet? It looked like you counted more than a hundred? Let's see." Naomi directs Clare's attention to the marks she made in her notebook and they total as Ben welcomes everyone to the meeting.

The crowd quiets and turns their attention to Ben. He looks up to see a group of parishioners led by Tony Mancuso enter the hall holding candles. The flames waver. They walk slowly to chairs near the front of the room and stand. People move out of their way to empty enough seats for the group. Ben offers the opening prayer and ends with an *Our Father*. The candle holding group speaks the prayer in a loud unified voice. The other parishioners, seated as people usually were for the meetings, look at the candles and speak the prayer softly looking back and forth between the candle holders, people seated nearby, and the facilitators. Naomi wants to leave and take Clare home. She keeps her hand on Clare's arm. When the prayer ends, they blow their candles out but remain standing. Ben reads the agenda and asks for additions or questions. Tony Mancuso breaks in before Ben finishes speaking. Naomi watches Clare.

"We demand that Elizabeth pay the legal expenses. We never agreed to the trial. We never agreed to the expenses. The expenses will cripple this parish!" His supporters mumble agreement.

Father Rogers stands to respond. Ben suggests that he add the question to the agenda and looks around the room for a response from the candle group and back at the seated group. "We understand your concern and we want to address your questions," Ben starts to say.

Father Rogers interrupts. When no one from Tony's group responded to Martha's calls and she made them repeatedly, Father Rogers anticipated the group would make a more public confrontation. He had spent the day in prayer. "Very good, Tony. People have moved to give you seats. Would you like to take them?"

At first no one moves. The room vibrates with silence. Father Rogers gestures toward the empty seats and looks directly at Gio. When Gio moves to sit, the others follow. Tony stands still, looks at an empty chair, folds his arms and remains standing.

"Can everyone see?" Father Rogers asks. Some heads nod. Tony remains in place and scowls at Gio. "Very good, very good. We must remember our roots." Tony opens his mouth. Father Rogers smiles at Tony and continues. "We started the school without knowing how we would pay the teachers' salaries and we have paid them every year. We trusted God to lead us and to find our way. We must continue to trust God." Father Rogers addresses Tony directly but looks at the group surrounding him intently.

Tony interrupts before Ben can prevent him, "Excuse me. This is different Father. We never agreed to the lawsuit and we certainly never agreed to pay the costs. We all agreed to keep the school open and we all agreed to do whatever it would take to do that."

"No one supported me." Elizabeth breaks in. "You" she looks directly at Tony Mancuso "After all I have done for this parish," she glares at Tony. "You abandoned me." Her gaze doesn't leave Tony's face as she speaks in a strident voice. "Where is your commitment to women? More important to Saint Luke's!" She pauses. "To the world, we live in now, not hundreds of years ago!"

Tony opens his mouth in surprise. His voice, compared to Elizabeth's, sounds relaxed, "Excuse me, Elizabeth. Women? Women, means more than just you. If, as you claim, you mean women, women would have participated in the decisions. In fact, you rejected many of the women in the parish. No, not women. This is all about you." Tony speaks calmly in sharp

270

contrast to Elizabeth's anger and volume and to his usual booming delivery.

Ben stands speechless and sees Clare raise her hand out of the corner of his eye. He glances over and she looks right at him. He nods and she stands up.

She turns to the people gathered and then she looks directly at Elizabeth. Her voice cracks as she starts. She clears her throat. Clearing it one more time and leaning in toward the microphone, she says, "I remember one time you told us that it is hard to forgive a transgressor. This sounds like the story you told us about our brothers and sisters doing things to us?"

Expectations

I learned that it is not God who changes; it is we who change.
Joan Chittister

    Bob Harrington, the fire chief, tells everyone, even if they don't ask. "We will never know exactly how the fire started which makes Minnie's death all the more tragic!" He knows the mayor will insist on an investigation. The investigation panel will include representatives from the fire department, the police department, and the mayor's office; but they won't find the ultimate cause. Bob leads enough investigations to know when they have adequate evidence to determine the cause and when they don't. This fire left no evidence. He scoured every inch of the church and found nothing. He explains this, again, to Father Rogers.

    "Very common." Father Rogers writes on a scrap of paper. "People think we can always find the cause." Bob watches Father Rogers nod his head. He pats Father Rogers' shoulder and smiles. "Maybe better that way?" He opts for fewer words of explanation figuring Father Rogers has his hands full with parishioners, the media, and the insurance company. Father Rogers takes a deep breath. "They won't ask me to investigate. As a parishioner, they automatically assume my prejudice. But whoever investigates will find nothing." He doesn't voice his worry about potential appointees. The previous months of turmoil at Saint Luke's have spilled over to his firehouses. He counts on the mayor's wisdom to avoid appointing Bob's officers who attend Saint Paul of the Cross. Some of them have brought accusations into the firehouse and confronted their Saint Luke's colleagues. Not even all his efforts to clarify the Saint Luke's situation at their weekly meetings with his division fire chiefs, quieted tensions at work. If appointed, he hopes they can rise above the acrimony and remain objective. Nevertheless, he worries.

"We can only hope, and a few prayers wouldn't hurt, that the investigation concludes quickly. We need to put this fire behind us. We still have work to do." At home, he calls this fire "a hot potato if ever there was one." He hopes the panel, whoever the mayor appoints, will not try to "stir the pot. God knows we've had enough pot stirring here." He doesn't say this to Father Rogers. He pats Father Rogers shoulder again and leaves.

Bob's words appear in the news stories. His honest assessment and willingness to extract himself from the center of the investigation seem to set a positive tone. The mayor chooses carefully from the community, avoiding the appointment of any Catholic members to the panel investigating the fire at Saint Luke's. Then, he asks the Catholic Bishop of Albany, a boyhood friend, to advise the panel. They work quickly. They interview all the firemen who responded to the call to put the fire out, parishioners who attended the meeting earlier in the evening, neighbors in surrounding houses, and Father Rogers. Their conclusion agrees with Bob Harrington's. Bob, as Fire Chief, makes the announcement to the public. "When we lose a person, any person, in a fire, we work extra hard to find a cause. Knowing the cause gives comfort to the loved ones, in addition to satisfying both the public and the insurance companies. This panel's investigation concludes without finding a probable cause. We know that without Minny Lord, the fire would have destroyed much more of the church. Now we, I say we because I attend church at Saint Luke's, must rebuild and continue our work in the community." He ponders what he will say at the next division chief's meeting. The newspapers feature Bob's statements printed over photos of the panel members. In TV coverage, the report cover fades into the fire at its height. A commercial for fire insurance grabs viewers' attention.

When Naomi Norton hears about the fire, trying to figure out the how, why, or who of the fire's origin stumps her. Calling Zack, she looks for advice on how to tell the children.

They remind each other to consider Clare's devotion to Elizabeth Winter and how she will respond. The parish meeting allowed her to meet an Elizabeth she didn't recognize. Naomi hasn't even spoken to Zack about Clare and the meeting. They agree to wait until they are all together before telling Clare and Mark.

She paces and eventually begins reading through the notes on her computer from parish meetings to find all of Minny's poems offered in the past. She smiles seeing how Minny in her simple poems captured both the conflict and the hopefulness she, herself, felt at recent parish meetings where attendance increased and angry words erupted. When Minny appeared, she didn't blame Elizabeth for creating a situation that set parishioners against each other. Instead, her words urged prayer and contemplation. She didn't list affronts; she urged thoughtfulness and listening.

Naomi welcomes the opportunity to call Fred and Mary, parish meeting facilitators, who resigned during the months following Elizabeth's removal from Saint Luke's, the contentious trial, and the conflicts that erupted in the parish. She asks for any poems they heard in previous years. Both respond enthusiastically and send her poems captured at meetings where they took notes. Fred, the lawyer, who tried to caution Elizabeth and help her to consider other options, offers to collect them all and create a book. He will print books and bring them to Father Rogers for parishioners. When Fred insists that he will pay for the books, Naomi wonders if he would consider joining the facilitation team again. She doesn't ask.

Father Rogers' homily at the first Mass after the fire proceeds smoothly centering on Christ the shepherd. "Minny Lord shepherded our precious home, our Saint Luke's. What we have pieced together from her coworkers, the fire investigation report, and her poems," he holds a copy of the book Fred handed him before the Mass, "gives us hope for the future." He pauses. Parishioners pull collars up against the cold, shift from foot to foot, and watch the sky for the predicted storm. He opens the book to the last page, looks up and down again. He looks at Fred standing next to boxes of books. "Very good, very good…" He nods. "And, I wanted to read this last poem, but –, I can't seem to read right now." He closes the book and breathes deeply scanning the gathered parishioners standing in the parking lot. "You see the cab of her truck still parked where she parked on the evening of the fire." He points across the parking lot to the large cab covered with flowers. He lifts up the book. "Her words, words of a very spiritual over-the-road truck driver." He shakes his head. "God brought Minny to us." He shrugs his shoulders. "Soon I can read her words aloud and I invite all of you to take a copy of the collection the facilitators put together. Thanks to Fred for printing copies for us." He takes another breath and continues with more certainty.

"She discovered the fire near midnight. As she drove home from a two-week trip, she passed Saint Luke's, noticed the smoke, parked her truck cab in the parking lot, and discovered the darkest smoke seeping from the side windows." He points to the section of the roof covered with large blue tarps, the shattered stain glass windows, and the flapping yellow tape that surrounds the church building. He pauses frequently trying to maintain his composure. "Before she woke me in the rectory, she located hoses and called the fire department. While we waited, she took a hose and went into the church. After removing the hosts, our Saint Luke's relic from the reliquary, and delivering them to me, she found what the firemen found moments later, the right side of the altar in flames. Her hose didn't have enough coverage to save her. They took her to the hospital immediately, but the flames had done too much damage. The hose she dragged with her slowed the flames' progress." Father Rogers rubs his hands and looks up at the church. "Bob tells us, they wouldn't have saved as much as they did without Minny Lord, without the hose directing water near the fire's source."

Stories among parishioners circulate about Minny's bravery. Other stories follow. Some describe scenarios and place blame. One thread of these stories reasons that Elizabeth and her strong supporters went overboard. "They knew they lost." Another version wishes for a different ending. "If only

275

Minny Lord had returned from that trip earlier, in time to attend that meeting and read one of her poems. Maybe whoever did it would have thought twice?" One story feeds on another. "Elizabeth threw a candle in anger at the Virgin Mary altar. She had the keys to the church!" In other gatherings people who objected to the trial and the burdensome costs got the blame. "Who had the candles? You saw them interrupting the meeting, shouting, ignoring any attempt to hear other comments. They objected to the cost of the trial!" What the fire investigation couldn't provide caused many others to fill that gap. "How much will it cost to repair that altar? No doubt, no doubt at all. I agree. Tony's crowd lost control!" At this point stories don't cross paths. The divisions grow deeper.

Minny's funeral preparations weigh on the parish. Father Rogers speaks quietly and pleads. The construction manager refuses the request to open the church. He lists all the dangers, shakes his head, and waits for Father Rogers to leave. When Father Rogers returns a second time, he brings Naomi with him. They don't argue. They ask for alternatives. They emphasize that they don't want to impede construction or create danger. They describe the significance of starting Minny's funeral in the church she saved. They watch the construction manager shake his head and wait for his expression to soften. When he finally looks up from his phone, they reemphasize their willingness to compromise and plead the need to include the church in the service, even if they must accept limits. They describe the service in detail and estimate the length of time people would stay in the building. They ask if they should eliminate the organ. When he agrees that the vibration could cause pieces of the ceiling to come loose, they ask about piano music. He sees the piano as a potential problem but suggests that very soft singing might not jar anything in the structure. They continue describing each part of the service checking how many songs he would consider too many. They ask for clarity on volume while in the building. They show the route of the casket into the church and down the center aisle. They ask if they should eliminate the procession, reduce the number of people accompanying the casket, carry it, or use the device the funeral home provides to roll it. As they notice the gradual change in the construction manager with each question, they ask about candles. "No candles, absolutely no candles," he insists. They fear they asked that question too soon. But they have an alternate idea, to carry candles at the cemetery. They will take her to the cemetery in the late afternoon as the sun sets. There parishioners will read the poems from Minny's book and hold candles.

Father Rogers' patience, Naomi's detailed description of the service, including the changes the construction manager suggests, secure permission for a limited service. Naomi thanks him and assures him that they will restrict the number of people in the church, and the amount and volume of the singing as he asked. They will complete the service within a half hour. She gives him a copy of Minny Lord's book as a thank you and they leave the chilly construction office.

Now they must create this funeral weighing both the construction safety and the parishioners' wishes. The divided congregation aches from the arguments about Elizabeth, the trial costs, and the tragedy of the fire. Everyone wants to attend this service. Any sign of exclusivity or special privileges will only aggravate or fuel controversies of the past months. Minny Lord stood outside the arguments as no one else did; and she urged concession, collaboration, and forgiveness. Her most recent poems ring with warnings of the dangerous road they traveled. Her death brings new recognition to each parishioner, to Father Rogers, to Elizabeth, to the facilitators, and to the press. But how that will or will not change people's entrenched opinions, no one knows. Naomi, Father Rogers, and Martha wonder what issues bother people the most. Without voicing their more troublesome questions to each other, they each avoid the more troubling questions and seek answers to the other questions. Naomi hopes, in this moment at least, they can put aside the more difficult challenges the parish faces to focus on the fire and honor Minny Lord.

"It's like walking on egg shells," Naomi remarks to Father Rogers as they return to the rectory. The fire didn't touch the rectory though the two roofs stood only feet apart. They walk slowly by the church grounds surrounded by an orange plastic fence. The construction manager will create an opening for the funeral at the side where the fire didn't touch the structure. They will carry the casket in with four people and sixteen people will follow. The service will take place on the side altar far from the fire and surrounding damage. No one has stepped inside the church since the fire. They will sing opening and closing songs outside.

"He made many concessions, many. Everyone must remain safe. We don't want to set the construction schedule back with a mishap or have anyone hurt. Minny wouldn't want that either." Father Rogers's face has acquired more wrinkles in the past year. His previously distinctive, black hair has turned mostly gray. He remains firm in his support of the Bishop and of Elizabeth. Striking the balance has taken a toll. He agrees to say the Mass alone with whispered responses from the parishioners. He looks forward to entering the church, returning to his home of the past twenty years, to his refuge and appreciates the extra care they take for this first step back.

"In the end, he seemed comfortable that we really wouldn't disturb the construction with the service. He even forgot to ask us to sign the paper relieving his company of all responsibility if anything happened. Now -" Naomi hesitates. Father Rogers surprised her with his request to accompany him. She notes more changes in his face and wonders about the pressure he has experienced. She suspects Father Rogers will rely on her to devise a method to eliminate a thousand people from attending the service, honoring Minny, and seeing their beloved church again. She has no viable ideas. If the press gets their way, they would send twenty people with heavy equipment. Her brow wrinkles as she rejects idea after idea.

Father Rogers guesses Naomi's thoughts, "Yes. Yes. I thought we might need to limit the attendance." He smiles as he notices Naomi's puzzled expression. "Very good, very good - we can include others at the cemetery. That allows everyone to participate in some part of the tribute."

"What about parking at the cemetery? Those narrow roads, but our parishioners never let parking keep them from anything! Zack always comments on crazy Catholic parking, a characteristic that might help in a situation like this." Naomi thinks of putting everyone's name in a hat, holding a parish meeting to choose people, and continues to discard one idea after another.

He watches Naomi turn away from her thoughts and towards him. He thinks through the logistics. "We could keep the information about the funeral off the website. I have written an obituary which will appear the day of the funeral. She didn't want any calling hours. Without that, we reduce the publicity." He watches Naomi and guesses she will come up with a solution if he talks long enough. "Ah, and we must think about the newspaper and television reporters, right? The reporters seem to call me every day, just in case they missed something." He shakes his head and points at the pile of messages on his desk. "Hopefully another event in the city will happen to distract them." He watches her face, pauses, and smiles. The thought that more talking will give her time to suggest an idea urges him to continue. "I did hear, they expect the mayor to make a decision about whether the city will add the school nurses back into the budget. That has upset a lot of people." He shakes his head. "Perhaps that announcement will get Saint Luke's off the front page."

"We can offer an extra prayer to the good Lord for that! Sometimes it seems like the mayor announces controversial decisions on purpose when something else has everyone's attention. She might be thinking Saint Luke's will distract people from this decision! Maybe it will work for us this time. We need a respectful service for Minny Lord without any outside influence or interruptions. Don't we?" Since the fire, Naomi checks the news more than once a day. She reads the newspapers word for word and watches the evening news constantly to anticipate parish and public reaction to Saint Luke's, dreading what she will find.

Father Rogers nods. Running out of things to say, he notices the wrinkles on Naomi's forehead, recognizes, perhaps, a

279

similar emotion he has experienced when he sat down to write his homilies during these months of upheaval in the parish. "I wonder if Martha has the old telephone tree, we used to contact parishioners before we had the website?"

"Why? Oh – letting people know beforehand the times and guidelines. Knowing Martha, she has it and can find it." Naomi frowns wondering how the message might change as it passes from one parishioner to the next. Then, she smiles and nods.

"Very good, very good." He watches Naomi and waits for her to speak. Watching her tired expression, he realizes that he has an idea to propose. "What if," he pauses. "What if, yes, what if, we ask the parishioners to name the twenty people?" Father Rogers muses. He sits at his desk. Naomi smiles. She takes a pen and a piece of paper from the printer and nods. He continues. "How does this message sound? *Minny Lord's funeral will be Saturday December 6 at 2 PM in the church. Only twenty people will attend the service inside the church. Thanks to our construction company for hearing our plea. We will hold another service at Queen of Peace in Pittstown at 3:30 and burial at 4:30 at Stanton Catholic Cemetery. Please confer among yourselves to choose the twenty attendees for the short Mass inside Saint Luke's. Please, thank the kind and safety-conscious construction manager and crew whenever you pass the site.* "Too long?" Naomi shakes her head. *"Call Martha at the rectory with your recommendation for the twenty attending at Saint Luke's."* He scratches his forehead. *"Since the Pittstown church has a small building, others should go directly to the Stanton Catholic Cemetery. Please bring candles and park safely."* He waits for Naomi to finish writing. "Not too long?" She shakes her head and continues writing. She reads it back to Father Rogers, and they both agree to give it to Martha. Father Rogers wonders if he will surprise Martha with his idea and whether she already has a list of alternatives. He sees he has surprised Naomi. He smiles.

"Hmm," Naomi wonders how the parishioners will decide among themselves without meeting, without resolving the rifts that have developed, and choose people. "Maybe a little complicated but ... no one group will make the decision." She sighs. "Now, we just trust God to solve this one. When you think of it, if they can make this kind of decision and more people go to the cemetery, we might be making the first step toward reconciliation." Her smile meets Father Rogers' nod.

"I have prayed every day for this. Do you think we should mention reconciliation?" Father Rogers picks up a piece of paper. He reaches for a pen. "No, we let Martha and God take it from here." He chuckles and puts the paper back. "They work well together."

Martha rolls her eyes when she hears the plan. Then, she goes to work. She has the old telephone tree lists and the list of parishioners with faxes. She sends an email to Naomi and Father Rogers, "God must have updated these old lists! Hardly any wrong numbers, even the fax numbers!"

The telephone tree works quickly. Conversations in homes and among neighbors happen throughout the evening and into the next day. Then, parishioners cross the branches and expand the reach of the telephone tree. New parishioners receive calls and assignments to call others. The first cross comes from a parishioner who supported Elizabeth. She tells the person who calls her that Tony Mancuso is a friend she lost during the months of division in the parish. "Put his name on the list." The caller agrees, "I haven't heard you say his name without anger recently. You make me want to suggest that child, the one who spoke up at a parish meeting. Or did she speak up at a Mass? We have to find a way to mend."

More questioning and the desire to reestablish a parish they believe in keeps Stanton telephone lines busy. Eventually Martha receives calls and writes names on a list. The day before the funeral, the list totals nineteen and each name has several marks beside it indicating that more than one person suggested the name. Martha watches the phone throughout the day. No one else calls. In the late afternoon, she calls people on the list. Many express surprise and wonder who chose them. Others offer to defer to another more worthy parishioner. Martha's smiles warm the pall that hangs over the rectory. With each call her smiles turn to chuckles remembering who suggested the person she speaks to and wondering if anyone will ask. No one does.

"Phone call for you Clare," Zack calls from the kitchen. He shrugs his shoulders in answer to Naomi's expression and Clare's request to identify the caller.

"An adult." Zack turns to Naomi as Clare takes the phone. He shrugs.

"Not her teacher I hope," Naomi wonders.

Zack scratches his head. His jaw drops when he recognizes the caller's voice speaking to Clare. "Martha, from Saint Luke's" he whispers to Naomi.

Clare hangs up the phone and turns to Zack and Naomi. "Someone chose me to attend Minny's funeral."

Naomi feels tears form. She doesn't speak. Neither does Zack.

"Did they choose Elizabeth? They should have chosen Elizabeth." Clare scowls.

Naomi and Zack notice each other's puzzled expressions.

"I don't know." Naomi responds slowly.

"But didn't you help plan the service?" Clare looks surprised.

"I did, but Martha asked parishioners to recommend the people to attend. People called her to suggest names. She collected all the names. I didn't call. She didn't give me the names on the list." Naomi speaks slowly to keep the tears from flowing.

Clare looks doubtful. Naomi finds herself without words wondering where Clare's anger comes from. She searches her mind assembling the information Clare could have accumulated over the previous months. She moves quickly to blame herself for not taking enough time with Clare to reflect on all the turmoil she might have experienced. All Naomi's doubts about Elizabeth surge forward to meet the enduring admiration for Elizabeth coming from Clare. "Tell me your thoughts, Clare." She sees Clare's hands form fists.

"Seems obvious how everyone in the parish has turned against Elizabeth, even you." She looks at Naomi without blinking and then at Zack. "How can we ever get women ordained if we can't ordain a woman who has worked so long for the church. Why don't you support her?"

Naomi can see Zack's forehead wrinkle, a sure sign he wants to set the record straight about Elizabeth including all the details they agreed should remain left unsaid. Many late-night conversations had them editing the sharp contradictions in Elizabeth's behavior that so many people reported and they experienced. She reaches for Clare's arm. "Clare we can't answer your question about who will attend the funeral. You can call Martha and ask. Or you can see who shows up there tomorrow." Clare's hands relax the tightness. "Remember that many people have worked hard to keep Elizabeth in the diocese. A condition for the job in Pittstown meant, for now, she can't attend anything at Saint Luke's. If people understood that, they might not recommend her name to protect her."

Clare looks away. She takes a deep breath. "She can go to the cemetery? Right?"

"Right."

Clare leaves the room.

Winter temperatures prevail the next morning. Naomi watches Clare join the others outside the rectory, to carry the casket, and whisper the responses. Naomi stands outside the church with Martha, Zack, and Mark as the small procession enters the side door of the church. She watches Clare, the only child, searching the people entering the church. Naomi catches a disappointed glance when Clare doesn't find Elizabeth. Naomi knows these people. People who insulted each other during the previous months stand side by side on the church sidewalk. Tony Mancuso carries the casket along with Bob Harrington, Ben, and Father Rogers. Naomi and the others huddle together outside during the service. She can't remember ever seeing Mark so still, despite having no toy to distract him, and the persistent wind that whisks by them. A few other parishioners stand on the sidewalk or sit in their cars.

Father Rogers whispers the Mass. His homily resonates. Martha gives copies of his homily to those standing outside. As she hands the last copy to one, others move together to share.

The Gospel of Matthew presents a woman who changes the attitude of Jesus. We say this woman had a prophetic voice. How many prophetic voices do we hear today? And did Minny speak with one of those voices?

So many of the Old Testament prophets were men, but Matthew describes a simple Canaanite woman challenging Jesus to help her and to see her faith. His apostles tell him to send her away. But he listens. He recognizes a prophetic voice, a voice saying something different from others. Did we send Minny away? Did we listen?

Minny used every opportunity to speak to us about listening to God and died in her final, heroic attempt to save our precious Saint Luke's. She wrote her poems. When she remained in town, she read them to us at parish meetings. When she traveled, she sent them to me. Did we listen?

Reading these poems last night, I realized that I did not listen carefully. Her death awakens in me the need to listen for these prophetic voices among us. Now, I will invite these voices, I will wrestle with the tough revelations these voices present, and I will work for the needed changes in a more spiritual way. Minny captured the challenging questions and the importance of prayer. She prayed, she encouraged us to pray especially during difficult changes. Challenge without prayer doesn't work. With prayer and trust in God, we can imagine both the change and the way to accomplish it.

Prophetic voices speak deeply from their hearts and give hope to accomplish the change together united in prayer. We have heard the voices of such prophets: Gandhi, Mandela, Frederick Douglass, Susan B. Anthony. Minny stands with them in her vision, her calls, and her actions. She reminds us that prophetic voices exist today even in our small city.

In her honor let us resolve to listen to each other and achieve the changes needed to go forward as thoughtful, caring people. Every change invites us to grow.

On Eagles Wings, led by Linda without her piano, greets the small group as they exit from the church and carry Minny Lord to the waiting hearse. The Nortons and Martha meet Clare coming out of the church. They watch the casket enter the hearse and climb into their own car. They follow the hearse in silence. Naomi realizes her children have never attended a funeral. She wonders what thoughts create the solemn expression on Clare's face. Mark's silence nags at her, but she doesn't engage them.

As they proceed south to Pittstown, Naomi notices other parishioner cars falling into line behind them with their headlights reflecting on the snow banks. At each intersection, more cars join the procession, too few police vehicles manage the long line from Saint Luke's. At the second traffic light with many cars now lined up, the hearse simply proceeds carefully through the red light without waiting for the police to catch up. The hearse driver can see the line stretched through both lights. He does the same at the next light and enters the highway cautiously to allow the following cars time to catch up.

"Good thing, it is a Saturday!" Mark says as he strains to see the line. "What would the school buses do with this long line?"

By the time the hearse reaches Pittstown, three hundred cars have joined the procession. Queen of Peace's small church and parking lot fill quickly. Some remain in their cars, while others gather outside the main church door. Father O'Malley, a gentle country priest with a small parish, stands on the altar facing a throng of people he has never seen and smiles to see the pews fill. Father Rogers joins the parishioners giving up his seat to one of the older members.

The Nortons remain in their car though Martha gets out to find a seat in the church. "I don't want to miss any part of this. We're getting this community back together with all the wounds healed and it will take a lot of work. Can't tell you what will happen, but I don't want anyone messing it up. Anyone!" Naomi watches Clare's expression. Then, Clare leaves the car and follows Martha into the church.

Elizabeth sits in a pew surrounded by those who supported her most actively, those who resisted her rough tactics, and those who stood on the sidelines reluctant to enter the fray. She keeps her gaze on the altar. Several adults push Clare to a position where she can see the altar. Clare sees Elizabeth, strains to catch a glance and bows her head.

Father O'Malley offers a brief blessing and invites an *Our Father*. Though he begins speaking it, the people in the front pews take it into song and those gathered outside the door join in, followed by those in their cars. The blessing at Queen of Peace avoids a collision with the Bishop's final edict that Elizabeth could not attend or visit Saint Luke's for a year. She goes to her car without speaking to anyone. Father Rogers thanks Father O'Malley and invites him to come to the cemetery. He declines as Saturday evening Mass will start, he imagines, before they would finish at the cemetery. They exchange hugs before Father Rogers returns to the hearse.

The Nortons wait while the casket returns to the hearse, the church empties and Martha and Clare climb into the car. "Amazing, amazing," Martha exclaims when she gets in the back with the kids. She glances at Naomi and back at the kids. She wonders how much they know. She thinks what a horrible example these adults have set for the children in the parish! Then, she lets go, "Elizabeth gave Father Rogers a hug on the way out! In fact, I think she didn't plan to. I saw her walking toward her car." Martha looks at the children on either side. "Isn't that wonderful? And she had to untangle herself from all the people gathered around her so that she got to him before he returned to the hearse!" She shrugs at Naomi.

"Oh, Rosa kept the kids informed." She looks at Clare who doesn't respond. "Thank goodness for Rosa. The kids have been talking about all this in their religious education classes. She started a question time with the children in each class. It helped, didn't it Clare? Mark?"

"Mom can't explain things when she has a headache or when she is upset." Clare shakes her head in sympathy. "Rosa can explain and my teacher lets us ask whatever we want." Clare continues. "I agree with you Martha, we have to get these things solved and we want Elizabeth back at Saint Luke's!"

286

Martha laughs. "Maybe all of us should have gone to these classes!"

Naomi breathes a sigh of relief that Clare's anger doesn't explode.

The hearse arrives at the cemetery, enters the gates, and proceeds along the narrow road to the small plot Minny purchased for herself when she bought her first truck. It stood at the corner of the old rundown cemetery on the east side of the city where she lived. The cars follow until the cemetery road fills. The remaining cars park in every available space around the perimeter of the cemetery. Zack gives up his place in line and parks on the perimeter leading cars to the pedestrian entrance. It's a longer walk from this entrance, but they follow each other easily to Minny's plot. Bob Harrington sits in a golf cart and points them toward the gathering. He offers rides to the older parish members.

"Mommy, what happened to my candle?" Mark feels his empty pocket.

"It must have fallen out in the car. Let's take a look." Naomi unlocks the car door. She finds the candle on the floor. Naomi hands it to Mark and he runs off to catch up with the others.

When the motors stop and the crowd quiets, a thousand people stand around the grave without TV cameras, news reporters, or people outside the parish. Father Rogers and Elizabeth stand together a sight no one has seen since the firing. Father Rogers gazes out and around at the faces reddened in the cold and the eyes filled with tears. He and Elizabeth start the burial together:

> As countless candles are lighted from a single flame, so we too as members of Christ's body will be what Christ is. Our human nature is transformed into the fullness of God; it becomes holy fire and light.

Their voices sway out of unison and back in, landing together on the words *fire and ligh'*. Elizabeth continues: "I" she continues without signaling a mistake, without looking at

287

Father Rogers her eyes fixed on the unlit wick, "we," pauses and repeats a little louder, "We light this candle as a symbol of renewal – renewal for Saint Luke's, renewal for women, renewal for Minny Lord's memories." Then, she does hesitate. "As flame destroys, it lights our way to new life," she turns to Father Rogers. He strikes a match and lights her candle. "It lights our way." They both turn to pass the light on to those gathered nearest. The light travels throughout the crowd.

Father Rogers continues: With this brief reading we will commend Minny Lord's soul to God. It comes from Romans Chapter 16:

> I commend to you Phoebe our sister, who is (also) a minister of the church at Cenchreae,
> that you may receive her in the Lord in a manner worthy of the holy ones, and help her in whatever she may need from you, for she has been a benefactor to many and to me as well.
> Greet Prisca and Aquila, my co-workers in Christ Jesus,
> who risked their necks for my life, to whom not only I am grateful but also all the churches of the Gentiles;
> greet also the church at their house. Greet my beloved Epaenetus, who was the first fruits in Asia for Christ.
> Greet Mary, who has worked hard for you.
> The Word of God."

The "Amen" response ripples through the crowd and floats on the still evening air. The sun slips behind the tall cemetery stones, and then behind the distant fence. A red glow lights the sky as a quiet line of candles flickers by the grave. The line arches as each person bends to take a handful of dirt and adds it to the grave.

Made in United States
North Haven, CT
09 November 2022

26456347R00163